Praise for
Pandemonium
by Daryl Gregory

Winner of the 2009 Crawford Award

"Believable characters, a multilayered plot and smooth prose define Gregory's darkly ambitious debut novel."
—*Publishers Weekly* (starred review)

"Wickedly clever entertainment."
—SF Gate (*San Francisco Chronicle*)

"Daryl Gregory can write like a son-of-a-bitch."
—Chris Roberson

"An unusually strong debut. . . Gregory's appropriation of pop-cultural icons is shrewd, amusing, and, as with Valis, often surprisingly poignant. As things get progressively weirder and wilder. . . *Pandemonium* bristles with frantic, feverish inventiveness, twist following twist at a dizzying rate."
—*Locus Magazine*

"[*Pandemonium*] breaks new ground while paying homage to some of the genre's most iconoclastic authors, A.E. Van Vogt and Philip K. Dick. . . . [A] bright new voice of the 21st century."
—*Library Journal* (starred review)

"*Pandemonium* rushes by like an out-of-control freight train. . . . [The novel] is the work of a young writer willing to play with the conventions of science fiction and fantasy and turn them in to a fresh, new vision of the world we live in."
—*New York Review of Science Fiction*

"A clever and fast-paced ride through the American pop-culture landscape. . . . Del's journey is both triumphant and heart-breaking."
—*Romantic Times* Book Reviews

PANDEMONIUM

Daryl Gregory

Ballantine Books · Del Rey · New York

A Del Rey Books Trade Paperback Original

Copyright © 2008 by Daryl Gregory

Published in the United States by Del Rey Books, an imprint of The Random House Publishing Group, a division of Random House, Inc., New York.

DEL REY is a registered trademark and the Del Rey colophon is a trademark of Random House, Inc.

ISBN 978-0-345-50116-5

Printed in the United States of America

www.delreybooks.com

9 8 7 6 5 4 3 2

Book design by Casey Hampton

To Kath, who knew before I did

PANDEMONIUM

The woman next to me said, It's the Kamikaze. Someone else said, No, it's the Painter—the Painter or the Fat Boy.

The river of people leaving the gates had log-jammed against a line of cops, and rumor rippled back through the crowd. A demon had possessed a man, and O'Hare security had sealed off the concourse between the gates and baggage claim. Reactions varied from exasperation to excitement. It was another travel delay, but at least it was an *interesting* delay.

I could see nothing beyond the end of the crowd but the cops' blue shoulders and the cavernous space of the United terminal. We couldn't go back: we'd just come through security, and more travelers were filling in behind us. There was nothing to do but wait for the demon to finish its business.

I dropped my blue nylon duffel bag between my feet and sat astride it, surrounded by a forest of legs and luggage. The scraping sensation in my head, quiet since morning, started up again. I stared at my shoes and tried to take clarifying breaths. My last doctor was big on clarifying breaths—that, and heavy meds.

I was tired. I'd been traveling all day, flying standby and catching one flight for every three, portaging the duffel through three airports, three sets of security shakedowns. At least I wasn't Japanese. Those poor bastards were practically strip-searched at every gate.

Someone backed into me, stumbled, and moved aside. I looked up, and the crowd shifted backward like spooked cattle. A path opened through the bodies, and suddenly I was alone in the middle of an aisle with the possessed man running toward me.

He was naked to the waist, his skinny chest and arms coated with gray dust, eyes wide and happy. He grinned, his mouth making words I couldn't hear. I got out of his way, leaving my bag in the middle of the floor.

He veered suddenly toward a popcorn vendor cart. Parents yanked children out of his way; people scattered. The crowd's mood had lurched from morbid curiosity to outright fear. A demon five hundred yards away was a lot different than one in your face.

He grabbed the cart by its handles and tipped it easily with the cartoon strength of the possessed. Someone screamed. The glass case shattered. Yellow popcorn blossomed into the air, and a metal pan bounced off the tile and rolled away like a hubcap.

The possessed man cackled and began to scoop up the popcorn, ignoring the shards of glass. He rose into a squat, arms full, and winked at me conspiratorially. His hands were bloody. He staggered back the way he'd come, hunched over his load. The cop let him pass without making a move.

What else could he do? He couldn't shoot the guy. It wasn't his fault, and if they obstructed him the demon might get pissed, jump to someone else (like a cop with a gun), and start hurting people. Nothing to do but keep the gawkers back and wait for it to burn itself out.

I picked up my bag and walked forward—plenty of room at the front of the line now—until I'd reached the temporary barrier, a ribbon of nylon strung between plastic posts. There was no one between me and the demon but a line of cops.

The United terminal was an art deco cathedral of steel and glass, shining ribs arcing under blue glass. I'd always liked it. The demon, trailing puffs of popcorn, shuffled to the middle of the concourse, stopped between the Starbucks and the shrine to the Kamikaze, and opened his arms. The popcorn spread over the marble with a susurrant *huff.*

He surveyed the mess for a moment, and then began to dance. He crushed the popcorn beneath his glossy black shoes. He paused, then danced again. When he was satisfied he dropped to hands and knees and began pushing the yellow powder into the borders of his sand painting, his collage, his sculpture—whatever the hell it was.

What it was, though, was a farm: a quaint white farmhouse, a red silo and barn, a line of trees, wide open fields. The farmhouse was powdered detergent or sugar or salt; the silo bits of red plastic and glass that could have been plucked from smashed exit signs; the trees cunningly arranged candy wrappers and strips of Styrofoam from coffee cups and junk food packages. The crumbled popcorn became the edge of a wheat field. The picture was simultaneously naturalistic and hazily distorted, a landscape seen through waves of heat.

The demon began to add details. I sat down on my duffel and watched him work. He fiddled with the shards of red glass to suggest the warp of barn wood; gently blew the white powder into the ghosts of gutters and window frames; scraped his shoe heel against the marble to create a smudge above the house that could have been a cloud or a large bird. The longer he worked, the more familiar the scene became. I'd never seen the place before—at least, I didn't remember ever seeing a farm like this—but the picture was so relentlessly quaint, so Norman Rockwell, that maybe it was the *idea* of the farm that I recognized. The Jungians thought demons were archetypes from the collective unconscious. Perhaps the subject matter of archetypal artists was archetypes.

And then he abruptly stood and walked away, not even glancing back at the finished picture. The man took maybe a dozen steps, and then collapsed. No one moved for perhaps a minute.

Finally a cop edged forward, his hand on his nightstick, and asked the man questions I couldn't catch. The man looked up, frightened. The cop helped him to his feet, and the man looked at his cut hands, then around at the crowds. The cop put an arm around his shoulder and led him away.

. . .

"Del!"

Lew, My Very Bigger Brother, bellowing from the other end of the atrium. His wife, Amra, shook her head in mock embarrassment. This was part of their shtick: Lew was loud and embarrassing, Amra was socially appropriate.

Lew met me halfway across the floor and grabbed me in a hug, his gut hitting me like a basketball. He'd always been bigger than me, but now he was six inches taller and a hundred pounds heavier. "Jesus Christ!" he said. "What took you so long? The board said your flight got in an hour ago." His beard was bushier than when I'd last seen him a year and a half ago, but it had still failed to colonize the barren patches between ear and chin.

"Sorry about that—something about four bags of heroin up my ass. Hey, Amra."

"Hello, Del."

I hugged her briefly. She smelled good as always. She'd cut her long, shiny black hair into something short and professional.

Lew grabbed the strap from my shoulder and tried to take it from me. "I got it," I said.

"Come on, you look like you haven't slept in a week." He yanked it from me. "Shit, this is heavy. How many more bags do you got?"

"That's it."

"What are you, a fuckin' hobo? Okay, we have to take a shuttle to the parking garage. Follow me." He charged ahead with the duffel on his back.

"Did you hear there was a demon in the airport?" Amra said.

"I was there. They wouldn't let us out of the terminal until he was gone. So what happened to the Cher hair?"

"Oh . . ." She made a gesture like shooing a fly. "Too much. You saw it? Which one was it—not the Kamikaze?" The news tracked them by name, like hurricanes. Most people went their whole lives without seeing one in person. I'd seen five—six, counting today's. I'm lucky that way.

"The Painter, I think. At least, it was making a picture."

Lew glanced back, gave Amra a look. He wanted her to stop talking about it. "Probably a faker," Lew said. "There's a possession conference going on downtown next week. The town'll be full of posers."

"I don't think this guy was faking," I said. That mad grin. That wink. "Afterward he was just crushed. Totally confused."

"I wonder if he even knows how to draw," Amra said.

The tram dropped us at a far parking lot, and then we shivered in the wind while Lew unlocked the car and loaded my duffel into the tiny trunk.

It was new, a bulbous silver Audi that looked futuristic and fast. I thought of my own car, crumpled like a beer can, and tried not to be jealous. The Audi was too small for Lew anyway. He enveloped the steering wheel, elbows out, like he was steering with his stomach. His seat was pushed all the way back, so I sat behind Amra. Lew flew down 294, swearing at drivers and juking between lanes. I should have been used to Lew's driving by then, but the speed and erratic turns had me gripping the back of Amra's seat. I grew up in the suburbs, but every time I came back to Chicago I experienced traffic shock. We were forty minutes from downtown, and there were four crammed lanes on each side of the road, and everyone moving at 70 mph. It was worse than Denver.

"So what have you been doing with yourself?" Lew asked. "You don't call, you don't write, you don't send flowers . . ."

"We missed you at Christmas," Amra said.

"See, Lew? From Amra, that actually means she missed me at Christmas. From you or Mom that would have meant 'How could you have let us down like that?' "

"Then she said it wrong."

They'd only been married for a year and a half, but they'd been dating on and off—mostly on—since college. "So when are you guys going to settle down and make Mom some multiracial grandbabies? The Cyclops has gotta be demanding a little baby action."

Amra groaned. "Do you have to call her that? And you're changing the subject."

"Yeah," Lew said. "Back to your faults as a son and brother. What have you been up to?"

"Well, that's a funny story."

Lew glanced at me in the rearview mirror. Amra turned in her seat to face me, frowning in concern.

"Jeez, guys." I forced a smile. "Can you at least let me segue into this?"

"What is it?" Amra said.

"It's not a big deal. I had a car accident in November, went through a guardrail in the snow, and then—"

Lew snorted in surprise. "Were you drunk?"

"Fuck you. The road was icy, and I just hit the curve too fast and lost control. I went through the rail, and then the car started flipping." My gut tightened, remembering that jolt. My vision had gone dark as I struck the rail, and I'd felt myself pitching forward, as if I were being sucked into a black well. "I ended up at the bottom of a ravine, upside down, and I couldn't get my seatbelt undone." I left out the caved-in roof, the icy water running through the car, my blind panic. "I just hung there until the cops got me out."

"Weren't you hurt?" Amra asked.

I shrugged. "My arms were scraped up, and my back was killing me, but that turned out to be just a pulled muscle. They kept me in the hospital for a day, and then they let me go. And afterward . . . well, all in all I was pretty lucky."

"Lucky?" Lew said. "Why do people say that? You get a tumor, and if it turns out that you can operate on it, people say, gee, that was lucky. No, lucky is *not* getting cancer. Lucky is not getting cancer, then finding ten bucks in your shoe."

"Are you done?" Amra said.

"He totaled his car. He's not that lucky."

Amra shook her head. "You were about to say something else, Del. What happened after the accident?"

"Yeah, afterward." I suddenly regretted bringing it up. I'd thought I could practice on Lew and Amra, get ready for the main event with Mom. Amra looked at me expectantly.

"After the accident, I had some, well, complications, and I needed to go to a different kind of hospital."

Amra frowned in concern. Lew said, "Holy shit, you mean like One-Flew-Over different?"

Amra shushed him. "Are you okay?" The tiny cabin and the high seat between us made the space simultaneously intimate and insulating.

"I'm fine. Everything worked out."

"Fine, he says. Holy shit. Does Mom know? No, of course not, she would have told me. She would have told me, wouldn't she? Holy shit." He swept down on the rear end of a truck, and for the first time in the trip he slowed down rather than change lanes. "So what were you in for? Did you check yourself in, or did they commit you? Does Mom know?"

"I'll tell her tonight. It's not a big deal."

"You don't have to talk about this if you don't want to," Amra said. "But you should feel free to talk about this. It's not a stigma."

"Come on, it's *sort of* a stigma," Lew said.

I nodded. "There *are* a lot of crazy people in there."

Amra turned back around. "I'm trying to talk seriously. This is important."

"It's not a big deal," I said.

Lew laughed. "Every time you say that it gets more convincing." He gunned the engine, swung around a station wagon, and swerved back right across two lanes, just in time to catch our exit. I braced myself against the door as we swooped into the hard curve of the off ramp.

"So what was it?" Lew asked. He glanced left and merged onto the street. "Thought you were Napoleon? Seeing pink elephants?"

"More like hearing things."

"No shit." I'd shocked him sober.

Amra looked at Lew, back at me. "Is this about the thing that happened when you were little?"

So Lew had told her. Which I should have expected—they were married. Family. "When I was possessed, you mean."

Amra looked so sad I made myself laugh. "Come on, I barely remember it."

"You ask me, he was faking," Lew said. He steered the car onto our block. Familiar trees scrolled past the windows, bare limbs raking a close, steely sky. "Del would always do anything to get Mom's attention."

Dinner had been waiting since 1985. The meal was straight out of my childhood—glazed ham, mashed potatoes, the mix of regular and creamed corn I loved, hot rolls. My mother brought it out of the oven—she'd been keeping it warm—two minutes after we walked in. We ate off the same white-and-green Corelle plates we'd always used.

We talked easily about trivia: changes to the neighborhood, the two winters I'd managed to miss. Lew and Amra didn't bring up demons or psych wards. My mother didn't ask why I hadn't shown up for Christmas, or why I'd suddenly decided to fly here with barely a day's notice.

Afterward, Mom tried to shoo us away while she cleaned up. Lew and Amra ran out to buy us ice cream, but I stayed to ferry dishes from the dining room to the kitchen. My mother loaded the dishwasher—it didn't work if anyone else did it.

She was a high-waisted, big-boned woman, built like a municipal building—solid, tall. Lew got his size from her. Her hair was feathered with gray, but when she smiled or spoke she seemed the same as the day I left for college. But when she wasn't concentrating—like during the long breath she took between sitting down and picking up her fork—her face sagged and she seemed to age twenty years.

"What did you do to your hand?" she asked.

I'd rolled up my sleeves to rinse the dishes. There was a long thin bruise like a bracelet around my left wrist. "Oh, that. That's nothing." She looked at me. I laughed. "I'd looped a rope around my wrist, I was— a friend of mine got stuck, we were trying to pull his car out. He hit the gas before I let go and—it's fine, it doesn't hurt, it just looks bad."

She tried to pat down the hair at the crown of my head, my eternal cowlick. "You're always getting in accidents. You look tired, too. Have you been sleeping?"

"It's just travel—I had to get up early and I lost two hours." I handed her another plate. "I can't believe you still have these dishes."

"I can't believe I have any left." Lew and I had dropped a lot of them over the years, and when they hit the tile they exploded into millions of needle-sharp slivers you could only find with your bare feet. I was uncritically nostalgic for everything in the house that I'd been oblivious to when I lived here: the cheap dishes, the Formica furniture, the thin carpets furrowed in the hallway. Every new thing in the house—like the oak magazine basket next to Dad's recliner—struck me as presumptuous and suspect, like a stranger wearing my mother's bathrobe.

Mom closed the dishwasher without switching it on—she wouldn't run it unless it was packed tight.

"What's wrong, Del." This was the first nontraditional thing either of us had said to each other since I'd arrived. The starting gun for the real conversation.

I had a plan. Start with the car crash. Hint at the stress I'd been under. Then bring up the hospital—I had to tell her about the hospital, it was too likely that she'd find out about it somehow—but make it seem like the visit was my idea. Just something I needed to clear my head. End of story.

"I've just had a tough winter." She didn't say anything, waiting for me to fill it in. "The first snowfall, I spun out and crashed into a guardrail—" I kept talking through her gasp. Thank God I hadn't said *through* the guardrail. "It's okay, I was fine, just scraped up my arms when the airbag went off. The car was pretty banged up, though. And after that, I had some trouble."

"Have the noises come back?" she said.

I opened my mouth, shut it. So much for the plan.

When I was a teenager I had a swimming accident, and after that I started hearing the noises. That's what I called them, anyway, what everyone in my family called them. But they weren't exactly sounds. I didn't hear voices, or humming, or music, or screams. It was more physical than that. I felt movement, vibration, like the scrape of a chair

across the floor, a fist pounding against a table. It felt like someone rattling a cage in my mind.

But that was too hard to explain, even to myself.

"Oh, honey." She dried her hand on a towel and pressed her
hand to my neck. "When do you hear them? At night, when you're
tired . . . ?"

"It comes and goes."

"Right now?"

"Right now, not so much." Another lie. Every few minutes, I felt a
lurch and a flurry of clawed scrabbling, like a raccoon in a cardboard
box.

She studied my face, as if by concentrating she could hear what
was happening in my head. Her left eye, the glass one, was fixed on a
point just beside my right ear. "You should talk to Dr. Aaron," she said.
"She helped you so much last time. You could do some therapy with
her."

"Mom, it's not like getting a lube job, you can't just drop in for
some quick therapy."

"You know what I mean. Talk to her. If you're worried about the
cost—"

"It's not the money."

"I can lend you the money."

"She's not going to charge me, Mom." I rubbed the side of my
head. "Listen, I already called her. I'm going to see her tomorrow."

"Then why are you arguing with me?"

"I'm not arguing! I'm just saying that I'm not 'doing therapy.' I'm
just going to stop in and say hello."

"Maybe she could recommend somebody in Colorado. There
must be good psychiatrists that—"

"*I'm not going to see anybody else.*"

She blinked, waited for me to calm down.

"I'm sorry," I said. "I didn't mean to . . ." I opened my hands, closed
them.

"What happened back there?" she asked quietly.

Amra and Lew were coming back soon. I didn't want to be in the middle of it when they walked in. I weighed what I could tell her. Enough to be plausible. But too much and I'd have to manage *her* reaction.

"It's complicated."

She waited. I sat down at the table, and she sat next to me.

"The noises weren't bad at first," I said. "They came mostly at night, but I was handling it okay. Then they started to get worse, more persistent. I missed some days of work." I kept my tone matter-of-fact. "So anyway, my car's totaled, the people at work want to fire me, I wasn't sleeping well . . . I knew I was stressed out. The doctor who took care of me after the accident referred me to a shrink, a psychiatrist. I told him my history, you know, the stuff from when I was five, and the stuff from high school. But if it's related to possession it's something he's never heard of before, so we had to spend a lot of time talking about what I think is going on. And in the meantime he's teaching me meditation techniques, ordering scans of my head, having me try out medications. And of course none of it worked. The MRIs and fMRIs and CAT scans didn't show anything, no tumors or blockages. The meditation exercises were all things Dr. Aaron taught me years ago, straight out of some post-possession handbook they all must read—and I'd *been* trying those.

"The drugs, though. He opened up the whole medicine cabinet: antianxiety, antipsychotics, anti-everything. Nothing was too horrible, but the worst combination made me sleep sixteen hours a day and then wake up with a dry mouth and a queasy stomach. But the noises didn't go away.

"After one particularly rough night I went in to see him and he says, why don't we try some environment that's less stressful, where people could watch out for you? Like on *Wild Kingdom*, why don't we tag you and bring you to a safer environment? And the next thing I know I'm in the psychiatric ward of the hospital, hanging out with schizophrenics. There was a guy there, Bertram—nice guy, maybe fifty, totally whacked. One minute we're having a perfectly normal conversation, talking about Pakistan or the weather or something, and the next second his head would jerk up and he'd stare at the lights and say, 'Did you *feel* that?' 'Feel what, Bertram?' 'They just scanned us.' See, he believed there were these super-telepaths named slans . . ."

I was rambling.

Mom sat silently, her mouth pulled tight. She'd sat through the recitation, absorbing the facts like blows. Her face had hardened, and her gaze had shifted from my face. I didn't know what I'd expected—not tears, my mother was not a crier—but not this. Not anger.

"What is it?" I said.

Headlights slid across the front window. Lew and Amra's Audi coasted into the driveway, bass pumping. The stereo cut off.

Mom stood up quickly, walked past without looking at me. "I'm going to make coffee," she said. "It has to be decaf, I can't drink caffeinated at night."

Amra followed me down the dimly lit stairs, one hand on my shoulder. Sometime during the run to Jewel, she and Lew had decided to stay the night instead of driving back to their house in Gurnee, about an hour away. Dinner had become a slumber party, and slumber parties required board games. Amra was trying very hard to treat me the same as she did before she knew I'd escaped the loony bin.

At the last step, I reached out and found the lightbulb chain. "The vault," I announced.

The basement was a maze of shelves, and the shelves were stacked with the treasure of our childhood—Lew's childhood and mine. Mom saved everything, not only every GI Joe and Matchbox car, but every Hot Wheels track, Tinkertoy, and puzzle piece. Anything that didn't stack neatly was sealed in clear plastic tubs. Farther into the dark were our baby clothes and old toys, Dad's army uniforms and paraphernalia, Mom's wedding dress, boxes of letters and books and tax returns, and odds and ends with irregular silhouettes: elementary school art projects, bicycle parts, an arbor of golf clubs and fishing poles. I was itching to explore farther, but not with Amra.

"The games are over here," I said.

I led her past the comic collection—eight long white cardboard boxes and one small brown box labeled in Magic Marker block letters:

"DeLew Comics." The small box was more than big enough to hold the complete output of our short-lived company. The winter I was in sixth grade and Lew was in eighth, we'd tried to sell our self-made comics for a quarter apiece to our friends. Our biggest seller, *RADAR Man*, made us maybe a dollar fifty.

"I never come down here," she said. "I can't believe your mother still has all this stuff."

"The Cyclops sees all, saves all."

She frowned at me—she hated that Lew and I called her that— and then spied a box on the game shelf. "Mousetrap! I used to have this!"

We pulled games from the shelf, comparing personal histories. I couldn't believe she'd never done battle with Rock'em Sock'em Robots, and we set it aside to bring upstairs. The games, I knew, were complete, down to every card and counter, even the gazillion red and white Battleship pegs.

"Here's the masterpiece," I said, and unfolded a massive, asymmetrical playing board taped together at odd angles. The tape was yellow and cracking. "Life and Death."

"What did you *do?*" she said.

"It's a game we made up, Lew and me. We cut up boards from Monopoly, Risk, and Life and—"

"Your mother must have killed you!"

I grinned. "Yeah." I sat down and pulled out Ziploc bags full of plastic pieces and dice. On the bottom was a sheaf of handwritten pages illustrated by pencil sketches of my preteen obsessions: soldiers, trains, and superheroes. The Official Rules.

Amra was oohing and ahing over her finds. "Ker-Plunk, Stay Alive, Don't Break the Ice—unbelievable." I flipped through the faded pages, trying to remember how to play.

"Bang."

I looked up, and Amra was aiming the slingshot at me, the rubber tube pulled back. There was nothing in the pocket, but she looked at my face and lowered the weapon. "What?" she said quietly.

I stood up, too quickly, and my pulse thumped in my temple. "Just put it back." My throat was constricted, and my voice came out strange. "That shouldn't—I didn't know that was down here."

I took it from her. The homemade weapon was small in my hands, just a Y of tree limb, a strip of black rubber, a patch of leather for the pocket.

"Are you okay?"

"Yeah, yeah." I tossed the slingshot back into the open box she'd found. I took her hands, dry and smooth and cold. "You just have to promise me one thing."

"What?"

"You've got to let me win in Rock'em Sock'em Robots. I've got a frail ego."

I lay on top of the covers in my sweats and T-shirt, staring at the night-time shapes surrounding my bed, waiting for the house to quiet. Mom had made my room into a sewing room, and the walls were lined with Rubbermaid boxes and stacks of fabric. Bolts of cloth leaned in the corners. When I was a kid, the walls were covered by my drawings, my homegrown superheroes and supervillains. In bed I'd stare up at RADAR Man and Dr. Awkward and Mister Twister, imagining them in motion, even when—especially when—the lines were too faint to make out. The pictures were better in the dark.

In the hospital my walls had been perfectly plain, though some of the long-term people had taped up posters (but no framed pictures: glass, nails, and framing wire were all big no-nos). I'd had no trouble falling asleep, though. At 9:30 every night they gave me two big yellow pills, and by ten I was unconscious. The nurses locked me in anyway: my shrink had told them about my sleepwalking problem, or as I liked to call it, wolfing out.

Every night since leaving the hospital I'd held a strategy session with myself. Did I need one pill tonight, or two? When should I take them? The last six capsules of Nembutal were in my duffel bag at the foot of the bed, and I didn't have a prescription for a refill. I was on war rations.

I hadn't taken anything tonight. I didn't want to fall asleep yet, and if I waited I might get lucky. The noises, usually most persistent after dark, were quiet for the first night in weeks. Maybe coming home had given me some control.

Around midnight, Lew finally clicked off the living room TV and clumped to bed. Mom and Amra had gone to bed hours ago. I waited a half hour more, breathing. The thing in my head kept still. I sat up slowly, afraid to wake it.

I opened the door and stood for a long moment peering into the dark, listening. Then I walked down the hallway with short steps, trailing fingers along the wall until I'd passed the bathroom and found the corner at the end of the hall. I turned in to the living room. Moved past the couch and around the end tables and footstools, navigating by the moonlight silvering the edges of the furniture. In the kitchen, the vent light above the stove had been left on like a nightlight. I unhooked the basement door, stepped down, and shut the door behind me. The stairs creaked as I went down.

I walked through the vault, the cold cement stinging my bare feet.

I went past the comics and the board games, past the box where Amra had found the slingshot, and turned farther into the maze, down a narrow path between the wood veneer cabinet stereo and the orange crates full of phonograph albums.

Two green dry-cleaning bags hung from a black pipe: my father's uniforms. The workbench was just behind them, against the far wall, near the water heater and sump pump. Tools hung from a peg board that had been screwed into the cinderblock. Only a few silhouettes were empty. The bench held the heavy red toolbox and stacks of Cool Whip containers full of screws and nails and orphaned hardware. A red Craftsman hammer lay on the bench like he'd left it minutes ago.

The safe was on the floor, under the workbench. It was a small steel box, about twelve inches to a side, painted black. I squatted down, and pulled on the door's little silver handle. It was locked, as I expected.

I leaned down on one forearm, and looked up at the underside of the workbench. It was too dark to see. I ran my fingers along the lip of the bench until they found the cuts in the wood. I smiled. I couldn't read the numbers etched there, but I didn't need to—Lew and I had memorized the combination long ago. Not that my father had made it difficult: 2-15-45 was my mother's birthday.

I leaned sideways to let the light hit the dial. The safe didn't open, and for a moment I wondered if Mom had changed the combination. I tried again, and this time it opened.

The inside of the safe seemed much smaller than the outside. A shelf divided the space into two small compartments. On top was a dark leather holster, flap closed, and a small box of ammunition. On the floor of the safe was the pistol swaddled in an oiled rag. I moved my hand under it, lifted it out like a baby, and unfolded the cloth with my free hand. A gleaming black .45 automatic, my dad's service sidearm in Korea. I fit my hand around the stubbly grip and aimed at the white cylinder of the water heater, feeling the weight of the Colt tug at the end of my arm. Before Lew and I had cracked the safe we'd held only plastic toy guns. The heaviness of the metal had come as a shock.

On the other side of the basement, the door to upstairs creaked open. I quickly folded the rag back over the gun and set it in the safe.

"Del?" It was my mother.

"Down here," I called. I was afraid to close the safe, sure that the metallic click would be immediately recognizable. I pushed the door to within an inch of closing. "Don't worry, I'll turn off the lights when I'm done."

The stairs complained as she stepped down. I did the only thing I could think of: I coughed and pressed the door shut. When she turned the corner I was walking toward her, a short stack of vinyl LPs in my hands. "I hope I didn't wake you up," I said. "You know, you could sell these on the Internet."

She was dressed in a housecoat and thick blue woolly socks. She glanced at the albums, then at my face. "You haven't slept at all yet."

I shrugged. "My circadian rhythms are all messed up. I don't sleep much anyway."

"I used to hear you walking around the house at all hours," she said. She took the top album from me, a painted photo of Bing Crosby in a Christmas stocking cap, and turned it over in her hands.

"You could have told me," she said.

"I know."

"I would have come."

"I know." She would have. She'd pulled me back from the brink twice before, and she could have done it again. She would have flown down, cleaned my apartment, counted out my pills, rubbed my head through the night.

But I couldn't tell her. I'd talked to her on the phone almost every week, and I'd never once said, Hey, I've lost my car and my job and my mind. And by the way, I'm calling you from the crazy house.

"It's not . . ."

I almost said it aloud: *It's not just noises.* I felt . . . vertiginous. Like my heels were rocking on the edge of a balcony rail. All I had to do was lean forward a few inches and let myself fall.

The thing's inside my head, Mom, and it's trying to get out.

"It's not that I didn't want to tell you," I said.

She picked up the hammer and hung it in its silhouette on the pegboard. "Well, you're home now." She touched my arm as she passed. "Don't forget to put everything back when you're done."

2

When I was fourteen I became famous in my high school for leaving so much blood in the pool that they had to drain it.

It was a fabulous head wound for such a stupid accident. I was at the side of the pool, trying to pull a canoe paddle out of another kid's hands, when I stepped back and put my foot down on a foam kickboard. The deck was wet, the kickboard shot out from under me, and I went down. I smacked my head against the cement lip of the pool and fell into the water. I didn't lose consciousness. I don't remember being afraid. I floated facedown for what seemed like a long time, unable to push my head out of the water. The bottom of the pool turned black, but maybe that was blood loss or oxygen deprivation.

Then a brilliant light as my classmates hauled me out. The gym teacher, I can't remember his name, laid me out on the deck and pressed towels to my head until the paramedics came.

The blow swelled the side of my head to the size of a softball and blurred my vision. But I wasn't paralyzed, or even badly injured. They kept me in the hospital overnight just to make sure, but they said I'd be home in the morning.

It was that night in the hospital that the "noises" began. The first thing I felt was a thump, like someone in the other room had knocked the wall behind my head. I turned, and it happened again, and this time there was nothing behind my head but my own room. I called for the nurse, asked her if someone was in the room with me. She thought I was dreaming.

Then the intermittent thumps grew louder, more frequent, and changed in character so that now it was like a baseball bat slamming repeatedly into a tree trunk—with the sting and burn of each impact running straight into my head.

I freaked out. They held me down and gave me something to knock me out.

The swelling from my concussion receded, my vision cleared, but the noises kept coming back. Sometimes it was the pounding; sometimes it was just a wordless whisper that scritched and scraped inside my skull. They took blood, made me lie still in expensive machines, changed my diet. Mostly they fed me pills. If I was asleep, I couldn't run out of the hospital.

Mom and Dad were there—Dad was alive then—but it was Mom I remember sleeping in the chair beside my bed. The doctors decided it wasn't a physical problem—not internal bleeding, not brain damage, not tumors—and it wasn't like any possession anyone had ever heard of. They suggested that it was time to bring in a psychiatrist. It was Mom who found Dr. Aaron.

Her office now was in an elegant two-story Victorian, a block from the train station. A big improvement over the flat-faced brick building she'd rented space in before.

"Is this it?" Lew said.

"This is the address." I levered myself out of the Audi.

"Comb your hair—it's sticking up in back."

I'd had trouble getting up this morning. I'd taken two pills to make sure I'd stay out, and it had worked. Lew had started pounding on my door at 10:30—he couldn't understand why the door was locked—and I'd finally stumbled out like a zombie.

"I'll be back in an hour to pick you up," Lew said.

"Is that a therapy hour or a real hour?"

"A TV hour. I'll see you in forty-two minutes."

Inside, the house seemed empty. There was no receptionist at the tiny desk out front. On the wall were a dozen plastic in-box trays labeled with other "doctor" names. I stood for a while looking up the big staircase, wondering which room might be Dr. Aaron's. It was a Saturday—maybe she wasn't even here yet.

I sat on the couch in the waiting room, a converted living room with a long-dormant fireplace and big windows that faced the street. I stared at the front door for a while, then picked up a copy of *Newsweek*. Marines were still in Kashmir. The Church of Scientology was suing the Church of Jesus Christ Informationalist for copyright infringement. Critics were panning *Exorcist: The Musical*. The issue was a month old, but it was all news to me—I'd lost touch with current events just before Christmas. I wondered if the demon from the airport had showed up in today's papers.

Somewhere upstairs a door opened and closed. I looked up, listening to the steps. A large woman in a black, knee-length sweater coat came down the stairs, and there was a moment before she turned and saw me.

My God, I thought, she's gotten fat. And then: I am such a jerk.

"Del?"

I stood up, stepped awkwardly around the coffee table. "Hi, Dr. Aaron."

I hadn't seen her since I was in high school. Then she'd been trim, serious, and in my fourteen-year-old eyes, seriously older: at least in her forties. But she was no older than forty-five *now*. Back then she would have been in her early thirties—probably only a few years out of med school.

I took her hand, unsure what was permissible—were we old acquaintances, or doctor and patient? Her open smile disarmed me. I leaned in and hugged her with my free arm, and she patted me on the back.

"It's good to see you, Del." Her face seemed to come into focus. Short black hair, thin dark eyebrows like French accent marks, pale pale skin. The woman in front of me overlaid the hazier version in my memory, replaced her.

She led me up the stairs. "I've thought a lot about you over the years, wondering how you were doing."

"I'm doing okay."

She glanced back, judging this for herself. "Come in and catch me up."

Her office was anchored in heavy colors: dark red walls, deeply stained oak floors and wainscoting, a barge of a desk. Everything else in the room strained to lighten it up. A Persian rug shot with Pepto-Bismol pink, pale floral loveseat, lacy white drapes and lamp shades. The only thing that remained from her old office that I remembered was the chocolate leather armchair.

She took my jacket and hung it behind the door. I sat on the loveseat, she sat in her armchair.

We smiled at each other again. Old times.

I said, "You're not going to take notes?"

"We're just visiting, right? Besides, I don't scribble as much as I used to. I found out I listen better without a notepad." She shifted her weight, crossed her legs. "So you live in Colorado now. How did you get out there? The last we'd talked—well, I got a letter from you when you went to college. You couldn't decide what to major in."

"I opted for a degree in Starving Artist." I shifted into Amusing Summary mode. After a dozen "Hi, my name is Del" introductions with doctors and fellow patients and various small groups, I'd decided that this was the least painful way to cover the arid territory between college and my current life. The long job hunt to turn my Illinois State graphics arts degree into a job offer, the ignominious move back into my mother's house, the series of low-paying jobs. I highlighted the most humiliating moments, such as deciding to move across the country with my girlfriend, then getting dumped as soon as we arrived.

"I think it was thirty minutes after we'd emptied the U-Haul that she broke up with me."

She laughed. Thank God she laughed. "Well, she wasn't going to break up with you until you unloaded, right?"

"Oh no, I only date the smart girls. Anyway, I decided I liked Colorado. I went through another string of dead-end jobs, office temp work, a few months at a web development shop that went bust, an even shorter stint drawing farm equipment ads for the PennySaver. My last job was at a decaling shop in Colorado Springs."

"Decaling?"

"It's like an automotive tattoo parlor. I tweaked the graphics files, managed this big Agfa film printer. And if I was a good boy, every few months I got to make up a new logo. I'm very proud of my Beaver in Hardhat with Wrench."

"You said, 'your last job.' You're not working there anymore?"

"Ah, no. They fired me officially a couple weeks ago. Of course, I'd stopped showing up weeks before, so I can't blame them. "

She nodded. "When you called, you sounded upset."

"I did?" That night I'd made sure to calm down before I dialed. "I may have been a little stressed."

"You said you needed a prescription refill on some sleeping pills. What are you taking?"

"Nembutal?"

"Okay." A slight pause, enough time to start me worrying. "When was this?" she asked. "How many milligrams?"

"Fifty, at first, though he upped me to a hundred. This was probably the middle of January." Her expression didn't change, but something made me backpedal. "Maybe the end of January. But not every night—just when I need it. Occasionally."

She frowned. "So that would be before you lost your job, then. What happened to make you look for a doctor?"

She hadn't said whether she was going to give me the prescription or not. I felt like a junkie on a job interview.

I described the crash at a level of detail between what I'd said to my mother and what I'd said to Lew and Amra. Smashing *through* the guardrail, yes, flipping and crunching to the bottom of the ravine and almost drowning, not so much.

"And the noises started again," she said. That's what we'd called them in therapy, too—the noises. She'd immediately noticed the parallels between the crash and my swimming pool accident, and leaped to meet me. I'd forgotten how quick she was, how in sync we could be. It was like we were picking up where we left off years ago.

"When did they start?" she asked. "While you were in the ER?"

"Faster this time. I was still in the car when they started."

She pursed her lips. "So how are you handling it? Are you using your exercises?"

"I've tried them." I'd worked with Dr. Aaron for months before she taught me something that could smother the sensations in my head. The exercises were mental plays I could enact. The one that worked best was one I called Helm's Deep. My mind was a fortress, and the noises—the pounding, the shaking, the metal-on-metal rasping—were orcs coming over the walls. All I had to do was knock them off the parapets. If they kept coming, I just had to back into the keep and seal the door. And if they came through the door, I retreated to the caves. Yeah, it was cowardly, but there were no frickin' elves to help me out. And it had worked—until now.

I ran a hand across my neck. "The door's closed, but I can still feel them."

"How are you getting through the day?"

I laughed. "I don't know. I can't just ignore it—sometimes it's the loudest thing in the room." *Loudest* was the wrong word, but she knew what I meant. "I've learned to not respond, at least in front of people. I keep my face blank; I try not to wince when it startles me. I just . . . concentrate on what people are saying. And I keep nodding."

"That must be incredibly tiring."

I laughed, ran a hand across my mouth. "You have no idea."

"The Nembutal . . . are you using that to help?"

"During the day? No. That's just to help me sleep. I mean, I can sleep most of the time, it's just that sometimes I can't sleep. Look, I know you're worried about the pills—"

"Nembutal's a heavy-duty barbiturate, Del. They use it to knock people out before operations. It's heavily addictive, and a hundred milligrams isn't far from overdose territory. You have a few beers when you take one, and you could end up like Marilyn Monroe."

"I'm not about to get addicted. Trust me, that's not what I'm worried about." I lifted my hands from my lap, dropped them. "Doctor. Do you think possession is real?"

"Of course." She tilted her head. I remembered that gesture from our sessions. "Del, I know you're not making this up. And neither are the thousands of people who've been affected by it. "

"That's not what I mean. Not possession the disorder. Old-fashioned possession. Do you believe you can be taken over by some outside force—some god or demon or whatever—or do you think it's all just . . . delusions of delusional people?"

"No one knows, Del. What matters is—"

"Just tell me what *you* believe, Doctor. Yes or no. Are people just going crazy, or is it something else?"

She frowned, seemed to weigh her answer. "I think that yes, there are people who are psychotic, or who have multiple personality disorder, who also say that they're possessed. There are even people who aren't psychotic who want so badly to be possessed, or want to explain some past trauma, that they convince themselves that they were seized by some higher power. I'm not talking about people who fake possession—there'll always be people who'll use the O. J. defense. But there are people like yourself, Del, who don't *want* to be possessed, and who aren't liars and aren't 'crazy.' The Jungians—"

"Oh God, not the Jungians."

"There's a reason eighty percent of psychotherapists are Jungians. The idea of the collective unconscious, continually recurring archetypes, the nonphysical independence of the soul—all that makes a lot of sense given the evidence. There are so many cases of possession where the victim displays knowledge or skills that they don't have access to, like seizing control of a plane, opening a bank vault. The literature is clear, and the Freudian explanation for possession just doesn't stack up, in my estimation. All these possessions can't be just the expression of the victim's innermost drives."

"Well, there's the Piper. He looks like pure id."

"But that's an archetype too—the satyr." She waved her hand. "We're getting off track. You want to know what I believe." She leaned back in her chair, crossed her hands in her lap. "I'm not a Jungian, and

I'm not convinced by the Freudians. I don't subscribe to any one theory—for me, the jury's still out. There's definitely scientific evidence to suggest that the disorder is not entirely triggered by internal factors."

" 'Not entirely.' " I laughed. "You mean it may not be all in my head."

She smiled. "The important thing, Del, is that I believe in your experience. I believe that when you were five years old you lost control of your body. Does that mean you were taken over by some vodun spirit or a Communist telepath or an archetype from the collective unconscious? I don't think so. But there are plenty of smart people who believe that's exactly what's going on. My own hope is that someday we'll discover that there's a biological trigger to possession—something viral, or genetic, or bacteriological—something we can fight. We already know that a few of the victims are Japanese, a few are girls, but the overwhelming majority are white men and boys—in America, anyway. Some are possessed repeatedly. Maybe there's a genetic predisposition that's triggered by something in the environment, some stressor, and that we can take steps to inoculate ourselves against. In fact, there are some researchers coming to ICOP this week—that's the International—"

"The conference on possession. I'm going."

"You are?" She frowned in confusion, then understood. "That's why you came back this week."

"There's a neurologist I want to talk to, Sunil Ram. From Stanford?"

"I've heard of him."

"Let me show you something." I got up and retrieved several folded papers from my jacket's inner pocket. "These are just copies, but I thought you might be interested."

She took them from me, and slowly paged through them. "These are MRIs of *your* brain, I presume."

"My doctor back in Colorado Springs did several fMRIs while I was staying at the hospital."

She looked up sharply.

"I've annotated the interesting bits," I said, moving on. "Do you know Dr. Ram's theory about possession? Look at the right temporal lobe."

She was looking at me with concern. She glanced at the pages again, then handed them back to me. "Del, I'm not a neurologist. Why don't you tell me what you think they mean."

What you *think* they mean.

I folded the pages again. "It doesn't matter," I said. "It's just a theory. Everybody's got a theory, right?" I put them back in my jacket pocket, pulled the jacket on.

"Del, were you hospitalized?"

"I was getting to that." I didn't move from the door. "I was in for two weeks, which coincidentally, was exactly as long as my insurance paid for."

"Please, sit down. Tell me what happened. Why did your doctor suggest that you be hospitalized? Did you try to hurt yourself?"

"No. Yes." I shook my head. "I didn't try to overdose, if that's what you're getting at. That's not why he had me committed."

She waited.

"If I tell you something, you have to promise not to do anything about it."

"Del, I can't promise something like that without knowing what you're going to tell me. Are you afraid I'm going to commit you?"

I put my hand on the doorknob. "I need an answer on the prescription."

She blinked slowly. "I can't just write you a prescription for a drug like that, Del. Sit down and talk to me. If you can explain to me what's going on, and I'm convinced you're not a danger to yourself or others, that might be a possibility. You're a strong person. If you tell me you're in control, I'll take you at your word."

"I'm in complete control," I said. "Almost all the time."

I'd walked halfway back to Randhurst Mall before Lew coasted up beside me. "Hey good lookin', be back to pick you up later."

Cars queued up behind him. No one had honked yet. I climbed in. "I need a beer, an Italian beef, and a beer."

"You know what would be good with that? Beer." He punched the accelerator, burping the tires, and then braked to a halt fifty yards later at a stoplight.

He looked over at me. "If this is what therapy does for you, sign me up."

"Where's Amra?"

"Shopping. There's this place called the Container Store that sells—"

"Lingerie?"

"Fish, but good guess. And Mom wants us to pick up groceries."

"Can you drive me into the city tomorrow?"

Lew stared at me. "Why don't you take the train?"

"I don't want to schlep my stuff through train stations."

"What, your one duffel bag? You are such a wuss."

"A wuss? You still say wuss? The light's green."

He rolled through the intersection, but the traffic ahead of us wasn't moving. "What are you going to do in the city?"

"I'm going to see some people."

"What people? You don't have any people."

"The Art Institute, then. Where are you going? You missed the turn."

"Nonsense. I have an unerring sense of direction."

"I'm driving on the way home."

"This car? Not a chance, Delacorte."

There was a strange car in the driveway—a dark blue Buick that looked freshly polished. We parked on the street. Lew opened the Audi's trunk with his remote ("Because I can"), and we carried the grocery bags into the house.

A man sat at the kitchen table across from my mother, his back to us. I didn't recognize him at first, but then he turned and smiled broadly. "Well look who's here," he said.

"Hi, Pastor Paul," Lew said.

The man pushed himself out of his seat. He was dressed in khakis and a striped golf shirt, his brown leather shoes too dressy for the rest of the outfit.

My mother stayed seated, her face pleasantly blank.

He came to me first. The groceries made a hug impossible, thank God. I shifted the bags slightly and held out a hand. He clasped my hand between his own. "Del, Del, Del." He slapped the back of my hand, then gripped my shoulder. "I can hardly believe it. You look just like your father."

I hadn't seen Pastor Paul since my father's funeral. My mother had stopped going to church when I was small, but my father had put on his suit every Sunday, dragging Lew with him. I stayed home to watch TV. I was jealous of Lew, but he begged to stay home so often that I knew I was getting the better deal.

I suddenly remembered a show I used to watch. It only played on Sunday mornings, and it was called something like *The Magic Door*. The magic was all done by green screen: a live-action guy with a guitar and a weird cap—an acorn?—who was magically shrunk down to the size of animal hand puppets. The guy would go through a door in a tree and come out in this magical forest, and sing songs where half the verses made no sense to me. It wasn't until high school that I realized it was a program for Jewish kids, and the mini guy was singing in Hebrew.

The pastor moved on to Lew, giving him his own hearty handshake. I remembered that aggressive enthusiasm. I never went to Sunday school, but I'd gotten to know Pastor Paul from his frequent visits. He'd arrive at odd times—the middle of a Saturday afternoon, or an hour after supper—and my parents would have to drop what they were doing and make him coffee. If I wasn't around he made a point of asking for me, and Dad would make me come in from the backyard. Pastor Paul always made a big fuss over me, asking me how I was doing, telling me how much I'd grown, even if I'd just seen him the week before. He was big into tousling my hair. He was a tousler.

"So what have you boys been up to?" he asked. "Your mother says you've moved out west, Del. Colorado. I hear it's real pretty."

"In the dark, it's a lot like Illinois." My stock answer.

He nodded, not really hearing me. "Those mountains are beautiful."

Lew put away the groceries while the pastor and I talked about nothing. Most of the nothing was handled by Pastor Paul. Whenever I started to answer a question or make a comment, his attention seemed to immediately move on to the next thing he was going to say.

After five minutes he announced that he had to be going, and five minutes later he announced it again. We gradually made our way to the front door, where he pulled on his elaborate winter coat and talked some more as he zipped, buttoned, snapped, and cinched. He pumped my hand again. "I've thought a lot about you over the years," he said. It was almost exactly what Dr. Aaron had said. "I'm glad to see you doing well."

I almost laughed at that.

He clapped me on the shoulder again. "I swear, you look just like your father. He was one of the 'Chosin Few,' you know. Not many men survived that battle."

"That's true." I didn't know what else to say to that. I don't remember my father talking about Korea.

"I always said, he was the one you wanted behind the wheel of the bus in a snowstorm." He nodded. "Well, I've got to be going."

I stayed on the porch, getting colder in the breeze, as he finally climbed into the Buick. I watched him pull away and then shut the door behind me.

"I don't like that guy," I said.

Lew laughed. "Pastor Paul? Come on, he's a nice old man." Mom shook her head, frowning. "What?" Lew said.

"How often does he come over?" I asked.

She shrugged, and carried the coffee cups to the sink. "Once a month. Maybe every few weeks."

Lew laughed. "Hey, he got the hots for the Widow Pierce?"

Mom gave him the look that Lew and I called the Brush-Back Pitch.

I followed her. "What's he want? Do you *like* him visiting you?"

"Not particularly."

"Then why do you put up with him?"

"He's just doing his job."

"What job? You're not even in the congregation anymore. Is he trying to get you to come back?"

"Oh no." Her voice was hard. "I'll never set foot in that church again."

I looked at Lew. Lew looked at his hands.

"Oh, and your friend Bertram called," Mom said. Her voice had shifted instantly back to normal. "He said he really needed to talk to you."

"*Bertram?*" I hadn't spoken to him since the nuthouse. How the hell had he gotten this number? Maybe the slans had beamed it to him.

"He said he really had to talk to you. I wrote his number on the fridge calendar."

"Mom, listen, if he calls again, just tell him I'm not in, okay?"

Mom gave me the Brush-Back Pitch (which Lew enjoyed—we were tied now at one apiece). She wasn't going to lie to anybody.

"Did you remember the sour cream?" she said.

Lew was already heading toward the door.

3

I awoke with a start and immediately groaned in pain. I was on the floor, my right arm and leg stretched up onto the bed, where my wrist and ankle were manacled to the frame. My elbow fired tracer shots of pain up the back of my arm.

"Del, open the door!" My mother. This wasn't the first time she'd called my name, I realized. Either her shouting or my fall had woken me up.

"It's okay," I said. My throat was raw. So I'd been screaming again. I pushed myself off the floor, got a knee under me. The dimly lit room whirlpooled around me—the Nembutal was still in my bloodstream— but the pain in my elbow lessened.

Louder, I said, "It's okay! I just fell out of bed."

I crawled back onto the mattress, my right arm and leg clumsy and dead as prosthetics. Circulation started to return, and every joint on the right side of my body ached in unison: shoulder to wrist, hip to ankle.

The foam-padded manacles were padlocked with Kryptonite combination locks. Blue polymer-wrapped bicycle chains looped from the manacles to the crossbars in the bed frame.

"You were yelling," Mom said. "Are you sure . . . ?"

I fumbled with the lock at my wrist. It was upside down, and my vision was fuzzy at the edges. I dialed the first number, and dragged my finger to the next tumbler. "It was just a nightmare," I said. I pushed the last number into line, until I was looking at "9-9-9." I pulled, and the lock opened. I tugged my hand free of the manacle.

"It's okay. Just go to bed, Mom."

I lay facedown, my heartbeat rushing in my ears, until she walked away from the door. I almost drifted asleep again, but forced myself to sit up, rub my face until I was awake enough to unlock my leg and get out of bed. The red LED alarm clock read 3:50. I was sleepy, but sleepy wasn't good enough.

I turned on the light, found my duffel bag, and swung it onto the bed. I fished out the orange pill bottle from the right-hand side, rattled it. Three pills. I'd taken only one before going to bed, but that had been a mistake. I needed to be either awake or *out*.

I looked at the clock again. Only a few hours until dawn. I dropped the bottle back into my bag without opening it.

When I came back from my walk, my mother was in the laundry room, moving my clothes from the washer to the dryer. I stopped short, then saw that they were the clothes I'd put into the washer before I left. It didn't look like she'd gone into my duffel bag.

"You don't have to do that," I said.

I turned sideways to move past her in the narrow space, a coffee cake under one arm and the three-pound Sunday edition of the *Chicago Tribune* under the other. The laundry room was really a breezeway that connected the garage to the house and did double duty as a mudroom. My dad had built it, under close supervision by my mother. She said he had hands of concrete, hell on anything smaller than a 2x4 or more fragile than sheet metal. He never worked on a piece of wood trim that didn't snap.

"You already got to the bakery?"

"Seven o'clock Sunday morning, and it was packed." I went into the kitchen, set the box on the counter. "Same old Polish ladies. That place hasn't changed a bit."

"You didn't go back to sleep, did you?"

I shook my head, even though she couldn't see me. "Sorry about that. I didn't mean to wake you up." I felt embarrassed and guilty, as if she'd caught me wandering around the house naked.

She started the dryer and came into the kitchen, drying her hands on a paper towel. She threw out the remains of the coffee I'd made at four—I'd needed plenty of caffeine—and started a fresh pot. I busied myself getting down plates and cutting slices of the coffee cake. We sat down at the table and divvied up sections of the *Trib*. The cake wasn't sweet in the center—nothing in the Polish bakery was as sugary as something from a regular bakery—but it tasted better to me than any roll or donut I'd found. Or maybe it was just nostalgia. We ate and read in silence for a long time.

The demon I'd seen at the airport two days ago was mentioned on page three. It was a brief story, a follow-up to whatever they'd run the day before. The victim was not going to be charged—nobody thought he was faking. Experts agreed it was the Painter strain of the disorder. (Those were the official terms—*strain, disorder*—as if marrying a medieval word like *possession* with more medical and modern-sounding partners tamed the idea, boxed it up into something tidy enough for science.) Best guess, there were perhaps a hundred distinct strains—a science-weasel way of saying one hundred demons.

The CDC recorded over twenty thousand cases of possession a year in the US, some lasting weeks and most lasting only minutes. Some people were hit repeatedly, as if being struck by lightning charged them for life. Most of the time they were seized by the same demon, but sometimes it was a different one every time.

The government hastened to add that the reports contained an unknown number of false positives, false negatives, incorrect diagnoses. Demons left behind no DNA, no wake of antibodies in the bloodstream, no cellular changes in the brain. A possession—especially a brief, one-time possession—was easy to hide and easier to fake. Different people were highly motivated to do either. Demons could make you do awful things—but awful things could make you famous. Possession survivors showed up on TV all the time.

Next to the airport story was a sidebar on the International Conference on Possession and its outlaw para-conference, DemoniCon. DemoniCon was not, technically, even a conference: it had no charter, no committees, no reservation agreements. It was an improvised annual party that followed ICOP around the globe. Demonology cranks, hobbyists, and demon fans bought up hotel rooms in whatever city ICOP was being held at that year, tried to crash the more interesting ICOP events, and then made nuisances of themselves.

People were worried about more cases of possession cropping up because of the conferences, or worse, more cases of copycat possessions. Nobody wanted armed impersonators of the Pirate King or the Truth running around. Security was supposed to be tight, though that would make no difference to a real demon. Nothing could stop a real demon.

"Lew's coming at ten?" Mom said.

"So he says." Amra and Lew had driven back to Gurnee last night. It was an hour up and an hour back, depending on traffic, but Chicagoans seemed to take this in stride.

"And you're staying in the city both nights?"

"Uh, yeah." I got up and refilled my cup. The "Self Clean" light was blinking. I hadn't told her about ICOP, or Dr. Ram. I hadn't even told her about seeing Dr. Aaron, except that we'd had a good visit, and that she'd gained a lot of weight.

I hadn't told her anything, and Mom hadn't pressed me. This wasn't like her.

"I'm worried about you, my son," she said.

My son. That always floored me.

"I'm going to be fine," I said automatically. "I've just been . . ." I sat down again, the coffee cup hot against my fingertips. "Mom, back when I was little . . . how *did* I snap out of it? If it wasn't the prayer thing, what happened? Did I just wake up one morning . . . back?"

"I suppose you were too young to remember."

"I was in bed for a long time, I remember that. There were these straps. Right?"

She gazed at the floor. "You were in the hospital for almost three weeks. All they knew how to do was sedate you and keep you tied up. We took you out of there, but even at home you had to be watched all the time, even at night, because you'd get up and tear around the house. You started a fire in the living room one night, to roast marshmallows. You were wild. And so *strong*.

"But you weren't mean—you didn't try to hurt anyone, not on purpose. You were just careless. You didn't know your own strength. Lew was seven, and much bigger than you, but even then, well, eventually your father . . . your father and I decided that you had to be kept in your room. Your father boarded up the windows to keep you from escaping, and we put a bolt on the outside of the door. A lot of that time, because of the tantrums, you had to be strapped down. We fed you in bed, though all you wanted to eat was peanut butter sandwiches and ice cream."

"I scream, you scream," I said, half singing it.

Mom looked up at me sharply, and then away. "You'd chant that at the top of your voice."

"Lovely."

She sighed. "You weren't easy to live with."

"So what changed? When did I get better?"

"It didn't happen in one day—it didn't happen in one *month*. The thing you liked, the thing we finally figured out, was stories—you'd lie still for stories. I read from picture books and the jokes from the paper, Lew would read you comic books. I told you stories from my childhood, talked about all the things you'd do when you grew up . . . oh, anything I could think of. We went through every book in the house, then went to the library every other day for a bag more. This was after my surgery, and it was a lot of strain, but some days I think I did nothing but read to you and take Tylenol."

"*Mike Mulligan and His Steam Shovel*," I said.

"Oh Lord yes. We must have read *Mike Mulligan* five hundred times."

I loved that book. "Okay, so then . . ."

"Then you calmed down. Gradually, we let you play more in the room, and you behaved yourself when you came out. You just got better and better."

I shook my head. "But how did you—when did you know I was me? What happened to let you know that the demon was gone?"

She smiled, shrugged. "I just knew. There was one thing, though. For the longest time you hadn't called us by our names. Lew was 'that big boy.' Your dad was 'mister,' and I was 'that tall lady.' And then one day I was feeding you lunch and you called me 'Mom.'" She shrugged. "That was enough for me. I knew then I had my little boy back."

Inside the shower I let the hot water beat on my skull and tried to drown myself in noise: the thrum and hiss of the shower; the indistinct male rumbling of the voice on the clock radio on the bathroom counter; the intermittent faint trill that could have been a telephone in the next room. It didn't help. Through all this, wired directly to my nervous system, was the rattling pressure of the thing in my head.

I twisted off the shower and slid open the glass door. The phone *was* ringing. It stopped a moment later.

Had to be Bertram. He'd left two more messages on Mom's machine while we were out last night, and I hadn't called him back. Why did he think it was okay to call me? We'd gotten to know each other in the hospital, as much as you could get to know someone nutty as a fruitcake. We'd had hours to fill with talk as we made circuits of the wing. But that was the extent of the relationship. We were hospital friends.

I opened the cabinet door under the sink and took a large, fluffy towel from the stack of large, fluffy towels, none of them older than a year. Mom had joined a towel club—a bunch of ladies who agreed to buy each other towels on their birthdays. For some reason Mom found this easier than just going out and buying herself ten new ones.

I dried off and started opening drawers, looking for a comb.

"Del, it's Dr. Aaron."

"Really?" I unlocked the door, opened it a crack. A lick of cool air against my shoulder. My mother stood there, covering the receiver with a hand. I shrugged and took it from her.

"Dr. Aaron?" My voice echoed in the small space. I leaned back, closed the door.

"Del, I'm sorry to bother you. But I've been looking at some of my old notes, and something occurred to me. Do you have time to talk today?"

I looked at my wrist, but I'd taken off my watch. It must have been about 9:30, though. "I don't know. My brother's coming by in a little bit, and I'm going into the city for a couple days." I'd already told Dr. Aaron about ICOP, but I didn't want to say it aloud. It seemed impossible to talk quietly in this echoing room. I picked up my watch from the sink top. It was 9:40.

"I think we need to talk before you go," she said. There was an edge to her voice. "It should take only a few minutes."

Was this about the sleeping pills? Maybe she'd reconsidered. Or maybe she'd decided what I really needed was to check into rehab. No, it sounded like something else.

"Okay, listen, let me get dressed and . . ." In the drawer was a gray earring box. I picked it up, ran my thumb over the velvet top. "How about the Borders by Randhurst Mall? They have a café. You live in town, right?" It was only two minutes' drive for me.

We agreed to meet at the bookstore in twenty minutes. Lew would probably be late anyway.

I put down the phone and looked at the little box. I used to sneak in here to show it to my friends. With great drama I'd lock the door and swear them to secrecy.

The box had a stiff spring hinge. I used both hands to open it.

My mother's spare eyeball.

I dried my fingers against the towel, then lifted the eye from its concave pad. It was lighter than I remembered. I held it up to the light, and my mother's eye stared down at me. Maybe it didn't fit right, or it was the wrong color, or she just wanted to have a spare around, but she got a new eye when I was in sixth grade, and kept the old one here in the bathroom. Lew and I called it the Eye of Agamoto, after

Dr. Strange's all-seeing amulet. It was my friend Jeff who said, "Is that the one she keeps in the back of her head?"

I leaned over the sink, wiped the fog from the mirror. I held the plastic up to my forehead, a big unblinking third eye, and looked at myself looking at myself. I couldn't imagine what it must have been like for my mother. Even after the possession, I was no angel. Even now. But during those months when I was running wild in the house and starting fires, or those long days when I was tied to the bed and she was tied to me . . . I don't know how she did it.

The demon that had possessed me was called the Hellion. It was a Dennis the Menace, a Spanky, a Katzenjammer Kid. It possessed boys who were at least four and never older than nine—towheaded kids with impish smiles and fly-away hair—and turned them into scampering brats with Woody Woodpecker laughs.

The Hellion was the eternal prankster. He booby-trapped doorways with paint buckets, threw baseballs through windows, slipped snakes into beds. Whipped out his homemade slingshot and knocked those glasses right off your head.

I grimaced. Pressed the eye back into its little bed. Closed the box with a snap.

"I want to go back to the car accident," Dr. Aaron said.

We sat at a table by the window, only a table away from the traditional yellow chair. Even Borders kept a yellow chair, as if the Fat Boy might burst in and start demanding lattés. There were maybe twenty people in the café, and at least half of them seemed to be seventy or older. We'd both ordered bottled water. Not usually my thing, but I'd had enough coffee this morning and I was feeling jittery.

"At any time during the crash," she said, "did you go unconscious? Maybe you struck your head?"

"Are we back to that theory?" I said. "I bonk my head, start hearing voices, wackiness ensues."

"Please, bear with me for a minute."

I leaned back in my chair. "I didn't hit my head—nothing like what happened in the pool. I mean, when I first hit the rail everything went black for a second—but just a second. I remember right after the air bag hit me, the car filled with this stuff like gray smoke. I found out later that it was the cornstarch they packed the air bag in to keep it from molding or something. Then I went through the rail and bounced against the air bag a few times, but afterward my forehead wasn't bleeding or anything. I didn't even get a black eye."

"When you say everything went black, you mean you blacked out?"

"No, I didn't go unconscious—I just couldn't see anything. I don't think I was knocked all the way under—it happened too fast. I just . . . saw black."

"Like 'a black well' opening up?"

Heat rolled up my chest, made my ears roar.

"Del, after we talked yesterday, I looked up my old notes from our sessions. When you first visited me, we spent a lot of time talking about your near drowning. You talked about a 'black well,' a deep hole that you saw at the bottom of the pool. You could feel it sucking you in."

"I did?"

"Do you remember that?"

"Not really." The shiver had passed. I pressed my palms into my knees. "Some."

"And this time?"

"Some." I looked up, smiled, but couldn't hold it. "There was something like that. Like a well. When I hit the guardrail I kind of lurched forward, and for a second there I saw it, this blackness, and I felt like I could . . . like it was sucking me in. But I held on. I stayed awake, and then I was getting whipped around inside the car. A second later I was at the bottom of the ravine." I shook my head. "You think that means something?"

"Del, both times after you saw this well, the noises came back. Some people when they have near-death experiences, they see a tun-nel, and perhaps—"

"The tunnel, the light, and Grandma and Jesus at the end of it with their arms open to greet me. I've read about this. That's just oxygen starvation."

"That's one theory—oxygen starvation and endorphin release. But say that the Jungians are right, and there are outside archetypes or memes that the brain is receptive to. One way to think of this black well is that it's a gateway—a gateway that opens when you're most vulnerable."

"So I'm near death, and the demon jumps back in."

"Maybe." She pursed her lips; it was killing her to agree with *demon*. Dr. Aaron liked things agnostic. But she nodded. "Maybe. It explains a lot. Each time the well opened, it came after you. It's like an opportunistic infection. But the good news is that you've fought it off before. And if the current exercises aren't working, that just means we've got to try new ones."

"It's a really good theory," I said flatly.

She blinked. "But you don't think so."

"I wish you were right, Doc. A couple of months ago I would have bought it."

"A couple of months ago—when you were hospitalized?"

I breathed in, breathed out. Cleansing breaths. "See, it's not just the noises now. I developed this sleepwalking problem."

She frowned, and I laughed. "Okay, that's not the right word," I said. "Sleep-*raging*, maybe. Wolfing out."

Her head tilted a fraction. This was what she used to do when I was fourteen. A little tilt, the right bit of leverage, and she could open me like a bottle.

"It didn't start until a couple months after the car accident," I said. "The noises had grown worse, but I was hanging on. I was getting to work most days. Then on a Thursday night I woke up, and my downstairs neighbor was pounding on my door." I smiled, remembering how it had taken me a few seconds to realize that the pounding wasn't coming from inside my head. "Anyway, I was on the floor in the front hallway, tangled in the bedsheets. I didn't know why I was in the hall, but I was furious at my neighbor for waking me up. I yanked open the door, and he told me I'd been screaming my head off for fifteen minutes. So, a nightmare, right? What do I know.

"It happened again a few nights later. I woke up in the kitchen this time, the phone ringing. I'd gone through the refrigerator, pulling out everything and breaking bottles and ripping open packages. I thought, Jesus Christ. So I started putting chairs in front of my bedroom door, turning my bed around—little obstacles to trip me and maybe wake me up. It didn't help. So I went to see that doctor in Colorado Springs I told you about. He started me on Ambien, but that didn't do anything for me, so he switched me to Nembutal. The attacks kept happening, though, and that's when I checked into the nuthouse. They kept watch on me, doped me to the gills, and I went a string of nights without any adventures. Of course, it was right about then that the insurance ran out."

"So you came back home. And it started happening again."

"It's still happening. Every night I—"

I started to say, Every night I chain myself to the bed. I could tell her everything: the bike chains, the combination locks (because keys could be lost thrashing around, or could be found by whatever was running my body at night), the whole Lawrence-Talbot-at-Full-Moon melodrama. But not yet. Not here in the coffee shop.

She waited for a long time, then said, "Del, tell me what's going on."

"I'm a little slow," I said, "but even I figured it out eventually. The Hellion, the demon that possessed me when I was five?"

She nodded. She knew I was stalling, and wasn't about to interrupt.

"He hasn't been seen since. Okay, a couple reports in the news when kids acted strange, but those were just guesses, they weren't confirmed possessions. And then, even those rumors died out. There's been nothing reported about the Hellion since the eighties."

I leaned forward. "Doctor, the Hellion didn't *come back* when I was fourteen. It didn't *come back* after the car accident." I made a noise that was something between a sigh and a laugh.

"It never left."

Dr. Aaron didn't move. I looked around at the quiet people quietly sipping their lattés and fruit smoothies.

Finally she said, "You know this."

"I can feel it in my head, Doctor. It's pissed off. Somehow when I was a little kid I . . . I trapped it. I think my mother helped me lock it down the first time. And you helped me the second time—we just thought that the exercises were helping me keep the noises out, when they were really helping me keep them *in*."

"Oh, Del. I'm so sorry. If you feel I've—"

I shook my head. "It's not your fault. I didn't mean it that way." I stood up, and pulled my jacket off the back of the chair. "You helped me a lot, got me through a really tough time. You were great."

"Del, you don't have to do this alone. I can help."

"You got your scrip pad with you?"

"Del, I'm talking about therapy. We can start meeting again, work on this together."

"I don't want to *work on this*, Doctor. I don't want to lock it down anymore." I yanked my arms through the jacket. Fuck the prescription. "I'm done with exercises. I need an exorcism."

Lew and Mom were in the kitchen, Lew talking on his cell phone and pouring a cup of coffee.

"I'll be ready in a second," I said, and moved past them quickly. They'd be able to read how upset I was from my face. "I just need to pack up."

"No way, no way it should be that slow," Lew said to the phone. "Did you ping it? Run a trace route?" There were crumbs in his beard. "Hey Mom, your 'Self Clean' light is blinking."

"I put your laundry on the bed," Mom called after me.

"Thanks."

"If it's self cleaning, why's it just blink at you? Shouldn't it just clean itself?"

My duffel bag was still zipped. My clothes were on the bed, folded and stacked with retail-quality precision. She'd made the bed, too. Why hadn't I done that? I closed the door behind me, and kneeled down.

I reached under the bed frame and up, feeling for the hole in the batting that covered the bottom of the box spring. I couldn't find it at first, and my heart raced. *Jesus, if Mom—*

My hand closed on the stubbled pistol grip. I pulled out the gun and the oilcloth, and quickly rewrapped it, resisting the urge to look at it.

I kept my back to the door as I unzipped the duffel bag. The loops of sheathed chain were coiled like snakes. I pushed them to the side and tucked the gun into the top of a pair of jeans. The pill bottle was still in its spot at the bottom of the bag.

Three pills. Three fucking pills.

I packed the newly cleaned clothes around and on top of all the incriminating evidence: the bottle, the locks and chains and manacles, the gun. I felt like a terrorist. A Mama's Boy terrorist, though; my mother had buttoned the collared shirts, double rolled the socks, and even folded my underwear.

I looked around at the room, checked under the bed again, and slung the bag onto my shoulder. It was suspiciously heavy.

My mother was in the hallway, coming toward me.

"Do you have everything?"

I glanced back at the room. "I think so."

"You can always pick it up when you get back. You're coming back before you leave, right?"

"Oh yeah. I'll see you in a couple days." I tried to make it sound casual.

We went into the kitchen. Lew was just putting away his phone. I carefully set down the bag—I didn't want to drop it, in case it clanked—and put an arm around Mom. She was still taller than me— no shrinking yet. "She folded my underwear," I said to Lew. "My mom folded my underwear."

"Big deal. She irons mine." He looked at me. Last night I'd told him about why I wanted to go into the city, but there was something else in his expression. "You ready now?" he said.

Ah. Mom must have told him I'd been with Dr. Aaron.

"I'm waiting on you," I said.

Mom pulled me into her, hugged me. "Drive safe. I'll see you in a couple days."

DEMONOLOGY

THE CAPTAIN

SRINAGAR, JAMMU AND KASHMIR, INDIA, 2004

The first vehicle in a four-vehicle U.S. Marine convoy had almost reached the west end of the bridge when the IEDs detonated. The four vehicles—three Humvees trailed by an M113 armored personnel carrier—were crossing the Fateh Kadal, one of nine two-lane bridges that crossed the Jhelum River in downtown Srinagar. It was 2:15 p.m., fifty degrees but sunny, the pavement still wet from the spring squall that had moved through a half hour before.

Private First Class Peter Gruen was driving the third vehicle in the convoy. He was squinting into the sun through the Humvee's narrow windshield when the vehicle in front of him suddenly catapulted into the air on a fountain of flame and broken cement. The shockwave was like a punch to the face. Gruen stomped on the brakes and twisted the wheel. His Humvee hit the cement wall and stopped dead, throwing him into the steering column. The hummer he'd been following came down on its side to Gruen's left, wheels burning. The circular hatch at the top of the vehicle bounced free, slammed into Gruen's door, and rolled to the other side of the roadway. Chunks of cement thundered down onto the hood and roof.

A ragged hole almost as big as his Humvee had been opened in the roadway between Gruen and the two lead vehicles. Twisted steel rods jutted up from the edge of the hole. Below was the black water of the Jhelum.

Sergeant Stevens, in the seat beside him, shouted into the radio, "Out! Out! Covering fire!"

Gruen felt like his lungs had flattened against the steering wheel. He wheezed, trying to suck air. Covering fire. His sidearm was on his hip, but his M-16 was stowed next to his seat, wedged between ammo boxes on the high hump that covered the drive shaft. The two marines in the back, Koslow and Mack, were carrying their assault rifles across their laps. Mack moved first. He kicked open his door and pulled himself out.

A sound like a shriek and a whistle. Gruen turned his face away, and the rocket-propelled grenade hit with a tremendous bang that rocked the Humvee up on its driver-side wheels. Gruen smashed into the door. The vehicle teetered for a moment, then fell back onto its wheels with a jolt.

Koslow yelled something Gruen couldn't make out. He could hear nothing but an intense ringing.

Blood covered the backseat, the front of Koslow's uniform. In the front seat, the sergeant slumped against the dash, almost on the floor, dead or unconscious. Where was Mack?

Gruen yanked on his door, and it opened with a squeal. He grabbed the sergeant under the arms and heaved backward, dragging the man into his lap. Through the ringing, he heard a distant percussive stutter. The .50-cal on top of the APC behind them had opened up.

Gruen dragged the sergeant out of the car and onto the pavement. He laid the man down on his back, his helmet propping up his head. They were out of the crossfire for the moment: the wall of the bridge against their backs, the overturned and burning Humvee blocking fire from the west, Gruen's Humvee blocking fire from the east. His vehicle was tilted oddly, the back right tire folded under it like an animal with a broken leg.

The sergeant's hand was bloody, the sleeve soaked. Gruen lifted the arm from Stevens' chest, and the man groaned. The hand felt pulpy, boneless. Gruen laid the arm on the ground, and ripped the sleeve open. "Koslow! Grab the medic kit!"

Koslow was still in the back of the Humvee. The man didn't seem to hear him for a moment, but then he ducked down to where the kit was bolted to the floor and came up with the metal box. He opened the door and stepped out. Bullets pinged the metal next to his head, and he squatted next to Gruen and the sergeant.

"Mack's dead," Koslow said loudly. He popped open the kit, and Gruen grabbed a roll of bandages and a roll of white medical tape. "Is the sarge hurt bad?"

"He'll be fine," Gruen said, but it was for the sarge's benefit; Gruen had no idea how bad he was hurt. He'd gotten first aid training like everybody else, but he was no medic. He put a pad of bandages into the man's palm, eliciting another grunt from him, and started wrapping the hand and wrist. The sergeant mumbled something, looking dazed. He was going into shock. "You're going to be all right, sir," Gruen said. Then to Koslow, "Where are they at?"

Koslow was peeking through the windows in the cab of the Humvee. "Both ends of the bridge, I think. Jesus, probably under us, too—I thought I saw water taxis down there before we crossed."

"Nazis," the sergeant said in a low voice.

"Uh, I don't think so, sir," Gruen said. That's all he needed, Sarge freaking out on him. Though really there was no telling who was shooting at them: Al-Fatah Force, PFL, LeT, any number of Pak-supported ultras. It could even be India-backed counterinsurgents. Everybody in the city—everybody in the entire J&K—wanted the marines out of there. He yanked off a length of tape, pressed one end to the bandage, and wrapped it three times around the sergeant's wrist like a cowboy roping a calf.

"We've got to get Mack and Sarge into the APC," Gruen said to Koslow. "Then go forward and find out who's alive ahead of us. We've got to get out of here."

"Gruen, they're building barricades."

Gruen stared at him. What the fuck?

He got into a crouch, then raised his head over the hood of the Humvee. The rear APC was still upright. It was a boxy, slab-sided thing on tracks, more heavily armored than the Humvees. More important, there were only four men in it, and room for eight more.

One of the APC's occupants was on the roof-mounted .50-caliber gun, firing back the way they'd come. Two other marines were on their bellies by the tires, firing as well. The fourth man was probably behind the wheel.

A hundred feet away at the end of the bridge, a jumble of car tires maybe three feet high had appeared like a magic trick, spanning the width of the bridge. More tires were being thrown onto the pile every second, even though the marines were filling the air with bullets. Locals swarmed out of the nearby buildings—five-story wooden shacks leaning into the river—and ran down the sloping streets toward the bridge, carrying tires, furniture, sheet metal. Like the entire city had been saving up junk in their backyards, waiting for this opportunity to personally fuck Private Gruen.

"The shooters are lining up back there," Koslow said. "Plenty of AK-47s, sounds like. They have us pinned down, at least until air support arrives. If we can get a gunship to clear—"

Gruen looked at the man with disgust. "Air support? We don't have time to camp here, Koslow. Forget the rifles—they've got RPGs. We've got to move *now,* before they frag us."

"Nazis!" the sergeant said. He was staring at the bridge wall behind Gruen. Gruen followed his stare. On the cement wall, a spray-painted red swastika. But that was like a holy symbol here, wasn't it? A Hindu thing or something.

"Go up front," Gruen said to Koslow. "See if you can get around the hole and find out what happened with the lead vehicle. We're going home in the APC." The M113 was Vietnam-era technology, slow and cranky, but it was armored to hell. "Get back here quick, okay?"

"Shit," Koslow said. He rose into a crouch, then moved into the smoke to the west.

Gruen turned back, and Sergeant Stevens was up, squatting on his haunches, the helmet off and on the pavement. Stevens tore a strip from the roll of medical tape and pressed it to the front of the helmet. Gruen wouldn't have thought that right hand was functional.

"What are you doing, Sarge? You need to get your helmet back on."

The sergeant ignored him. He pressed a second piece of tape onto the helmet, making an upside down V, and tore another strip from the roll.

"Sergeant, please . . ."

Stevens thumbed the third strip into place and suddenly jumped to his feet, all trace of shock gone. Spine straight, shoulders back, he looked half a foot taller. Bullets ripped through the air around his head, but he ignored them. He gazed down at Gruen with a confident smile. Gruen had never noticed how blue the man's eyes were.

"Oh, shit," Gruen said. He felt sick to his stomach. "I need you to sit down, Sergeant."

"Not Sergeant," Stevens said.

He placed the helmet firmly on his head. The tape on the forehead formed a blocky letter A.

"It's Captain."

Stevens stalked across the road to the steel roof hatch that had come loose from the overturned Humvee. He gripped the inside handle with his left hand and lifted it like a shield. It must have weighed thirty or forty pounds, but he held it easily by that one awkward handle.

"Round up the men," Stevens said. There was no arguing with that voice. "I'll clear the barricade."

And then he ran toward the end of the bridge, into a hail of bullets. Gruen stood up, shouting, "Sarge! Sarge!" He'd never seen a man run so fast, so beautifully, covering the length of the bridge in what seemed to be a series of still frames. Stevens raised the makeshift shield in front of him, and bullets sparked off the steel and whined away—once, twice, and then a hailstorm. Several times rounds seemed to strike his legs and arms, causing a barely perceptible stutter, but if anything his speed increased.

Ten feet from the barricade he leaped, legs spread in a V, his shield in front of him like a battering ram, his bandaged right fist outstretched. Two gunmen went flying, another three collapsed under him. And then he was gone, vanished behind the wall of smoke and tires, into the mass of attackers.

Gruen looked around wildly. Koslow came back through the smoke, his arms around another marine, and two others followed. One of the followers carried a dead man. "Let's go!" Gruen shouted. "Go, go, go!" He ran around the hummer and picked up Mack's blood-soaked body. Mack's left arm was missing, but Gruen didn't see it anywhere on the pavement. The overturned hummer was still burning. There was nothing they could do for the bodies inside.

The marines ran toward the only remaining vehicle, the APC. The soldiers had stopped firing. Automatic gunfire still crackled from the west end of the bridge, but no one on this side seemed to be firing anymore. The driver opened the hatch from the inside, and the marines clambered into the rumbling vehicle, stepping on one another. It seemed to take minutes to load and get situated. Gruen sat on the bench seat, Mack cradled in his arms. The APC slowly backed up and swung around.

"Hold on," the driver said. The engine whined, and the tracks scraped and squealed. The APC jerked into motion, picked up speed. Through his window slit Gruen could see the ground moving past them. The vehicle jolted as it went over something—a tire, a body?—and then they were into the barricade.

The APC struck the wall of tires, sending debris exploding away from them. Gruen gripped a handle above his head with one hand and held on to Mack with the other. The nose of the APC went up, banged down hard. The vehicle stopped. Gruen pulled himself off the floor, then bent to peer through the windows, looking for the sergeant.

There.

Stevens stood in the middle of an unmoving pile of bodies, the circular hatch still on his left arm. The edge of the shield was stained a solid stripe of red. His uniform hung in tatters. The flesh above his waist had been torn into red ribbons, as if he'd taken several rounds directly to the chest. There was nothing left of his right arm below the elbow.

Gruen couldn't understand why he hadn't bled out by now.

Stevens grinned, his teeth impossibly bright, and raised the stump of his arm into the suggestion of a salute. The marines stared at him through the windows. No one spoke.

Then the shield dropped from his grip. Stevens fell to his knees, and pitched forward.

4

Half a block from the Hyatt Regency, traffic came to a dead stop. We were on Wacker, just above Michigan Avenue, almost in the shadow of the Hyatt's black steel and gray-tinted glass towers. Competing mobs of protesters and costumed counterprotesters had overrun their sawhorse-delimited camps on the sidewalks in front of the hotel and were spilling into the street, compressing police officers and un-aligned audience members between them. The protesters had signs and bullhorns, but the less organized countercrowd—DemoniCon attendees in trench coats, nightgowns, and red, white, and blue jumpsuits—looked to be having more fun.

"Just drop me off here," I said. There was nowhere to go except back the way we'd come, or maybe a hard left into the river.

"Hold on," Lew said. His phone was still plugged into his ear, and for a moment I couldn't tell who he was talking to. He'd spent half the drive on the cell, interrogating a series of underlings who either couldn't or wouldn't install something called a domain controller. It was weird to think of Lew, disorganized geek, as a *boss*. But it was clearly killing him to be away from the office. "I'll circle around and come back on Wacker."

I'd already opened the door. "Just pop the trunk. You can get back to work."

"It's just these guys, if you don't watch them they do it half-assed, and then you've got to scrape the servers and start over."

If you don't watch them? I laughed. "Lew, Lew. You the man. And I don't mean, you the man. You the *man*."

"Get a job, slacker."

The Audi's trunk yawned open. I swung the duffel onto one shoulder, and the weight nearly tipped me off balance and onto the hood of the car behind me. Lew stepped out of the car, careful to keep his door from dinging the SUV next to him.

He shook my hand and clapped me on the back. "So this doctor guy—call me and let me know how it goes. Good or bad, okay? Maybe me and Amra can cancel our thing, come back down, have dinner."

"No, don't do that. Seriously." He'd already apologized for having to do something with Amra's friends tonight, and even one apology was very un-Lew. "I'm going to get an Uno's pizza, a beer, watch some hotel porn, and go to sleep." The cars next to us started rolling forward, and honks erupted from the line of cars stopped behind us. "I'll call you tomorrow."

I got to the sidewalk, and watched the cop wave Lew's Audi into the opposing lanes and send him back the way we'd come.

"Well shit," I said. On my own again.

I turned and hiked up the hill toward the hotel, the duffel feeling like a dead body on my shoulder. The frigid wind lashed my hair and ruffled my spring jacket, a nylon, no-name thing from T. J. Maxx. Though I couldn't see it, somewhere a few hundred yards ahead of me was the lake.

As I reached the edge of the crowd, a huge man wheeled suddenly and I had to put out an arm to avoid colliding with him. He was big, over three hundred pounds. I would have taken him for a Fat Boy impersonator if not for the rest of his costume. He wore the Truth's broad-brimmed fedora and a black trench coat cinched tight as a sausage casing. He grinned down at me, his face huge as a moon. Maybe he wasn't possessed, but there definitely seemed to be more than one person in there.

"Sorry," I said, and moved sideways, nudging between a teenage boy wearing horns (the Piper?) and a chaps-wearing Lariat. I shifted the duffel to my front and used it like a bumper to plow through a sea of impersonators: a Pirate King; a pair of white-gowned, curly-haired Little Angels; a Smokestack Johnny in pinstriped overalls; a half dozen shield-carrying Captains; two more Truths; a Beggar (pockets stuffed with Monopoly money); a goggle-eyed Kamikaze; a bare-chested Jungle Lord.

The religious protesters were outnumbered, but made up for it in noise and passion. They were stacked up behind a row of sawhorses, shouting back at the DemoniCon fans, singing hymns, and waving signs:

THOU SHALT NOT HAVE ANY GOD BEFORE ME

LET JESUS INTO YOUR HEART — NOT SATAN

SIMON SAYS: NO AMERICAN IDOLOTARS

DON'T BE DEMONI-CONNED

The protesters could have been from any number of denominations, from Roman Catholics to Latter-day Saints, but the flavor of the signs struck me as distinctly fundamentalist. Possession was the perfect disease for the postmetaphorical wings of the church. Most Anabaptist strains of Protestantism incorporated possession into their theology, and quite a few used the disorder on both ends of the equation: demons could take you, true, but so could Jesus. "Asking Jesus into your heart" wasn't just a turn of phrase—he *took* you. The Pentecostals favored the spiritual third of the Trinity over Jesus himself, with the Holy Ghost repossessing believers at regular intervals, overriding their vocal cords to inflict glossolalia, and then moving on, leaving the suddenly empty vessels to collapse in the pews.

A funkily dressed woman in hoop earrings—I never would have taken her for a fundamentalist—held a sign that said, THE BODY IS GODS' TEMPLE. I smiled at the punctuation, and the woman took this as interest and flipped the sign over: NOT THE DEVILS PLAYGROUND. She wore a gold brooch in the shape of two Christian fish intersecting like an eye:

I nodded—yes, very nice, have to be going now—and stepped past her. The brooch marked her as a Rapturist—and maybe they all were. It made sense for them to be here. The Rapturists saw possession as one more sign of the end days, clearly described in Revelations, and they'd taken possession logic a step further than most sects: Armageddon was being waged now, between angels and demons, with human bodies as the battlefield. To a Rapturist, DemoniCon attendees weren't just misguided kids; they were plots of enemy territory to be captured.

I wondered what they'd make of me. To a Rapturist, I was fucking Iwo Jima.

A minute more of nudging and sidestepping got me past the last sawhorse, through the fundamentalists, and onto the mostly clear cement patio surrounding the Hyatt entrance. I pushed through the revolving door and stopped, dazed by the sudden absence of sunlight, bullhorns, and wind.

My eyes adjusted to the dimness. The atrium was an immense glass box. The furnishings projected a bland veneer of luxury, like a Ford Crown Victoria with deluxe trim. Gleaming floors, stiff couches, a long front desk in dark wood.

ICOP should have already started its sessions, but the lobby was largely empty of people. There was no one at the front desk, and only seven or eight people sat in the couches and chairs arranged in constellations around the room.

I crossed the marbled floors until I could see around a large column to the far end of the lobby. Past the elevators was a set of escalators, one leading up and another two leading down to the underground ballrooms. The area in front of the escalators was cordoned off by burgundy velvet ropes like the kind used in movie theaters. The only way past was through a metal detector guarded by a rent-a-cop, a black man in a gray uniform parked on a high stool.

I shifted the duffel bag and deliberately looked away from the guard. I was okay. I could get to the elevators, and my room, without going through the metal detector.

As I waited at the front desk I flipped through the credit cards in my wallet, trying to remember which card I'd used to reserve the room, and whether any of the cards could cover it. My mother used to talk about her "flood of bills" every month, and maybe that was why I'd started picturing my own debt as water rising in a sinking ship—with me trapped in the lower holds. The ship was going down, no doubt about that, but a few cabins still had pockets of air, and my job was to swim to the ones that had enough breathing room, like Shelley Winters in *The Poseidon Adventure*.

"One night?" the clerk asked me. She was a mocha-skinned woman in a tailored blue suit. I nodded, wondering if she thought I was a fan trying to sneak into the legit conference. I should have worn a tie. "And will this be on the Visa?"

I stifled the urge to say, "Which one?" My credit union Visa was dead, and the airline tickets had sucked the last of the oxygen out of my Lands' End card, but there might still be a few inches of breathing space near the ceiling of my Citibank. "Let's do Discover Card," I said. I had maybe $800 left on that one.

I kept my relaxed smile in place until the transaction cleared.

Ten minutes in the room and I didn't know what to do with myself. I didn't want to unpack, so I'd toured the bathroom (fantastically clean) and closets (oddly small), then inspected the mandatory hotel room equipment—TV, telephone, minibar—each with its own tented instructional card. Some poor slob with the same college degree as me had probably spent weeks designing each card. Or even sadder, they'd fired the poor slob with the useless degree and hired a high school kid who could use Microsoft Publisher.

I opened the drapes, and sat on the king-sized bed. I was thirty floors up. The second Hyatt tower blocked my direct view, but to either side I could see Lake Michigan: a broad plain the color of steel stretching to the horizon, scored with whitecaps. So huge. Repeated exposure to maps had never eradicated my boyhood conviction that this was no lake, not even a "great" one, but a third ocean.

The thing in my head paced back and forth, running a stick along the bars.

I got up, closed the drapes. Sat down in one of the chairs. Got up and looked through the drawers in the bedside table. Empty, not even a Gideon Bible. There hadn't been one in the last hotel I'd stayed at, either. Maybe the Gideons were falling down on the job.

I opened the duffel and looked through the printouts from the ICOP website.

Dr. Ram only showed up on the schedule for two events. The first, in less than an hour, was a poster session (whatever that was) with several of his grad students. The important event was his talk at 3:00 p.m. today in the Concorde room, one of the underground conference rooms.

So. Ambush him at the poster session, at the talk, or somewhere in between?

I pulled out the two collared shirts I'd brought—one blue, one white—both of them wrinkled as hell. I couldn't decide which one to wear and decided to iron both of them. The room's iron, annoyingly, was heavier and more fully featured than any I'd ever owned.

I didn't know when it would be best to approach Dr. Ram, or what I would say. This part of my plan had been hazy, even though I'd written over a dozen letters to him since I'd first read about his research, explaining my situation and proposing that my condition and his research interests seemed to intersect. Some of these letters were eloquent and cogent. Some were written from inside the white-noise cocoon of Nembutal.

I hadn't sent any of them. The problem was this: Demons didn't write letters to neurologists; therefore I wasn't possessed. Perhaps I had *been* possessed, but in that I was no different than thousands of other victims. There was no such thing in the literature as half-possessed — demi-demons weren't on the menu. So I was either a possession victim unique in the annals of the disorder, or I was crazy — and frankly, my credentials for crazy were impeccable.

I had managed to work up the courage once to call his office. He wasn't accepting patients — at least not walk-ins like me. I'd considered flying to California and pitching my case personally, but then I'd read on his website that he'd be attending this year's ICOP. I'd convinced myself that this was my best chance to get to him.

I put on the blue shirt and hung up the white one, and changed from jeans to beige, wrinkle-free khakis. I looked in the mirror. My hair was sticking up in the back, but otherwise I looked perfectly normal. Just another sane, reasonable person who had every right to walk up to a neurologist and introduce himself.

The thing in my head shifted like a toolbox sliding around the bed of a truck.

In the lobby I acknowledged the security guard with a nod and tired smile and walked through the frame of the metal detector. Detector and detective were silent. I followed the registration signs down an escalator to a long windowless room. A line of registration booths divided up the alphabet.

ICOP registration procedures were designed to keep out curiosity seekers, religious nuts, and especially the attendees of DemoniCon, ICOP's shadow conference. The $185-a-day fee immediately scared off the merely curious and the average fanboy. But even if you had the cash, only members and guests of ICOP sponsoring organizations (APA, AMA, WHO, and a dozen other acronyms) were allowed to register.

Fortunately, a DemoniCon fan site had offered an alternate entrance mechanism.

Go to www.apa.org and apply for a $45-a-year student member-
ship—don't worry, you're not going to pay for it. Choose Check
or Money Order not credit card. Enter a disposable e-mail address (you just need it for a couple minutes) and a fictitious street
address. After the site tells you that your membership is inactive
pending payment, go to the site's Forgot My Password page and
enter your temp e-mail address. That's right, the site automatically generated an account for you when you applied. Thanks,
morons! The site will e-mail you the password (in plain text of
course—these people haven't heard of encryption). Now log in
to the Members Only section and go to Edit My Account. See
that 15-digit membership ID? Copy that bad boy to the clip-
board. Next, go to the ICOP website. In the conference registration form, choose APA from the organization dropdown list, and
on the next screen, paste in that membership ID (evidently this
is a web service to APA's server, because it actually checks if the
ID's in their database—fake IDs don't work). Last, pay $15 via
credit card (sorry folks, there's no "check or money order" option
here). Voila. Your only problem: now that they have your credit
card, if they ever bother to check that you're not a student,
they've got you for FRAUD. Enjoy the conference!

I stepped up to the "M-N-O-P" booth, and presented my driver's li-
cense and web receipt. The woman spent a long minute looking over
the receipt and studying a laptop in front of her. I realized I'd made a
mistake. Anyone from ICOP could have run across the site. How
many DemoniConners had tried this scam? How could they not notice the unusual number of APA student registrations?

The woman handed me a conference badge. "Keep this with you
at all times," she said. Then she gave me a program book and compli-
mentary nylon tote bag.

I walked a short distance away and sat heavily on a couch. I looked
at the program book first. Most of the speeches and panels were being
held in the dozens of small rooms under the Hyatt, but the bigger

events—the keynote address, the Vatican panel, the speech by O. J.'s lawyer, Robert Shapiro—were hosted in the ballrooms. The poster sessions were in one of the main ballrooms.

Okay then. Ready for ambush?

I eventually found the right ballroom. People drifted in and out of the big double doors, watched by a security guard glancing at badges. I took a cleansing breath and went inside. I found myself in the middle of a seventh-grade science fair.

The room was filled with double rows of tables, their surfaces walled off into individual display booths by cloth-covered boards. The mysterious poster sessions, I realized, though there were few actual posters: almost all the visual aids—graphs, data tables, diagrams— were printed in off-tint ink-jet colors on 8½ x 11 sheets and stapled into the cloth. Titles were usually in huge type, printed a few letters at a time across several pages.

The tables were numbered. I walked down the aisles, looking for the one assigned to Dr. Ram in the conference guide. The topics I passed were all over the map: reports of UFO abductions correlated with incidents of possession; demographics of possession victims by country; a demon cosmology based on aspects of Tarot; a pictorial history of Kamikaze airport shrines; thematic similarities in victim abuse stories; postpossession Kirlian aura distortions; genetic predisposition for possession in twins; recurrence of folkloric devices in the *New England Journal of Medicine* articles; Indian asuras contrasted with American demons; a theory of telepathy through quantum entanglement maintained in Penrose microtubules; Joan of Arc as an early example of possession disorder; an airborne vector for possession explained by wind patterns over Superfund sites . . .

My own demon's name caught my eye, in a paper called "Expanding the Post-War Cohort: A Bayesian Analysis of Incident Reports, 1944–1950." The bearded guy in front of the table was having an energetic discussion with another bearded guy, so I took time to skim the abstract. I couldn't figure out what the point of the article was. Everybody knew that the big three—the Kamikaze, the Captain, and the

Truth—had all appeared around the same time. The paper was arguing that several more ought to be included: Smokestack Johnny, the Painter, the Little Angel, some demon named the Boy Marvel, and my own Hellion. Okay, knock yourself out. What did it matter? I imagined bearded guys all over academia working themselves into a lather over this, precisely because the stakes were so low.

A few minutes later I'd found the row that had to contain Dr. Ram's table. Three numbers down from it I slowed my pace, took another deep breath, and slowly exhaled.

No one was there.

I checked the number: 32. Definitely his table. I was immediately ashamed at how relieved I felt that he was gone.

The table wasn't empty, though. A thin stack of articles was set on the white cloth: "Voxel-Based Morphometry of Gray Matter Abnormalities in Post-Possession Patients." Dr. Ram's name was on it, followed by three others. I'd already read it online, and could only follow every third sentence.

I couldn't see the doctor anywhere in the aisles, and I was pretty sure I'd recognize him from his pictures. My relief turned to annoyance. Where the hell was he?

"*We are*," the woman at the next table said. She was leaning against the edge of the table, a sheaf of pages in her hands.

I glanced around, but I was the only person there. She smiled at me expectantly. She was about my age, short brown hair, triple-pierced right ear, but dressed semiformally in long dark skirt and chocolate boots.

"Excuse me?" I said.

She nodded at my badge. "*We are . . .*"

I looked down at my badge. "Del Pierce?" I said.

She laughed. "*Penn State.* I did my undergrad there."

"Oh, sure, yeah." My fake alma mater. But I had no idea what the "we are" thing was about.

Her booth featured a series of seven photographs—snapshots enlarged to blurriness, printed on slick ink-jet sheets—each of a young

girl in a white nightgown. Several seemed to have been taken in hospital rooms. The research paper's title, in 78-point Futura, was "Cases
for Nonlocal Intelligence," followed by the smaller subtitle, "Information Transfer and Persistence among 'Little Angel' Possessions."

"You're looking for Dr. Ram," she said. "Are you into the neu-
ropsych end of things?"

"Yeah, kind of. And you're working on the Little Angel?"

Otherwise known as the Angel of Mercy and the Girl in White.
The demon possessed pretty, prepubescent girls, dressed up in lacy
nightgowns, and went around visiting people on their deathbeds: cancer patients, motorcycle accident victims, burn unit residents. The
Angel's kiss killed them. Urban myth had it that her touch relieved
these unfortunates of pain and gave them an overwhelming sense of
calm. The deceased were silent on the matter.

"I know," she said. "Been done to death."

"No, no, I wouldn't say that." (Why not?) I picked up a copy from
her own stack of articles. It was stapled, maybe twenty pages long. I
looked at the abstract, something about how some girls possessed by
the Angel knew things that only other Angels—Angels that had appeared in other states, in other times—would know.

"So you haven't seen him, have you?" I said. "Dr. Ram?"

She shook her head. "Those papers were on the table when I got
here to set up. But if I see someone I can tell them you stopped by."

"No, don't do that," I said quickly. "I'll catch him later." I lifted her
article and said, "Thanks for this. It looks interesting."

I turned and walked away, making a show of reading the rest of the
abstract with great interest. The research team had interviewed eyewit-
nesses to the visitations going back to the forties, concentrating on
what the Angel had said that wasn't reported in the media. Then they'd
interviewed families of patients who had died during the visitations.
They found out a couple things: One, Angels knew things about the
patients that no stranger would reasonably know; and two, Angels
knew details from previous visits that had never been broadcast or published.

I reached the end of the row, glanced back. She wasn't looking at me, but there was no one between us. I tucked the paper into my tote bag. There was a garbage can ten feet away, but I didn't want to hurt her feelings by throwing it out in front of her.

And the paper *was* garbage. So these "nonlocal intelligences" knew things they shouldn't know, and seemed to be the same "person" possession after possession. In any decent junior high science fair, the appropriate response to those claims would be, *Duh.*

And that pseudo-scientific phrase: *Nonlocal intelligence.* Every booth lobbied for some new term, each more ungainly than the last: meme, archetype, viral persona, possession disorder variant (PDV), intermittent shared consciousness (ISC), socially constructed alternate identity (SCAID) . . .

None of the names would catch on. *Demon* fit. *Possession* fit. A seventh grader could diagram that sentence: Demons possess *you.* Subject, verb, object.

I circled through the big room, shuffling sideways around clumps of people having minireunions—this must be quite the social occasion for academics who only saw each other at conferences. I couldn't look at the poster titles anymore; I was just trying to get back to the only open door, where I'd come in. The bag dug into my shoulder. My face felt hot.

Ten feet from the door the way was blocked by people watching a slideshow projected onto the white wall. I shouldered my way through the crowd, and looked up as the picture changed. It was a picture of the farm the Painter had created in the airport—the same white farmhouse, the red silo and red-brown barn, golden fields bounded by lines of trees—but rendered in paint on a brick wall in some city, and on a much larger scale: judging by the garage door at the edge of the slide, the painting was at least fifty feet long and maybe twenty feet high. Then the picture changed, to a chalk drawing of a boy in swim trunks, arms around his knees, perched on a rounded boulder in a stream. A towel was draped over his back like a cape.

The thing in my head jerked and shuddered, and I clamped down on a wave of nausea. I pushed out of the crowd, not caring that people were staring at me. I reached the hallway and went down the stairs, heading for the exit and cold lake wind.

Some academic would write a paper about the recurring subjects of the Painter. There were probably factions arguing about the meaning of the farm images, and young turks proposing radical interpretations of the boy on the rock. Trying desperately to make it all *mean* something.

The truth was scarier: nobody in there knew what the fuck was going on. Or else everybody was right and it was all true: aliens and archetypes and asuras, psychosis and psionics, hellfire and hallucinations.

Pandemonium.

"Have you heard the poem about the dog who had a bone in his mouth?" the bag lady said. She had no shopping cart or bags, but she clutched an oversize vinyl purse the size of an artist's portfolio, which I decided met the minimum qualifications for the position.

She wasn't talking to me, and I kept my head down. The concrete bench was cold against my butt and thighs, but I still wasn't ready to go back inside.

The woman spoke at a notch above normal volume, her words delivered with the overenunciated deliberateness of the borderline autistics I'd met in the hospital. She was impossible to tune out. She wore a red hooded sweatshirt, a blue-striped winter jacket over that, and a long checked skirt over gray sweatpants. The tops of her rubber boots were trimmed with leopard-print fur.

She was addressing a bearded old man who sat at the next bench. He could have been any age between seventy and ninety. He sat like a sculpture, hands folded in his lap, and listened patiently. Seated next to him was a strikingly handsome white woman I took to be his daughter, or maybe granddaughter. She studied a program booklet, though she didn't look like an academic: long black hair that reminded me of Amra's before she cut it, tanned legs crossed under a tight skirt.

"It's a *very* good poem," the bag lady said. The old man said nothing. The black-haired woman glanced up, then exchanged a look with the only other person outside with us, a man about a dozen feet away. He was a florid, fiftyish man in jeans and a blazer, with boyishly long sandy hair. One hand was jammed in his jeans pocket; the other held both a Mountain Dew can and a lit cigarette. He'd been pacing and smoking, somehow managing to drink and smoke with the same hand. He took a drag from his cigarette, looked at the bag lady, and shrugged.

"The dog came to a puddle and saw his reflection," the bag lady said. "He looked in the reflection and what he *thought* he saw was a dog with a bone in his mouth, but he didn't recognize that the dog was *himself*, he thought it was *another* dog with a *bigger* bone in his mouth. So he dropped *his* bone to get the *other dog's* bone, and lost *his* bone in the water. Now there were *two* dogs without bones. The moral of the story is that the grass is always greener, you see?"

"This is the way of the world," the old man said. His voice was strangely flattened, like a satellite phone call digitally processed for maximum compression. "Objects in mirror are closer than they appear."

"I've read all of Philip K. Dick's books," she said. As if this were the natural follow-up to a dog poem. "*Flow My Tears, Ubik, The Owl in Daylight.* I've read *VALIS* twenty-two times. I carry the book with me at all times. Look."

I glanced up. She'd pulled a paperback from her purse. "Would you sign it for me?"

She opened the cover and thrust it at him, inches from his face. He didn't flinch or pull back. He slowly took a pen from the inside of his jacket, supported the spine of the book, and made a series of curving strokes, finishing with an X through the middle. I couldn't see what he'd drawn, but I doubted it was an ordinary signature.

"Thank you very much," the woman said, and closed the book without looking at it. "I hope you find Felix. I have to go now." She turned abruptly and nearly walked into the grille of a cab pulling into the drive. The cab jerked to a stop. The woman paused for a long moment, staring at the driver, and then she moved around the hood, heading for the Hyatt.

I glanced at the old man, and he caught me looking. His eyes were set back into his skull, but they were glittering and sharp. One eye closed, reopened. A wink.

I thought of the Painter back at O'Hare. That same wink.

"A fan," he said. His lips gravitated into a slight smile, and he seemed to shrug without moving his shoulders. "I have certain responsibilities."

The cab's rear door opened, and a dark-skinned man stepped out, hefting an oversize laptop bag. I recognized him from his book jacket photo, especially that expanse of wavy, oil-black hair, just shy of Elvis length.

Dr. Ram strode in my direction, nodding vigorously at something being said by the person who had stepped out of the cab after him. His companion was a priest: a bald head above a clerical collar and a long, black, loose-sleeved cassock.

No, not a priest—or at least not a Roman Catholic one. It was a woman. Her head had been shaved down to stubble, but that only revealed a fine, elfin bone structure: high cheekbones, a pointed chin. She walked with her head bent close to the doctor, matching his intensity. Although Dr. Ram was nodding, they seemed to be having an argument.

I stood up. I hadn't expected to see him just now, but this was the time to talk to him, before he went to his presentation, before he was surrounded by students and colleagues.

The bald woman glanced at me, but then she noticed the old man on the bench, and stopped. "Hello, Valis," she said evenly. She sounded Australian, or maybe Irish. Her ears were beautiful.

"Good afternoon, Mother Mariette," Valis said.

Dr. Ram had already pushed through the revolving door. She followed after him. I hadn't even moved.

Valis's friend (son? son-in-law?), still carrying the Mountain Dew and cigarette, stalked over. "What the hell's O'Connell doing here?" he said, amused. "I thought she retired, became a hermit or something."

"She's an exorcist, Tom," Valis said in his long-distance voice. "One can't retire from a calling."

"I have to go now," I said. "I . . . it was nice to meet you."

Valis inclined his head in a nod. The woman smiled and the other man—Tom, Valis had called him—raised his pop can and cigarette in a salute.

5

Dr. Ram was mobbed before he left the podium. I hung back, waiting for my moment to get his attention, but his admirers—fellow scientists, students, fans?—kept asking him questions, and he kept nodding and answering as he unhooked his microphone, packed up his laptop, and made for the exit. The crowd moved with him, forcing him to go slowly, like a man underwater.

The bald woman that Valis had called an exorcist, Mother Mariette, wasn't among them. She hadn't shown up for his presentation.

You didn't have to be there to know the talk would be a success. Dr. Ram was already a celebrity in the neuroscience world. The field had failed to come up with a hypothesis for possession disorder that would stand up to repeated testing. For the past few years researchers had hung their theoretical hats on linking possession to artificially induced OBEs: out-of-body experiences. Most research teams were looking for a chemical explanation, but then a team from Sweden, during surgery to implant electrodes inside a woman's skull in order to alleviate her debilitating seizures, had zapped the woman's parietal lobe, in a structure called the angular gyrus. The woman, who was awake during the operation, reported floating above her body. A few other researchers replicated the experiment, but most groups were constrained by ethical considerations: without some extreme medical necessity, they couldn't just open up the skull of someone and start zapping.

Dr. Ram had taken another approach, and started running former possession victims through functional MRIs, hoping to see heightened activity in the angular gyrus, or perhaps some deformation in the area that these patients had in common. Perhaps they all shared some mutation that made them prone to possession; perhaps they suffered some damage from being possessed. He examined over eighty possession victims in a two-year span.

And found nothing. Nothing for twenty-four months.

Then Dr. Ram got "lucky." One of his patients (name withheld, of course) was possessed by the Piper *while* receiving the fMRI. The session went to hell. Dr. Ram never spelled out the details in any of his papers, but somehow he was driven from the room, and a female nurse was "harmed." Given that the demon was the Piper, everyone understood this to mean rape.

The MRI, however, recorded what had happened inside the patient's brain moments before he pulled his head out of the MRI tunnel, yanked off the headphones, and started singing. This was the first time this had happened anywhere; MRIs had only been around since the eighties, and demons didn't submit willingly to medical examinations.

Dr. Ram had posted still pictures and a few mini-movies of the famous scan on his website. They reminded me of the radar weather maps on TV: colorful high-pressure systems of thought rolling over a cauliflower-shaped island, blossoming in reds and yellows and virulent greens. When Dr. Ram finally went back to replay the scan, he was shocked: the parietal lobe and the angular gyrus had stayed dark, but a portion of the *temporal* lobe had lit up like a thunderstorm.

Brain function (or malfunction), Dr. Ram argued, might be able to completely explain the disorder, wresting the disease from the grip of faith healers, Jungians, and UFOlogists. Once you had a way to attack the disease scientifically, anything was possible: demon detectors, unequivocal diagnoses of possession, testable treatments . . . a cure.

"Dr. Ram."

He didn't hear me. I followed him down the hall toward the elevators, persisting even as he shed members of his entourage by ones and twos. One of his shoes was untied, but he didn't seem to notice.

"Dr. Ram, if you have just a second—"

He glanced at me, then was immediately distracted by a scruffy-bearded man at his elbow. Dr. Ram grunted at something he said, and then the elevator opened and the people around them shuffled forward, and Dr. Ram and the bearded man went with them. Dr. Ram looked up, and waved me inside. I put out a hand to stop the door from closing, and wedged inside.

"Thanks! I enjoyed your talk. I was—"

But the bearded man was still talking, something about calcium channel blockers. We went up.

At the eighteenth floor Dr. Ram stepped out, and the bearded man was still talking as the doors started to slide shut. I abruptly jumped forward, and Dr. Ram's eyes widened. The doors closed behind me.

Dr. Ram didn't move. Maybe he didn't want me to know where his room was. I opened my mouth, shut it. I fought the urge to say, "I am not a stalker."

"Are you a student of Dr. Slaney's?" he said.

"What?"

He nodded at my badge. "Dr. Slaney. Or perhaps Dr. Morgan?" His accent was pure California, vowels stretched a bit longer than a Midwesterner's.

"I want to show you something," I said. I unzipped the tote bag, flipped through the other pages I'd picked up, and withdrew the fMRI printouts. I held them out to him. "I'd like you to look at these."

"I'm sorry, I really don't have time. I have to meet someone . . ."

I stood there, holding them out to him. Finally he took them.

He looked at the first one, shuffled it to the back, looked at the next one.

"Where did these come from?" he said intently. He studied the first scan again.

"Me."

He looked up, his expression guarded.

"I've been following your work," I said. "What you noticed about activity in the temporal lobe—you see it there?"

"I see *something*." He flipped a page, tilted his head. "But even if I take these scans as valid—which I would not—they could mean almost anything. You could have been experiencing fond memories of your birthday, or simply contemplating a new haircut." He handed the pages back to me, but his voice was kinder. "I know these scans might be alarming to the layman, but heightened activity in the temporal lobe by no means suggests that you were possessed while getting your MRI."

My cheeks flushed in embarrassment. "I'm not—" I breathed in. "I don't know how to put this. I'm possessed *now*. I can feel . . . I can sense this presence inside me. I know that it just *feels* this way, that it's just a subjective sensation that could be a symptom of the disorder, but—" I smiled tightly. "It's just that I feel like I've *trapped* this thing in there."

I had to give him credit; he didn't immediately dismiss me. What I was saying was impossible—no one that I'd ever heard of walked around saying that they're possessed.

But he thought for a moment, and then said, "What would you have me do about this?"

"I was thinking. If your theory is correct—" I almost ran into a Jurassic-size potted plant, and stepped around it. "If this section of the brain is responsible for possession, then if we disable that section—"

"Disable? How?"

I looked at him. He lifted his hand. "No. No." He turned and started down the hallway, the laces of one shoe whipping along the floor. I hurried after him.

"At least consider it, Doctor. There are similar operations being done for tumor victims."

"You don't have a tumor! I can't just cut into your brain based on a *theory*. It's not even a theory, it's a hypothesis, and an unproven one at that. Maybe, years from now, there will be some surgical option—"

"So you have thought about it."

He stopped in front of a door. He seemed genuinely angry now. "Young man. No one would do what you're asking, no respectable doctor. You're grasping at straws."

I shoved the papers back into his hands. "Please, just *look* at them. Maybe we're not talking about surgery; maybe there's some chemical way to—I don't know, interrupt the process."

He shook his head, fishing in his pocket for a key card. "Even if I believed you, there is no way to do what you're asking."

"I'm not making this up. Just look at them. My name's on there, and I wrote down a couple phone numbers where I can be reached." He looked at his door, then down the hallway, anywhere but at me or at the pages in his hand. "Please," I said.

"I'm sorry," Dr. Ram said. "I cannot help you." He stepped inside and closed the door without looking at me again.

"Liar," I said.

Later, my new friend Tom steered me toward the bar.

"Trust me," he said. "You need another fucking beer."

"No, I'm okay . . ."

"Three more Coors Light," he told the bartender. Then he turned to me. "Seriously, you look like somebody just ran over your cat."

I laughed, shrugged. "So is your friend really a demon?"

Tom looked back toward the table. We were in a lounge on the second floor of the Hyatt. The place was crowded, half the people in costume. Valis, with his neatly trimmed beard and tweed jacket, looked like an Oxford don. He sat next to the handsome woman—Tom's wife, Selena. They were surrounded by half a dozen people who had coalesced around Valis in the past hour. Tom had spotted me sitting alone by the bar and had sucked me into their gravitational field.

Tom sighed. "Phil's had a complicated life. Ever since the stroke— well, even before the stroke, he heard voices. Imaginary friends, you know? Then in eighty-two, the first thing he said when he got his speech back was that we should refer to him from now on as Valis." He shrugged. "I asked an exorcist to talk to him—"

"Mother Mariette?"

Tom's eyebrows shot up. "Yeah, that's right, you saw her! Anyway, she declared him a fake. Valis didn't jump, he wasn't in the public record, and it was simpler to say that Phil had finally . . . well, Phil had taken a lot of medications in his life, and this wasn't his first hallucination. And frankly, Valis's arrival wasn't all bad. Look at him—you can't even tell that half of him used to be paralyzed. Total recovery. Better than total! He eats better than he used to, he exercises, doesn't take pills. He lives with Selena and me, but he takes care of us as much as we take care of him. I mean, shit, he's enjoying himself! He can't help it. He tries to do the silent Valis thing, but then somebody hits one of his hot topics, and he's off, man."

The bartender returned with three tall glasses filled with faintly discolored tap water. We carried the beers back to the table, navigating around bodies, through the smoke. Selena barely seemed to speak, Tom talked constantly, and Valis mostly listened, though when he did speak, as he was doing now, people shut up. A glass of ginger ale sat on the low table in front of him, untouched.

"But you cannot separate science fiction from fantasy," Valis said, "and a moment's thought will show why. Take psionics; take mutants such as we find in *More Than Human*. If the reader believes that such mutants could exist, then he will view Sturgeon's novel as science fiction. If, however, he believes that such mutants are, like wizards and dragons, not possible, nor will ever be possible, then he is reading a fantasy novel. Fantasy involves that which general opinion regards as impossible; science fiction involves that which general opinion regards as possible under the right circumstances. This is in essence a judgment call, since what is possible and what is not cannot be objectively known but is, rather, a subjective belief on the part of the reader."

There was a slight pause, and then a Hispanic kid younger than me, dressed in a black T-shirt and immaculately pressed khakis, spoke up. "But does it matter what the readers think is possible? It seems to me that it's how the characters in the novel behave that determines what kind of book it is. A character in a science fiction novel believes that the world is rational, that you can find the answer, the ultimate truth, and goes about finding it. In *More Than Human*, the characters think that they're the next step in evolution, part of a scientific process—"

"No, it's the fact that there *is* no ultimate truth that makes it SF." This from a tall, bony man who looked as old as Valis. He sat on a low chair, his knees at the same height as his shoulders. "You can always ask one more question. But magic is fundamentally unexplainable."

Behind him, I saw the back of a shaved head, weaving through the crowd. Mother Mariette? I stepped sideways, trying to get a glimpse of her profile. If I could catch her . . .

"Nobody in a fantasy novel tries to figure out *why* magic works," the bony man said. "It just does. Jesus turns the water into wine, end of story. In the real world—"

"In the real world most people don't try to figure out how things work, either," the Hispanic kid said. "Electricity works by flipping a switch."

I'd lost her. If it was her at all. I turned back to the group, and Selena was looking at me curiously. I shrugged.

The tall man said, "Yes, most people are philistines. But if they *wanted* to find out, nothing is presumed to be unexplainable."

A frizzy-haired woman in a peasant skirt said, "Wait, *most* of the important things in life are unexplainable. The soul is unexplainable; demons are unexplainable; consciousness is unexplainable . . ."

Somebody laughed—the pale young man in the eyeliner and tuxedo shirt leaning on the arm of a chair. "That just means you're a confused fantasy character intruding in a science fictional world. Most scientists—most scientists at ICOP, anyway—think that we'll eventually be able to understand all of that. Just because we don't understand it *now*—"

"Man in his present state is not able to comprehend," Valis said in his distant voice. "Or if he comprehends, he is unable to hold on to that comprehension. The Eye of Shiva opens, then closes." His voice seemed to carry much farther than it ought to at such low volume, like a radio signal catching a lucky bounce off the ionosphere. Or maybe it was just that people strained to hear him. He was famous, he was rich, he wrote books. At least he used to, before he decided he was possessed by a Vast Active Living Intelligence System. I hadn't read the books, but I'd seen a couple of the movies.

"Okay, so we get maybe one second of total enlightenment, now *that's* depressing." I couldn't see who was talking. "At least in a fantasy novel, everybody gets to *know* the truth. Moral order is restored, the One True King returns, Jesus rises from the dead."

Somebody else said, "You're confusing theme with genre."

"No, he's talking about destiny," Tom said. "As soon as you introduce destiny, you're in a fantasy, even if you dress it up as *The Matrix* or *Star Wars*. As soon as the universe starts responding to you personally, that's magic—you only get to draw the sword out of the stone if you're King Arthur—"

"—or Bugsy Siegel," someone said.

"Yeah, sure," Tom said, waving him off. "But in an impersonal science fictional world, anybody who knows the trick, the technology of sword extraction, gets to be King of All Britain."

"Or else you scuba dive down and wrestle the Lady of the Lake for it."

" 'Strange women lyin' in ponds distributin' swords,' " the pale man said in a not-quite British accent. " 'Is no basis for a system of government.' "

The conversation instantly degenerated into a flurry of *Monty Python* quotes, then fragmented into a variety of smaller conversations. The tall man had left with the frizzy-haired woman, but other people joined the group. Tom seemed to know everyone, and everyone at least recognized Valis. The volume of noise and smoke climbed, and it wasn't just our little band; DemoniCon partiers were descending from all levels of the Hyatt towers. At some point in the night—1 a.m.? Certainly past midnight—I found myself in the john, Valis at the urinal next to me. I was pissing away what seemed to be gallons of Coors Light, amused by the fact that it looked almost exactly the same going out as coming in.

On the wall above the urinal, someone had written DOGMA: I AM GOD.

"So . . . ," I said. "You piss." I realized at this point that I was a little more buzzed than I'd thought.

He nodded without turning to face me. "The body has its own imperatives," he said.

I couldn't argue with that. Out in the bar, someone shrieked in laughter.

"People don't treat you like a demon," I said. "They like talking to you."

"They like talking to Phil." He stepped back from the urinal, zipped up, and walked toward the sink. "They prefer to think of me as their old friend who is not gone, but merely gone crazy. It comforts them."

"Wait—you let them *think* you're faking, but you're really . . ." I processed this for a second. "A demon pretending to be a man pretending to be a demon."

"Exactly. A fake fake." He turned on the faucet. Hot only.

I was surprised to realize that I believed him—or at least didn't disbelieve him.

"Okay, so if you're really a demon," I said, "how come you never possess anybody else? Jumping would pretty much settle the matter, wouldn't it?"

He addressed me through the mirror as he washed, steam rising past his face. The water temperature didn't seem to bother him. "Divine intervention is not always divine invasion. I have intervened in Phil's life twenty-two times. Nineteen of those disruptions involved simple transmission of information, compressed into cipher signals that would trigger anamnesis."

"Say what?"

"Anamnesis. The loss of forgetfulness."

I blinked at him.

"Total recall."

"Oh."

"A few times it was necessary to take more direct action. The first time he tried to kill himself," he continued in that distant voice, "I seized his body, wrote the emergency room number on the palm of his hand, and awakened him. But the watershed moment came in 1982. Phil experienced a stroke followed by cardiac arrest, his third and most damaging attack. In order to restart his heart and resume blood flow to the brain, I had to seize complete control of biological functions. It was necessary for me to install a holographic shard of my essence."

"You possessed him."

He shook water from his hands—two economical flicks of his wrists—and drew a paper towel from the stack above the sink. Outside, someone was shouting, but I couldn't make out the words. "I continue to pump this heart, to work these lungs. I fear that if I left this body for very long, he would die."

"Okay, but . . ." I shook my head. "Why?" I laughed. He regarded me calmly, and that only made me laugh harder. "I mean, why not just let him die? It was his time, right? What good are you doing him walking around in his body?"

His head tilted, and he smiled. "That's the question each of us must ask."

He pushed open the bathroom door and the noise from the bar rushed in: angry shouts, amused catcalls, drunken hoots. A crash as some very large piece of glass—or maybe a hundred smaller pieces—struck something hard and shattered.

Valis held the door for me. Across the room, a bare-chested man hung above the bar by one arm, legs tucked up under him, swinging from the rack of wineglasses. The rack alongside the short end of the bar had already been pulled down.

The swinging man was clad only in a kind of leaf-covered loincloth. His face was painted red, and little horns protruded from his skull. In his free hand he held a wooden panpipe. At the top of his swing he let go, arced through the air, and came down feetfirst on a round table.

"Time to dance, my revelers!" he shouted.

"Jesus, it's just like the Olympics," someone near me said.

It was the same thing the Piper had shouted back in 2002. A Finnish speed skater, Arttu Heikkinen, was on the last thousand meters of the 5000-meter race, half a lap ahead of the nearest competitor, on pace to break the world record. Suddenly Heikkinen slowed, looked around until he spotted the TV cameras, and beamed. The second-place skater started to pass on the outside. Heikkinen tripped him, sending him sliding into the padded walls, and burst out laughing. He ripped his Lycra suit down the middle and let it hang like a half-shed skin. And then he turned in a circle, and commanded the spectators in the arena to dance. Heikkinen never recovered from the shame and never appeared in another race.

Most of the people in the bar were trying to get away now, but others were frozen in their seats. I pushed through the outrushing crowd, bouncing off bodies, trying to get closer. The Piper hopped onto the bar's yellow chair, and then leaped over the back of a couch, landing next to a red-haired woman. She screamed.

"I . . . said . . . *dance!*" the Piper exclaimed. He yanked her to her feet, laughing maniacally. The woman, thin and perhaps forty years old, shook her head frantically, tears already running down her cheeks.

"Hey mister," I said.

The Piper turned and leered down at me. "Ye-es?"

I didn't know what was in the glass—water, 7Up, vodka—something clear. I shoved it at him, splashing his face. He sputtered, blinked. The woman yanked her arm free.

"Get the hell out of here," I said. "You're not fooling anyone."

He stared at me. Whatever he'd used to paint his face was running onto his chest in scarlet streaks.

"I said, get out."

He stepped down off the couch. "Jeez, take it easy. Take a fucking joke." He slumped toward the open end of the room that connected to the hotel proper. A long moment, and one of the male bartenders ran past me, trying to catch him.

Someone slapped me on the back. Someone else pushed a shot glass into my hand. Tom, laughing. "How'd you know, man? How'd you fucking know?"

. . .

"—wouldn't even listen to me. He just walked away. All I'm talking about is taking down the antenna. There's some hardware in our heads that's picking up broadcasts from the All Demon Network, and we just have to figure out a way to pull the plug, or at least change the fucking channel. I'm not even talking about real surgery. We wouldn't have to even drill into the lobe, you could do it with microwaves, the way they can kill off tumors with these intersecting microwaves, all of 'em too low powered to hurt you except at the exact point where they overlap. Is that so much to ask, to just *consider* it?"

Selena nodded sympathetically. Or maybe she was just humoring me. I chose to take the sympathy.

"You can't do that," the Hispanic kid said, interrupting. Who wasn't Hispanic, it had turned out, but Armenian. "I've read about this Dr. Ram guy, and what he's talking about is cutting out the Eye of Shiva."

"The whatsis?" I dimly remembered somebody mentioning that earlier.

"The hidden eye that the ancients believed opened them up to God," Tom said. "In Phil's terms, it was the thing that allowed him to receive the information that Valis was firing at him. If you look back at—"

Tom suddenly lurched forward, his drink sloshing onto the carpet. A huge man in a T-shirt and cargo shorts had backed into him. "Someone stole my costume! It was right here! Who stole my costume?" He turned, and I recognized the fat man from in front of the Hyatt this morning, the one dressed as the Truth.

"Nobody here, man," Tom said.

The fat man scowled, then shoved off in a new direction. "Where's my fucking fedora!"

The Hispa—*Armenian* kid gripped me by the arm. "Del, look at me. Do you really want some quack to cut out your connection to God?"

"*God*? You think this—you think these things are *God*? Smokestack Johnny, the Piper, the Fat Boy?" I reached for my glass, my glass of brown something. "Then God is a fucking whack job." I had to concentrate: the tips of my fingers had gone numb, as had my lips, and getting the glass to my mouth involved levels of concentration I usually reserved for winning kewpie dolls with the Claw. Drop a quarter, win a Wild Turkey.

Whose hotel room was this?

"The Eye can destroy, too," the kid said. "Valis says that the carrier signal is also harmful radiation. Maybe some people can't *handle* the information when it hits them. These deviants get overridden by the purity of the info-stream."

"We should go," Selena said.

"Or maybe that's the real message getting through," Tom said. "Shiva's two-sided, man—protector of the weak, but destroyer of the wicked. If you try to shut that down, you're removing the divine essence from humanity."

"Divine essence?" I said. "Hey, I'm Fat Boy, I'll possess a guy and make him eat ten pounds of chocolate at one sitting! Yeah, that's divine, that's fucking deep, that's like . . ." I couldn't think what that was like. It was like something, though. "All I'm saying, we shouldn't have to live in fear like this. I mean, Christ, ever since Eisenhower's assassination, the Japanese have been treated like dogs, and the president *still* can't appear on live television—everything's a fucking tape delay! And the Secret Service guys are standing by with tranqs in case he gets all Nixon on them!"

"Nixon wasn't possessed," somebody said. "He was just crazy."

"*All I am saying*—"

"Is that we can't live like this," the kid said. "But we can. We *do*. Even the Israelis get back on the bus."

"We should go," Selena said again. Not just for the second time— she'd been saying it since Valis left an hour ago, escorted by a trio of young people.

"Let me get one for the road," Tom said. He pulled another Coors Light can from the case, then took something from his pocket—a flap of vinyl. He wrapped it around the beer, transforming it into a publicly respectable Mountain Dew can. A RePubliCan.

"You know," I said, struck by a brilliant thought. "If you poured the beer out now, and replaced it with Mountain Dew, then you'd have a fake fake."

"You don't say," Tom said.

"A Valis Special!"

Selena said, "You're not driving anywhere, are you, Del?" I shook my head vigorously and waved good-bye.

Sometime later I looked around and realized I didn't know the name of anyone in the room. Even the Armenian kid had vanished. I left the party and started looking for a way up to my floor. I passed a sandwich sign announcing possession movies playing in a ballroom— *Omen, Being John Malkovich, Fail-Safe, 2001: A Space Odyssey*—and veered toward the doors, but then I saw the bank of elevators and corrected course. A door opened and a bunch of us pressed inside. "Eighteenth floor," I said. A minute later the elevator hissed open like an airlock, and someone behind me tapped me between my shoulder blades. That bit of kinetic energy sent me slowly drifting down the hall.

My vision had tunneled down to the wrong end of a cheap telescope: everything was too small and too far away. I drifted down to my door.

The key card eventually appeared in my hand, a clumsy magic trick. I slid it in, slid it out, slid it in again . . . Door sex. The red light blinked at me, refusing to turn green. I grabbed the handle, stared into the bubble lens of the peephole. The thing in my head stomped and rattled. Open the pod bay doors, Hal. Open the fucking—

I leaned back from the door, squinted at the number.

This wasn't my floor. But I'd been here earlier; I'd walked past that prehistoric-size plant . . .

Oh, right. Dr. Ram.

Dr. Fucking Ram.

The demon thrashed in my head. I was crashing. Lucite banks of processors began to shut down in my brain, one by one, overwhelmed by alcohol and demons. *Daisy, Daisy . . .*

Then I remembered the chains. I couldn't be wandering around like this. Had to get them chains.

I turned, unsure now which way led back to the elevators. The hallway stretched into the distance, door after door after door, the infinite regress of a mirrored mirror.

6

I woke up screaming, limbs paralyzed by restraints. This wasn't unusual. Over the past few months, it had become routine.

What was new was the intense light in my eyes, the number of people around me, and the particular quality of the pain. Someone just out of sight—a tall, blond nurse with blue eyes, I think—was scraping the skin off my hands with a carpenter's file, or perhaps playing a butane torch over my knuckles. Another tall, blond person was working behind me. The holes in the top of my skull had already been drilled, and now she was inserting the tiny wires that would carry electricity into the folds of the angular gyrus. Other Scandinavians, dressed in brilliant white, moved in and out of the light, haloed and indistinct, murmuring in Swedish. However, when I shut my mouth and stopped screaming, a female voice said, "*Thank* you." So at least one of them was bilingual.

The butane treatment went on for a long time. I waited for the electricity to travel down the wires into my gray matter and jolt me out of my body. I was looking forward to seeing what the room looked like from the ceiling: my body stretched out on a tasteful pine gurney by IKEA, the sensuous nurses bent over my empty tin can of a body, their crisp uniforms unbuttoned to expose milky white cleavage.

"Hit me!" I commanded in my best James Brown.

"Okay, that's it," a male voice said. In English again, unless my hy-perstimulated lobes, drawing on race memory encoded in my DNA, were automatically translating. "Take him down to the drunk tank."

That's right, I'd been drinking. Coors Light, mostly. Coors Fuck-ing Light! Was it even possible to get drunk on Coors Light?

Evidently.

Walls zipped past. Elevators dropped and rose. The ambulance rumbled. Time progressed in a series of jump-cuts: *Now, Now, Now.*

Something bad had happened. Several bad things. I was almost sure of it.

I needed to remember something important. Or unforget it. What was that word again?

I looked into the upside-down face of the man pushing my gurney into the building.

"Anamnesis," I said proudly.

"Uh-huh," he said.

Amra and My Very Bigger Brother were waiting for me in the busy front room of the First District Police Station.

"Good morning, starshine," Lew said.

I smiled weakly. I felt nauseous, still slightly drunk. My body felt like it had been yanked apart and snapped back together by clumsy children. My hands ached fiercely. I suspected the pain would only get worse as the alcohol wore off.

"Thanks for this," I said. *This:* driving downtown on a Monday morning; putting up money for bail; existing. "Did you tell Mom?"

"What, and kill her?" he said.

"Thank you," I said. I didn't have the energy for banter.

Amra lightly touched one bandaged hand. "Does it hurt?"

"Little bit." I'd woken up with my right hand wrapped from wrist to fingers, turning it into a club. My left hand was only partially wrapped, but blood had seeped through the bandages on my palm like a stig-mata. The tips of my fingers were stained black from the fingerprint-ing. Or so I assumed. I couldn't remember that.

The bandages had made it difficult to sign the I-Bond, the piece of paper releasing me on my own recognizance until my court date on April 20. My thought was that if I was still cognizant of anything by then, I'd be more than happy to show up.

We walked slowly toward the front door. I shuffled like an old man. I'd pulled a muscle in my lower back, and my shoulders felt shredded, as if I'd tried to bench press a piano. I hadn't felt this bad since the car accident.

"I think something bad happened last night," I said.

Lew laughed. "You think? They told us you tore up a hotel room and half a hallway. Mirrors, TV, broken furniture. Total rock star. And I guess you also banged up three security guards before they tied you down."

"Oh."

"Oh yeah."

Amra opened the door for me. Sunlight smacked me in the face. "The cop we talked to said they haven't filed assault charges yet, though that could be coming," she said. "As for the damages, he said we should talk to the hotel, sometimes they'll drop the criminal mischief charge if—"

I stopped them. "Where's my bag?"

"What, your duffel bag?" Lew said.

"I need my bag."

"Jesus Christ, Del, you're worried about your fucking luggage?" he said. "Forget that shit. You can buy some more clothes. Your bigger problem is that you're about to do time. We've got to get you a lawyer, maybe find a—"

"Do the cops have it? I need my bag, Lew. Find out what happened to my bag."

He blinked, lowered his voice. "What's the matter with you? You got drugs in there or something?"

"No," I said scornfully. But then realized that wasn't true. The Nembutal. But that was legal, and it wasn't what I was worried about.

"Please," I said. "Just find out what they did with it. See if the cops have it."

He shook his head in disgust, but then he turned and went back to the counter. I sat down on one of the red plastic chairs and rested my arms on my knees. I could feel every pulse in my hands.

"He's worried about you," Amra said, after a while. "We're both worried. This is not just about getting drunk, is it?"

"Nope."

"This sounds like possession, Del."

"Yep." I couldn't look up. The thing in my head was dormant; whether it was because it was worn down by the night's exertions or masked by the hangover, I couldn't tell. I wanted to lie down on the dusty linoleum, because it looked smooth and cool.

Lew walked back. "They say they don't have anything of yours besides what you had in your pockets."

"Fuck," I said.

"Come on, I'll loan you some clothes when we get to my house." He was already half out the door.

"We have to go back to the Hyatt," I said.

Lew, outlined in harsh sunlight, stopped, sighed, then slowly shook his head again, signaling a new level of disgust. I wished he would stop doing that.

"On the way there," I said, "I'll tell you everything."

I told them everything. Almost everything. Something, anyway.

"And that's what happened last night?" Lew said. "This wolfing out thing?"

Lew was driving again, but I was too nauseous to sit in the back, so Amra had let me take the front passenger seat. I spent most of the drive with the side of my head pressed to the cool window.

"I must have passed out before I got back to my room," I said. "Or I got back to my room and couldn't get the restraints on. Either way, I lost control." Lost it completely. It wasn't just property damage this time. I'd beaten up security guards.

Amra said, "And you're sure that this demon is the Hellion, the same one who possessed you when you were a kid?"

"I think so. I don't know."

But I did know. It had always been in there, sleeping, even when I couldn't feel it. The car accident had merely woken it up.

"You said it was just noises," Lew said. "You said it was no big deal—this Dr. Ram guy was just going to help you with the noises. You didn't say anything about surgery, or exorcism, or any of that shit."

"I know."

"So you're Mister Big Fat Liar Pants."

"Basically."

And there was more. I told them about getting turned down by Dr. Ram and going out drinking, but I didn't mention meeting Valis, throwing a drink in the fake Piper's face, or the rest of the night's wanderings. Not because I was embarrassed, but because I didn't have the energy.

The Audi's tiny dashboard clock said that it was almost 10 a.m. The street in front of the Hyatt was clear of pedestrian protesters; evidently even Rapturists had to go to their real jobs on Monday. The Demoni-Conners were probably sleeping off hangovers.

Lew parked under the glass canopy protecting the entrance and turned on his flashers. He glanced at Amra, then looked at me. "You want me to go in with you?"

"No, I'll be right back." Lew's cell had rung three times during the drive, and it had pained him to ignore the calls. Lew was the Man now, and for all I knew, Amra was the Man too. The fact that both of them had taken off work to bail me out heightened my humiliation. Gourmet shame.

"I'll go in," Amra said. She climbed out of the backseat. "It's pretty cramped back there. Lew, give him your jacket."

Ah: the bloody shirt. I slid my huge mummy hands through the sleeves of the golf jacket, gritting in pain as I forced them through the narrow wrists, and Amra zipped me.

We went arm in arm to the front desk. Three clerks were huddled in the doorway to the back office, their blue-uniformed backs to us, talking to someone deeper inside the office. Their words were too low to hear, but the conversation seemed intense.

I stood for a full minute waiting for them to notice us. I kept my arms down to hide the bandages. The lobby was too cold; chills ran up my neck. With each passing moment, I felt sicker.

Finally, Amra said, "Excuse me? Can someone help us?"

One of the clerks, a black woman much taller than me, reluctantly broke away from the group. "Checking out?" she said. She barely looked at us; her attention was still back with the huddle.

"Hi," I said. My voice was gravelly, and I was conscious of the stink of my breath. "Uh, last night . . ."

Last night what? I trashed your hotel, pummeled some security guards, and was arrested, but I *really* need the bag I left behind. Jesus, even if they had the duffel, they might not give it to me. How many thousands of dollars did I owe them?

Amra spoke up again. "Last night, when we left the hotel, we left a bag behind in the room."

I looked at her. That "we" touched me.

"What room was it?" the clerk asked.

Amra looked up at me. I blanked, then tried to reel it out of memory. "The thirtieth floor," I said. "Thirty fifteen?"

She typed on a keyboard tucked under the lip of the desk; typed again; then studied the screen, her expression suddenly cold. There was no way to see what she was looking at, but it didn't require much of a guess.

"Delacorte Pierce?" she said.

I nodded, feeling a stone drop into my gut.

"Could you wait one moment. The manager would like to speak with you about the bill."

It was not a request.

The clerk went to the doorway and leaned in past the other clerks.

The wall behind the desk strobed with colored light. I looked over my shoulder, the movement hurting, and froze. Outside, a police car had pulled into the entranceway, lights flashing. A second squad car pulled in behind it, then an ambulance. The lobby pulsed with blues and reds.

"Del?" Amra put her warm hand to my damp neck. Sweat had broken out down my back. I finally put a name to the emotion that had been growing in me since I'd woken up in the drunk tank: dread. Something bad had happened last night.

"Dr. Ram," I said, almost whispering it.

"What?"

Two paramedics came through the door with a wheeled stretcher between them, escorted by four police officers. Everyone in the lobby stepped out of the way and froze, the pedestrian version of pulling onto the shoulder.

A few yards from me, the wall opened—a door disguised as paneling—and a short white man with precisely cut white hair strode out, followed by two other uniformed clerks. They intercepted the paramedics and police in the middle of the lobby. The white-haired man, some kind of manager, exchanged a few words with the paramedics, then led the group to the elevators.

I suddenly recognized a face among the onlookers: Mother Mariette, the bald priest I'd seen talking with Dr. Ram yesterday. She wore a gray smocklike thing with baggy sleeves, black leggings, heavy boots. No clerical collar. She pressed back against a column until the cops and paramedics passed. She watched them for a second, then strode toward me and the exit, pulling a wheeled suitcase behind her. Her eyes were fixed on the exit, her expression determined. I fought the urge to duck behind Amra. But I had to know.

"Amra, just try to get my bag. Please."

I walked away quickly—as quickly as I could, with the muscles of my back seized tight—until I was in the priest's path.

"Mother Mariette," I said.

Her eyes flicked toward me, but she kept moving, angling to step around me.

She didn't recognize me, and I wasn't surprised. She'd barely glanced at me when she spoke to Valis on the way into the hotel, and she hadn't even seen me in the bar.

I stepped directly into her way, forcing her to stop. She looked me in the face for the first time. She was not tall, just past my shoulder. From anything farther than ten feet, her narrow face and long neck made her seem much taller. Her lips were set in a hard line, her eyes rimmed in red. She'd been crying.

"Mother Mariette, is it Dr. Ram?"

Her lips parted; her eyes widened. Red and blue lights played over her pale skin.

"Is he dead?"

Just as quickly her expression changed. Flat, controlled rage slammed down like a welder's mask. "Step away," she hissed. She pushed past me, not quite running.

I glanced back at Amra. She was staring at me, frowning in confusion.

I started after the priest, running a few steps before the pain forced me into a walk. Mother Mariette reached the door as another car pulled into the entranceway, this one an unmarked vehicle with a blue light on the dash.

By the time I got outside she was ten yards down the sidewalk, the gray smock rippling in the wind, the wheels of the suitcase rumbling over the cement. Lew was in the car, the cell phone pressed to his ear, his eyes on the police cars. He hadn't seen me.

I hurried after Mother Mariette, making small, involuntary grunting noises as I went. I forced myself to catch up to her, and when I was a few feet away I put out an arm and touched her shoulder.

She spun away from me, throwing out a straight arm that struck my bandaged hand, knocking my arm aside, and I yelped in pain.

"What is it you want?" she said.

I cradled my hand, blinking away tears. "Jesus, you didn't have to—"

"Out with it. Who are ye?"

"You don't know me. I was—"

"Speak your name," she commanded.

She was so angry, and I was still distracted by the throb in my hand, but that Irish voice was knocking me out. "Speak" and "name" were near rhymes, stuffed with extra vowels.

"Del," I said. I sucked air, coughed. "Del Pierce."

She stared at me, large eyes set wide in that finely shaped skull. Thirty seconds of silence.

"You've been possessed," she said finally. "Recently, too."

She sensed it in me, sensed the Hellion. She misunderstood it, thought it was something else—a residue, a taint—but she saw it. I'd never met anyone who could do that.

"How do you know?" I asked.

"You're one of those goat boys." She righted her bag, gripped the handle firmly. "Wanting a bit of *cosplay*, scaring yourself with penta-grams and incantations, praying to some god that you don't wake up as yourself in the morning. Only now it's happened, and you don't know what kind of shite you've gotten into."

I wanted to rub my hand, but it would only hurt more. "I don't un-derstand half of what you're saying."

"Sure you do. You wanted Dr. Ram to tell you you were special. And then what happened? Got a little angry? Maybe you're going to tell the police that you blacked out. You just woke up with the gun in your hand."

"Dr. Ram was shot?"

Another emergency vehicle, this one a white-and-red van, rolled past us. Mother Mariette turned her back to me and started walking, away from the hotel. I hurried after, but keeping an arm's length be-tween us.

"Please tell me," I said. "How did he die? Was it a demon? Which one?"

"The one that uses forty-five automatics," she said.

"Oh shit," I said. My father's gun was a .45.

I had no memory of getting out the pistol. I'd left the party, tried to find my room . . . and then nothing. But the demon would have had no trouble finding it.

"Only rumor, of course," she said. "Perhaps it wasn't the Truth. I'm sure you'll read the definitive account in the papers." We reached the light at Lake Street, at a confluence of silver skyscrapers. A park of some kind lay off to our right.

She gestured at the window behind me. "Get me a coffee to take away, Mr. Pierce." The corner of the ground floor was taken up by a café.

"*What?*"

"Black, two sugars."

She stood there, waiting to see if I'd move. No, waiting *until* I moved.

Maybe it was the Priest thing, maybe the Woman thing. Maybe it was the Woman Priest thing. I obeyed.

The line at the counter stretched almost to the door, and I suddenly remembered that for thousands of people—millions of people—nothing unusual had happened last night. They'd woken up in the same bed they'd gone to sleep in, next to the same people they'd slept with for years. Now it was just another coffee break, another venti latté and lemon honey seed muffin, then back to the cubicle to delete an hour's worth of spam. Poor deluded sheep. They weren't any safer from demons than the poor fuck who'd gotten taken by the Truth last night, but they refused to admit it. They weren't immune; they were just undiagnosed.

The line moved quickly, and in a minute the venti paper cup was burning my fingers. (But only the fingers: I held the cup in my left hand, but my palm was too thickly wrapped to feel the heat.) She wanted two sugars, but there weren't any cubes. Of course not; when was the last time I'd seen sugar cubes anywhere? I poured some sugar into the cup, but that didn't seem like enough, and I poured again. Now it seemed like too much.

What the hell was I doing?

I snapped down the plastic lid, then sidestepped the tables and incoming customers until I was outside again.

Mother Mariette was leaning against the wall, eyes closed.

"Your coffee," I said.

She opened her eyes, took the cup from me, and held it up to her lips, but didn't drink. She closed her eyes again and let the steam from the slit mouth of the cup pass over her face. Her breathing slowed; her body grew still. I realized that from the moment I'd seen her in the lobby she'd been in a state of high excitation, an electron ready to jump. And now, moment by moment—praying, meditating?—she was dumping energy. Blowing off steam.

She opened her eyes again.

There were a dozen things I needed to tell her. About the Hellion, my slipping control, the solution I'd worked out from Dr. Ram's research. But Dr. Ram was dead, and I was running out of time.

"I need your help," I said. "When I was five years old I was possessed by a demon. And ever since then, it's stayed with me. Inside me. And when I read about Dr. Ram, I got an idea for a surgical technique—"

"We wrestle not with flesh and blood," she said. Not looking at me. "But against principalities, against powers, against the rulers of darkness in this world."

I waited, but she didn't say more.

"See, that doesn't really help," I said.

She sighed. "I know where you're going with this," she said, not unkindly. Her anger had dissipated, and now she seemed merely tired. "You're not the only person to see the possibilities of Dr. Ram's work. Spiritual amputation, chemical inoculation, surgical exorcism . . . at the very least a method to positively identify cases of possession. And thanks to Dr. Ram's death, his line of research is closed, and I doubt anyone will pick it up."

"What do you mean, closed? If anything, this proves he was on the right track. The demons feared him so much they killed him to stop him."

She looked at me, smiled faintly. "The demons have no master plan, Mr. Pierce. They don't work together toward some agenda. Each of them is an obsessive, each of them wants what it wants. If the Truth killed Dr. Ram, it was for one reason—he said he had a cure, and he was lying." She shrugged. "That's the Truth's job. Punish the liars."

She grabbed the handle of her bag. "Good day, Mr. Pierce. This is the last day of our acquaintance." She stepped off the curb, between the bumpers of the stopped cars, and the roller bag dropped and bounced behind her.

"Wait! You've got to help me! What am I supposed to do?"

She stopped halfway across the intersection, looked back at me. "There's nothing you *can* do," she called back to me. "At least not against the demons, for they do with ye what they will. But if I were you . . ." The light turned green, but she took no notice. "I'd hire a good lawyer."

She strode the rest of the way across the street, holding up traffic. Someone was going to run her down, or at least lay on the horn—this was Chicago, for Christ's sake.

But no. She reached the far curb without incident and walked north, toward Lake Michigan, the plastic wheels of the suitcase clattering over each crack and crevice of the sidewalk.

Lew and Amra lived in Gurnee, a far northern suburb that was home to the biggest amusement park in Illinois, Six Flags Great America. From the guest bedroom I could see the hump of the highest section of the American Eagle roller coaster rising up over the bare trees. It was actually two roller coasters, on twin wooden tracks, so that theoretically the coasters could race each other, but in practice they never ran near the same speed.

"Do you ever go?" I said. When Lew and I were growing up, we had gotten to go to the park once or twice every summer, starting back when it was called Marriott's Great America.

He looked up, saw what I was talking about, then went back to work clearing the bed. "No." He'd been using the bed as an extra desk, loaded with stacks of papers, technical manuals, and foam-filled boxes that could have transported high-tech pizzas. Most of this garbage went into the closet.

Lew was mad at me, but trying not to be, an unnatural state that he couldn't maintain for long. He'd only be himself after he'd blown up. "Did Amra tell you yet?" I said.

"Tell me what?" he said.

But I knew she had. The hour-long ride home had been nearly silent, but right after we'd arrived at their house she and Lew had stayed in the kitchen while I went to the guest room with the blue duffel bag and the black nylon convention bag, shut the door behind me, and unzipped the duffel. Some of my clothes were missing—when the hotel people had grabbed my luggage from the room, they hadn't bothered retrieving the shirts and pants I'd hung up in the closet. But better that than trying to pack them up; I didn't want them going through my bag. The important things were there: the bike chains, the Kryptonite locks, and my father's gun. Still there.

I had almost broken down then. Tears welled up, goggling my vision. I unwrapped the oil rag around the pistol, hefted it in my hand. I lifted it to my face, wiped at my nose, and sniffed. A gun after it's fired smells like cordite or something, doesn't it? My knowledge of guns came only from television and Elmore Leonard novels.

I couldn't smell anything. The weapon didn't seem any different from when I'd wrapped it up at Mom's. Nobody had used the gun, I told myself. Not me, not the Hellion, not even the Truth.

I'd rewrapped it, weak with relief. As I'd stuffed it deep in the duffel bag, on the other side of the door Lew had been making outraged noises he barely tried to conceal. Amra had told him. The hotel bill had been four thousand and some-odd bucks. None of my cards would cover it.

And now Lew couldn't even look at me. He pulled the bedspread off the bed, spilling white kernels of foam and paper clips, and bunched it up. "I'll get you a fresh blanket," he said, and carried the bundle to the hallway.

I tried to empty my pockets, fumbling with bandaged fingers. Wallet, keys, crumpled ones and fives, change, a folded card from the Hyatt that said "Please tell us how we're doing." I used my palm to spread open the card. Inside I'd written "T & S" and a phone number. Tom and Selena. I dimly remembered promising to call them when I got to California, but why did I say I was going to California?

Lew stalked back into the room and without a word started spreading the blanket out.

"I'll pay you back," I said, which we both knew was bullshit.

We'd understood from high school on that it was Lew's job to make good grades, find a high-paying career, buy a two-story house in the suburbs, and generally become Dad. It was my job to fuck up. Occasionally this annoyed me, but most of the time I was comfortable with the division of labor. Lew's job was nearly impossible, and mine came naturally.

"Don't worry about it," he said.

"At least you'll get the bail money back."

I couldn't help it; I just wanted to poke him until he burst.

"There are towels in the bathroom," he said. "And I'll get you some clothes that—"

"Lew! Del! You should see this!" It was Amra. I followed Lew to the kitchen. A small TV on the counter was showing a picture of Dr. Ram. I recognized the photo from his book jacket. Almost immediately the story switched to a report on fighting in Pakistan.

"Somebody was shot at the Hyatt last night," Amra said. She was shook up. "That's why all the police were there. His name was Ram, he was a neurologist or something."

Lew turned to face me. His anger was gone, replaced by shock, or something like it.

"It wasn't me," I said.

"This guy who was murdered—you went ballistic last night, and they have you on file. How do you know you weren't involved?"

"Oh, it's worse than that." I carefully sat down on a kitchen chair. My back was still torqued. Not only had I lost control, I told them, but people had seen me with Dr. Ram, and later heard me ranting about how he wouldn't help me. Then I'd gotten off on the wrong floor—Dr. Ram's floor—no doubt around the time he was shot. "To top it off," I said, "I gave him my MRI reports. Somewhere in his room are a bunch of papers with my name on them. See? It's practically an open-and-shut case."

Lew and Amra exchanged a look. I admired that marital telepathy, the way they could check in with each other without speaking.

"We know a lawyer," Amra said.

"I don't have time for that," I said. "I'm not going to turn myself in."

Lew pulled out a chair and sat down. "Del, listen to me—"

"There's a woman who can help me," I said. "Mother Mariette. I need to find her, look her up on the Internet or something, find out where she lives—"

"That bald woman you went off after?" Amra said. "How can she possibly help you?"

"She's an exorcist."

Lew made a dismissive noise. "Jesus, Del, you can't just latch on to some religious quack. You've got to get serious, we're talking about murder here. This Mother Mary—"

"Mother Mariette," I said. "She's Irish, I think—she's the only person I've ever met who actually says *ye*. And she's a priest of some kind. I'm not exactly sure what church she's in, we'd have to find that out."

He sat back in his chair, looking pained. "Let me get this straight," he said. "A bald Irish exorcist nun . . ."

"Lew, she saw the Hellion in me. Nobody else has ever done that before—none of the shrinks, none of the doctors, not even Dr. Aaron." I leaned forward. "This woman is *the shit*."

No one said anything for a long moment.

Then Lew said, "You're going after her, I guess?" He saw something in my face, and shook his head. "Where does she live, fucking Dublin?"

"I don't know. Yet."

He sighed, got up, and left the room. A moment later he came back with his laptop. "Go take a shower," he said. "I'll Google her ass."

DEMONOLOGY

THE TRUTH

LOS ANGELES, 1995

Later, when the videotape played on every news channel in a seemingly continuous loop, it was easy enough to hear: a percussive sound like a cough, picked up by the microphones inside the courtroom. But no one watching the scene live on television, and no one inside the crowded chambers at the time, seemed to recognize it as a gunshot.

In the minutes before the attack, the single television camera allowed in the courtroom was focused on the defendant's table. O. J. Simpson—or Orenthal James Simpson, as the prosecution had repeatedly referred to him during the trial—stood impassively as Judge Ito issued his instructions. On the tape, many people are partially visible behind Simpson, including three California State police officers in brown uniforms, but it is Johnnie Cochran who is directly behind him. Cochran was not the architect of Simpson's possession defense—that was Robert Shapiro—but it was Cochran who had successfully sold the jury on it. The blood, the glove, the black bag: the obviousness of it had made his case. Who else but a man possessed would leave so clear a trail?

When the court officer read the verdict for the first count—for the murder of "Nicole Simpson, a human being"—Cochran gripped Simpson's shoulder and pressed his forehead into the taller man's back. Simpson smiled in relief, and nodded. Murmurs rolled through the courtroom. Then the second verdict was read for the murder of Ronald Goldman.

It was at that moment that Marc Janusek, a building janitor for over fifteen years, shot Officer Steve Mercer as he stood guard outside the courtroom. A few seconds later, out of sight of the camera, the door to the courtroom was pushed open. Cochran looked over Simpson's shoulder at the movement, but at that moment Simpson was lifting his hand and waving to the jury. He mouthed the words, "Thank you."

The first clue to the television audience that something was amiss was when one of the police officers, Dan Fiore, ran toward the defendant's table. He grabbed Robert Shapiro by the shoulders and shouted, "Get down! Get down!"

Janusek, the janitor, moved into the frame, his back to the camera. He was dressed in a black trench coat and a wide-brimmed fedora, and was carrying two silver pistols, though only one is visible on the tape. The next gunshots, however, were from Officer Tanya Brandt. Brandt, an African-American and the only female officer providing security inside the courtroom, fired her service revolver twice into the possessed man's back.

Janusek turned quickly, the trench coat fanning around him. He raised his arm, and fired once. Officer Brandt fell to the ground, out of the camera's sight.

Troopers converged from all corners of the courtroom. One officer tried to tackle the possessed man, but was immediately thrown off. Another officer fired at nearly point-blank range, but Janusek was spinning, and only later was it determined that the shot had missed. The bullet tore through Janusek's coat and struck the wall only inches from where prosecution lawyer Christopher Darden was standing. Janusek, however, abruptly stopped moving, and three officers immediately threw themselves onto him, smashing him to the ground.

The following moments were chaotic, but a rough order of events was reconstructed from the tape and from later interviews.

Every person in the courtroom, with the exception of the three troopers restraining the possessed man on the floor, was trying to exit by any means possible. Most were heading toward the large door at the rear of the court, but many were also moving forward, toward the bench, to the three doors that led to the judge's chamber, the jury room, and the hallway.

The camera swung from the pile of officers wrestling with Janusek and focused on Simpson. Fiore and another officer were pulling and pushing the defendant toward the judge's chambers. Simpson stayed hunched as he moved, his hands on the back of Fiore. Cochran, Shapiro, and Simpson attorney Robert Kardashian were just behind. Fiore suddenly stopped, and Simpson stumbled into the officer's side.

Fiore turned, reached over Simpson, and grabbed the other bailiff by the front of his shirt. Fiore lifted the bailiff off his feet and tossed him sideways. He hit the floor and skidded into the prosecutor's table.

Cochran seemed to be the first to realize that the demon had jumped. Cochran grabbed Simpson by the arm and pulled him backward. Officer Fiore stepped forward and punched Cochran in the face, breaking his glasses and sending him to the ground. Simpson stared at Cochran, then looked up at Fiore. There was a long moment in which neither man moved. Then Fiore smiled, opened his mouth, and laughed: a deep, rolling laugh that seemed to go on and on, filling the room.

Only a few yards away, Janusek had gone still, and at least one of the officers holding him down seemed to understand what had happened. The camera showed one of them abruptly stand and move toward Fiore, his arms out.

It was impossible to determine how many bodies the demon occupied in the next thirty seconds. Suddenly, officers were turning on each other. Faces collapsed under vicious punches, leg and foot bones snapped from kicks delivered near the mechanical maximum of human force, disabling both attacker and target. As soon as one man struck, he would abruptly lose concentration, his hands would drop—and another man would take him down. Within half a minute, every police officer but one was unconscious.

The middle of the courtroom was empty except for Simpson and Fiore. Both men seemed frozen in place. Then Fiore knelt down, and calmly smashed his forehead into the floor.

Fiore would survive, as would all of the officers, including the two who were shot, Steve Mercer and Tanya Brandt.

Janusek, motionless since being tackled by the police, got to his feet. His face was bloody, his nose smashed flat. He straightened the trench coat and recinched the belt. Then he stooped to pick up the fedora from where it had been pushed under a chair. He placed the hat firmly on his head, and then, facing Simpson, tilted the brim down in a kind of salute. Then he lifted both hands, the silver pistols plainly visible. O. J. Simpson, forty-eight years old and one of the greatest rushers in collegiate and NFL history, did not run.

7

Lew swung onto the shoulder and hit the brakes, sliding on loose gravel. We came to a stop under the dark rectangle of an unlit billboard, the road walled on both sides by forest.

Lew slapped on the dome light. "Give me the directions," he said.

"These directions?" Lew hadn't wanted me to print them out. We didn't need any fucking MapQuest directions, he'd said. The Audi had GPS.

"Shut up and give me the fucking printouts."

"It says the same thing it did the last twenty times I read it to you," I said. "Highway Twelve, then thirty-five point two miles to Branch Road, then—"

"There is no fucking Branch Road!"

"Maybe not on your little blue screen there—"

"Jesus Christ, would you shut the fuck up about the GPS?" For the past two hours our little yellow arrow had glided across a blank blue screen. The satellite connection still seemed to be working, but the DVD of map data had nothing to say about this patch of Appalachia.

I said, "You spent what, fifty thousand dollars on this car? How much would it cost to get one of those that showed actual roads?"

He gripped the steering wheel with both hands and stared out through the windshield. "Give—me—the fucking—"

"Take 'em." I slapped the pages onto his lap, then got out and slammed the door behind me.

It was 1:30 a.m., forty degrees, and dark, no light but the fingernail moon slicing in and out of high, opaque clouds. I felt like I had the flu: nausea, headache, aching joints. My hands still burned in their bandages.

We'd left Gurnee just after 5 a.m., ahead of the morning rush, zipping down the skyway through the heart of Chicago and riding a cresting wave of traffic onto I-80, heading east into the rising sun. Lew barely slowed through the toll plaza; thanks to the I-Pass on the Audi's dash, each toll automatically deducted from his credit card. The female voice of the Audi's GPS prompted us before every turn. So twenty-first century. If I weren't so nervous about being pulled over by the cops, I might have enjoyed it.

Ten miles past Gary, Indiana, we drove into a wall of lake-effect snow and lost WXRT just as the angels were coveting Elvis Costello's red shoes. We emerged twenty minutes later to sun and sweet driving. Ohio had been colonized at forty-mile intervals by glass-and-concrete flying saucers—the nicest oases I'd ever seen. Spacious and clean, appointed with shiny restaurants, arcades, and gleaming restrooms that clairvoyantly flushed, rinsed, and blow dried—everything but wiped your ass. We assembled a multivendor breakfast of Burger King hashbrowns, Panera's asiago bagels, and Starbucks venti lattés. Then while Lew revisited the auto-john, I stopped into the gift shop for ibuprofen and other medical supplies, and also picked up a newspaper. There was a short article on the Hyatt shooting.

"Did they catch the shooter?" Lew said.

"No arrests, no suspects, but they're interviewing 'persons of interest.'"

"It's not too late to call the cops," Lew said.

"No. No way."

"Fine then," Lew said, and handed me the keys. "You drive."

"Really?"

The offer wasn't entirely altruistic. As soon as he got in the passenger seat he set his beautiful silver laptop atop his lap and proceeded to daisy-chain himself to the car: cigarette lighter to laptop to cell phone to headset to ear.

"Smile," he said, and took my picture with his phone. "I'm sending this to Amra."

"You guys do this all the time?"

"Sure. We send each other pictures during the day. Or just IM. And e-mail, of course."

"Lew?"

"Del?"

"What do you do when you two have sex, put on body suits and touch serial ports?"

"Nobody's had sex through serial ports since 1987. We're strictly FireWire, bro. My baby needs the bandwidth. Don't you, baby?"

I hadn't even realized Amra was on the line. I tried to ignore Lew while they talked, but it was impossible. There were several *really*s? and sudden glances at me that kept me on my toes.

"Okay," Lew said, and pulled off the earphones and mike. "The cops called, but Amra thinks it was just routine, they were calling everybody who stayed in the hotel."

"Do they know who did it yet?" I asked.

"It doesn't sound like it, but I'll check the online news in a sec. But here's the weird thing. Did you call any of your friends and tell them that you were at our house last night?"

"What are you talking about? Of course not."

"A guy stopped by this morning as Amra was getting ready for work. He said his name was Bertram Beech. This is the same guy who was calling Mom's house, right?"

"He was at your *house*?"

"She said the guy creeped her out. Very intense, said he had to speak with you, said it was a matter of life or death."

"No way."

"Uh, *way*. What kind of head case says 'a matter of life or death'?"

"The Bertram kind," I said. "Did she tell him where I went?"

"Of course not. But listen, man, you can't have him coming by the house again. Call him and tell him that it's not cool."

"All right, I'll call him." What could Bertram want? The phone calls were bad enough, but now he'd traveled all the way to Chicago, and somehow found Lew's house. Well, that maybe wasn't that difficult. I'd talked about my family with him in the hospital, and these days it wasn't hard to find a phone number for almost anybody.

I suddenly realized that I was coming up on the bumper of an RV, and switched over to the left lane.

"Who is this guy?" Lew said. "Somebody from Colorado?"

"I met him in the hospital." I saw the eyebrow raise in my peripheral vision. "Yeah, that hospital. He believes that powerful telepaths are secretly in charge of the planet, and that they're possessing people for their own entertainment."

"Powerful telepaths . . . ," Lew said.

"Slans," I said.

Lew burst out laughing.

"You mean you didn't know that *Slan* was nonfiction?" I said. "Bertram belongs to an organization that believes that Van Vogt intentionally—"

"What did you say—Van Vaht? It's Van Voh."

"No it's not. You've gotta pronounce the *T* at least."

"What, Van Vote? Don't be an idiot. I bet you still say Submareener."

"My *point*—," I said.

"And 'Mag-*net*-o.' "

"—is that Bertram thinks *Van Voggatuh* used fiction to cloak the truth."

"As opposed to, say, your friend P. K. Dick, and Whitley Strieber, and—"

"Streeber."

"And L. Ron Hubbard, who just made up shit and said it was the truth."

"Exactly."

Lew nodded. "I find your ideas intriguing, and I'd like to subscribe to your newsletter. What's the name of this fine organization?"

"It gets better," I said. "The Human League."

"No way."

"I'm not sure they realized the name was taken."

"My God," Lew said. "It's the perfect cover for an elite fighting force—an eighties New Wave band! This is so *Buckaroo Banzai*." He refolded his legs, no easy task in the Audi. "So this Bertram guy must have been thrilled to meet you, one of the pawns of the overlords. Did he explain why the masters of Earth would bother possessing an underemployed graphic artist and not, say, the national security advisor?"

"Oh yeah. He was convinced that my possession—well, all the showy possessions, like the Captain?—were for the entertainment of the other slans, kinda like theater for superhumans. The slans came to power in the forties, and they're long-lived, and that's why so many of the demons are so old-fashioned. They like their old radio shows and comic books—the Shadow, Captain America."

Lew snorted. "Sure, that makes sense. They keep it a secret that they're running the world, then they blow their cover by playing dress-up like Trekkers?"

"Only Trekkies say Trekkers," I said. "There must be two types of slans—the responsible, world-dominating type, and the role-playing, geek slans."

"White-boy racist geeks, judging from how my black friends reacted to the O. J. killing."

I snorted. "Like you have black friends."

"So did you tell Bert your theory that you'd trapped a demon?"

"We had a lot of time to talk."

Lou sighed. "Well no wonder."

"No wonder what? And it's not a theory."

"Say the slans are in charge," he said. "These telepaths can invade any mind they want, bouncing around people's heads like packets on a network. They go wherever they want, dropping into your personal hardware like a virus. But you, you're special."

"I'm antiviral?"

"Not exactly. You didn't kill the demon, you just quarantined it, like a sandbox that keeps Trojan horse programs from dialing out."

"You really gotta work on your metaphors," I said. "How's a sandbox supposed to stop a Trojan horse?"

"Shut up," he explained. "The important thing is that you've trapped one. It can't get out and infect other people. If you could teach people how to do that—"

"I don't *want* to teach people how to trap one. It's awful. Even if I knew what the trick was, which I *don't*, nobody would want this thing in their head."

"It can't be worse than being possessed," he said.

"You don't get to have an opinion."

"Okay, okay. Fine. But say that once you get this thing out of you, you could use the same trick that kept it in to keep it out. You'd own the world's only demonic firewall."

I rolled my eyes.

He pointed at me. "You, my friend, may be the ultimate weapon in the war against the slans."

"Oh my God," I said, my voice going spooky with awe. "That would make me . . ."

"The Chosen One!" we said simultaneously.

We rode in silence for a while. Then Lew said, "But seriously. Bertram can't come to the house, not while Amra's there alone. You gotta call him and tell him to cut that shit out."

"I told you, I'll call him."

"Okay," Lew said.

"Okay."

We made great time crossing Ohio and Pennsylvania. My thoughts kept jumping from Dr. Ram to Valis to Mother Mariette. Lew distracted me by reading from some of the more tangential web pages we'd only skimmed the night before when we were looking up the priestess. Then he started streaming music from his laptop to the car radio.

"You got to hear this one," Lew said. It started with a U2 guitar blast from "Vertigo" overdubbed with their spoken intro to "Helter Skelter," which abruptly became Jet's "Are You Gonna Be My Girl." And all the chords matched. I hadn't realized they were so similar.

"Hey, that's cool," I said, and then shut up, because suddenly Paul McCartney was singing "Lady Madonna" over that thrash of Jet chords, and it sounded like *those* two songs were meant for each other. And then as soon as I settled into that, a guitar riff from the Joe Walsh song kicked in—that one about "life's been good to me so far," I couldn't recall the name. And then it was all three—Beatles, Jet, and Joe Walsh—punctuated at random by distant shouts of "What the fuck is going on!" that sounded like snippets from a Sex Pistols track. I couldn't stop giggling.

"Holy shit!" I said to Lew. "Where did you get this stuff?"

"Downloaded it. They call 'em mash-ups."

"I think I'm in love."

He had hours of this stuff on his hard drive. We cut northeast into New York, and Lew played me Doors versus Blondie, Depeche Mode versus Marvin Gaye versus Cypress Hill, Madonna versus Sex Pistols, and on and on. It was like these DJs had tapped into all the pop songs in my brain, into the collective radio in all our brains, and remixed and relayered until the songs were having sex and making strange, beautiful babies.

Eventually we left the interstate behind and the music ran out, along with Lew's cell phone service. For the past few hours we'd been twisting and bobbing along two-lane back roads, rollercoastering through pitch-black forests. And now we were lost. Or rather, the world was lost. The GPS told us exactly where we were, but had no idea where anything else was.

Permanent Global Position: You Are Here.

I walked away from the car, toward the trees, sucking in cold air. A few feet away from the headlights, it got very dark. I stood there, letting my eyes adjust. What had looked like a solid wall of shadow resolved into individual trees, evergreens interspersed with bare-limbed things with interlocking branches. Snow was still mounded under some of the trunks. Somewhere out there was a town called Harmonia Lake, and presumably a lake to go with it, and a house or trailer or tent that might have been, and might still be, Mother Mariette O'Connell's home.

I crossed my arms against the cold, turned my back to the woods, and started back to the car. Lew, illuminated by the dome light, was flipping through pages of printouts and cursing.

Suddenly a light above the billboard sputtered to life, silvering the grass. I realized I wasn't alone, and looked up.

A gray-green humanoid monster reached toward me with huge webbed hands. It was hairless, with a wide, pale belly like a toad's, caught in midstride as it stalked out of some dimly rendered swamp on thickly muscled thighs, its crotch conveniently shadowed. The head was bald and round, mouth agape, neck gills fanned. It stared down at me with black goggly eyes.

"Oh Lew?" I called out. "Lew!"

He looked at me, scowling. I nodded at the sign.

The billboard was faded and peeling, but below the painted monster the huge block letters were clear enough: HAVE YOU SEEN THE SHUG?! And then below that, slightly smaller: MUSEUM & GIFT SHOP— HARMONIA LAKE MOTEL 2 MI. ON RIGHT.

Lew shook his head, then crumpled the remaining pages and tossed them in the backseat. "Fucking MapQuest," he said.

The Harmonia Lake Motel and Shu'garath Museum and Gift Shop was a Victorian stack of narrow windows and peaked roofs disappearing into black sky. A long, slope-roofed porch wrapped the house in a shadow mouth, toothed by gray posts. The windows were dark except for two narrow, faintly glowing panes on either side of the front door.

A light high on a telephone pole shone weakly on the empty parking lot. Two gravel roads, not much wider than walking paths, led from each end of the lot and disappeared into the woods; signs pointed toward cabins 1–2 and 3–5.

On the lawn in front of the house, a man-size wooden cutout of the Shug held its own rectangular sign, white letters dimly visible: BAIT.

Lew put the Audi in park. "You've got to be fucking kidding me."

"Come on, you want to sleep in the car?" I got out and crunched toward the house, hands in my armpits, shivering. Lew reluctantly followed me. The air smelled faintly of rotting fish; the lake was somewhere behind the hotel.

I patted the plywood shoulder of the Shug as I passed and went up the front steps. The porch creaked, naturally. Next to the door were a pair of broad-backed rocking chairs, a wicker table between them, and farther down, a porch swing on metal chains.

The front door was a two-part affair, a screen door in front of a wooden one. Nailed to the face of the wooden door, where the knocker would be, was a glossy hunk of driftwood, vaguely squidlike: bulbous and shiny on top, multiple twisting limbs below, each limb turning up at the end into a sharpened point like a fish hook. The black wood gleamed like it was still in water.

The screen door was ajar. I opened it, tried the knob of the wooden door, and found it locked.

Lew cupped his hands to one of the narrow windows beside the door. "Can't see a thing through these curtains," he said. "But I think the night clerk's been laid off."

I touched the driftwood and ran my finger along the bulb and down one limb. It wasn't wet, exactly, but the wood seemed oily and slightly gritty. I delicately touched the tip of the tentacle, dimpling the skin of my finger, and the porch light came on.

I jumped, Lew jerked upright—and then we looked at each other and cracked up.

The lock clacked significantly and we stifled ourselves. The door opened six inches on a chain. A small white-haired woman glared up at me, mouth agape. She was seventy, seventy-five years old, a small bony face on a striated, skinny neck: bright eyes, sharp nose, and skin intricately webbed from too much sun or wind or cigarettes. She looked like one of those orphaned baby condors that has to be fed by puppets.

"What are you, drunk?" she said. Her voice was surprisingly low and sharp.

"No! No ma'am." I glanced at Lew, daring him to laugh. "You just startled us."

Lew sidled up behind me, raised a hand. "Hi."

"Do you know what time it is? " she said. "You shouldn't be out at this time of night."

"We'd like rooms," I said.

"Or cabins," Lew said.

"I don't check in people after eleven," she said. "I can't put you into cabins that aren't prepared."

"Please," I said. "We'll take anything you have. You don't have to do anything to the cabins."

She stared at me for a second, blinked. "You're the boy who called."

"That's true," I said, politely allowing the "boy" comment to slide. Last night we'd searched for every Harmonia Lake number we could find. The town had no chamber of commerce, no police station, not even a gas station. We came up with six phone numbers, five of them residential, none of them O'Connell's. The remaining number was for the motel.

"I told you I'd give her your message," the old woman said.

"I know, I just thought we'd—"

"She hasn't stopped in yet."

"That's fine, I understand," I said. "For tonight, though, we'd just like to—"

"She hasn't got a phone."

"You mentioned that, yeah."

Her eyes looked past me, and then she seemed to come to a decision. She shook her head, disgusted.

I said, "Listen—"

She shut the door. A chain slid back, then she opened it again a few inches. "All right, then. It's almost morning. I suppose I can check you in. Besides, I'm already awake."

She disappeared from the doorway. I looked at Lew, then pushed open the door. The old woman was already in the next room, walking away from us. Her silver hair, I could see now, was waist-length, and braided. She wore a pink bathrobe over red sweatpants.

The front of the old house was divided into three sections. The middle area was taken up by a picnic table covered by a red-and-white checked vinyl tablecloth. To the right was a dark room illuminated only by a red Coca-Cola sign over the beverage cooler in the corner: the gift shop? Shadows suggested many shelves stocked with cheap crap. The old woman went left, into what I supposed was the hotel lobby, crossing the room to step behind a pressboard-and-veneer front desk. If not for the desk, the room would have passed for any homey cottage circa 1972: oval braided throw rug, a cockeyed green cloth swivel chair, and a plaid couch-and-loveseat combo. Covering the dark paneled walls were dozens of small framed photographs, interspersed with mounted, waxy fish of alarming size, nailed to the wall in midgasp.

"You should have told me you were coming," she said. "You could have made reservations."

"You're full?" Lew asked incredulously.

"Cash or credit?" she said.

I reached for my back pocket, not looking at Lew. The bastard let me pull the wallet all the way out before he said, "Credit."

"And we need two rooms," I said. Lew shook his head but didn't press me on it. Maybe he wanted his privacy as much as I did.

She laid his credit card on a hand machine, racked it like a shotgun. I picked up one of the brochures on the desk, a photocopied trifold, black print on 30-pound yellow paper. The front had the same picture and logo as the billboard. Had I seen the Shug?! Yes, and too many times. These people could use a graphic designer.

"You don't have Internet access, do you?" Lew said. "It doesn't have to be high speed."

She squinted at him. People either got Lew or they didn't.

She handed his card back to him. "You're in three, he's in four, next to the washhouse. Breakfast starts at five-thirty."

Lew looked at me, one eyebrow raised. Washhouse?

The old woman escorted us outside, pointed down the gravel trail to the left, and waited on the porch while Lew and I got in the car and rolled slowly in the correct direction. The first cabin, barely visible in the dark, was only a dozen yards from the parking lot. Lew pulled in at the next gap in the trees. The Audi's headlights revealed a miniature peak-roofed house, maybe twenty-five feet long and fifteen wide, set on cinder blocks, surrounded by trees except for the grassy parking space out front.

Lew sighed. "You so fucking owe me."

He kept the headlights on as we got our bags out of the trunk. The lake was a faint gleam through the trees behind the cabin.

He handed me my key, wired to a wooden block big enough to be used as either a flotation device or mace, depending on the emergency.

Lew glanced at the duffel and said, "You going to be okay?" Talking about the chains. Last night in their house Lew had watched, aghast, as I looped the chains through the bed frame, adjusting the slack.

"I'll be fine," I said. "Listen, thanks for coming with me. I know you hate to take off work."

He waved me toward my cabin and turned away from me. "Go to bed."

"Fair enough," I said. I was tired enough to fall over.

My cabin was only fifty feet from Lew's, connected by a stone path through the trees, but a few steps away from the headlights I could barely see a thing. I kept my eyes wide and one hand out to stop me from ramming into trees. I eventually recognized the outline of a small porch, went up the three short steps, and nearly impaled myself: hanging on the door was another one of those squid-shaped driftwood eye-stabbers. My hand moved lower, found the knob, turned.

The door was unlocked. I wasn't sure how I felt about that.

I found the switch inside the room, and an overhead light came on. Something small and long-tailed darted into a hole in the wall.

The room was floored with specked linoleum, and some of the specks were dubious. A double bed took up most of the room, its brown-and-yellow polyester bedspread nicely complementing, in both style and time period, a small yellow Formica table with aluminum legs and a couple of matching chairs padded in split vinyl. A small square window opposite the door mirrored the light. There was no bathroom: no bath, no room, not even room for a bath. From the smell, the walls were insulated with old fish wrap.

"You in?" Lew called.

"Does yours have a Jacuzzi too?" I shouted back.

"Sleep tight, now."

Outside, the headlights switched off (Lew's magical remote control). I shut the door and dropped my duffel bag on the floor. It clanked.

Oh. Sleep tight. Very funny.

I could hear the lake creeping toward the cabin. The longer I sat in the little room, the clearer I could hear it, until it seemed to be lapping at the floorboards beneath my bed. *Bloop. Blurp. Blu-doop.*

I sat on the bed, propped up and staring at the dead flies in the bowl of the overhead light. My rodent roommate stayed demurely out of sight.

The Hellion banged around inside my head like a drunk in a dark room.

On the ride today I'd realized that I'd been going about this all wrong. Knocking myself out with Nembutal obviously wasn't the answer, because the demon was busting out anyway at irregular intervals. Besides, I was almost out of pills. And alcohol seemed to have no effect, because after infusing my gray matter with Coors Light I'd managed to not only black out but go rock-'n'-roll on a hotel.

No, the only way to ensure a demon-free night was to stay awake.

The question, then, was how long could a human being stay awake? Keith Richards could party for three days straight, but I wasn't sure if he counted as a human being. I kept myself alert for a good hour by peeling off my bandages and poking at my poor beat-up hands. I re-covered the bigger cuts with fresh bits of gauze taped down with Band-Aids, and left the smaller abrasions to air out.

The pain was useful, but for any long-term attempt at uninterrupted consciousness I needed chemical assistance. At the Ohio oasis I'd stocked up on packages of NoDoz and chased a few pills with my latté. I'd dry-swallowed a few more after getting into the cabin, but sooner or later I'd need to find something with a bit more oomph. Addiction didn't scare me. That was like worrying about tetanus after a bullet to the head. I just needed to stay awake long enough to convince Mother Mariette to cure me. NoDoz wouldn't cut it for long, though. If we didn't find the exorcist quick, I'd have to build my own crystal meth lab.

Mother Mariette O'Connell, we'd learned (thank you, Google), was an Irish citizen and a priest in the Latin Tridentine Church, an Irish splinter group of the Church of Palmar de Troya in Spain, which itself (thanks again, Big G) was an apocalyptic cult that had broken away from mainstream Catholicism.

The Palmarians were run by "Bishop" Clemente Gómez who, upon the death of Pope Paul VI, declared himself to be Pope Gregory XVII of the Holy Palmarian Church. Gómez, a gay priest with abstinence problems, had been known in Seville as El Voltio—"too much voltage"—before a vision of Mary in the nearby village of Palmar de Troya triggered his religious conversion. He'd invented the Palmarian Catechism, which taught, among other things, that somewhere in space was the Planet of Mary—home to Elijah, Moses, and Saint John—where human sin had not yet reached, and that elsewhere was the Planet of the Anti-Christ, where salvation was impossible and demons from the fourth dimension were readying for Armageddon. Gómez lost his sight in a car accident in 1976, then declared that Mary would heal him, which she declined to do before he died.

O'Connell had appeared in the United States sometime in the late eighties or early nineties. A San Jose Mercury News article from 1992 said that she'd performed a successful exorcism on a young girl who'd been possessed by the Little Angel, and that the priest had performed several other exorcisms in the States. Over the next few years she racked up a series of wins, saving two other girls from the Angel, but also casting out demons as various as the Pirate King and the Painter. After 1999 she'd dropped out of sight—or at least, out of sight of the media and the web. We could find no phone number or e-mail address in the directories. The last known address came from a mention in the Spring, 1998, issue of the C. G. Jung Psychological Club of Philadelphia newsletter, which said that she was Mariette O'Connell "of" Harmonia Lake, New York.

That's when I found the hotel phone number. After the failed conversation with the old lady clerk, I told Lew that I had to go there, I had to find O'Connell. Lew looked at me, shook his head, and shuffled off to bed. To Amra. He came out ten minutes later, said we should leave in the morning before rush hour, and went back to the bedroom.

The overhead light suddenly flared bright, making me wince.

I sat up, heart pounding. I'd been dead asleep. Shit.

I lurched out of bed before I could fall asleep again. The room was freezing. The little window had grown more translucent; the sky had grown marginally lighter.

I pulled on my shoes, tugged a sweatshirt out of my duffel, and opened the door to damp gray chill. A thick fog soaked up the light spilling past me, absorbed the feeble predawn glow forcing its way into the sky. I could see only the porch's wooden steps and the suggestion of tree limbs—everything else was gray milk. I walked around the open space in front of the cabin, working my arms and flexing my neck like a boxer, as the grass wet my shins and the air lightened around me. Next to the cabin I found a path of stepping stones and followed them around the shack to a wooden dock that jutted into cloud. I walked down the creaking dock, hands jammed in my pockets.

A slap and splash as something hit the water.

The Shug!

That was my first thought. I stood there, heart racing—and then got a mental image of me standing there shaking like Don Knotts, and laughed. Wait till I tell Lew.

Ripples tocked against the pilings. I could see only a few feet into the fog. The ripples died. The narrow patch of water visible at the end of the dock smoothed, turned glossy black.

"Oooh-kay," I said to myself. "Time to—"

Something big moved under the water, a pale expanse of flesh twice the size of a man, gliding just under the surface . . . and abruptly nosed down, diving, a smooth hump like a whale's back barely breaking the surface.

I screamed, fell back on my ass. Scrambled backward like a crab. I twisted sideways, somehow got my feet under me, and ran.

The dock did not quite meet the shore; my foot fell into the gap, a drop of six inches, and I plunged headlong into the rocky dirt. Somehow I managed to tuck my bandaged hands into my midriff and hit with my right shoulder and cheek, a two-point landing that left me stunned and stupid.

A handful of seconds. I rolled onto my back and pushed myself up on my elbows. I scanned left, right, left, watching for movement in the shifting fog, ears straining. I heard nothing but the rasp of my own breath. The water lapped against the shore. I got up, backed my butt against a tree, and hunched there, panting.

Jesus Christ. Jesus Fucking Christ.

I eventually realized I was saying that out loud, and shut up. The sun had finally edged over the surface of the lake, and trees emerged from the fog. My breathing slowed to the point where I could stand up straight. To my left, behind the clump of trees where Lew's cabin sat, another dock became visible. The expanse of water between the docks was smooth and empty.

I shook my head, and a low chuckle started in my chest. I couldn't stop it. Oh Jesus. Wait till I tell Lew.

Still laughing, I turned toward the path back to the cabin. Twenty yards down the shoreline, the Shug waded out of the water.

8

Eventually I realized Lew was calling my name. I looked back toward shore to see him stumble through the bushes and nearly put his foot into the water. He clumped toward the dock. Even at this distance I could tell he was annoyed. I waved at him and went back to my conversation. The next time I looked back Lew had stopped midway down the landing. He was staring, but not at me.

The Shu'garath sat with his legs over the side, ankles in water, naked except for black plastic goggles on his forehead and a pair of dark nylon trunks. A gigantic baby, hairless and pale as a cave fish.

I gestured Lew forward. My brother raised an eyebrow.

"Lew, I'd like you to meet the Beast from the Depths, the Terror of the Northern Lakes, the Shu'garath himself—Toby Larsen. Toby, this is my brother, Lew."

Toby stood slowly, rising up to nearly seven feet. An expanse of milk-white skin. Huge thighs. A keg torso pregnant with a Buddha belly: glossy and tight and almost translucent, like something extruded by a glass blower. He gave off a powerful, yeasty odor.

Lew had to look up at the man, a rare experience for Lew.

And Toby looked down. Broad nose, tiny ears that seemed almost vestigial, rubbery pink lips. He blinked. His eyes seemed tiny compared to the black goggles perched on his smooth, Beluga forehead.

Toby lifted one arm, a slablike thing with none of the comic book definition of a body builder's. A weightlifter arm, a blacksmith arm.

I gave Lew an admonishing look. Lew came to his senses and took the man's giant paw in his own.

"Pleased to meet you," Lew said. Without looking away from him, he said to me, "I couldn't find you. I looked in your cabin . . ."

"I was out here and Toby swam right by me, scared the shit out of me! Do you know this man can hold his breath for nearly eight minutes?"

Toby shrugged; a ripple of meat.

"So," Lew said. "You're the Shug."

"For thirty-five years," Toby said. His voice was surprisingly soft.

"Shug number five," I said.

I gave Lew the abbreviated version of the story Toby had told me over the past hour. Back in the twenties, Harmonia Lake had been a popular stop on the road between New York City and Montreal. Hotels, gas stations, resorts. Oliver Hardy had fished there. When the first Shu'garath was sighted in 1925, the indistinct photographs and breathless newspaper accounts only made the place more popular. Somebody got the idea of swimming around as the Shug, and for a while there was even an annual Shug festival: fireworks and eating contests and a boat parade. But in the fifties the interstate went through to the west, and then the only people who stopped into town were the Shug watchers. They still got a few tourists—the museum's listed on the web, he said proudly—but most business came from fishing.

"So what does being the Shug involve, exactly?" Lew said, deadpan. "I mean, you swim around in fifty-degree water—"

"No, no," Toby said. "It's about forty-eight right now. But I've been in there colder than that. I can take the cold. I've got the insulation."

"Sure, sure. But still . . . swimming around and scaring the shit out of people. That's not exactly a full-time job."

Toby stared at him. I lifted a hand, started to say something.

Toby said, "I also do children's parties."

I barked a laugh. Lew nodded, keeping a straight face.

The big man pulled the goggles down over his eyes. "Besides, somebody's got to do it. As long as there's a Harmonia Lake, there's gotta be a Shug."

He padded to the end of the dock, stopped, looked over his shoulder. His head like a planetoid embedded on rolls of neck fat. "Oh, try Louise's walnut hotcakes."

He dove in, vanishing beneath the water. When he didn't come up, Lew and I walked to the end of the dock. The fog had burned down to wisps. Harmonia Lake was much larger than we had suspected last night. The opposite shore was dimly visible across the water, on the other end of a road of sunlight. I couldn't guess at the lake's shape; left and right the shoreline disappeared and reappeared as it traced scallops of land, the gaps hiding anything from shallow coves to vast expanses of water.

Lew and I watched for a few minutes, then started walking back up the dock, but both of us kept looking over our shoulders to see if the water had broken. At the shore we stood and waited: eight minutes, ten. We never saw him surface.

"Are you sure it was him?" Lew said. He was trying to pace, but the short metal leash of the pay phone kept yanking him back. Lew's cell phone still hadn't managed to find a signal, and it was cramping his style.

I stabbed another triple-stacked wedge of pancake, smeared it through the syrup. I'd stopped being even faintly hungry fifteen minutes ago. Now I was stuffed, engorged, infused . . . and I couldn't stop putting the food in my mouth. The coffee was terrible and the bacon was ordinary, but the pancakes were avatars of some perfect Ur-cake whose existence until now could only be deduced from the statistical variations in other, lesser pancakes.

"Have you called the police?" Lew said into the phone. He glanced up at me, glared, then pivoted away. "I think you should call the police."

I stabbed, I smeared, I swallowed. The Baby Condor woman,

Louise, poured me more coffee and pointedly ignored Lew, who was obviously making too much noise.

Lew carefully put the phone back on the hook. He didn't immediately come back to the table. He walked toward the gift shop, stopped, and then walked back. He leaned into the table, arms straight, and addressed the salt and pepper shakers in the middle of the table. "He's sitting in a *van* outside our goddamn *house*."

I didn't have to ask who he was talking about.

"This van's been parked on our street," Lew said. "Amra passed it on the way to work, saw him sitting there. He's fucking *stalking* her now."

"Is he still there?"

"She called the cops, but the van was gone by the time they got there." Lew stared at the checked vinyl.

I started to say: Bertram's harmless, afraid of his own shadow.

"This is unacceptable, Del."

"Okay," I said.

"*Okay?!*"

"Okay!"

I got up awkwardly, levering my feet over the bench. A pound of weapons-grade carbohydrates sank lower in my gut.

I sifted through my wallet until I'd found the ATM receipt where I'd written Bertram's number after he'd called Mom's house. My calling card was right there, but I didn't know how many minutes were left, and why should I pay for it? I called collect.

It rang only once—then there was a silence as whoever picked up negotiated with the computer to accept the call.

"Oh my God, is it really you, Del?" The connection had the clipped metallic sound of a cheap cell phone. His voice sounded strange—Bertram and I had never talked on the phone before—but I recognized him. "Where are you?" he asked.

There was no way I was telling him—the next day he'd be outside my cabin door. "What are you doing, Bertram? How the hell did you get to Chicago?"

In the hospital he'd always been hunched over the phone by the nurses' station: a little white guy, bald with a fringe of sandy hair, pudgy except for skinny legs. Every phone call he received was critical, every discussion freighted with meaning. To Bertram, *casual conversation* was a contradiction in terms.

But Bertram wasn't in the hospital in Fort Morgan; he was in a van in Chicago.

"It's imperative that you and I talk," Bertram said. "In person."

"I don't think that's going to happen. I can call you in a couple weeks, but right now I need you to—"

"You don't understand, this is *important*," Bertram said. "I told my commander about your, uh, situation. This someone—I can't say his name over the phone—very much wants to meet you. He has a solution, a kind of *procedure* that would allow you to be free of your, your . . ."

"Situation."

"Exactly! I can hear in your voice that we understand each other."

Understand each other? All I could think was, Bertram has a *commander*. Commander of the Human League.

"This is bigger than just you," Bertram continued. "With your help, we can change the world."

Jesus, Lew was right. Bertram, and all his fellow Human Leaguers, thought I was the Anti-Slan Firewall.

In the background of the call I heard a male voice say something I couldn't pick up, and then Bertram said, "Del, if you would just tell us where you are, we could meet you."

"Bertram, if this is about the—"

"Don't say their name!" he said, panicked. "For goodness' sake, you have no idea of the range of their scans. In 2004—"

"Bertram."

"—a soldier in Srinagar—"

"Bertram, I need you to focus."

"Focus?" he said, wounded. He exhaled loudly into the phone. I could picture him bent over his knees, the cell phone mashed into his face. "I am more focused than I have ever been in my life."

I stepped away from the phone, shaking my head, and the receiver cord brought me up short. I turned around as Mother Mariette O'Connell walked through the front door.

She was dressed in a silver nylon jacket, padded and stitched in a diamond pattern, zipped up to her neck. She glanced in our direction and then went left, toward the front desk.

She stopped.

"Here's the deal," I said to Bertram, speaking quickly. "Don't call my mother. Don't call my brother or sister-in-law. And do *not*, under any circumstances, go near their houses. The next time they see you, they're going to call the cops. Do you understand?"

O'Connell turned, frowning. Her eyes narrowed.

Bertram breathed into the phone. "Del, I'm just trying to—"

I thunked the big receiver onto the metal hook—an old-fashioned pleasure that cell phones couldn't match—and then O'Connell was marching toward me. "What *the fuck* are you doing here?" she said.

Lew didn't budge from the table. The coward.

"It's imperative that you and I talk," I said. A moment later I was sitting on the ground.

"Ouch," Lew said.

"Can somebubby gib me a nabkin?"

Louise came out of the kitchen holding the coffee pot, and froze. O'Connell turned away, shaking out her hand. My teeth must have broken the skin of her knuckles.

Lew pulled a tuft of napkins from the chrome dispenser, dropped them on my lap. I dabbed gingerly at my lower lip. I was in no hurry to get up.

"What did you do to her?" Louise demanded.

O'Connell spun back toward us. "And who are you?" she asked Lew.

He held up his hands. "I'm the driver."

"Then you know your way back," she said. Without turning away from Lew she looked at me, raised her arm, and pointed: a wrath-of-God, get-thee-to-a-nunnery point. I didn't know anyone outside of the nuthouse who looked comfortable wielding a gesture like that, but she was a natural.

"I told you in Chicago," she said. "I can't help you. You were traumatized by a demon as a child? See a therapist. You have no right to come to my hometown, bother my friends, and harass us. Go home, Mr. Pierce."

I carefully peeled the napkins away from my lip, stared at the bright red blot. My mouth still stung, and more blood welled to the surface. I looked up at her until she dropped the finger.

"I guess Toby had you pegged wrong," I said.

"*Who?*" Louise said, shocked.

"The Shu'garath? The gigantic guy who swims around in the lake?"

Louise said, "Toby talked to you?"

"Toby doesn't talk to people," O'Connell said.

"Well he talked to me. He's a nice guy, though I wish he had warned me about your right hook." A warm dollop of blood seeped over my lip like gravy, and I patted at it. "He said that *of course* you'd help me. Said that if anybody could help me, it was you."

"I'm retired," O'Connell said.

Louise looked from me to O'Connell, her bird eyes expectant.

We followed O'Connell's Toyota pickup down the highway. Gray primer blotches covered the once-blue truck like a tropical disease. A few miles north of the motel she turned onto a steep dirt road that looked like it had been shelled by artillery. The pits were much deeper than the Audi's clearance, and Lew had to ease in and out of them at an angle to avoid bottoming out. O'Connell immediately left us behind, and the next time we saw the pickup it was parked in a muddy clearing. On one side of the clearing was a steep drop-off, Harmonia Lake spread out below. On the other side was a collection of low, ramshackle structures. Or maybe one complex structure. It was hard to tell.

At the center of the cluster was a mass of rounded aluminum that used to be a silver Airstream trailer. The trailer had grown several new rooms, as well as a couple of porches, a deck, two open-sided sheds, and many awnings, constructed of barn-wood planks, vinyl siding, and rusting sheet metal. Covered walkways, roofed in thick green plastic and floored with sections of warped plywood, connected to a Plexiglas-walled greenhouse and two garages. One garage door was open, revealing an old pontoon boat surrounded floor to ceiling by industrial junk.

Lew and I walked gingerly over the muddied driveway and reached one of the front porches. A door had been left open for us. Next to the frame was a driftwood sculpture like those at the motel, all glossy hooks and barbs. The wall below it was stained, the deck glittering with fish scales, as if she'd been hanging her catch of the day on the thing. Lew gave me an appalled look.

I knocked on the frame, and could see O'Connell moving in a distant room.

"Take off your shoes and have a seat," she called.

"What are these sculpture things, folk art?" I said. "They were at the motel, too."

She didn't answer. The front room was long and low-ceilinged, three barn-plank walls secured to the naked, curved side of the Airstream trailer by angle irons. The wooden walls were insulated almost floor to ceiling by books, on shelves built out of the same knotted wood as the planks. A few spaces had been hollowed out of books to make room for odd bits: two huge open-faced stereo speakers like the kind I used to have in high school; an undersized, cheap-looking electronic organ that looked like a starter instrument for ten-year-olds; a framed picture of the pope.

The largest hole accommodated a cast-iron wood stove squatting on a platform of bricks. The books were kept back from the stove and the big pipe that ran up to the ceiling, but not far enough for my comfort. The room looked like it could go up in a flash.

Arrayed around the stove were four worn, comfortable-looking armchairs upholstered in oranges and browns, on a carpet of 1974 gold shag. Lew sniffed and rubbed his nose. Dust mites that had been evolving for decades in the room's substratum clacked their mandibles in anticipation.

Something about the picture of the pope looked off, and I leaned closer. It was John Paul II, looking saintly. The picture had been ripped into ragged pieces and then carefully taped back together.

O'Connell came through the hatchlike doorway in the side of the trailer. For some reason I expected her to offer tea, but her hands were empty except for a pack of cigarettes. The jacket was gone. She wore a knobby silver cross over a faded black concert T-shirt for Tonton Macoute, a band I'd never heard of.

It was the first time I'd seen her without the voluminous cassock or some other bulk hiding her shape. I couldn't decide her age: Thirty-three? Forty-two? She was a small thing, with thin arms and a narrow waist. She had breasts.

"Sit," she said.

We both sat. I didn't look at Lew—I was afraid he was rolling his eyes. O'Connell remained standing, her arm on the back of the armchair opposite us. Next to the chair was a floor lamp with a round glass table at its middle. The tabletop had just enough space for an ashtray heaped with ashes and broken-spined butts. *Her* chair, obviously.

"So what is it you want from me, then?" she asked.

I looked at Lew, but he was studying his hands.

O'Connell made a disgusted noise. "Come on now, you can say it. You think you're the first person to come after me with that religious glow on his face?"

"When I was a kid I was possessed," I said slowly.

"So you said." I'd told her as much in Chicago.

"I was five, and for a while we thought it had gone away. But recently I figured out that it never left. It's still here."

"All this time," O'Connell said, nonplussed.

"And lately," I said, plunging on, "it's been trying to get out—it *has* gotten out, a few times. I don't think I can hold it back anymore."

She laughed. "If it wanted out, me boy, it would *be* out."

"Listen," Lew said testily. "All he wants is for you to get rid of this thing, okay?"

"Get rid of it? And put it where?" she said in the tone of a school-master. She sat on the arm of the chair. "You can't destroy a demon. You can't kill it. You can't even send it back to the fiery depths. All you can do is try to persuade it to go somewhere else. To someone else. For-get about everything you saw in those *Exorcist* movies—pentagrams and holy water and 'the power of Christ compels you' and all that shite. It doesn't work. Even Jesus, when he cast out demons, just sent them into swine—and no, I can't manage that trick. No one else has figured it out either."

"There's got to be something you can do," I said. Trying to make it sound like a statement, not a plea. "You've exorcised other people. The Little Angel in New Jersey, the Pirate King in San Diego." Wit-nesses had *seen* her cast out demons—Lew and I had read the stories, and they were from reliable sources—newspaper and magazine sites, not crackpot websites and free-for-all discussion boards. "I know you can help me," I said. "You saw the demon in me."

"What are you talking about?"

"Back at the hotel. You looked at me, and you knew I'd been pos-sessed."

"Mother of God, you think I have magical powers. Has it crossed your mind that you're not possessed at all, that you've simply got men-tal problems?"

"Are you kidding? All the fucking time." I ran a hand through my hair. "All I want is what you did for them, for those other people. I want you to get this out of me. Whatever the cost."

Her mouth turned down in what could have been restrained anger, or disgust. She tapped a cigarette from the pack. "All right then," she said. She lit the cigarette, inhaled. She held it between her index and middle finger, the other fingers folded against her palm. "The standard rate is five hundred dollars an hour. Two hours up front."

Lew leaned forward on his elbows. "Uh, a thousand bucks would buy this house, your pickup, and all the pot you're probably growing in that greenhouse."

"It would be a donation to the Church," she said evenly—or as

evenly as she could with all those Irish notes in her voice. I loved the
way she said "church." She said, "I've taken a vow of poverty."

Lew opened his hands. "Obviously."

"It's a deal," I said.

Lew looked sideways at me. "Del . . ."

"I said, it's a deal."

"You'd be wise to listen to your driver," O'Connell said. "I've told
you twice—I can't help ye. It'd just be throwing your money away."

"It's all right, I'm broke anyway."

O'Connell stared at me, then laughed quietly, smoke tumbling
over her lips.

"Sounds fair to me," Lew said to her. "You can't help him, and he
can't pay."

"As long as we understand each other," she said. She put her smile
away like a wallet. She slid into the chair, crossed her legs, and leaned
back into the upholstery. She tapped her ashes into the ashtray beside
her.

"A demonology lesson, then. Start the clock."

There are three ways to get a demon out, she said. Four, actually, but
only three were viable.

All of them depended on persuading the demon to leave. There
was no forcing the thing out, no *compelling*. The demon had to leave
of its own free will.

But it was persuasion at the emotional level. Demons weren't rational. You couldn't reason with them, argue with them. They weren't
people, they were archetypes—two-dimensional characters acting out
a familiar, ever-repeating script. Their goals were always the same,
their methods predictable. The hosts changed, the specifics changed,
but the story was always the same.

First, you could try to give the demon what it wanted—accede to
its demands. If you brought the current story to a satisfactory conclu-
sion, then perhaps it would move on to the next victim, to play out the
next episode.

Or you could convince the demon that it wouldn't get the story it

wanted. Frustrate it; deprive it of its fun. You could try sensory deprivation and drive it out with boredom. Or you could simply put it in an
environment it didn't like, a setting or situation that ruined the story:
take the Little Angel out of the hospital, take the Pirate King off the
ship. Or you could make the victim into an unattractive host. It depended on the demon. The key was to learn the story, then subvert it.

The third way was to use a goat: some other host to take on the
demon. Someone who more perfectly matched the demon's needs,
both physically and emotionally; someone the demon found irre-
sistible. It wasn't necessary to kidnap anyone, or trick them into shaking hands with the devil. There were plenty of volunteers, people
who'd love to be a God toy. Probably half of the people at DemoniCon
were praying that some demon would choose them, make them special. There were even professionals who'd dress up to lure a demon,
though their success rate wasn't high; the demons seemed to recognize hacks. No, a good goat was an earnest volunteer. All you had to do
then was introduce the goat to the demon and let nature take its
course.

"Think of possession as a hostage situation," she said. "The bad
man is inside the house, holding the girl with a gun to her head. You
can't rush the house. All you can do is give in to his demands, or try to
convince him that the demands will never be met. Or, you can broker
an exchange of hostages."

"You said there were four ways," Lew said. "What if exchanging
hostages doesn't work?"

O'Connell waved a hand. "Kill the hostage," she said.

I got up from my seat, paced the floor. The carpet under my stocking
feet felt greasy. Lew steepled his hands, thinking. O'Connell lit another cigarette.

"We need something else," I said finally. "None of those will work
for me."

"Except the last one," the priest said.

"Hey," Lew warned her. Then: "Besides, they're all the same idea.

If all demons do is jump to the next host, then all we're *ever* doing is exchanging hostages."

O'Connell gave him a nod, the cigarette between her knuckles. "The driver's got it."

"So we have to find the right goat," Lew said. "It's like rigging a honey pot on a mail server." O'Connell gave him a look, and he started to explain. "I work on computer networks. Sometimes to protect everybody else from spam, you put a new mail account on the server, and have it respond to all kinds of shit—mailing lists, Nigerian banking scandals, penis enlargement ads. The spam pours in. We collect all the addresses, blocking those from hitting the good mail accounts." He sat up in his chair, warming to his idea. "Except that spam is infinite, and demons aren't. If the demon's in the honey pot, it's not in you. And hey, there are people who'll *volunteer* to take the hit for us. All we need is the right goat."

"We can't do that," I said.

"All we're talking about is doing it sooner, not later," he said. "One way or another, the demon's going to find its way to another host. Maybe years from now, maybe tomorrow, but shouldn't *you* get to choose? You've done your time, man. Let somebody else have it for a while."

I shook my head, but Lew was no longer looking at me. "So how do we find a goat?" he said to O'Connell. "What kind of person are we looking for?"

She shrugged. "Depends on the demon. The goat may be a particular type of person, or just somebody who happens to be in the right place at the right time. The Captain takes only soldiers, Smokestack Johnny appears only on trains, the Shug . . ."

"Let me guess," Lew said. "Only takes fat, bald guys."

She nodded. "Who live around the lake."

"So this Shug thing," he said. "It's not a publicity gimmick—like, Nessie of the Finger Lakes. It's a real demon."

For some reason, this didn't surprise me. I think I'd known from the moment I'd met Toby.

"The Shug protects the lake," she said. "It's tradition."

Lew shook his head. "Some tradition. You know, you'd think any guy with a weight problem or a receding hairline would move out of the neighborhood pretty damn fast. I mean, the minute that Toby—"

"You don't know what you're talking about," she said.

"—started losing his hair he shoulda got out of Dodge. Or started dieting. A big white boy like that—"

"Toby knew what he was doing!"

Lew sat back in his chair, clearly skeptical.

"Let me tell you about Toby," O'Connell said. "One day when he's seventeen, eighteen years old, this fine, good-looking lad suddenly shaves his head, starts eating everything in sight. He starts taking midnight swims. He works on his lung capacity, trying to stay fit despite the weight. Obesity and extreme exercise don't mix, after all. The Shug hosts tend to die of heart attacks, or drowning, or both."

"Wait a minute," Lew said. "He *wanted* to be Shug?"

"He was making himself into the perfect host. His family was upset, of course. Toby's father especially. He was a big man, and he had a temper."

"A big man?" I asked. "A big, bald man?"

O'Connell smiled tightly, and made a small gesture with the hand holding the cigarette. "He wasn't going to leave, he'd lived here his whole life. And he wasn't in the best of health. Toby knew what he had to do, and he did it."

"Holy shit," Lew said.

As long as there's a Harmonia Lake, there's gotta be a Shug.

O'Connell looked at me. "So you see, it's just a matter of knowing your enemy. Which one is yours, Mr. Pierce? Why don't you sit down and tell us which demon you think has set up house in your soul."

I didn't sit down. The air between us was hazed with smoke. Inside my head, the demon scraped and shuffled, restless. I pressed my hand against the cool, curved side of the Airstream, breathing through my teeth.

I can't live like this, I thought.

"It's a demon called the Hellion," I said. "It usually strikes kids who—"

"I know the Hellion," O'Connell said shortly. "It's certainly a clever choice."

"I didn't *choose* anything," I said.

"The Hellion was part of the postwar cohort. Very active from the forties until about twenty years ago, when sightings suddenly became scarce. You're the right age, and your story's a tidy explanation for why it's been so shy lately. Of course, you have a slight problem in that the Hellion didn't disappear with you. There were dozens of sightings in the eighties—"

"Unconfirmed," I said.

"Oh please, what's confirmation? Parents are swearing that their child is possessed. Sure, the likeliest answer is that their little darlin' just has attention deficit disorder, or maybe he never 'attached' to his mother, or maybe he's just throwing a tantrum. But that still leaves a lot of cases. And there's really no way to tell one way or another, is there? Who gets to decide who's possessed and who's not?"

"You do," I said. "You know."

"What does it matter?" Lew said, exasperated. "If the goat thing works, that ends the argument. All we need to be talking about now is how to find a replacement."

"*We can't do that,*" I said again.

Lew sat back, shocked at something in my voice.

"The Hellion only takes children," O'Connell told him. "Specifically, fair-haired lads about waist high."

"Oh," Lew said. "Right."

Lew and I didn't talk on the way back to the motel. When we pulled into the parking lot he said, "We're done here, right?" *Here:* the middle of the woods in Bumfuck, New York.

O'Connell had made it clear she thought I was faking, and even if I wasn't, she didn't have much to offer. No rites, no rituals, no magic spells. Just the bargaining skills of a hostage negotiator, and a chance to sacrifice some innocent kid for my sake.

"Let's go home," I said.

But Lew was too worn out from yesterday's day-long drive to start back tonight. We decided to get some sleep and head out early tomorrow. He went to his cabin for a nap while I walked the edge of the lake, one eye out for the Shug. The water was mirror-still. I felt fragile from lack of sleep, my limbs connected by misfiring circuits. The Hellion shuddered behind my eyeballs, reminding me: I'm here. I am with you always.

That evening we stopped at the front desk to check for messages, just in case O'Connell had suddenly remembered a handy incantation from the *Necronomicon*. Louise gave us directions to a restaurant. Lew complained that there were mice in his room.

"The mice aren't in your room," Louise said. "Your room's out with the mice."

We ate dinner fifteen miles away in a town called Merrett, at a storefront Italian restaurant with five tables—and one of those was the yellow chair table permanently reserved for the Fat Boy. The garlic bread was buttered French bread sprinkled with garlic powder, and the tomato sauce looked orange. I was glad I wasn't hungry. My stomach had tightened from lack of sleep and the constant agitation of the Hellion. The demon had been in motion since O'Connell's place, a ceaseless scrabbling. I wanted to pound my forehead against the table.

Lew took my plate and started finishing off my lasagna, just like when we were kids.

I said, "You know what I saw down in the basement the other day?"

"*RADAR Man* comics?"

"Close. I mean, that too. But I opened up Life and Death."

"Heh," Lew said. "The Cyclops threw a fit."

"I was thinking, you could use the oceans on the Risk board to have naval battles. You know, with the stuff from Battleship." I'd had this idea weeks ago, staring at the ceiling from my bed in the psych ward.

He nodded, chewing. "You'd have to figure out how to hide the ships. Maybe draw a grid on the oceans, but still use the Battleship boards to keep track of them."

"But the ships should be able to deliver troops, or fire on the countries."

"Oh yeah, for sure."

We headed back to Harmonia Lake, Lew driving, and despite the distraction of the demon I found myself nodding off, only to wake up with a jerk, as if I were the one behind the wheel. My plan to stay awake until cured was not going to work, but I couldn't afford to fall asleep, not like this. I'd have to strap myself in tonight. Tie a gag around my mouth and hope that it stopped the Hellion from screaming. I'd have to do this every night for the rest of my life.

Lew and I sorted out by dashboard light our key and block sets. Lew said he was going into the main house to call Amra. "Give her a kiss for me," I said. "Tell her I'm sorry I stole her husband."

I walked down the gravel road to my cabin. With each step, the demon threw itself against the cage of my skull. Thunder rumbled in the distance, and cold air gusted from the lake. I found the cabin steps in the dark, and started up. Lightning flashed silently from somewhere out of sight, briefly revealing the silhouettes of trees and a cloud-packed sky.

A fish was impaled on my door. A skinny, foot-long thing with an alligatorish snout. Fresh.

I stared at the door, wondering if I'd imagined it, but my eyes picked out the details in the gloom. Two of the barbs of the driftwood were poking through the fish's white belly. There didn't seem to be much blood. In the next stutter-flash of lightning, I made out two dark, dried trails running down from the puncture wounds like tear-driven mascara. The thunder rolled, louder and closer.

Okay. There's a fish on my door.

I kept my head back as I inserted the key, turned it, and pushed open the door.

I flicked on the lights. The room was empty. The only place where there was room for anyone to hide was under the double bed. I knelt quickly, lifted up the bedspread. Dust and dark.

I shut the door slowly, so as not to dislodge the fish. I wasn't sure I wanted it on my door, but I knew I didn't want it lying on my stoop like some banana peel primed for Dagwood's return home.

I sat down on the bed, pulled the duffel bag toward me, and rustled through my clothing, pulling out bike chains and locks and piling them next to me on the bed. When I came across the oil rag at the bottom of the bag, I set it on my lap. Unwrapped it like a baby.

The gleaming gun, a box of ammunition.

I opened the ammunition box. The bullets looked shiny and new, but who knew how old they were: ten years, twenty? I couldn't remember Dad firing this thing. Maybe the gunpowder was unstable. Maybe the gun would explode the first time it fired.

At first I couldn't eject the clip, but then my thumb found a latch at the top of the grip and the magazine pulled free. It was empty.

I picked a bullet from the ammo box, lined it up with the mouth of the magazine, and pressed it down into the spring-loaded chamber. I fed another bullet into the slot, and another. There was a possibility that no one had mentioned. Maybe only I could let the demon out. Maybe it needed me to open the gate. And if my brain shut down before it opened, then maybe it couldn't get back into the world. Maybe it would end with me. That would be some kind of accomplishment, wouldn't it? The first guy to erase a demon from the world.

I pushed the eighth bullet down into the spring-loaded magazine, then slipped the magazine back into the gun with a solid *clack*. The Hellion jumped at the sound, and I shut my eyes until it settled down.

Rain began to clatter against the roof, sounding like applause.

I slid my hand around the grip, lifted the gun, and touched the mouth of the barrel to my lips. The barrel was shaking, and I had to steady it with my free hand. I opened my mouth slightly, my upper lip sliding over the nub of the gun sight, then opened wider, let the metal slide between my teeth. I wanted my teeth out of the way, even though that couldn't make much of a difference. I sat there, breathing in the smell of oil, tasting iron.

A simple thing. A little pressure on the trigger.

I thought about Lew. He'd be so pissed. He'd have to call Mom, try to explain. I couldn't think about Mom.

I pulled out the gun, wiped my lips, then my eyes. My eyes were flooded. I moved the gun to the side of my head and pressed the muzzle to my temple.

Breathe in. Breathe out. Squeeze.

Ah, who the fuck was I kidding? I dropped my hand to my lap, still holding the gun. I couldn't walk up to that cliff, couldn't throw myself off. I was paralyzed. Too infatuated with my addiction to breathing, unable to extinguish my irrational belief that there was another way out.

Hope wasn't a thing with feathers, it was a hundred-pound ball and chain. All you had to do was drag that sucker to the edge and throw it over first.

A hard knock on the door. I jerked at the sound. Jesus Fucking Christ, I could have fired the thing accidentally. I looked down at the .45, and embarrassment swept over me, as if I'd been caught masturbating. I had to hide the gun.

I stood up, quickly wrapped the pistol and ammo back in the oil rag, and stuffed the bundle deep into the duffel. The knock sounded again. What the hell does it take for a guy to get a couple minutes alone these days?

I smeared the tears from my eyes and lurched toward the door, then realized the chains and locks were still piled on the bed like a nest of snakes. Fuck it. Lew knew about the chains. I yanked open the door.

O'Connell stood there, the hood of her silver jacket pulled over her head, the rain ricocheting from her shoulders and head, forming a nimbus. The fish was still in place, one eye watching us.

"Yeah?" I said stupidly.

"I have a question, Mr. Pierce," O'Connell said. "How did your mother lose her eye?"

DEMONOLOGY

SMOKESTACK JOHNNY

SAND CREEK, KANSAS, 1983

He came walking out of the middle of nowhere, ambling down the snow-lined tracks with a pipe in his teeth, huffing clouds like a steam train. Despite the terrible cold, no jacket or gloves, just overalls and a blue flannel shirt and a blue-striped cap.

The conductor of the train saw him first. He stood in the cab, looking out the frosted window as he talked on the radio with the dispatcher, explaining why the train wasn't moving. Even with the heaters on and the train stopped, it was only forty degrees in the cab. The toilet in the nose was frozen over.

"I think we've got a bigger problem," the conductor said, and signed off. The pipe-smoking stranger waved jauntily up at the windows, then walked right up under the nose of the diesel, out of sight. The conductor went to one of the side windows, then the other, but couldn't see anyone. He quickly pulled on his gloves, opened the cab door, and leaned out, squinting into the icy wind. The freight train stretched back in a straight line over the blank white plain, a hundred and sixty cars—twice too long for such cold weather, but the Rock Island was going into its third bankruptcy and the company was running everything they could.

The stranger and the two other members of the crew—the train ran with just a conductor, engineer, and one brakeman—were nowhere to be seen.

The conductor hopped down and hustled around the front of the train to the other side. It was twenty below, but he'd already started to sweat.

About ten cars down, the engineer and brakeman crouched beside a boxcar, waving a flashlight at its underbelly. The stranger was halfway to them, striding through the snow beside the tracks.

"What's the problem, boys?" the stranger called out heartily. "Outta air?"

The engineer looked up, surprised, then stood up. "Who the hell are you?" he said, his voice carrying easily in the cold air. The conductor frantically waved his arms as he ran, trying to get the engineer to shut up.

The stranger didn't seem to take offense. "Why, I'm the king of the rails, that's who! I've got coal in my teeth and steam in my lungs! There's never been an engine I couldn't fix or a locomotive I couldn't drive. No grade too steep, no snow too deep. I'm Smokestack Johnny, and I ride the high iron!"

A moment of stunned silence, and then the brakeman said, "Who?"

The engineer said nothing. He'd been a railroad man for fifteen years, but the brakeman was a kid only a month into the job.

The conductor finally caught up to them. He was breathing hard and he felt sick to his stomach, but he forced a shaky smile onto his face. "What can we do for you, Johnny?"

The stranger whipped around. "Hey there!" he said, beaming. "You must be the conductor." He was a handsome man, his jaw as square and clean shaven as a Burma-Shave ad, his hair as black as axle grease. "Say, we rode together once, didn't we?"

The conductor gulped, nodded. "Back in forty-eight. You took us through Chicago." He still got the nightmares.

"Right!" Johnny said, then laughed his big laugh. "Course, not everybody on that crew was all that polite." He winked at the other two men. "A few of those boys had to be dropped off a little early, if you know what I mean. But we made it across the ol' Mississip, didn't we? Record time!"

The conductor tried to laugh with him. "Yessir, record time."

"Right! Now let's see about getting this iron horse moving."

Johnny marched off toward the end of the train.

The engineer looked at the conductor with fear in his eyes. He must have seen the pictures from the last time Johnny had ridden the Rock Island line, two years before: a hundred derailed cars flung over the bridge and onto a Missouri highway. The new kid, though, still didn't seem to grasp the seriousness of the situation.

"Why don't you go up to the head end and keep the engine ready," the conductor told the engineer, loudly enough for Johnny to hear. The engineer knew who to talk to at dispatch.

The engineer glanced back at Johnny. "You sure?"

"Just go."

The conductor and the brakeman jogged to catch up with the demon. Every few cars Johnny ducked under, took a quick look around, and sometimes rapped the air brake pipes with his knuckles. At the thirtieth car, a piggyback flatbed with a truck trailer latched onto it, he said, "I think I see your problem."

All three of them squatted down under the car. It was still cold, but they were out of the wind.

Johnny stuck his finger into an ice-encrusted ventilator. "Your A-1's frozen open. Musta popped when you dumped your air at the yard." He turned to the young brakeman. "I need a pipe wrench, son, and a coupla fusees."

The brakeman looked at the conductor, and the conductor nodded.

A few minutes later the kid came back lugging a tool chest as big as a suitcase, and a smaller red plastic case. The stranger popped open the plastic case and took out a long red fusee.

"Watch your eyes," he said, and broke off the butt of the flare. The end sparked, and began to hiss red flame and white smoke. He held it like a magic wand, playing the fire over the frozen valve, and started to sing:

"Johnny told the brakeman, get your hand off that wheel,
Johnny told the brakeman, get your hand off that wheel,
We're going through Altoona

At a hundred and ten,
And if we don't get up that mountain
We ain't comin' down again."

His voice was rough and big. He didn't hit all the notes, but he got near enough. Then the fusee sputtered out, and he tossed it into the snow behind them.

"Let's see you use that wrench," he said to the brakeman, and the kid hefted a pipe wrench two feet long. The stranger showed him where to grip the vent. The kid yanked on the end of the wrench, but it didn't budge. He pulled and pulled and even bent over it to put his weight into it, but the wrench didn't move.

"Let me give you a hand with that," the stranger said. He gripped the cold metal in one naked hand and jerked down. The valve end popped off with a squeal and bounced against the ground. The demon laughed. "Don't feel bad, son—you loosened it for me!"

The conductor picked up the valve in his gloved hands, heard a rattle, and shook it. Something black fell out of it. The conductor picked it up, regarded it suspiciously. It was a lump of coal. Who would have jammed a lump of coal into the ventilator?

"I'll show you a trick," the stranger said. He took the valve end from the conductor, turned it sideways, and fit it back on the pipe, capping it. "It ain't legal, but it'll get you home."

It took an hour and a half to pump the pipes back up to the minimum PSI. Johnny sat in the cab with them, filling the air with smoke, stories, and old railroader jokes that only the brakeman hadn't heard before. "Know why the conductor's got the best job on the train?" Johnny asked. "Because he don't have to work with the conductor!" He'd slap his knees and laugh hard. No one else could manage more than a forced chuckle. Finally the conductor sent the brakeman running to the back of the train to release the handbrake, and the engineer started bringing the electricals online.

"So," the conductor said casually. "How far you riding with us today, Johnny?"

"Just as far as Olympia," the demon said.

The engineer said, "We ain't going to—"

The conductor cut him off. "If that's where you're going, Johnny, that'll be just fine. I'll radio the dispatcher."

The engineer's eyes were wide. "We can't just switch over," he said quietly. "That's not even our road."

"It is now," the conductor said.

Johnny whooped his approval. "Get outta my way, boys," the demon said. "I'll show you how to drive." He started the bell, then pulled twice on the air horns and set the throttle to notch 1—all as natural as a man pulling on his shirt. The train started to move, and the brakeman had to run to get back in the cab.

Johnny moved smoothly through the notches. The train picked up speed, and then he started to sing. He bellowed "Rock Island Line" and "Casey Jones" and "I've Been Working on the Railroad."

They hit the Hutchinson switch much too fast—the conductor thought he could feel the cars swaying off the curve—but the wheels held and they rocketed onto Kansas & Oklahoma's north-running track.

Johnny had them on notch 8 by then, running faster and faster, like a twelve-year-old happy to let his Lionel fly off the track. They flashed past little towns like Nickerson, Sterling, and Ellinwood, the crew holding their breath at every crossing. One of the K&O peddlers ahead of them just managed to pull into a side-out, its last car almost jutting past the switch, and they cleared it by two feet, whistling past at a hundred miles per hour.

The track turned west, running straight into the dropping sun. The snow lit up like fields of crushed glass. And then he picked up the song he'd been singing while working on the ventilator:

"Johnny told the fireman to shovel that coal,
Johnny told the fireman to shovel that coal,
We're stokin' up that firebox
Until the smokestack screams,
And if the boiler blows, boys,
Be sure to save the steam."

Olympia was a little bump of a town that came up on their left. The demon laid on the air horns and kept blowing, a long wail that must have been heard all the way to Dodge City. He sang out:

"Johnny told the conductor, better say your prayers,
Johnny told the conductor, better say your prayers,
There's a diesel train a-comin'
And it's riding on our track.
We won't be here much longer, boys,
But I'll be comin' back,
Lord, I'll be comin' back."

He set the throttle and marched to the cabin door. The brakeman stood up in alarm, but the conductor and the engineer didn't move.

"It's been a great ride, boys!" Smokestack Johnny said. His smile was bright as a headlamp. Then he yanked open the door and stepped into the wind.

9

I opened my mouth, closed it.

O'Connell made a disgusted noise and pushed past me. She went to the table, pulled off her jacket, and draped it across the chair back. She wiped the water from her face, and her gaze fell on the pile of chains on the bed. She looked at me, eyebrows raised, as if to say, Are those yours?

"Make yourself at home," I said. I stood near the open doorway, rain splattering the back of my shirt, and nodded toward the fish. "Mind telling me what this thing is supposed to be?"

"Northern pike."

"I can see that," I said. Though I'd had no idea what kind of fish it was. "Who put it there?"

"You can thank Louise. It's a service of the motel, like a mint on your pillow."

I don't check in people after eleven. I can't put you into cabins that aren't prepared.

"And that would be because . . . ?"

"Think Passover," she said. I frowned. "Blood over the door, angel of death? Children of Israel?"

"I missed a lot of Sunday school," I said.

"Consider it a sign of respect, then. Part of our tradition."

I got an image of those wooden barbs, nailed up at every house around Harmonia Lake.

"You haven't answered my question, Mr. Pierce."

I closed the door, went to the bed, and started pushing the chains into my duffel. "So how do you know about my mom?"

"You want genealogy, call the Mormons," she said. "You want demonology, you call Red Book."

"Who?"

"Hardcore Jungians. Possession's their specialty." She sat down and fished through the inner pockets of her jacket, finally drawing out a pack of Marlboros and a lighter. "They keep records of every possession, every witness too." She leaned forward, light glinting off her still-wet scalp, and tapped a cigarette from the pack. "You were in there more than once, I might add."

Not just for the Hellion, I guessed. I'd witnessed a few possessions, and my name must have shown up in a few police reports.

I zipped the duffel and stood there, unwilling to sit down at the table with her, or to sit on the low bed and have her look down at me. O'Connell lit the cigarette with the quick motion of a longtime smoker. Rain drummed the roof.

"You were evaluated by a psychiatrist when you were first possessed, right after your mother's surgery," she said, leaning back again. "The doctor wrote it up as a case study in the *Journal of Abnormal Psychology*. You honestly haven't heard of this before now? He didn't use your name, of course, but the time periods match your story. Someone in the Red Book Society helpfully made the connection to your mother's accident years ago. When I called, it only took minutes to pull out your name.

"After all, the doctor could change your name, but he couldn't change your sex, or your age; all that's pertinent to the profile. Like that little slingshot—that's a signature prop of the Hellion. But even more than the slingshot, there's that particular move—shooting the glasses off someone's face. Now, that's something that can't be easily faked. The little kid's gotta have strength, coordination. Of course, you probably didn't mean to smash her eye to a pulp. But still, it's a hell of a shot."

"*It wasn't me,*" I said.

"I know," she said. Resigned to it.

Fuck you, I thought. *Now* you believe me?

I turned away from her, but the room was too small to pace. There was nowhere to go but outside.

"Before you were possessed," she went on in that new, weary voice, "dozens of adults were injured by the Hellion firing that thing at people's faces. But after you, even though people kept reporting appearances of the Hellion, not a one. In the twenty-one years since your mother was injured, no child has done what you did." She paused, and when I looked at her, she was watching my eyes. The weariness was a pose; her body was relaxed, but her eyes were filled with the same energy I'd felt back at the hotel. "You were the last one, Del. You trapped it."

"Jesus Christ!" I shouted, then started laughing. "What do you think I've been trying to tell you!"

We sat in the small room as the rain came down and the ceiling clouded with cigarette smoke. O'Connell asked pointed questions and I answered at length, making this something between a clinical intake session and a confession. I was tired of choosing my words, sparing the gory details, managing everyone's reactions. With a kind of escalating, giddy recklessness, I told her everything, daring her to disbelieve me. The first possession, the wild behavior, the way they'd strapped me down until they thought they'd driven the Hellion out. I told her about the accidents that brought it back to my awareness, the black well that wanted to pull me in, the pressure in my skull, the wolf-out sessions. I enumerated the ways I'd tried to keep the demon strapped down: the therapy sessions with Dr. Aaron, the stay in the psych ward, the drugs. My bid to get Dr. Ram to cut the thing out of me.

"The receptors in the brain that Dr. Ram identified, I think they're like . . . antennas. Broadcasting stations. Remove them, and you—"

Something in her face told me this was old news to her. I remembered the first time I had seen her, walking into the hotel with Dr.
Ram, deep in conversation. "You thought he was on the right track
too."

"I did, until the Truth killed him. I'm not sure why or how Dr.
Ram was lying. Maybe he was faking his data." She shrugged. "We'll
find out sooner or later, I imagine." She put out the stub of her cigarette, reached for her pack. "Now. Tell me again how your family
drove the Hellion away. They strapped you down and read you
books?"

"Lew read me comics. My mom read me *Mike Mulligan and His
Steam Shovel*. I loved it."

"What do you mean, you loved it?" Before I could answer she
stood up, frowning. She leaned into the little window that overlooked
the lake and cupped her hand to the glass.

I heard it then, over the pattering rain. The chop of helicopter
blades. The sound grew louder, until it was directly overhead: a deep,
thumping drone. The helicopter was either very close, or very, very
big. It passed on, but we could still hear it.

"Search and rescue?" I asked.

"I don't think so."

The sound grew loud again as the helicopter circled back. I went
to the door and opened it. Fifty yards away, over the motel parking lot,
a circle of lights descended through the dark and rain like a UFO, set-
tling behind the silhouettes of trees.

The helicopter filled almost the entire parking lot, the blades of its
twin rotors nearly brushing the tree limbs. It looked like a Huey, one
of those huge transports the army used, but it was newer and sleeker
than that. A Huey redesigned by Audi.

Lew came up behind me. We were ten feet from the edge of the
parking lot, back in the trees. "What the fuck is going on?" he said.
"What's she doing here?" Meaning O'Connell. The priest had pulled
on her silver jacket and was jogging for the porch of the main house,

where Louise stood with a long coat pulled around her. The old woman looked pissed.

The only marking visible on the helicopter was a logo painted onto the side door and the nose: a gold H in a gold circle.

"We're being invaded by Hilton?" Lew said.

"Maybe they're buying out the motel."

The rotors gradually slowed. Louise stepped down from the porch and stalked toward the helicopter, past the plywood cutout of the Shug. O'Connell called to her and then reluctantly followed.

The side hatch slid open and five bulky, helmeted men jumped to the ground and fanned out. Lew and I instinctively crouched. The men wore some kind of blue-black camouflage, and they were heavily encumbered with packs, belts, and bandoliers. Jutting from the back of each helmet was a thick black cable that ran down the man's back to connect to the pack at his waist, giving the men the appearance of ponytailed warriors from a Chinese martial arts flick.

In their hands they carried bulbous things that looked like Star Trek phasers. None of them seemed to have seen me or Lew, but they were scanning the trees.

Lew grabbed my shoulder. "Let's get the fuck out of here," he said into my ear.

"No, wait," I said.

Two more men appeared in the open hatch of the helicopter. The first man was square-shaped, waist as wide as his broad shoulders, belt cinched tight under his gut, making his legs look skinny. He was completely bald. He wore a silky flight jacket over the same camo gear as the other men, but he was helmetless. There was something on his face, though—a kind of metal mesh, as if he'd made a form-fitting mask of chicken wire.

The man next to him was much shorter. He was dressed in street clothes—dark chinos and a gray, fuzzy sweater—but his head was covered by the same black helmet as the camo goons. His face was scrunched in concern, and he kept glancing up at the bigger man.

"The *H* doesn't stand for Hilton," I said under my breath.

Louise shouted something, and several of the men shouted back—commando shit like "Get down! Freeze!"—aiming their little science fiction weapons at her and O'Connell.

I stood up and Lew grabbed my arm. "What the fuck are you doing?" he said.

"They're here for me!" I said.

I stepped forward, and some of the men swiveled to face me, barking orders to halt. I lifted my hands in the air and stepped onto the gravel of the parking lot. The foot soldiers surrounded me. I resisted the urge to glance backward at Lew, hoping they wouldn't notice him, but no—they yelled for him to come out with me.

From the helicopter doorway the smaller man waved excitedly. I waggled a hand, but only slightly—I didn't want to give these guys an excuse to shoot.

The man with the chicken-wire face hopped down and strode toward me with an assured smile, like a pastor welcoming a sinner back to church. He was fifty, maybe sixty years old, the stubble on his scalp gray. A few feet from him I realized that the metal on his face was no mask; copper wire was stitched into his skin, threaded over and under. The skin was raw and peeling.

He held out a hand, and the skin there was embroidered too—a mesh glove.

"Delacorte Pierce," he said in a booming, theatrical voice. "I am Commander Stoltz of the Human League."

He stood there, hand out and smile steady, waiting for me to shake. The goons—I could only think of them as goons—seemed to aim their phasers a little more forcefully, if that was possible. They were all white men, faces wide and puffy beneath their black helmets. Some of the bulk that I'd attributed to body armor turned out to be beer gut and man boobs: most of these guys were seriously overweight.

I gripped Commander Stoltz's hand. The commander didn't wince, exactly, but his smile faltered for a moment. The ridged skin of his palms felt like scar tissue, and was alarmingly hot, like a waffle iron warming up.

The short man in the sweater looked up at me, beaming. "Hi, Del!"

I sighed. "Let me guess: Caller ID."

He shook his head, smiling. "You called collect. But the calling number shows up on my bill. I got it on the web."

I'm an idiot. I never should have called from a landline. "I thought we had an agreement, Bertram."

"You're going to thank me later," he said.

I didn't think so. I nodded toward the goon to my right, at the thing in his hand that looked like a plastic bar of soap. "What are those supposed to be?"

"Show him," Commander Stoltz said.

No boom or pop: just a delicate *zip!* and my vision went white. I hit the gravel on my side, my limbs useless. The pain, when it caught up to me a second later, was mathematically pure. And it didn't stop. A thin wire connected my chest to the mouth of the goon's gun, and the pain flowed for an absurdly long time.

The goon must have released the trigger at some point, but it was several seconds before thoughts could tumble into the void where the pain had been. My body felt like a pile of cooked, boneless meat. One of the camouflaged men did complicated things to my wrists, and commented on all the bandages on my hands. The other man fastened one of those helmets onto my head. I couldn't marshal the neuromuscular resources for even a feeble thrash.

Bertram leaned down into my line of sight. "I'm really sorry about this, Del. I really am."

Fuck you! I shouted. *You just fucking Tasered me!* Converted through my nonworking vocal cords, this came out; *"Faaagaaah!"*

Somewhere above me in the unseen land of the vertical, much shouting. Lew, O'Connell, the goons, even Louise—all of them yelling. God, they wouldn't Taser an old woman, would they? The shock would kill her.

"Take these people inside," the commander ordered.

"You're making a terrible mistake," O'Connell said. Those hard Irish r's.

"There's no mistake," Stoltz said. "You have no idea how dangerous this man is. But don't worry, we have no intention of harming him. Bertram, go with your colleagues and explain the situation to these people."

I should have been scared, or angry, but all I could think was : *Colleagues. Co-leagues. Heh.*

"Shouldn't I stay out here with Del?" Bertram said. "I could help—"

"That's an order," Stoltz said.

The man behind me pulled my torso into a sitting position. My helmeted head lolled forward like a bowling ball.

Two goons herded the group to the main house. Lew glanced back as they reached the top of the steps, and hesitated. The gunman behind him gestured with his Taser, and Lew reluctantly went inside.

The commander patted me on the shoulder. "Let's walk and talk."

"At first I didn't believe Bertram's story," Commander Stoltz said. "He has a history of mental troubles, as you know."

I was too afraid of being Tasered again to point out that this was coming from a human hot plate who got his operating instructions from a pulp science fiction novel. We were walking slowly down the gravel road toward my cabin, one Human Leaguer a few feet ahead of us and two behind, their flashlights bouncing along the ground with us, skidding up into the trees. It had taken a few minutes to get my land legs back. My hands were cinched behind me in some kind of plastic cuffs, and they'd also fastened one of those packs onto my back. It was heavier than it had looked on the fat boys; the thing must be all battery.

"The independent evidence, however, was irrefutable. And considering your recent troubles in Chicago, it seemed as if indeed you were losing control for good. You must understand that we had to act quickly."

"Oh, sure, of course," I said, keeping the sarcasm out of my voice. I tried to subtly flex my hands, but the cuffs, whatever they were made of, had no give. I needed to stay calm, think my way out of this, but all I wanted to do was run screaming into the trees.

"The helmet you're wearing operates on the same principles as my own personal integrity system," he continued. "The constantly shifting electromagnetic field creates a kind of Faraday cage that interferes with the psionic frequencies of the *GedankenKinder*. Not only does it—"

"The who?"

"The Thought Children. A parallel race, descended from Neanderthals, with psychic abilities far beyond our own. The source of the so-called demons."

What the fuck? Neanderthals?

We'd passed Lew's cabin and my own. The yellow light shining through the trees ahead of us came from the safety light above the washhouse door.

"I thought you guys were all about the slans," I said. "Bertram said—"

"Bertram's only been a member of the league for a year. He's not been fully authorized, and his personal integrity system is not up to the required level." The commander touched me on the shoulder, trying to impart the seriousness of the matter. "We're at war with telepaths, Del—intelligence can't be trusted to an unsecured medium."

"But you're telling *me*," I said.

"This is on a need-to-know basis—and I very much want you to understand some things, my friend. Bertram's already told you that Van Vogt"—he pronounced the name *Van Vote*—"used the word 'slan' as a code for what popular culture has mislabeled 'demons.' That much is obvious, even to the casual reader. What Bertram has not been trusted with are the many other coded meanings embedded in the text. For example . . ."

There was no way of stopping the commander now.

". . . consider the tendriled and tendrilless slans in the book. Van

Vogt made the tendrils external, which is excellent melodrama, but does that mean we should be on the alert for people with actual snake-like appendages growing out of their heads?" He laughed dismissively. Oh yeah, how silly. "Only now do we understand that 'tendrils' represent the physical structures present in the brains of the *Gedanken-Kinder*, deformations that human neuroscientists have only recently confirmed. And think about the emphasis in the book on electronic thought broadcasters and receivers, and all the uses of numerical combinations and codes. Once I understood how Van Vogt had sowed the book with clues to the psionic blocking frequencies, it was only a matter of time until I could build our own versions of the Porgrave devices. That helmet you're wearing—while it's not quite up to the level of the three-sixty system I use—is more than adequate to block their telepathic scans. And as for 'possession,' mental transference in *either* direction, what Van Vogt called 'hypnotic control,' is completely impossible."

My God, I thought. It's always the same. One day this guy's the assistant manager at Home Depot, the next he's a prophet with a direct line on eternal truth. It didn't matter if it was John 3:16 or the Kabala or No Money Down Real Estate audio tapes. It all came down to the Book, the Mission, and the absolute fucking Certainty.

I tilted my helmeted head toward him. "And you've tested these things," I said skeptically.

"My system has never been penetrated," he said, clapping a hand on my shoulder. "Not once in the ten years since I discovered the frequencies. It's our greatest weapon against them, Del." We went past the washhouse, all the lights behind us now. I'd walked this way earlier, but nothing seemed familiar in the dark. The road ended somewhere ahead of us—it couldn't be more than fifty yards—at a cabin that had looked vacant to me this afternoon. At least, its eye-stabber door decoration hadn't had a fish on it. Beyond the cabin was a short pier, and beyond that was nothing but water and forest and a footpath snaking through the trees, roughly skirting the lake. "The field generator accomplishes with technology what you've managed to do on your own, by accident. But it's not perfect. Which brings us to our problem."

"There's no problem," I said earnestly. I didn't know what this walk in the woods was about, but I did *not* like being tied up and jerked through the forest like a squealer in a mob film. "The demon's totally under control."

"Del, Del." He chuckled condescendingly. "We know your control's slipping. Bertram told us all about it. Isn't that how you two ended up meeting each other in the first place?" He was pleased with this point. "No, your system isn't working at all."

"You want to put me in a cage, is that it? Or you want to wire me up like you. That's the solution Bertram was talking about."

He shook his head, but I couldn't make out his expression. It was dark, and the helmet had slid down, obscuring my vision. He gripped the back of my arm and tugged me forward.

"I wish it were that easy. Or rather, that simple. Installing a three-sixty system is no trivial matter. It's painful—I can attest to that—and the chance of infection is very high. But once you're fully wired, there's no better defense on the planet. However . . ."

I didn't like the sound of "however."

"As good as the three-sixty system is, it's not secure enough for your needs. Now, most of us, we're only trying to keep the slans out, whenever they might turn their attention to us. And if they succeeded in psychically seizing me, I'm only one man, a citizen no more important than any member of the league." He'd delivered the speech before. No doubt the Man of the People thing went over real big with the troops. "But with you, Del, the beast is already inside the cage. Say that we fitted you with the three-sixty system—what if the power supply fails? What if you cut yourself and break the field? These are dangers I constantly live with, but with you, the stakes are much higher. Can we risk letting the beast out? Can we allow the Hellion to ruin the lives of untold children?"

Oh shit.

Bertram was a nut job, but he was my friend, and all this time I'd been banking on the fact that he wouldn't go along with something that would do me real harm. But the commander knew that too. So they'd lied to Bertram. And they'd made sure he wasn't along on our little walk in the woods.

I stopped in the road, head down, fighting a wave of nausea. The men behind us pointed their flashlights at our feet. "You said—you said you weren't going to—"

"You can't let fear rule this moment," the commander said. "I know what you're going through. I was possessed twice when I was not much older than yourself, and I spent years dealing with the sense of helplessness, the loss of control. You have an opportunity here, an opportunity to change the world. If the *GedankenKinder* dies in its cage, we've removed one of the overlords that rule this planet. We've taken a huge step toward freeing mankind."

"But I can help," I said. "I can teach you what I do. It's a skill Dr. Aaron taught me, it's like a mental firewall—"

The commander was shaking his head. "I'm sorry, Del. We can't risk it. There's no other way."

He was right. There was no other way. I'd known it when I picked up the gun in the cabin. The only difference between me and the commander was that he could pull the trigger.

One of the lights illuminating our feet suddenly flicked away. From behind us I heard the snap of a tree branch, and the sound of something heavy crashing through the brush.

I stood up, looked behind us. One of the men behind us was gone. The other man swept the beam of his flashlight across the trees at the edge of the road. "Jared, you okay?" he said.

The Human Leaguer in front of us cast around until his beam picked up his colleague behind us. He stared into the light, blinking. "Sir, I think Jared fell down."

"Oh for goodness' sake," the commander said, disgusted. "Mr. Torrence!" he called. "Back in position! Mr. Torrence!"

There was no answer. The man behind us raked his light over the trees.

Something dark crashed through the bushes farther back. Both flashlight beams swung toward it.

A man in a black helmet stumbled into the road. "Sorry, sir!" he said. "There was a ditch alongside the road I didn't see, and then I—"

"Never mind," the commander said. "Just get your light on and catch up."

The commander fastened a hand on my neck. All the flashlight beams were focused away from me, and I'd glanced toward the trees to my left, judging the odds of losing them with my hands tied behind me . . . but somehow he'd seen the movement and anticipated my plan. "Courage, Del," the commander said. "You can do this."

"There's something I should tell you," I said. "It's not safe to be out at this time of night."

The second flashlight came on, then went off. The commander looked back, and I followed his gaze. There was only one man in the road. Jared Torrence had disappeared again.

"Where in the world did he go now?" the commander said. And louder: "Mr. Harp, please help Mr. Torrence—"

Something hit the dirt near my feet and I jumped back. It was black and shiny, with a frayed tail. One of the helmets, its cable snapped.

The commander stared at it for a second, then nudged the helmet with his boot. It rolled over, lopsided. Mr. Torrence's head was still inside it.

"Oh, Jared," the commander said sadly.

I ran. The leading soldier jerked his light toward me, raised the hand that held the Taser. I ducked and barreled into him. My shoulder struck him in the gut, and we both went down. I twisted as I hit the ground, and my elbow jolted painfully. I kept rolling, got my knees under me, lurched to my feet again. The guard was on his back, his flashlight several feet away on the ground, pointing away from me, illuminating a wedge of road and forest. Somewhere behind us one of the other soldiers—Mr. Harp?—screamed.

I ran again, bent over and wobbling. The last cabin was in front of me, a slab of pitch black against the slightly lighter sky. I dodged right, remembering that the path started just behind the cabin. I threw myself forward, spinning to avoid trees that materialized out of the dark, inches from my face.

Something crashed through the bushes next to me. I stifled my own scream and leaped away from it. My right foot came down on something slick—log, moss-covered rock?—and I went down again, off balance. I came down backward. The battery pack hit first, wedging into my spine, and then my head whipped back and struck a rock with a sound like a hammer going through ice. The impact stunned me, but I wasn't dead. The helmet had saved my life.

A shape appeared above me. Arms grabbed my shirt, hauled me to a sitting position.

"Are you doing this, Del?" the commander hissed. "Are you doing this?"

You're making a terrible mistake, O'Connell had told Stoltz.

I tried to shake my head, but my neck muscles wouldn't respond. "Passover," I said.

"What?"

"Blood over the door."

The commander pulled me erect, and dragged me onto the wooden pier. The soldier I'd slammed into ran toward us out of the woods. He hadn't picked up his flashlight, but the Taser was in his hand, swinging wildly.

"Shoot it!" the commander told the man.

The soldier leaped onto the pier, stopped. "Shoot what?"

The commander pointed toward the shore. "Anything!" The soldier obediently turned and dropped to one knee. He held his little Star Trek gun with both hands, aiming down the length of the pier.

I should be safe. Louise had made the sacrifice for me, hadn't she? Put the blood over the door. But the Human League had no such protection. Their rooms hadn't been made up. They were intruders here.

"Toby protects this place," I said.

"Who's Toby?" the commander said.

A slab of white flesh launched from the water beside the pier, rose in a spray of water. Blacksmith arms thrown wide, goggled eyes black and glinting. His mouth stretched open, inhumanly long, loose-hinged as an orca's.

The soldier didn't have time to move. He was struck and carried over the side of the pier before he could even scream. The two of them splashed into the black water and disappeared.

"Toby," I said. But it wasn't. Not now. "The Shu'garath," I said.

The commander looked at me, aghast. The copper wires stitched into his face caught the moonlight. "See?" he said. "*See?*"

He grabbed the cables attached to the back of my helmet and yanked, pulling me off my feet. The battery pack banged again into my lower back. He dragged me backward toward the end of the pier, splinters slicing into my forearms and wrists. I screamed, swore, shouted, my voice high and keening like a toddler throwing a tantrum. I kicked my legs, trying to dig my heels into the planks, but he yanked me along without difficulty.

"It never ends," he said. "The terror never ends. We can't live like this, Del. We can't live with these monsters."

Behind us, at the midpoint of the pier, a white hand gripped the edge, and the Shug pulled itself effortlessly up. It turned, opened its mouth, and roared.

"*Stop!*" I screamed. But I didn't know who I was screaming to. Both of them. Everyone.

"I'm sorry, Del," the commander said. "We can't live like this."

He jerked me to my feet, and tossed me backward over his leg. For a moment I was airborne, looking back: the commander on the edge of the pier, bent with the effort of his throw, his eyes on me. And behind him, the huge figure of the Shug, slouching toward the commander, mouth agape.

I struck the water. Icy water engulfed me and I grunted in shock, coughing air. I thrashed, trying to bring my arms out from behind me, but the plastic cuffs were unyielding. The weight of the battery pack pulled me down, reeling me into the dark.

.   .   .

I could see nothing but black, feel nothing but cold. Terror was a white noise, a static roar. I tried to drown it out with inner shouts, chants of *Oh fuck Oh fuck* and then *The Shug will save me The Shug will save me* . . .

I touched bottom, ass first, and then the bottom gave way. I sank into mud, silky and unknowably deep. Fresh panic coursed through me. I twisted, trying to bring my feet up, and then slid onto my chest. My face pressed into the mud, and I recoiled in horror. I couldn't take that. I couldn't die suffocating in mud.

I convulsed like a fish, finally ended on my side, in mud as deep as my breastbone. I lifted my helmeted head, shook it to clear the mud from my eyes.

I opened my eyes but there was nothing, black in all directions. And silence.

No splash in the water above me, no cloud of white as Toby came for me through the silty water. Toby wasn't coming. The Shug wasn't going to save me.

The Shug is a monster. That's its job. Terrorize people, kill them, enforce the rituals. It doesn't rescue people. It doesn't retrieve cats from trees, fight fires, show up for potlucks. That's not part of the bargain, no matter how many fish you nail to the door. The deal is, if you make the sign, the angel of death passes by your house. The angel of death doesn't pull you out of the pool, or cut through the steel of your car door and carry you out of the ravine. It's the fucking angel of *death*.

My chest burned; my ears pounded. It took all my strength to keep my lips clamped shut. I searched the water for some sign of movement—if not the Shug, then Lew, somehow escaped from the Human Leaguers. Come on, Lew. You're running through the forest, you're at the pier, you're diving . . .

There. Floating in the middle distance, a quavering circle of deeper black.

The black well.

As I watched, it blossomed, rushed toward me, filled my vision. The hole was bottomless, a twisting tunnel that branched and split into an infinite number of side shafts, but there was something waiting at the end of each of them. The mouth hovered above me, or I hovered over it, ready to fall, the gravity sucking at me like a whirlpool. It was a door, a gate—to something. Death, or the Hellion's cage inside my head, or some false paradise generated by my oxygen-starved brain. I didn't care, as long as it was somewhere else.

I let go, and fell.

10

Oh my God, did you shoot him? The commander didn't say to—
    Shut the fuck up, Bertram, I didn't fucking touch him!
    For God's sake just get him up, pull the chair up—
    I don't understand. Del never said his brother was epileptic . . .
    Everyone shut up! It's a trick, dammit. Don't fucking go near him!
    It's not a seizure.
    —please, at least hold his head so he won't—
    What'd she say, "say-zure?"

I could feel him. There, in the dark, I reached for him. I reached and
I *grabbed—*

Light.
    An expanse of braided carpet, stretching like a plain. Voices: O'Con-
nell, Louise, Bertram, other men.
    I'm telling you, don't go near him!
    Black boots appear, large as houses. A giant's hand.
    Another male voice, closer: If this is a trick, we're going to Taser you,
do you understand? Can you talk?
    I—

Lew's voice. Resonating oddly, a microphone turned too loud in a small room.

I'm drowning, the voice said.

He struggled, trying to throw me off, and I clamped down tighter, tighter still, like the bear hugs he always used against me to end our wrestling matches.

His arms were stretched backward, wrists touching, bound in hard plastic.

Flex.

Lew's arms flexed.

"You're not drowning," the guard said. "You fell over."

Pull.

The arms yanked away from each other. Plastic snapped. The pain speared up the arms.

Ignore the pain. Grab him.

The hand seized the guard's ankle, pulled. Small bones popped. The man screamed, hit the ground.

Get up.

The perspective lurched. A Human Leaguer in midnight camo, firing. The Taser dart embedded somewhere out of sight. The leaguer pulled the trigger, pulled it again. His expression changed from anger to confusion.

Punch.

The fist knocked the gunman back into a wall. The framed photographs clattered to the floor, coughing glass.

Bertram, still in helmet and pack, seemed to be in shock, his eyes on the man who'd collapsed against the wall. Louise pressed far back into the couch. O'Connell, beside her, wore a tight-lipped expression that could have masked anything: fear, shock, anger.

"And who are *you?*" O'Connell asked.

Lew's hands pulled the dart-tipped wire from his chest, tossed it aside.

"I'm dying," Lew's voice said.

Run.

The body knew what to do. It crossed the room in three long
strides, pushed through the door, leaped over the steps, and landed in
the gravel. Something popped in its right leg. It turned, ran toward
Cabin 5.

Faster.

The body obeyed, though it ran jerkily now, its gait thrown off balance by the malfunctioning knee. Lungs heaved oxygen into the
bloodstream; the heart forced it down, through clogged arteries, flood-
ing large muscles with oxygen and chemicals. Pain signals traveled up
the spine and went unanswered.

The body knew what to do, even though it had never done it so
completely, so forcefully.

Trees whipped past. The yellow light of the washhouse illuminated a crumpled body in the middle of the road, one arm missing, the
shoulder ending in a pool of blood like a rain puddle.

It leaped over the dead man, clearing it by ten feet. Ten more seconds and it reached the last cabin, three more and it was through the
trees, onto the wooden pier, and charging toward the water.

The Shu'garath squatted at the end of the pier, pulling apart pieces
of meat strung together with copper wire, as if deboning a fish. It
looked up, white chest slicked with blood. It opened its mouth, and
roared a challenge.

Out of my way.

"Out of my way," Lew's voice said.

The Shug threw down the loglike chunk it had been worrying and
stood to face the running man. A moment before the two big men
struck, the Shug melted aside and slipped into the water without a ripple. The running man didn't break stride.

Dive.

The icy water slapped the skin. Lew's body was buoyant with fat
and trapped air, but the big legs kicked and forced it into the dark. Ten
feet down, then fifteen feet, the arms plowed into mud.

The hands pushed through the silt, overturning rocks, waterlogged
sticks, sharp-edged bits of ancient garbage. Eyes opened wide, gather-
ing as much light as possible, but the water was too dim, too silted, to

see more than a few inches. The body, already depleted of oxygen from the sprint, had to keep kicking to stay close to the bottom. The hands kept moving, fanning through the mud.

The pier. Closer to the pier.

Legs kicked toward the shore. Hands touched the first pylon, then the body swung back, moving low over the lake floor like a manatee. It worked on, commanded to ignore the burning in its chest, the blood trickling from its nose.

Fingers brushed a rubber-covered cable. The hand closed on the cable, traced it to the helmet and backpack, then to the body of the drowned man still attached to them. Both hands grabbed the body under the arms and heaved it out of the muck.

The shore.

Lew's body held on to the man with one arm and beat upward, angling toward land. A few moments more and its head broke the surface, gulped automatically for air. It ducked again and lifted Del's body out of the water. It strode out of the lake, carrying the drowned man like a bride.

O'Connell was there at the shoreline, and Bertram appeared a moment later, breathing heavily. He'd removed the helmet and pack, and his bald head was damp with sweat.

"Set him down," O'Connell said.

Its head tilted down, looked down at the ground. Blood spattered onto the drowned man's chest. It was Lew's blood, gushing from his nose. A moment's concentration stopped the flow.

"*Listen to me!*" she shouted.

Its head rose again.

O'Connell jumped down a short ledge, her eyes on Lew's, and began to pull off her jacket. "Set him down. Set the body down. He's not breathing. Let me help."

Set it down.

Arms and legs and back muscles coordinated to lay the man on the jacket O'Connell had stretched out. The drowned man's face

—my face—

was white and translucent as rice paper, tinged with blue: blue eye-
lids, blue lips. He wasn't breathing.

O'Connell bent over him, delicately pulled the helmet from his
head. She pushed up the soaked sweatshirt and T-shirt to his
armpits—his arms were still bound behind him—and laid her cheek
on his chest. She stayed in that position for a very long time. "I can't
hear anything," she said, almost to herself. She tilted his head and ran
a finger deep inside his mouth, spooned out a wad of oily black that
might have been mud, mucous, blood, or a mix of all those things. She
adjusted his head, breathed into him, one hand pinching his nose.
Moments later she switched and compressed his chest, three times
quickly, then moved back to his face.

"He's too cold," she said without pausing. "We've got to strip him."
She gestured at Bertram. "*You.* Give me that sweater."

Bertram obeyed. O'Connell paused in her CPR to unbelt the
drowned man and yank down his pants. "We need blankets, lots of
them. Find Louise. Go!"

Bertram turned to go just as one of the Human League guards—
the one who had been thrown back into the wall by Lew's punch—
came through the bushes at the shoreline. His beefy face was sweaty
and flushed. He stared at the big man at the edge of the water, then
down at O'Connell busy on the ground over the naked man. "They're
all dead," he said to Bertram. "Harp, Torrence, Parrish. We've got to
find the commander. We've got to get—"

Bertram nodded toward the pier, at the mass of cloth and flesh and
wire. The Leaguer took a step forward before registering what he was
seeing. He made a whining, despairing sound, then turned to Bertram
in confusion.

"Go!" O'Connell ordered.

Bertram hustled toward the woods. The Leaguer hesitated, then
bolted after him.

O'Connell resumed CPR, alternating breaths with compressions.
In a few minutes she was panting with the effort.

She sat up. "This isn't working," she said, trying to catch her

breath. She looked at Lew's body. It listed to the right because of the
damaged leg but remained standing. It was shivering, but otherwise
unmoving. Awaiting commands.

"Del, you've got to go back in."

Lew's body didn't respond.

"You've done this before. The pool, Del. You saved yourself before.
You have to go back in."

How?

"I don't know how," Lew's voice said.

"Dammit, you got out, you can get back in." She got to her feet.
"You can't stay—" She made a slashing gesture, aimed at Lew's chest.
"*In there.* In someone else. Get back in your body, Del."

My body.

A rumble of big engines. The rumble grew louder, then was joined
by a rising whine. The helicopter lifted over the treetops in a ring of
lights. It turned on its axis, tilted toward the lake, and zoomed away.

In Lew's vision, where the vehicle had disappeared was an absence, a dot of deeper black.

The mouth of the well opened, edges fitfully expanding, eating the
sky. The twisting shaft like a gullet, dropping, or rising, until it exploded into an infinity of tributaries that divided and divided again:
black fireworks.

The well tugged at me, but less forcefully than it had under the
water. I could resist it, or I could fall into it. All that was required was
that I be willing to die, again.

Somehow O'Connell got us to the hospital in Louise's '92 Taurus station wagon, the only car big enough for all of us.

Bertram rode with O'Connell up front. I lay diagonally in the
back, covered with blankets. Lew rode in the middle seat, leaning
against the window, Louise next to him holding towels to his nose.
The muscles of Lew's triceps were torn, and he couldn't lift his arms.

I was conscious, my eyes open. I could hear everything that was
said, but couldn't make myself move or talk. Just as well.

The hospital was an underfunded, fifties-era county institution forty-five minutes from Harmonia Lake. When I arrived in the ER my core temperature was 83 degrees, my heart rate somewhere near twenty beats per minute. I was breathing slowly but regularly, which surprised them. At that temperature, my central nervous system should have shut down like a carnival in winter.

The staff was small, but they knew hypothermia; plenty of drunk fishermen falling out of their boats. They fastened a mask over me that hissed hot, humidified oxygen into my lungs, and set up an IV of warmed saline.

They didn't know what to make of Lew's injuries, though. O'Connell told them that he'd dived in to rescue me from drowning, but he looked as if he'd been in a car accident. He'd burst dozens of arteries in his nose and cheeks, creating a full-faucet nosebleed that was surprisingly hard to stop. His face had swelled with blood, turning his eyes into piggy slits. As well as the torn triceps, several muscles in his back were pulled. His right kneecap had popped loose from the tendons, floating under the skin, and would require orthopedic surgery. Worse, blood tests showed that he'd suffered a heart attack. Only the massive amounts of adrenaline in his system had kept him from dying on the spot.

My shiver reaction came back online after thirty minutes of oxygen and IVs, and my core temp started to rise. This seemed to make the ER doctor very relieved. By morning I was breathing without the mask, and the rectal thermometer pegged me at a toasty 94.2.

My first visitor was Bertram. He wouldn't stop apologizing. "I swear to God, Del, that was never part of the plan! It's—it's—completely against the League philosophy! We use only humane, nonlethal weapons."

"Humane? Have you ever been shot by a Taser?"

"But we'd never *hurt* you. 'The use of force is a black crime.' It's one of our core beliefs. Killing you was never in the plan."

"Bertram, you weren't *in* on the plan, you were *part* of the plan."

He was crushed, and for a moment I felt sorry for him. A moment.
I got him out of the room by telling him I was tired. If you're in a hospital bed, you're entitled to a range of efficient social tactics.

Later in the morning O'Connell appeared in my doorway looking
like Super Exorcist. She was back in her voluminous black cassock,
which served as a matte backdrop to the gigantic hunk of silver that
hung from her neck on industrial-gauge chain. The crucifix was a
nine-inch-long naturalist rendition of Jesus in maximum agony mode.
It looked like it weighed five pounds.

I didn't know how long she'd been standing there. It was too late to
pretend to be sleeping.

"Hi," I said.

"How are you feeling?" she said. This was probably a required
question for clerical visits. The forms must apply even to dubiously or-
dained priests of schismatic sects.

"Not bad," I lied. My mouth felt cottony, and I cleared my throat.
"Warmer." They'd put some kind of hot-water tube vest around my
chest, and now that my temperature was above the danger zone, they
let me heat up my extremities too. The nurses had piled four or five
blankets onto me, covered them with a sheet, and tucked the edges
tight, creating a perfectly smooth mound that hid any suggestion of
legs or arms. I hadn't moved enough to disturb their handiwork.

"Your doctor's amazed at your progress."

"This morning I impressed my nurses by sipping chicken broth.
Very exciting." I smiled, but I didn't have the energy to sell it. I
changed the subject. "Have you seen Lew?"

"I stopped in just now. He's fairly medicated at the moment, not in
any pain." She walked to the end of the bed. She didn't seem to know
what to do with her hands. "He doesn't remember rescuing you.
That's standard."

Standard for possession, she meant.

I tried to change the subject again. "That's good in a way," I said.
"The less he knows, the less he'll get sucked into the investigation."

"What investigation would that be?" O'Connell's face was set into an expression of mild curiosity. There was no one else in the room, but she was performing just the same.

I didn't know what to say. Commander Stoltz and at least three of his men were dead, killed by the Shug. The rest of the Human League, all except Bertram, had fled in the helicopter. True, they'd come to kill me, so they weren't about to go to the police. But there were still four dead men. You couldn't have people die in your town and just pretend it didn't happen. You had to at least look into it, didn't you?

But no. If they called in the cops, what could they do? Arrest Toby, kill him? And then the Shug would just move on to the next host.

This couldn't have been the first time people had disappeared at the lake. It wouldn't be the last.

O'Connell watched my face, saw me get it.

"It's Harmonia Lake, Del," she said.

Holy shit.

"You'll still have to answer some questions, though," she said. She paced to the window, leaned against it. "Lew wants to know what happened to him. He wasn't happy with my answers."

"What'd you tell him?" I said.

"Exactly what I saw," she said. The morning light was behind her, and I couldn't make out her face. "I saw him snap handcuffs like chopsticks, shrug off a Taser, disable two armed men. I saw him save his brother from drowning." She paused. "That's what I saw. Now why don't you tell me what *happened*."

"I was at the bottom of the lake, remember? I was unconscious until—"

"Don't lie, not to me," she said quietly.

It was too hard to look into the sunlight. I stared down at the mound of bedclothes covering me from chest to toes like a white casket.

"How'd you do it, Del?"

"What the *fuck* are you talking about?"

"You might want to keep your voice down." She stood up, but her face was still in shadow. "You jumped. You possessed your brother, you controlled him, and then you jumped back into your own body. You can try to pretend it didn't happen, you can pretend it was some near-death hallucination. But you did it."

"Look, I'm not saying that . . ." I took a breath.

"Okay," I said. "Something happened. But I don't know how—it just *did*, okay?" I bought myself time to think by closing my eyes and opening them slowly, as if dealing with some internal perturbation. Hospital Bed Tactic 12.

"I told you about the black well," I said. "I saw it again. And this time I went into it. I . . . rode it. And at the end of it was . . . Lew."

"You're telling me," she said, "that you just clicked your heels and wished real hard."

"*I don't know how it works*," I said. "What the hell do you want from me?"

She stepped away from my window, circled my bed. I could see her face again, and it was sealed tight, the same mask I'd seen her use too many times now.

"So what now, then?" she said icily. She crossed her arms under her breasts; the crucified Jesus tilted up, his eyes on mine. "You're all cured?"

"No," I said. "It's still here." I sat up in bed, felt a wave of dizziness, and shut my eyes. "The Hellion's still inside. I can feel it."

"Now, that's interesting." She went to the door, looked over her shoulder at me. "So why didn't it jump when you left it? You weren't holding it back anymore. That's what you've been doing all this time, isn't it, holding it back?"

Lew was only two doors down, but it might as well have been a mile. We could have called each other, I guess, but I didn't want to bother him. They'd told me he could barely lift his arms, so how would he pick up the phone? He must have made at least one call, though. My mother called me at noon to tell me that she and Amra would be there by this evening—tomorrow morning at the latest. They were driving in, and they didn't know if they could get there by the end of visiting hours. She asked only a few questions—just enough to confirm the basic story she'd gotten from Amra, who'd gotten it from Lew. Mom was restraining herself. For now.

I spent most of the day inert as a statue, falling in and out of sleep without moving my head. Nurses came in at two-hour intervals to take my temperature, but their questions didn't require more than a grunt or a nod. I thought about Christopher Reeve. I tried to imagine lying there paralyzed, watching each day's sunlight track across the wall. But Reeve hadn't stayed in bed. Okay, he was rich—high-tech wheelchair, staff of nurses, as many physical therapists as he wanted—but he was determined. *People* magazine said he worked for a year just to learn to move his pinky. How motivated was *that*? Eventually he even retaught his body to breathe on its own. Inch by inch, he was clawing his way out of that chair.

And then? Superman gets killed by a fucking bedsore infection.

The sky outside the window darkened. Visiting hours came and went, without Mom and Amra. I closed my eyes in relief.

"You snuck up on me," Lew said.

I sat in the dark in the chair beside his bed. I'd been watching him sleep for a long time, trying to decide if I should wake him. It was past midnight. The night staff seemed to be skeletal, and no one had noticed me shuffling down the hallway like an old man. It was only two doors, but it took me forever. I felt like my muscles had turned to jelly under the water, but I forced myself to keep lifting one foot, then the other. *Move the pinky, Mr. Reeve.*

"Sorry about that," I said.

"Didn't know you were mobile." His voice was slowed a notch from painkillers.

My face heated with embarrassment. "You got the worst of it."

He tilted his head in a suggestion of a shrug. "I guess."

He was propped up in bed, his arms unmoving at his sides. His right leg was in a cast from thigh to calf, to stabilize the knee. My eyes had adjusted to the dark, but I couldn't read his expression past the bandages, the bruises that looked like deeper shadows.

"O'Connell says you don't remember anything," I said.

"One minute I was with her and Louise and the guards. The next, lying there next to the water, screaming my head off."

"You don't remember anything else—running after me, diving in?"

"Should I remember something?"

Run.

Faster.

"Nah. Get some sleep." I pushed myself slowly out of the chair. "Mom'll be here in the morning and your sleeping days will be over."

"But now you've woken me up."

"You want me to read you a comic book?" I said.

"Hm?"

"Nothing. Mom told me about when we were kids. She said you used to sit with me and read me—" I got a clear image of Lew, holding up a page from *The Flash*. It was Flash versus Dr. Light, and Flash was moving in a red-and-yellow blur that was *faster* than light.

"You okay?" Lew said.

"I just . . ." My voice caught. "I just need to get to bed. I'll see you in the morning."

I used the door frame for support and shuffled into the hallway, managed to make it back to my room without getting busted by the nurses. I sat on the edge of the bed, unable to get that image out of my head: seven-year-old Lew in the chair, holding that *Flash* comic. How many nights had he sat there, waiting for his little brother to come back? Waiting for the wild boy who'd maimed his mother to go away.

And Mom, reading *Mike Mulligan and His Steam Shovel* over and over.

O'Connell asking, *What do you mean, you loved it?*

I clicked on the bedside lamp. My vision was blurred, and it was hard to make out the instructions on the phone's faceplate, but I finally got an outside line. The call was picked up after only two rings. Louise sounded exactly as she had the night I'd phoned from Lew's house in Gurnee: tired and annoyed.

"This is Del," I said, trying to control my voice. "Del Pierce." Stupid: How many Dels could she know? How many had she just taken to the hospital? "I need to reach Mother Mariette. Can you tell her to call me at the hospital as soon you see her? Hello?"

The phone had gone silent. I thought she'd hung up, and then O'Connell came on the line. "What is it? What's happened?"

I cleared my throat, ran the back of my hand over my eyes. "You knew, didn't you? You knew before the commander showed up."

"Knew what, Del?"

"I shouldn't remember them reading to me. I shouldn't remember being the Hellion."

"No. Probably not."

"When I took Lew, I could feel him, feel him fighting me. Fighting me just like—"

"Del, I'm coming over there. Don't do anything. I'm giving the phone to Louise for a minute, so please stay on the phone . . ."

Oh God. The Hellion was still inside me, clawing at my skull. Kicking out the posts. And the walls were coming down.

DEMONOLOGY

THE LITTLE ANGEL

BROOKLYN, NEW YORK, 1977

When the large black Mercedes pulled up to the curb, Dr. Wayne Randolph left the shelter of the awning and hurried into the rain like an eager doorman, umbrella at the ready. He didn't care if he looked desperate. He liked to think he was smart enough not to pretend.

He opened the passenger door, and the old woman looked up at him from under her hat. She favored him with a brief smile. "You must be Dr. Randolph," she said in a soft Swiss-German accent. They'd met years before at the first ICOP, but of course she wouldn't remember him; he'd been just a medical student then. Dr. Toni Wolff, however, was the same as he remembered her from twenty years before: ancient, tiny, and somehow invulnerable, like a well-preserved insect specimen. She wore a formal black evening gown, and held a very informal brown leather bag on her lap.

"Thank God you could come so quickly," he said. She'd made it across town in only twenty-five minutes, a New York miracle. "I'm sorry to interrupt your evening."

"Thank you for calling Red Book," she said. "Some of your colleagues

stubbornly refuse our help." Her voice, too, was as he remembered it: cigarettes and Switzerland.

The driver, a trim, fortyish man dressed in a tuxedo, hefted an old-
fashioned wooden wheelchair from the car's voluminous trunk and set it up
beside the car. "Hi, I'm Frederick," he said. He'd just gotten Dr. Wolff into
the chair when headlights slewed into the entranceway. A small white MG
skidded to a stop just inches from the Mercedes' rear bumper.

A young woman in a sleek red dress hopped out from behind the wheel
and ran around the back of the sports car, somehow managing to move
gracefully in six-inch clogs. "Sorry I'm late!" she said. Her black hair
seemed to shine in the rain. The dress was some kind of silky wrap, tied at
the hip, that threatened at any moment to become not a dress at all.

"And this is Margarete," Dr. Wolff said.

Frederick leaned close to Dr. Randolph's ear. "We're getting a bit wet,"
he said.

Dr. Randolph came to himself and hopped forward to lead them
through the sliding doors. "We've got her locked in one of the observation
rooms. I told her we lost the keys, as you suggested on the phone, but she's
not very happy. She's, uh, throwing a bit of a tantrum."

"What does she look like?" Margarete asked.

"Just like in the papers—little girl, maybe ten years old, white nightgown. Beautiful long curls." He turned right and led them into the oncology
wing. "She looks like Shirley Temple."

"Has she kissed or touched any of the patients?" she asked.

"One, we think," Dr. Randolph said.

"You think?" Frederick said.

"We're not sure if the girl did it, or if the excitement was too much for
the woman. She was very old." He suddenly realized what he'd said, but Dr.
Wolff didn't seem to take offense. "Anyway, we can't get in there with her."

"She's still in the room with the patient?" Dr. Wolff said.

Dr. Randolph winced inwardly. "We had no choice. That was the room
the girl was in when we found her."

They heard pounding, then shouting. A high-pitched voice yelled, "Or
else, mister!"

A small crowd of nurses, orderlies, and patients had gathered in the hallway outside the room, but they were standing well back from the door and the door's little window. The door shook every time the girl inside kicked it. Frederick said, "Step aside, please! Thank you!"

"Dr. Randolph?" Margarete said. He turned and forced his eyes to stay on her face. The neck of her dress seemed to plunge almost to her navel. "We need to get these people out of harm's way," she said.

He nodded.

"So why don't you do that?"

"Of course, of course."

After Dr. Randolph had cleared the hallway—twenty feet of it, at least— he came back to find Dr. Wolff paging through a small notebook, and Margarete and Frederick conferring in low voices. Were they married? he wondered. Dating? Perhaps they were only colleagues.

"It's the Long Island girl, all right," Frederick was saying. "I'd recognize those cheekbones anywhere." He leaned against the wall beside the door, arms crossed. "God only knows how she gets across the city barefoot and in a nightgown with nobody seeing her. Or into the damn hospital."

"No one reads our alerts," Margarete said.

"Dr. Randolph does," Dr. Wolff said without looking up. He hadn't realized she'd seen him return. "And for that we are thankful."

Inside the room the girl kicked and yelled something Dr. Randolph couldn't make out.

"We have to move before the demon damages the girl," Dr. Wolff said. "So the question: temporary or permanent?"

"She's done this for three years," Margarete said. "She's paid her dues."

"I agree," Frederick said.

"Temporary or permanent what?" Dr. Randolph asked. "Exorcism?"

"Let me out of here!" the girl yelled.

"To use a word freighted with misunderstanding," Frederick said.

"But why *wouldn't* you choose permanent?" Dr. Randolph sounded exasperated.

Dr. Wolff opened her purse. "How heavy would you say she is, Doctor? Forty pounds? Forty-five?"

"About that."

"Oh, and I'm going to need scissors," she said. "Margarete, could you fetch a pair? This place should be full of them." Margarete spun away, the skirt of her dress parting to expose a length of tanned thigh. "And Doctor, I need you to unlock the door for me."

Frederick straightened. "I should be the one to go, she's not going to do anything to me."

"I need to talk to her before she leaves," Dr. Wolff said. "However, I won't leave you out, Frederick. You can play bodyguard. In a few minutes I'll need you and the doctor to hold her down for me."

Dr. Randolph felt his stomach clench. "I'm not sure I should—"

"Don't worry, Doctor," Dr. Wolff said. "You're not her type."

Dr. Randolph pulled the keys from his pocket, then struggled to find the right one. He could feel the hospital staff watching him. When he placed the key in the lock, the girl inside suddenly quieted.

"Please, Dr. Wolff, I don't think it's a good idea for you to go in there," Frederick said.

"Pffft!" she said. Then louder, "My little angel! We've found the keys. We're going to have you out in a jiffy." She pronounced it *zhiffy.*

"It's about time!" the little girl said.

Dr. Randolph pulled the door open, and Dr. Wolff immediately rolled forward, blocking the doorway. "My, aren't you a pretty little girl!"

Dr. Randolph looked at her through the window. She was a pretty girl. Her face was pale and elfin. Her hair hung in long, golden brown ringlets.

The girl looked at Dr. Wolff suspiciously. "I know you," she said. "You were at that other place."

"That's right, we met last year."

"You're old," the little girl said. "Very old."

"Yes I am." She rolled forward a few inches. "But let's talk about you, my little angel. Tell me about the first place you ever visited. Can you remember that?"

The girl tilted her head. "You're sick, too, aren't you? You're *dying.*"

Margarete came up behind Dr. Randolph. "Oh no," she said quietly.

"Don't worry about me," Dr. Wolff said. "Tell me a story about your adventures. Do you remember visiting Kansas City?" She rolled farther into the room. Margarete and Frederick exchanged a look.

"You're really 'fraid," the girl said. She stepped forward, her filmy white nightgown swishing around her mud-stained legs.

Dr. Wolff said, "I have something in my purse I'd like to show you. Do you like surprises?"

"You can't fool me," the little girl said. "You're afraid it's going to hurt when you die. You're afraid it's going to take a long, long time."

Frederick spun around the frame of the door and grabbed the handles of the wheelchair. The little girl screamed. Frederick hauled Dr. Wolff backward out the door, her legs kicking up. As soon as the chair had cleared the doorway Margarete lunged into the room and tackled the little girl to the floor.

You weren't supposed to touch the Little Angel, Dr. Randolph thought. That was the first rule.

"Frederick!" Dr. Wolff said. "Get Margarete out of there!"

The demon threw off Margarete and sent her crashing against the far bed. Her strength, for a child, was enormous. Dr. Randolph ducked back out of sight.

"Meg!" Frederick said.

Dr. Wolff took the purse from her lap and tossed it at Dr. Randolph. "Doctor, get the syringe."

Dr. Randolph stared at her.

"Twenty cc's should do it," Dr Wolff said. "Enough to slow her down without killing the girl."

Dr. Randolph opened the purse and withdrew a syringe. "What's in this?" He withdrew the plastic cap from the needle.

"She's u-up," Frederick said quietly.

"You," Dr. Randolph heard the girl say. "You were mean to me last time."

"Sorry about that," Frederick said. He raised his arms and stood in front of Dr. Wolff. Dr. Randolph pressed his back against the wall, out of sight of the girl. He gripped the syringe tightly in his damp hands.

The girl walked forward. "You're young," she said. "Not sick at all."

"That's right. Fit as a fiddle."

"But you're mean."

The girl walked out of the room. Dr. Randolph held the syringe at his side, unable to move. She was only two feet away from him, her back to him, and still he couldn't move.

He must have made a noise. The little girl glanced at him over her shoulder. She frowned. The syringe slipped from his fingers and clattered away.

The girl turned her attention back to Frederick and Dr. Wolff. "I just want to *help* her," the girl said. She reached out her hand. "But mean people are always stopping me."

Suddenly the girl squealed in pain. She wheeled around, turned again, as if the needle were still stuck in her behind. "What did you do?" the girl said.

Margarete held the syringe between two fingers like a cigar. "Nighty night," she said.

The demon stumbled, and Frederick caught her before her head struck the ground.

"Oh my goodness," Dr. Randolph said. "She was going to kill us. Kill us all."

Frederick made a face. "She wasn't going to go after you." He looked at Dr. Wolff. "But you, Doctor. I didn't like the way she was talking. If she comes for you—"

"Summoned or not, the god will be there," Dr. Wolff said. "Now, before she wakes up, Margarete?"

"Already on it," Margarete said, and snipped the air with a pair of scissors. She kneeled beside the unconscious girl, lifted up one of the long, springy curls, and clipped it off near the base of the skull.

"Is that necessary?" Dr. Randolph asked.

Margarete smiled up at him. "The Little Angel has a thing about hair. Won't go anywhere without it."

"Ah," Dr. Randolph said, though he wasn't sure he understood. "What's going to happen to her?"

"First we try to find her parents," Dr. Wolff said. "And then the hard work begins."

11

I woke to darkness and thumping bass and synthesized strings: an eighties funk power ballad. The male falsetto had to be Prince—nothing compares to Prince—but I didn't recognize the song. The woman's voice singing along with the recording was breathy and keening at the same time, threatening at any moment to veer off key.

The thing in my head was quiet. Still there, though: it breathed warily, an animal crouched in the corner of a dark room.

I lay there inhaling the powdery, foreign scents of an unknown bed. I had no idea how long I'd slept. It'd been almost 2 a.m. before I'd gotten out of the hospital—the nurses hadn't wanted to let me check out, but O'Connell was formidable. I'd fallen asleep only minutes after getting into her truck, and had woken up briefly to navigate through a series of small rooms. She'd insisted I sleep here, rather than on the couch, and I hadn't argued.

There was a window above me on the curved wall to my right, but it was dark on the other side—which meant that the window looked out on another room, or that it was still night, or worse, night *again*—and the deep ache in my arms and legs told me I'd been sleeping too long in one position.

Holy shit. Mom had to be freaking out.

The song ended, and in the break, I yelled out, "Hel-lo!" The next song started—another eighties number, but U2 this time. A minute later the door opened and O'Connell leaned in. She was in rock-chick mode again: black T-shirt, black jeans. Despite the singing a moment ago, she didn't look happy.

I wasn't in the bed so much as on it: I lay on top of the covers, with several blankets thrown over me. I lifted one arm a few inches, as far as it would go.

"You can untie me now," I said.

She stepped back and closed the door, leaving me alone in the dark again.

Ooookay.

Sometime last night, after I'd babbled and cried for a couple hours and finally fallen asleep, O'Connell had tied me spread-eagled to the bed frame with the combination locks tucked out of sight and out of reach, an arrangement impossible for me to set up on my own—and one I didn't much like now. The situation put me in mind of more than one Stephen King novel, and I'd had enough of horror stories.

Bono was emoting through the second verse when she came back into the room carrying a vinyl-padded kitchen chair in one hand and my blue duffel bag in the other. She set the chair near the foot of the bed and dropped the duffel onto the bed between my spread legs. She made no move toward the chains.

"I really need to pee," I said.

"Let's talk first," she said.

"About what?"

"Oh, I hardly know where to start." She sounded peeved. "The county sheriff stopped by for a talk this morning. Not about the Shug, about Dr. Ram. They found the killer."

"What? That's great!"

"Some DemoniCon fanboy named Eliot Kasparian. He claims he was possessed, woke up wearing a trench coat and holding a pair of guns. He's in custody."

"So was he possessed by the Truth, or is he faking?"

"I hope for his sake that he's not lying," she said.

Good point, I thought. The Truth didn't like fakers. But if he really was possessed, then it was Dr. Ram who'd been the liar.

O'Connell said, "We're not completely off the hook, boyo. The sheriff says that the police still want to talk to all the hotel guests who were there that night, especially the ones that checked out that morning. Especially the ones that might be showing up on security camera tapes."

"You told him I was here?"

"Her. I didn't have to—she's smart enough to figure out where you went when you checked yourself out of the hospital. Plus, you were snoring."

"She didn't think it odd that I was chained up in your bedroom?"

"I didn't open the door. Officially, she doesn't know where you are."

"Why would—why would she go along with that?" And why would O'Connell stick her neck out for me?

"She's a friend. And she lives here. The ladies of the lake watch out for each other."

I didn't know what she meant by that. Were there any male residents of Harmonia Lake? I hadn't met any. Maybe only women stayed, because they weren't candidates to be the next Shug.

"This is a huge relief, though," I said. "So you want to unlock me?"

"We're not quite finished with our conversation," O'Connell said, and unzipped the duffel. I tried to sit up, but the chains kept me from raising more than my head. "Hey, that's my stuff!"

She ignored me. And then I realized that of course she'd already been into the duffel—she'd gotten the chains and locks.

Shit.

"I have rules, Del." She pulled something else out of the duffel, a rectangle of cloth. Ah. The oil rag that had been wrapped around the pistol. "One of them is, I will not have guns in my house."

"I'll take care of it."

"Oh, I've already taken care of it."

"What'd you do with it? That was my dad's army pistol!"

"It was also a forty-five automatic, the same model the Truth uses. The same model that killed Dr. Ram."

"But that's over now—you know it wasn't me!" I tried to sit up, but all I could do was lift my head in a forceful manner.

"You still can't go around carrying ready-made *props*—especially ones that put holes in people. The demons can possess *anyone*—whoever they want, whenever they want. They're especially attracted to those who've been possessed before, even by another demon. You're already marked, Del. So, let's not make it so easy on them, eh?"

"What did you do with the gun?" I said.

"I heaved it into the lake."

I blinked at her. I didn't know whether to be angry or relieved.

"Next," she said. She pulled out the black nylon bag I'd gotten at the ICOP conference. She withdrew from it a sheaf of stapled papers and started slowly turning the pages. "Now *these* are interesting souvenirs," she said. "Out of all the academic crap at the conference, this is what you take with you. What did you think you'd do with these, apply a little guilt, a little leverage to get me to take your case?"

"I don't know what the hell you're talking about," I said.

She spun the packet at me. The pages landed on my chest, open to the page she'd been looking at. At this angle I couldn't read the words, but I saw the photocopied picture and realized what I was looking at. The "Little Angel" paper from the Penn State woman.

"What are you mad about?" I said. "This is just some research paper I picked up."

But there was something about the girl in the picture, even viewed sideways. She was maybe nine years old, dressed in a white gown. Even in black and white, after multiple generations of photocopying, the girl's beauty was evident. Pale skin, high cheekbones, a head bursting with curls.

"When was this taken?" I said.

"Nineteen seventy-seven," she said. "I was eleven."

"I didn't know," I said. I looked up. "I swear it, it's just something I picked up and put in my bag. I thought you grew up in Ireland."

"My mother and I moved to New York when I was eight, after my parents divorced. The Little Angel found me soon after. I didn't move back to Ireland until I was a teenager."

"I'm sorry," I said. "I didn't—"

"Stop it. Whatever you had in mind, it doesn't matter. I don't require *motivation*, Del. I don't need to be manipulated into helping you, and I don't respond to pity. There are thousands of people who've been possessed, and it doesn't matter if I was one of them—the job's the same."

"The job . . . ," I said, unsure. "Being an exorcist?"

"Being your pastor."

"Oh. I mean, that's nice and everything, but I don't think I need—"

"Del."

She walked to the side of the bed near my head, put her hands on her hips. "Last night you were afraid you were going insane. You said the Hellion's memories were breaking through into your own. You were losing yourself."

"I was a little freaked out last night, but I'm fine now. I can handle this."

"You are so far from handling this." She crouched, bringing her head even with mine.

"Now . . ." She lifted one of the bike chains into view. "Three numbers. What's the combination?"

"Uh, that would be six, followed by six . . . and I'm sure you can guess the last one."

She shook her head, opened the first lock. Then she walked around the bed to my other arm. While she was working on the next combination, I peeked under the blankets. Boxer briefs, my erection as clearly delineated as the trunk of a cartoon elephant. My need to pee had turned into an ache.

She undid the second chain. Hands finally free, I began to unfasten the manacles, leather-padded medieval things I'd purchased from a fetish website. The steel loops were big enough for a shower curtain rod to be threaded through them—I'd seen the pictures—and more than wide enough for the bike chain. My shoulders were stiff, but I felt a hundred times better than yesterday. The cuts in my fingers barely hurt. "What if I'd died in my sleep?" I said. "These chains are pretty strong—I'd be attached to your bed for weeks."

"Oh, I wouldn't cut through the *chains.*"

She gave no indication she was joking.

I scooted down to the edge of the bed and started reeling in the chain so I could get at the lock. "Do you know what time it is? My mother's got to be at the hospital by now. She'll be frantic."

She didn't answer, and I looked at her.

"They arrived this morning," she said. "I called Lew and told him you had to get out of the hospital because you were losing control of the Hellion." She tossed a length of chain onto the bed. "Hardly an exaggeration. I said you'd be back in touch after we returned from the city."

"Wait—what city? New York City?"

"Get dressed," she said. "We have an appointment at Red Book."

I didn't think she meant the magazine.

As soon as she left the room, I pulled open the duffel bag and started sifting through the clothes, running my hands through the folds. Nothing. I started pulling out the clothes, shaking them one by one.

"Oh, one more thing," O'Connell called back. "I threw out the Nembutal too."

The three-story brownstone was buried somewhere in the heart of the city—I had no idea where, and I didn't think O'Connell did either. Once we'd squeezed through the George Washington Bridge, slow as toothpaste, she began taking unpredictable rights and lefts, shouldering across lanes, dodging down side streets, and merging onto four-lane avenues. Nearly midnight and the traffic was still dense.

O'Connell was the worst driver I'd ever ridden with—worse than

Lew, worse than even me, and I'd driven through guardrails. Several times I found myself inches from sheet metal or the scowling face of a taxi driver. She seemed oblivious to the other cars, and even to the road in front of her, one hand on the steering wheel, the other pinching a cigarette, navigating by temperature, or road texture, or smell— anything but street signs.

"You know," I said casually, "there's this thing called MapQuest." But O'Connell had stopped talking to me. She hummed and muttered to herself. Maybe she was praying.

An hour and a half after crossing the river, and seven hours after leaving Harmonia Lake, O'Connell braked to a stop in the center of a dark street double-lined with parked cars. Without saying anything she got out of the truck, leaving it running. I opened my door and stepped out, as much to get air as to see where she was going; O'Connell had smoked the entire way, and my eyeballs felt like gritty ball bearings.

O'Connell walked up the steps of one of the brick apartment buildings we'd passed and pressed a doorbell. Above the door, a circular window of stained glass glowed like an eye surveying the street: red and blue and purple panes outlined in dark-leaded curves, swirling out from the center like petals dragged through water.

I looked away from the window, feeling queasy.

The apartment door opened, and an older woman with short white hair stepped out, hugged O'Connell. The women exchanged a few words, and then O'Connell strode back to me. "We can park around back," she said.

"Was that one of the shrinks?" I asked. She'd told me that the people we were visiting were psychiatrists, "absolutely brilliant." They'd become her therapists when she was eleven, after the first string of possessions. "They saved my life," she said. She'd been vague on how exactly they'd helped her, or what she expected me to get out of meeting them. "Just be honest with them," she said. "They'll be able to straighten this out."

She steered the truck into an alley. An iron gate swung open automatically and closed behind us. She parked diagonally on a small brick-paved patio, and we pulled our bags from the bed of the truck.

The white-haired woman met us at the back door, ushered us in, and set the alarm behind us. O'Connell said, "Del, this is Dr. Margarete Waldheim."

"Meg," the woman said, and shook my hand. I must have winced. She glanced down, turned my hand in hers, looking at the cuts. "Have you been fighting?"

"Just with furniture," I said.

"Ah. I always stick with the softer pieces—seat cushions, pillows."

She was younger than I had thought from the street, maybe in her fifties—the white hair had thrown me off. A ruddy, apple-shaped face. Shorter than O'Connell, not fat but sturdy. She wore a green-striped man's dress shirt untucked over black stretch pants, and thin black shoes like dance slippers.

"Anyway, welcome to Bollingen," she said.

I glanced at O'Connell. What happened to Red Book?

"Bollingen is the name of the house," O'Connell said. I still didn't know if Red Book was the name of a cult, an institute, or a giant computer that would tell me my future.

She led us down a dark-paneled hallway, past a tiled kitchen and half a dozen closed doors, while O'Connell talked about the trip in. She didn't mention the labyrinthine tour of Manhattan.

We arrived in a high-ceilinged foyer at the front of the house. Set into the floor was a slab of granite inscribed in Latin: VOCATUS ATQUE NON VOCATUS DEUS ADERIT. *Non vocatus deus*—no vacations for God?

I made the mistake of looking up. High above the door was the circular window I'd seen from the street. The panes, viewed from the inside, were bruise-dark and glinting, like half-seen blades about to spin.

"You okay, Pierce?" O'Connell said.

I looked away from the window, ran a damp hand through my hair. "What? Oh, yeah. Tired I guess."

"The design came from one of Dr. Jung's paintings," Meg said. "During his Nekyia period, he became fascinated with circular forms, circles within circles. Some of his works resemble Indian mandalas."

I didn't know what to say to that. And what the hell was a Nekyia? One thing was clear: Jungians loved yargon.

O'Connell said to Meg, "Is the old man upstairs?"

At first I thought she meant Jung himself, but that couldn't be—he'd died in the fifties or sixties. She must have meant the other Dr. Waldheim.

"He's turned in for the night," Meg said. "And I'm about to collapse myself. I'll show you to your rooms. If you're hungry, though, make yourself at home. Siobhan can show you the kitchen."

"Wait a minute—*Shavawn?*" I repeated phonetically.

O'Connell looked at me. "Mariette is the name I took when I became a priest."

Meg laughed quietly. "I can never remember to call her that." She led us to side-by-side rooms on the second floor. "There's a journal in the desk," Meg said. "In case you have any dreams."

"Okay," I said, as if she'd told me where the towels were. "Thanks."

I closed the door, dropped my duffel on the floor. Outside, Meg and O'Connell murmured together, their words indistinct.

The room was a cozy space smaller than my dorm room at Illinois State, but bigger than my hospital room in Colorado. There was one skinny door besides the one I'd come through, but I didn't feel like hanging up my clothes. Most of the room was taken up by a high bed on a cast-iron frame (convenient for chaining), an armless wooden chair, a small writing desk with a lid unfolded to reveal—yes indeed—a handsome leather-bound journal and two fat pens. I flipped through the thick oatmeal-colored pages, but although a few pages had been torn out, nobody had left behind any nighttime notes.

Outside, the women stopped talking. O'Connell's door opened and closed.

I sat down on the bed, and the mattress sank beneath me. The thing in my head shifted slightly. It had stayed quiet all day, as if the long drive had jostled it to sleep, and I pushed my thoughts away from it before it could wake up. Thinking about the demon seemed too much like summoning it.

I stared at the walls instead: dark rose wallpaper that looked like it had been put up in the forties. Opposite me was a large water stain in the shape of a heart—and not a valentine heart. A fat smear sprouting from its top was disturbingly aortic.

Someone knocked on the door—but it wasn't the hallway door. I curled out of the bed and cautiously opened the skinny door I'd taken for a closet. O'Connell stood there, holding a big folded white towel and a washcloth.

"I was wondering where those were," I said.

Behind her was a bathroom tiled in checkerboard black and white, and another open door. Her room looked bigger than mine.

"Will you be singing in the shower tomorrow?" I asked.

Her face tightened. "Of course not."

Jesus, she could get pissed so *fast*. "You have a beautiful voice," I said. She made a dismissive sound like a cough. "No, really," I said. "You could have been a singer."

"And you could have been a bicycle repairman." She pressed the towel and washcloth into my hands, and while I put them on the desk she stood in the doorway, looking around at the space. I bet her room really was bigger.

"So. Shavawn."

"No, it's—" And she said it in a subtly different way. I made a face and she spelled it for me.

"Ohhh," I said. "*Siobhan*. You know, I've seen that in print but I never knew how it was pronounced."

She didn't quite roll her eyes. "Any other questions?"

"Nope. Yes! The Latin thing by the door."

"*Vocatus atque non vocatus deus aderit*," O'Connell said. "Dr. Jung wrote that above the door to his house. 'Summoned or not, the god will be there.' "

"That's what I thought."

"Goodnight, Mr. Pierce." She walked toward the bathroom door. "And please don't oversleep, the Waldheims are early risers, and we'll want to get started." She nodded at the bed. "Need someone to strap you down? Or do you need to have a wank first?"

I barked a laugh. My face heated. "What?"

"It must be difficult with your hands tied down." Her tone was clinical. "And it will help you sleep." The muscle behind my balls thumped like a bass string.

"Thanks," I said. "I'm fine."

"Suit yourself. I'll see you in the morning." She turned and disappeared into the bathroom, closing the door behind her. A moment later I heard her own door close.

I sat down on the bed and let the collapsing springs roll me backward. *Siobhan.* I lay there, staring at the ceiling, my dick as hard as the Washington Monument.

The sound was like a faint, drawn-out squeak, repeating rhythmically like a rusty hand pump. Very faint at first, then growing slowly louder.

I sat up in my cocoon bed. In the windowless room I couldn't guess what time it was, but it felt like hours since I'd threaded the chains through the bed frame and lain down, waiting for sleep. The manacles lay open and unattached.

I'd tried O'Connell's sleep advice. She'd been wrong.

The sound grew louder—*chirr-up, chirr-up*—and then passed by my door and moved on.

I eased out of the bed, pressed my ear to the hallway door. I thought I heard the squeak again, very faint, then the sound of a door opening. A half minute passed in silence.

I turned and found my jeans in the dark, felt around for my T-shirt, pulled them on. I went to the door again. Nothing. I slowly twisted the knob and eased the door open.

The hallway was slightly brighter than my room, soft light coming from around the corner where the balcony overlooked the foyer. To my left, the corridor was darker, running perhaps twenty feet before it ended in an oversized door. I headed toward the light, in the same direction the sound had been moving. I passed O'Connell's door, then two other doors, my bare feet quiet on the narrow Turkish runners. I felt like a teenager sneaking past his parents.

I leaned around the corner. The balcony was empty, the row of doors along it all closed. There was one door opposite me that was ajar, the room dark. Had it been open when Meg showed us to our rooms? I couldn't remember if I'd looked down that way.

I stepped onto the balcony. I could hear no one on the stairs, no one on the floors above or below. I glanced down at the empty foyer, then at the open door. "Summoned or not, here I come," I said to myself.

The circular window, hanging level with the balcony, glinted like a waking eye.

I trailed one hand along the polished banister until I reached the open door. "Hello?" I said, and rapped lightly on the door frame. I didn't expect an answer, but I felt it was good to go through the motions, just in case I was cross-examined later: Did you knock before you went in? Yes, Your Honor, I even announced my presence.

I glanced behind me once more, then reached inside to the left-hand wall. I found a light switch, flicked it on.

Directly in front of me, the Black Well.

"Shit!" I said aloud.

It was only a painting, but it still took me a moment to calm down. I stepped inside the room, put a hand against the wall.

I was in some kind of cathedral-ceilinged library. The walls cut in and out, creating dozens of nooks and multiplying the wall space. Towering bookshelves alternated with narrow, green-draped windows, and the remaining spaces were filled by paintings and tapestries and glass frames of every size. In the center of the room were several fat leather chairs surrounded by long tables that held stacks of books, small glass cases, Tiffany-style desk lamps. The centerpiece seemed to be a podium holding an open book the size of my mom's family Bible.

The Black Well painting hung on the wall opposite the door, in a dark frame maybe three feet wide and four feet tall. I walked around the crenellated edge of the room, distracted by all the exotics hanging on the walls: African masks; pen-and-ink drawings of mythological animals and armored knights; tapestries of unicorns and demons and lines of pilgrims; plaques and awards in German and French and English; black-and-white photographs of bespectacled men with pipes and dark-eyed women in large hats; honorary degrees; framed prints from old books, some illustrated with arcane symbols.

Most striking were the dozens of paintings, many of them multi-colored mandalas but others art-nouveau-style renderings of fantastic characters: a winged man with a devil-horned forehead; a bearded man in robes; a long-haired woman naked except for a black snake draped over her shoulders.

But my attention kept returning to the Black Well painting. I approached it obliquely like a swimmer fighting the current, and stopped a few feet away.

The well wasn't rendered exactly as it had appeared to me under the lake, but the painting caught the essence. Bands of black and red and purple spiraled and twisted away from the eye, promising an infinite regress. I put a hand out, hovering above the canvas. I pictured my hand plunging into it, the well sucking in my arm, my body. I stepped back, feeling nauseous.

Behind me, the chirp of rusty hinges. I whipped my head toward the door.

An old man pushed an antique wooden wheelchair into the room.

"I'm sorry," I said. "I didn't mean to—"

He held up a hand—to silence or reassure me, I wasn't sure which—and rolled the chair toward me. It was an ungainly, slat-backed thing like a steamship deck chair mounted on rusting bicycle wheels. The man pushing looked as old as the chair. He was thin, all forehead and white hair, dressed in a loose white shirt and blue pants that could have been pajamas or hospital scrubs. His hair started at ear level and dropped to his shoulders, clouding into a white beard that fanned his chest.

"December of 1912," he said. His voice was quiet but penetrating. "Dr. Jung experienced what some people call a break*down*, and what others call a break*through*."

He pushed the empty wheelchair to a spot between a chair and couch. "The doctor referred to it as his Nekyia, his Ulysses-like descent into the underworld."

Oh, Nekyia, I thought. Right. Of course.

"He said it was as if the floor literally gave way beneath him, and he *chose* to fall," the old man said. As he talked he carefully adjusted the chair's angle, backing and filling until it was aimed directly at me. "Into the depths. Into the womb of primordial life."

He straightened, then nodded at the Black Well painting. "Can you imagine, *choosing* to fall into that?"

There was a wink in his voice. I couldn't tell if he was laughing at me or trying to convince me he was in on the joke.

"You must be Dr. Waldheim," I said. O'Connell had told me they were a married couple.

He shook his head. "No, no, I'm the other Dr. Waldheim. Call me Fred." He walked toward one of the protrusions of wall I'd passed. He moved slowly, but he didn't seem to be in any need of a walker. "After the doctor fell, he was introduced to several independent personalities who became his guides through the underworld." He indicated the picture of the old man beside the naked girl and her black snake. "First were Elijah and Salome. They were the first to anoint him as the Christ—the Christ within each of us." He smiled. "Well, maybe not all of us."

He moved on to the winged old man with the horns. "This is Philemon, the doctor's most important advisor. You notice the four keys he holds, representing the quaternity: the Father, the Son, the Holy Ghost—and the Devil. Dr. Jung came to realize that the separation between God and Satan was an artificial construction of later Christians. The Gnostics understood that there was one God—some call him Abraxas, but he has many names—and that truth and falsehood were aspects of the same universal nature."

I stood there, trying to figure out how I could get out of the room. The Black Well hovered just behind me, a dizzying void like the edge of a roof under my heels. "Yeah, well . . ."

"However . . . ," the old man said, drawing out the word. "The doctor could have just been, what's the word, *whacked*." He rolled his eyes toward the wheelchair and then laughed, a long, dry chuckle.

I forced a thin smile. "I really should get back to bed."

"Wait, you're missing the best piece." He gestured toward the podium and the huge book on it.

The pages were old and thick, and looked like they'd been hand-bound to the leather cover. The leather was a dark, burnished red.

"Oh," I said. "This must be that Red Book I've heard so much about."

The old man laughed, delighted. "This is just a copy, but we've tried to make it as accurate as possible."

One page was a large illustration, the other handwritten text. I moved around to the other side. The picture was of an angelic crea-ture with a crown of stars and great wings behind it—like the Phile-mon character, but more refined. Someone had written in the margin: *Ka*. What kind of word was that—more Greek? The dense scrawl on the opposite page was harder to decipher, but at least it was in English. Someone had underlined this:

The archetype is a figure—a demon, a human being, or a process—that recurs constantly throughout history. It appears whenever creative fantasy is expressed freely.

"After the Nekyia he recorded his innermost findings about his ex-periences here," Fred said. "The book's never been shared with biog-raphers—it could too easily be misunderstood by the masses. Gnostic texts such as these are like mandalas, wheels within wheels. But I have a feeling you would find it enlightening." He made a flipping gesture—go on, go on—and I started turning over pages, just humoring him.

"The problem of possession concerned him from the beginning," Fred said. "In 1895 he attended a séance in which his thirteen-year-old cousin Helly was controlled by the spirit of their mutual grand-father, Samuel Preiswerk—the first of many possessions. Later the doctor learned to call down personalities himself, exercising what he called the 'transcendent function.' However, soon after he began to fear that these archetypes, these 'invisible persons,' would overwhelm him, and he engaged in elaborate rituals to ward them off. He spent days building miniature villages of stone and sand, peopling them with tiny figures, token humans to attract the spirits. And then he destroyed the figures in a symbolic sacrifice."

I looked up from the book. "And did it work?"

He shrugged. "Evidently."

"So what do you want me to do? Buy some Legos?"

He laughed. "It might not hurt. But we've found that it usually helps just to talk."

"Talk," I said skeptically.

"Others have come to us in worse shape. You'd be surprised."

"Like O'Connell?"

"Siobhan was only eleven when she came to us. She'd been possessed many, many times. The damage . . ." He shook his head. "In some ways the Hellion and the Little Angel are the cruelest of the demons, because they go after the children. But I think we were able to help."

"Why'd she become a priest then, and not a shrink?"

"I think she found our methods a bit slow, and . . . indirect. We're scientists. The church promised, Whoosh!" He shook a hand at me. "Get thee behind me! Boogedy-boogedy." He laughed again. "It doesn't work, but it's quick. All we could offer was the promise of years of research."

"Sure," I said, thinking, *Years?* I didn't have time for these people either. "Listen, thank you for showing me, well, all this. But I need to get back to bed." I walked toward the door, making sure to angle around the wheelchair.

As I reached the door the old man called out, "Mr. Pierce."

"Yes?"

"Siobhan told us you suspect that the barriers between you and your demon are crumbling. Your memories are bleeding over."

I laughed, embarrassed. "I wasn't in the best shape last night. I probably said a lot of things that didn't make sense. I'm just a little stressed out."

"For good reason."

O'Connell must have told them everything—the jump into Lew, the memories I shouldn't have, the wolf-out sessions. My growing fear that the Hellion was knocking down the walls that kept us apart.

I ran a hand back through my hair. "Did Jung really paint that thing?"

He nodded.

"Okay." I turned away from him, took a breath, held it. Some destabilizing emotion threatened to wash me away. Fear, or maybe relief. I exhaled. "Okay."

"Ah," the old man said. "You thought you were the only one who'd seen it."

"Let your arms rest at your sides," Dr. Waldheim said. "Let your shoulders relax. Good. Now relax the muscles of your jaw, your forehead . . . Good."

The Other Dr. Waldheim said nothing, but nodded encouragingly. The wheelchair was parked next to him, and beside that was the tripod holding the tiny digital video camera. They'd asked me if I minded recording the session, and it was fine with me; I was interested to see what I looked like under hypnosis.

I had no trouble relaxing—I was dead tired. It had taken me forever to fall asleep last night. O'Connell had finally woken me at noon, fed me take-out deli sandwiches, and led me back to the library, where she left me in the care of the Waldheims. The drapes had been pushed back, and bright lozenges of sunlight warmed the floors. Meg Waldheim's voice was low and rhythmic, almost a murmur.

"You're not going to lose control, Del. You're not going to hurt anyone. You can come back any time. Do you understand?"

I said, "Sure." At least I think I did. I may have only nodded.

Dr. Waldheim said, "All right, Del. Let us talk to the Hellion."

The doctor, it turned out, was wrong about several things.

The next time I opened my eyes—when did I close my eyes?—I was wedged into a corner of the room, the edge of a bookshelf sharp against the back of my head, and books heavy on my chest and shoulders, spilled around and under my arms . . . and the Waldheims were staring down at me with frozen faces. For a long moment I couldn't make sense of their expressions. Shock, that was clear enough. And sadness. But there was something else there—something deeper than sadness.

Grief.

12

O'Connell brought me meals as regular as a jailer, and took away trays almost always as full as they'd come in. It wasn't that I was on a hunger strike, or that I was trying to prove some point. I just wasn't interested in food. O'Connell would chat me up, trying to get me to tell her what I was thinking. Meg Waldheim stopped by a couple times too. I found that if I ignored them, they eventually went away.

On the morning of the third day O'Connell came to my room, but there was no breakfast tray. She was dressed in full Kabuki priest mode, her pale face floating like a moon over the expanse of black cassock. She leaned against the writing desk, blocking my view of the Waldheims' laptop. "Enough of this," she said, and yanked the electric cord from the wall. When the video continued to play on-screen—the laptop had a battery—O'Connell slammed down the lid. "Time to get out of bed."

"I was watching that," I said sulkily.

"Really?" she said. This was sarcasm. I'd been watching the loop of four-minute video pretty much nonstop for the past few days. I knew this was pathological behavior, Howard Hughes–quality OCD. However, my interest in sanity had gone the way of my appetite.

"Get up, Mr. Pierce." That killed me: *Mr. Pierce.* "It's time to take a shower, change your clothes, and leave your little spider hole."

"Could you turn the laptop back on, please?"

She made a noise that was something between a growl and a stifled scream and shoved the laptop off the desk. It hit the floor with a terrible crack.

"That was Fred's," I said. It was only an old Compaq, but still.

"Get your arse out of bed, Del. Now."

I closed my eyes. I didn't have the energy to fight with her. Maybe later I could leave her a note: *Dear Pastor, You're fired.*

She yanked the covers off my bed. "You have forty-five minutes to get ready, Mr. Pierce."

"What happens in forty-five minutes?"

"That's when your mother is expecting your call."

This got one eye open. "What? I can't do that. Not right now. Listen, just tell her I'll call in a couple days."

"She said that unless she talks to you herself, *today*, she'll assume you've been abducted and contact the police. Which is ludicrous, of course." She pursed her lips. O'Connell may have thought she was a tough Irish girl, but she'd never gone toe-to-toe with the Cyclops. "She may be serious, however, and we can't afford more legal trouble."

"She's serious all right," I said. I put my arm over my eyes. "Listen, just bring me the phone. I don't need to take a shower to—"

She gripped my shirt and hauled me to a sitting position. "Mr. Pierce . . ." She stepped back, pulling me off the bed. I would have crashed onto the floor but just barely got my legs under me. Which was how she tricked me into standing.

". . . you've begun to *turn.*"

Her fists were still bunched in my shirt, ready to haul me into the shower like a drunk.

"All right," I said. "Fine. You want to give me a little privacy?"

She cocked an eyebrow, clearly not trusting me.

"Suit yourself," I said, and pulled up my T-shirt, which got her to release her grip. She watched me until the shirt was off and I reached for the waistband of my running shorts.

She turned and walked to the door. "I want to hear running water in thirty seconds," she said, and closed the door behind her.

I sighed, went to the bathroom. The tile was cold on my bare feet. I crossed the small space and twisted the lock on the door that led to her bedroom.

The bathtub was a decent old-fashioned kind, sliding glass doors and two sprocket knobs, none of this single-handle hardware that made it impossible to set the water temperature. When it was hot, I pulled up on the plunger, and the spray drummed the bottom of the tub.

I walked back into my bedroom and shut the bathroom door behind me.

I carried the laptop back to the bed, set it on my knee. The lid crackled as I opened it. I rebooted, and while the rest of the screen seemed okay, the lower left section had turned black. Windows finished loading, though, and in a minute I had the video running again.

The subject sits on the couch. His arms are at his sides, forgotten. The camera is to his right, but he's gazing straight ahead of him. He's wearing blue jeans, a gray John Hersey High School sweatshirt unraveling at the cuffs, a blue T-shirt visible at the neck. His smile is slightly self-conscious. He needs a shave and his hair's a little too long; the back of his head is roostering where he's slept on it.

Meg Waldheim's voice, off camera: Let your shoulders relax. Good.

She continues to speak, and the subject does seem to relax. The smile fades. His expression grows distant, as if he's listening to soothing music.

Meg Waldheim says, All right, Del. Let us talk to the Hellion.

The subject doesn't change expression. He gazes straight ahead, as if considering their request.

And then he lurches forward, throwing himself off the couch. He's on all fours, his chest heaving, as if he's gasping for air.

The side of Meg Waldheim's head appears in the frame; she's leaning forward. Tell us your name, she says.

The subject looks up at her. His eyes are wide in animal terror. He doesn't recognize them.

Tell us your name, she says again.

The subject screams. The sound is raw, unmodulated. He scrambles away from her. Only his leg is visible now. And then he's up, back in the frame, running and half stumbling for one of the outcroppings of wall. Suddenly he drops out of sight of the camera.

A dark blur as Fred Waldheim crosses in front of the camera. A moment later he's back in view on the other side of the couch, moving deliberately to where the subject is, somewhere on the floor. He says something the camera doesn't pick up. He raises one arm, and says louder, There there, we aren't going to hurt you.

The subject screams, and this time he's screaming a word at the top of his lungs, the same word over and over: Mahhhhhm! Mahhhhhm! Mahhhhhm!

Meg Waldheim, still off-camera, says again, What is your name?

This part of the video annoyed me. They must have realized his name by then—how much more obvious could he be?

"Del," I said to the screen. "His name is Del."

Over the past few days, whenever I'd grown tired of watching the laptop, or staring at the water-stain heart on my wall, or trying to sleep, I'd spent a few hours composing pages for a mental scrapbook called Things I Shouldn't Remember. Alongside "Lew reads Del *The Flash*" and "Mom Reads Del *Mike Mulligan and His Steam Shovel*" was a jumbled collage of a page called "My First Exorcism."

First the hands: touching my head, my shoulders, my legs, trying to soothe me but hold me down, too, to stop me from bucking and twisting out of their grip. A circle of faces around the bed, all men, and my father among them, calling my name. And through it all the preacher's voice, rising and falling, rising and falling. In that moment my mouth is open and my chest is full, ready to scream or laugh.

That was it. A fragment, a leftover, like a dusty playing piece from a lost board game. It wasn't something I'd *suppressed*. It was just that I hadn't *recalled* it lately.

Because this wasn't the first time I'd remembered the exorcism. Every once in a while when I was a kid I'd stumble across the image in my brain—those disembodied hands, those floating faces—and then, unable to make anything of it, let it fall back into my mental toy box. I didn't even know anymore if I was recalling the original event or the memory of a memory, a distorted and embroidered version fed by the fears of a kid growing up in a religion-charged family. The scene had a lurid quality that suggested it'd been lifted from one of those hellfire-and-brimstone evangelistic comic books Lew brought home from Vacation Bible School. It was easy to convince myself I'd made it up. Easier to let it sit in a box, unlooked-for.

Until now. Now I didn't have any choice but to abandon amnesia. Anamnesis, baby.

All clear?

Yeah, me too. Me the fuck too.

The first thing I said to her was, "How's Lew?" I wanted to know, but I also wanted to short-circuit any talk about me. It was a tactic I'd used to great effect during long-distance calls from the psych ward.

"He's doing better," Mom said. She told me about blood tests, ACE inhibitors, the *real* cardiologists he'd be seeing as soon as they got back to Chicago. But as soon as she'd run through the headlines in Lew's recovery, she was back on me. "Where are you? What are you doing with that woman?"

"That woman" was twenty feet away, a stack of folders and thick books the size of photo albums in her arms. She'd been ferrying them into the dining room while Dr. Waldheim sorted them into piles on the long table, and the Other Dr. Waldheim sat at the table studying the screen of a laptop newer and thinner than the one O'Connell had broken. The empty wheelchair took up the spot next to him. O'Connell set down her load and glanced up at me. I stepped out of the archway, out of her line of sight, and leaned against the stainless steel face of the refrigerator.

It took me many minutes to explain to Mom that I'd left of my own free will, that I was working out things with these new therapists O'Connell knew, that I was *fine*. It was clear that she didn't believe me. Or if she believed me, she didn't understand. How could I sneak out of the hospital when I was still hurt? How could I leave Lew alone like that?

"So when are they letting him out?" I said. A second distraction attempt.

"He's going to be released tomorrow. We're going to start driving back in the afternoon. But if you come back, we'll wait for you. We have both cars."

"Mom, I wish I could, but I can't right now."

"Del, you're only getting deeper in trouble." Her voice shook, and I realized it had been years—maybe as far back as my pool accident in high school—since I'd heard her sound so sad, so truly dismayed. "The police want to talk to you about that doctor who died downtown. And the people you've been seeing—this Bertram person won't stop visiting Lew, and that old woman at the motel. There are things they're not saying, Del. It's not just me, Amra thinks so too. And this woman you left with—she's a priest?"

I started to answer and she interrupted me. "Del, you need to be careful. These people will tell you they have all the answers. They'll make all kinds of promises. But they can't help you. Come home, talk to someone objective, someone we trust. I'll call Dr. Aaron. I'm sure she can—"

"I'm sorry, Mom. I can't."

She kept talking. All I could do was repeat that I was sorry, that I couldn't come back home, that she shouldn't worry about me. I couldn't tell her that she was talking to an imposter.

"Take care of Lew," I said. "I'll call again as soon as I can."

I hung up the phone. Braced myself against the stove, leaning over the cold cast-iron burners. Breathing. Still fucking breathing.

O'Connell moved into my peripheral vision. After a while she said, "We have some things we'd like you to look at."

"Sure," I said. "Why not?"

Meg and Fred Waldheim looked up as I came in, seemed to study me as I sat opposite the wheelchair. I had to give them this much: they didn't look afraid. Fred seemed positively fascinated, like a bomb-sniffing dog nosing a dubious suitcase.

Meg said, "You must be struggling to come to terms with the situation."

I picked up one of the books. *Smokestack Johnny Routes, 1946–1986.* "What situation is that, exactly?" I said.

Fred nodded, as if I'd made an excellent point. "We only saw what happened during the session, what you saw on the video," he said. His beard obscured his mouth so that it was hard to tell when his lips were moving. Maybe it was a ventriloquist act, and I was supposed to play along and talk to the wheelchair. "We can make guesses, but no one can tell us what it means but you."

"Bullshit. We all know what's going on."

"Why don't you tell us?" Meg said. Soft, comforting Meg.

I shook my head. They might be grand wizards of an elite Gnostic/Jungian secret society, but they sounded like every psychiatrist I'd ever met.

"All right then, let me explain it to you. I'm a fucking *demon*, okay?" Meg blinked, but didn't interrupt me. "Something happened when I was—when *Del* was five. The Hellion took him, but it didn't let go. He stayed. He went native."

I was crying again, dammit. I never had controlled everything about this body. Not the way I'd controlled Lew.

I wiped a hand across my eyes. "Hey, what do they call it when the hostage falls in love with his captors? The Patty Hearst thing."

"Stockholm syndrome," Fred said.

"That's it. That's what happened to me. I fell in love with the people who strapped me to that bed. Lew, my dad, my mom—" *My mom.* I couldn't get my grammar straight. *My* dad. *My* mom. *My* life. A problem with possessives.

"But here's the kicker," I said. "I used to think, hey, if things get really bad, at least I have suicide as an exit strategy. But now—" I started to laugh. "Now I don't even know how to kill myself."

O'Connell put a hand on my arm. "Del . . ."

"Don't *touch* me," I said, and yanked my arm away from her. The three of them looked at me in shock.

I sighed. Nodded toward the stacks of folders.

"So what's the deal?" I said. "You guys have something in your X-files that'll help me with that?"

The Other Dr. Waldheim shrugged. "You never know."

The Red Book files contained the details of every possession since 1895—and it eventually became clear to me that they wanted me to look at every damn one of them. And comment. About what? Anything that came to mind. They were big into free association.

"Synchronicity," Fred kept saying. "Everything's connected." Meg Waldheim kept a tape recorder rolling at all times.

We worked past supper the first night, then picked up again at breakfast. The Waldheims tag-teamed their way through lectures on the epidemiology of possession. Jungians saw evidence that archetypes had been seizing human minds since prehistory. In America demon sightings had been recorded since the Pilgrims, but most scholars pegged the start of the modern possession epidemic at the first publicized appearance of the Captain on July 12, 1944. The Truth and the Kamikaze came soon after. By 1949, the Hellion, Smokestack Johnny, the Painter, the Little Angel, and an infrequently seen demon called the Boy Marvel had all taken victims, though the exact dates of their first appearances were in dispute.

"How about this one?" O'Connell said. She kept coming back to a particular stack of pictures, like a cop pressing mug shots into my hands. Except these were all pictures of the victims.

"No," I said for the hundredth time. I had my own favorite pictures, from an overstuffed folder called *Nixon's War on Possession:* clinical shots from the fifties and sixties of dark-suited "psychics" wired up to refrigerator-sized boxes; bare-chested Japanese men—God help the Japanese after Eisenhower—surrounded by pentagrams, a Tesla coil at each point in the star; dog-collared priests holding jumper cables to steel mesh satellite dishes. If Nixon's Secret Service guys hadn't taken their boss out in '74 he'd probably still be president and the internment camps would still be open.

O'Connell held up a black-and-white photo. It looked as if it had been taken in the fifties. "You're hardly looking. Are you sure he's not familiar?"

The problem was that they were all familiar. A parade of boys with sharp noses and mischievous smiles and blond, cowlicked hair.

"I told you," I said. "I don't remember being any of these kids."

"Give it time, Del," Fred said. They all still called me Del.

"Your conscious mind is only one part of the psyche," Meg said, picking up the attack. "That conscious shard is constrained by space and time, but the rest of the psyche—"

"I know, I know, the rest has its tail in the collective unconscious."

God was I tired of talking about the collective unconscious. Talking about it, reading about it, dreaming about it. O'Connell and Meg Waldheim pushed books into my hands like missionaries.

Jungians described the CU as a kind of aboriginal dreamtime tarted up with quantum mechanical theory—a late ornamentation, after Wolfgang Pauli became one of Jung's patients. This vast reservoir of human thought was a primordial soup that gave birth to the archetypes—which were either just patterns or objectively real independent personalities, depending on which of Jung's books you were reading, and who his audience was at the time. Jung seized upon demons and possession as confirmation of his ideas, and his public pronouncements began to match his private beliefs. Ghosts entangled themselves in the nervous systems of the living; telepathy and precognition worked by virtue of the trans-spatial, faster-than-light medium of the collective unconscious; archetypes stalked the Earth.

"Look," I said. "What if there is no connecting medium? What if the demons have nothing to do with archetypes?" I pushed away from the table. We'd been camped out in the dining room all this time, because that's where the files were. "The philosophizing angels and snake women Jung saw don't have much in common with American demons. How many gun-toting vigilantes did Jung meet when he was touring the underworld?"

"Now you're just being difficult," O'Connell said.

"The archetypes don't change," Meg said, voice even as always. "But their expression at any given time is filtered through culture. The Truth is an imago of the father, the destroyer and protector, like Shiva and Abraxas. The Captain is our Siegfried, the eternal hero. And the Piper, obviously, is just an aspect of the Trickster."

"There are no new ideas," Fred said from behind his book. "There's only repackaging."

"What about Valis?" I said.

"A purely rational being, absent of emotion," Meg said. "The representation of thought itself, dressed in technological garb."

"You said Valis was a fake," I said to O'Connell.

"He is. Dick made him up—writers do that."

"Maybe he did make him up, but that doesn't mean he isn't a demon. Maybe he'll disappear when Dick dies—kill the author, kill the demon."

"You can't kill an archetype," Fred said.

I stood up. "You know what? I don't feel like a fucking archetype." I walked around the end of the table and pulled out the wheelchair. Fred looked up from his book with alarm.

"I don't know what the hell I am," I said. "But I know one thing. I don't belong here." O'Connell tried to interrupt, but I cut her off. "Here. In this body." I gripped the edge of the wheelchair, rolled it into me. "It's not mine. There's a kid who got it taken away from him. So." I pushed the chair forward again, pulled it back. I couldn't look at their faces. "So why don't we do something useful and find me a body. My own goat. Maybe a murderer or something, somebody who doesn't deserve their skin anymore." I looked up. "How about that? Got any serial killers in those files?"

"This isn't all about you and the boy," O'Connell said.

"*No?* Who the hell is it about then?"

She gestured at the fan of pictures on the table. "Those kids. Toby. Dr. Ram. Everybody who's been possessed, everybody who's had their lives ruined by the demons."

"You mean *you.*"

"Yes, me too!" She was on her feet now, her pale skin flushed. "And your brother, and your mother, and everyone who's ever—"

Meg said, "Siobhan, please . . ."

O'Connell stalked toward me. "We have a chance here—maybe the first real chance we've ever had. You're one of them, Del. What they know, you know. We can find out how the demons do what they do; we can find out how to turn you—"

She shut her mouth.

I raised my eyebrows. "You were about to say, turn me *off.*"

The Waldheims watched us. No one said anything.

"Okay." I nodded, ran a hand through my hair. "I can get behind that. That's what I want too. Tell me how."

O'Connell and Fred exchanged a look.

"You already have a plan," I said.

"We think you should try to jump again," O'Connell said.

"What—now?"

"If you're ever going to leave your current body, you're going to have to practice," she said. "Better to do it into the body of a volunteer, in a controlled environment surrounded by people who could take care of the boy."

"Who's the volunteer? You?"

O'Connell seemed embarrassed at this. Meg looked away. Then the Other Dr. Waldheim raised his hand.

"*Fred?!*"

My head swiveled between the old man and the women. "Are you all crazy? O'Connell, you saw what happened last time—I almost killed my brother. There's no telling what I would do to, to—"

"An old fart," Fred said agreeably. He laid his book on the table.

"I don't think the plan is perfect either," Meg said. "But we can't bring others into this."

"I've been possessed before," Fred said.

"How long ago?" I said.

"We don't think you'd repeat the mistakes of your first time," O'Connell said. "That was a dire situation—you were drowning, and you panicked. This time . . ."

"No. We find another way. We—" I stared at the open page of the book Fred had put down. "What is that?" I said.

"Painter artifacts," Fred said. "From 1985 to 1992."

"No, that picture." I picked up the binder, looked at the photograph in its plastic sleeve. A drawing had been scratched and scraped with coal or black dirt, onto a slab of concrete that could have been a section of highway. The drawing was hardly more than an outline, a fuzzed sketch of a woman.

She leaned into the corner of an armchair. Her hair had fallen across her face, hiding one eye. The other eye was closed. Her lips were slightly parted. A book lay splayed open on the floor, as if it had slipped from her fingers. It was a picture book: a few smudges suggested paragraphs; faint lines hinted at a brontosaurus neck, a boxy head, tractor-tread feet. *Mike Mulligan and His Steam Shovel.*

There weren't any distinguishing details that would allow a stranger to match the woman in the picture to a real person. But the way her hair fell across her face, the way her legs were tucked under the chair . . .

"I need to borrow this," I said. I nodded toward the stack of albums. "I need all of them."

An hour in, I realized my project required more space, and I moved from my bedroom to the library. Under the gaze of the Black Well painting I laid out the piles of plastic-wrapped pictures into clusters and series, setting out trails of stepping stones that ran in and out of the niches, around the furniture, turning the room into a giant game board. The chronology of the pictures' creation had nothing to do with my organizational scheme, and neither did geography. Or style and material, for that matter: the same subject could be tackled in sculptures, chalk drawings, paintings, collages. The demon's name was the Painter, but that was a misnomer.

I crouched over the smallest series, only three pictures. The first was the sketch of my mother—Del's mother. The label on the back of its cover sheet said it had been created in Moab, Utah, on September 8, 1991. Next to it, from two years earlier and several states away, a sculpture made out of wood and bits of tin and barbed wire that somehow looked like a young, chubby Lew. Last, a smear of yellow and green paint created in Hammond, Indiana, 2001 that I recognized as my father's 1966 Mustang gleaming in the driveway. None of them created anywhere near the times they depicted—Lew was a high schooler by '89, my mother sold my father's Mustang when he died in '95—but that seemed to be the point. These weren't snapshots from a moment in time. None of them were *photorealistic*. These were interpretations, images fished from my memory, distorted and glossed by emotion.

"Are you finding what you need?" a soft voice said behind me. Meg had appeared in the room, silent as a cat.

"I don't know," I said. I looked at my watch—already past 1 a.m. I should probably be in bed, but I wasn't tired. This body was just a vehicle. I could drive it as fast as I wanted until the gas ran out. "I feel like there's gotta be some kind of message here."

"You aren't the first to be fascinated by the Painter's work," Meg said. "Most of the originals are in the hands of private collectors, though Red Book has tried to acquire as many as possible. Everyone is searching for clues in them—the government, academics, hundreds of hobbyists on the Internet. A theory for everyone, and everyone with a theory."

I had suspected as much at IPOC—all those academics were the tip of the iceberg.

"The Boy on the Rock, for example." She stooped, picked up a picture from one of the trails I'd laid, and showed it to me.

I'd found a dozen pictures of a kid maybe eleven or twelve, at a stream. Sometimes he sat with his arms around his knees, sometimes standing, about to dive, sometimes climbing up onto a boulder, a towel draped across his back. I'd first seen one of the pictures in the ICOP slideshow.

The kid wasn't me, wasn't Lew, didn't seem to be any of the Hellion victims. I didn't know what to make of him, but he seemed important to the Painter.

"He's got the most regular features of any of the subjects," Meg said. "Everyone's tried to identify him, match him to a photo of somebody real. The government interviewed thousands of people back in the seventies. Lots of near misses—you can find plenty of fresh-faced boys, and even plenty in bathing suits—but no hundred-percent matches. Still, there are theories. It's a self-portrait of the original Painter. Or he's the Painter's son. Or he's the archetype of innocence, a cherub. Or he's not even been born yet; he's the one the Painter is waiting for."

"To do what?"

She shrugged, smiled. "You know how it is with messiah stories." She set the picture down again and grunted as she stood up.

"So I'm wasting my time here," I said.

She shook her head. "Oh no. None of us have ever had your resources. No one's been able to ask a demon what they mean. The Painter is always silent."

Meg came to the source pile, the clump of pictures I couldn't sort. I kept returning to the pictures, sifting through them, waiting for the moment that something resonated, some synapse fired—and then I'd carry the picture to another part of the room. She frowned at the pile—perhaps thinking of all the work of putting these back in their binders—and moved on, her eyes following the horizontal exhibition on the floor.

"How is the boy?" Meg said casually. She didn't mean the boy on the rock. "Do you still feel him straining to get out?" They couldn't call him the Hellion anymore, and they wouldn't stop calling me Del. So the person in my head was like an unnamed fetus: *the boy*, or just *he, him.*

"Quiet," I said. He'd been silent and unmoving since the hypnosis session. I didn't think time passed in there. He wasn't conscious, stalking his cage and scheming his escape. He was like a fitful sleeper, and sometimes when his nightmares came on strong, or there was light coming into the cage from some hole I'd opened up, that's when he got agitated. Since my car accident I'd been leaving the cage door open at night, and I hadn't even known it.

After the session with the Waldheims, though, I had slammed the doors and tripled the locks. I clamped down on him as tightly as I had in those years when I thought he'd vanished—the years between Dr. Aaron's "cure" and my plunge through the guardrail in Colorado. Now that I knew what I was doing, maybe I could hold him down for years. Maybe I could throw him so deep in the dungeon that he'd never come back up.

All I'd have to do then was live with *myself.*

"What's the theory on the farmhouses?" I asked. I stood and led her to the twenty or so pictures. I picked up the most recent one. "This one I saw the Painter do at O'Hare Airport a couple weeks ago." No, less than that—today was Tuesday. I'd arrived in Chicago ten days ago.

The police or maybe a reporter had gotten an overhead picture of the popcorn–and-litter collage: the quaint clapboard house, the red silo and barn, the tree-edged fields. I was struck by the same sense of familiarity that I'd felt at the airport, but it wasn't as strong as the pictures of Lew or Mom. It wasn't anyplace I'd lived.

"Have you wondered about the smudge?" she said. She pointed to the dark blur in the sky above the house. At O'Hare the Painter had created it by scraping the heel of his shoe across the tile. "It's in all the pictures."

"It is?" I picked up another one of the series, then another. Each picture showed the same farm, but in winter, in summer, at night. And she was right—the smudge was always there. In the nighttime pictures it was a faint glow.

"We could call in our experts to help you," Meg said. "We didn't want to bring anyone in until you were comfortable, but perhaps—"

"No. No more people."

Meg frowned slightly. Of course they wanted to call in their experts. The entire secret society would be in a lather to meet me.

"Promise me," I said.

She touched my shoulder. "No one else. I promise."

I moved away from her, my neck hot, and bent to pick up another picture. "About this smudge," I said without looking at her. "What are the theories on that one?"

"It's never distinct enough to be a signature," Meg said, easing gracefully back into scholar mode. "But it's always there. It could be a bird, but because it also shows up at night, most people think it's a plane . . ."

"Holy shit," I said.

I stared at her. "I know where I've seen this," I said. I scooped up several of the plastic-coated pictures and started for the library door.

"What is it?" Meg asked.

"There's something I need from my mom's—from her basement." I had to wake O'Connell. If she wouldn't go with me I'd just take the keys to her truck. "I've got to get to Chicago."

DEMONOLOGY

THE KAMIKAZE

OUTSIDE DENVER, COLORADO, 1955

A plane roared up from behind them, so low it blew off the president's ball cap. Eisenhower was in midswing. He sliced badly, sending the ball into the trees, and jerked his head up to stare at the underbelly of the aircraft. He could make out rivets.

The plane zoomed away, disappeared over the next hill. The president cursed, something he rarely did. He turned to his golfing partner that day, George E. Allen, and said, "What the hell do those boys think they're doing?"

"Those boys" referred to the pilots of nearby Lowry Air Force Base, where Eisenhower kept his summer White House. Planes were frequently overhead, but they'd never buzzed the golf course.

Allen laughed. "You ought to say something to their commander-in-chief." Even though Allen was a former secretary of the Democratic National Committee and an advisor to Truman, the two men rarely talked politics. Eisenhower valued their friendship, as well as the fact that Allen's handicap was larger than Eisenhower's fourteen.

The president placed another ball on the tee, and grunted as he stood up. The eighth tee box was on a slight rise, and he had a clear view of the green. He leaned on his club and mopped his forehead with a handkerchief. It was unusually hot for late September, almost tropical. In a few days they'd have to go back to Washington, back to the political swamp. The Republicans had taken a beating in the off-year elections a year ago, and his own reelection campaign was about to begin. He'd have to figure out what to do with Nixon. His staff wanted the man off the ticket.

The drone of the plane grew louder again. Allen and Eisenhower looked around, saw the plane circling back, banking around to their left. They could see its glass canopy, the tops of its wings. The plane was just a Beechcraft trainer, but the air force seals had been overpainted with large red circles. Eisenhower squinted, said, "George, is there a man on that thing?"

A figure in red clung to the outside of the plane's canopy. A white cape, perhaps a shredded parachute, rippled behind him. One hand seemed to be flailing at the glass that covered the pilot.

The two secret service agents who'd been trailing the president ran up the hill toward them. One of them said, "Mr. President—," and grabbed Eisenhower's arm.

The plane came out of its turn. It wobbled, then straightened, the nose aiming down at them. Eisenhower could see the pilot's face—he wore a white scarf around his forehead—and the face of the daredevil riding the plane's back. The glass canopy had shattered, and the red-clad man was reaching down into the cockpit.

The agents hauled Eisenhower and Allen backward and pushed them down the hill. Eisenhower ran several steps and suddenly fell to his knees. One of the agents pulled the president to his feet. The plane struck a moment later.

The next morning, Vice President Richard Nixon came across a short item in the paper noting that the president had suffered an attack of indigestion. Nixon turned the page without thinking much about it; Eisenhower was prone to that sort of thing. It wasn't until Sherman Adams, the assistant to the president and White House chief of staff, called an hour later that Nixon realized the seriousness of the situation.

"There's been an accident," Adams said. "The president's had a coronary."

Five minutes later Nixon entered a basement room of the White House already crowded with staff: Jim Hagerty, Len Hall, Jerry Persons, the Dulles brothers, and several men he didn't recognize. It was clear that they'd been talking for some time, perhaps hours.

Adams pulled Nixon aside and said, "Dick, you may be president within the hour."

The chief of staff told Nixon what they knew: a plane crash, a dead secret service agent, another badly burned. Eisenhower had been struck by shrapnel and suffered a heart attack sometime after the crash. He'd lapsed into unconsciousness soon after reaching the hospital. George Allen was wounded but in good condition. Allen confirmed that the plane had dived for them, and that they'd been saved by a "daredevil" clinging to the plane. "If he hadn't made that kamikaze hit that hill we'd be dead," he said.

Nixon scowled. "What daredevil? What do you mean, 'kamikaze'?"

The men in the room turned to the Dulles brothers. Allen, director of the recently created Central Intelligence Agency, handed a folder to his brother, John Foster Dulles, the secretary of state. "The plane was one of ours, stolen from Lowry Air Force Base," Foster said. "But it was painted like a Japanese Zero."

Nixon frowned but said nothing.

"The pilot was Lawrence Hideki, an Air Force helicopter mechanic of Japanese descent. The 'daredevil' is unknown at the moment—perhaps he was another airman on base. We're checking to see if Hideki was troubled by psychological problems, or if he had any links to Japanese extremist groups. But frankly, we don't expect to find anything along those lines."

Again Nixon said nothing.

"This is not the first such attack on American soil," Foster said. "Yesterday Allen ordered a search for similar cases." He laid out several folders, and briefly described three previous attacks: May 1947, a Japanese man dressed as a kamikaze pilot stole a crop-duster plane in Kansas and crashed it an hour later, killing eight people attending a farm auction. July, 1949, a plane painted like a Zero crashed into the side of the USS *Cun-*

ningham in San Diego, killing eighteen sailors. And in 1953, a second-generation Japanese sailor working on the aircraft carrier *Antietam* tried to hijack a fighter plane but was stopped before he could take off.

"There may be more," Foster said, almost apologetically. "We're pulling records of all plane crashes and hijackings right now."

The room was quiet for a long moment. Finally Nixon spoke: "Did the president know about these attacks?"

Allen Dulles stepped forward. "You have to understand, Mr. Vice President, nobody thought these events were related. In each of these cases, the pilots were men with no criminal record, no history of mental illness, and no obvious links to Japanese nationals. We had a handful of coincidences, nothing that rose to a level worth the president's attention."

"Let me see the folders," Nixon said.

Word came of Eisenhower's death at 8:00 p.m. A short time later, Nixon was brought into an adjacent room where several people waited: his wife, Pat; his secretary, Rose Mary Woods; Nelson Pym, a staff photographer; and Justice Hugo Black. Pat had brought the Milhous family Bible from their apartment. In the official photo, Nixon is listening to the justice, his expression tight-lipped and grim.

After taking the oath of office, Nixon hugged his wife and returned to the briefing room. He didn't have to call for attention; the atmosphere had already changed.

President Nixon stood silently for a long time, arms folded tightly across his chest, staring at the table. When he spoke, he didn't look up.

"I'm no general," he said quietly. "I can't be the kind of leader President Eisenhower was."

Sherman Adams looked at Jim Hagerty with a worried expression. No one needed to tell them that Nixon was no Ike.

"But I know conspiracies," Nixon said. "I understand how the Japanese, a defeated people, may turn desperate. How even the most innocent-seeming of men can be secretly plotting the destruction of the nation." He didn't have to explain: Nixon was the man who had brought down Alger Hiss, the man who'd held the reins of the Un-American Activities Committee. "This is a new kind of war, a new enemy, whose weapon is fear."

Nixon looked up, into the faces of men who'd been plotting his political death a day before. He showed his teeth, a twitch of a smile. Some of the men looked away uncomfortably.

"I promise you," Nixon said. "We will root out this new enemy, wherever he is among us."

13

"Let's swing by again," O'Connell said.

"It's not even been ten minutes," I said. "We can't do it too often, you know that."

We were parked in front of the Jewel grocery not a quarter mile from my mother's house. I couldn't see any way to "stake out" the house from any closer than that, not without getting caught in the same way that Amra had busted Bertram and the Human Leaguers. My neighborhood was a triangular clump of houses bounded by three very busy streets, the houses with their backs turned resolutely to the traffic. One road ran through the development, a wobbly horseshoe infested with cul-de-sacs. The place brimmed with retired people, the parents of the kids I'd grown up with. If my mom didn't notice two people hanging out in an unfamiliar pickup, one of her understimulated neighbors definitely would. Worst-case scenario: they call the cops.

So every twenty-five minutes or so we drove past my mother's house to see if her Chevy Corsica was still in the driveway, then headed back to Jewel. We'd done this since 8 a.m. and it was almost noon. Her car hadn't budged. We knew she was there, because I'd called from a pay phone and hung up when she answered. We just didn't know when she'd leave.

I'm not saying it was a particularly well-thought-out plan.

"Why don't you just walk up to the front door?" O'Connell said. "Ring the bell and say, 'Hello, Mother, I just need to look at something in the basement.' "

"I'm not going to do that. I can't just . . ." I shook my head. "I can't."

"She's still your mother, Del. She's still the same person who raised you."

But I'm not the same person she raised, I thought.

O'Connell made a disgusted noise. "I'm out of cigarettes," she said, and slammed the cab door behind her.

We were tired of driving, tired of each other.

She hadn't wanted to come to Chicago. She was sure the Waldheims could help me figure out more about my nature, about all demon nature, if only I gave them time. But I'd begged, told her I'd do it with or without her, and she'd given in surprisingly easily. Maybe she knew I needed her.

She also didn't fight me on the need to drive rather than fly. Neither of us wanted to put our names down on an airline ticket and get picked up for "questioning" as soon as we stepped off the plane.

Eighty percent of the trip retraced the route Lew and I had taken out of Chicago. O'Connell's rattling pickup was a lot slower than Lew's Audi, but at least my chin wasn't banging against my knees the whole way. We'd spent last night at a Days Inn just off the interstate— separate rooms—and had driven the rest of the way in this morning.

The number of things we didn't talk about was enormous.

O'Connell opened the truck door and dropped a *Tribune* on my lap. "Eliot Kasparian confessed," she said.

"Who?"

"Dr. Ram's killer. He admitted he made up the possession. He was fully conscious when he killed him."

I looked at the picture under the headline and recognized the face.

"Holy shit," I said. It was the Armenian kid. "I talked to this guy that night. He was at the party—a big fan of Valis'. He said Dr. Ram was trying to cut out our connection to God." I skimmed the article and found the phrase I was looking for. In his confession, Kasparian said that Ram was trying to close the "Eye of Shiva."

"He wasn't lying," I said.

"Kasparian?" She tapped a cigarette from the pack.

"Dr. Ram. He was on to something. The cure. He could have helped me."

"Somebody else, maybe," she said. "Not you." She lit the cigarette, exhaled in the direction of the half-open window, but the smoke seemed to eddy in the cab. I think I was up to a pack a day in second-hand smoke. "It's been twenty-five minutes," she said.

"Okay, fine," I said. "Go by the house again, and I'll scrunch down."

"Fine." She put the truck in reverse, turned to look over her shoulder as she started to roll, and hit the brakes. I looked up in time to see a maroon Corsica cruise by, the driver oblivious to the near crash.

"Was that . . . ?" O'Connell said.

"Yep."

"Oh my."

"Her peripheral vision's not so good on that side."

"Then I suppose we should go."

O'Connell pulled into the driveway and I hopped out. It was Thursday, and I didn't know anymore when Mom did her big shopping. She could have just been running to the store for milk. She could be back any minute.

"Keep it running," I said. I'd always wanted to say that.

I walked briskly around to the back of the house, pushed through the chain link gate that never stayed shut, and stepped up to the back door, ready at any moment for SWAT teams to burst from the bushes. How in the world did people work up the nerve to break into *strangers'* houses?

The key was under the windowsill to the right of the door, in the notch my dad had cut out for that purpose. I dropped the key, finally got it into the lock, and quietly pushed open the door.

The kitchen smelled like chocolate chip cookies. *Warm* cookies.

On the counter was a cookie rack loaded with six rows of happy, chunky mounds. Mom never made them just for herself—they were always for company, or for some special occasion. I couldn't count the number of times she'd slapped our hands away from the plate. If we begged, she'd give us one apiece—*one*—and then banish us from the kitchen.

I reached out, stopped, my hand hovering over the rack. Heat rose off them. She must have pulled them out of the oven right before leaving for the grocery store.

She wouldn't have *counted* them, would she?

I pulled back my hand. Not yet. Take one on the way out. And one for O'Connell. That would be our reward. Surely Mom wouldn't miss two.

I went down the basement steps, my hand automatically finding the lightbulb chain.

The brown box marked "DeLew Comics" was right where I remembered seeing it with Amra. The box was suspiciously light. I set it on the ground and pulled off the lid.

Inside, a thin stack of comics, maybe twenty issues, fewer than a dozen pages each of faded, 8½-by-11 sheets. I picked up the top issue. A muscular man in red-and-yellow striped spandex floated above a city street, surrounded below the waist by a massively overinked tornado. Shakily drawn cars flew through the air; bystanders cowered.

Mister Twister #2. There'd never been a #3.

I exhaled, laughed to myself. I'd been afraid the comics would be gone, evaporated like an imaginary friend. There were fewer copies than I remembered—weren't there like a hundred left over?—but at least they existed. I wanted to sit down and read them right there, but there was no time. I fit the lid back onto the box and tucked it under my arm.

I glanced around to see if there was anything else I needed, and noticed a Ziploc bag on the floor. I picked it up, realized it was the set of white plastic buildings from the game of Life. Well, what used to be Life before Lew and I chopped it up for our own game. I scanned the shelves for the Life and Death boards and noticed the piece of wood jutting from an open plastic tub.

The Hellion's slingshot. My slingshot.

I dropped the bag of playing pieces and picked up the knotty, untrimmed handle of the weapon. Before I could change my mind I tucked it into the back pocket of my jeans, grabbed the comic box, and headed upstairs.

"Del!"

"Shit!" I bobbled the box, caught it.

Bertram stood at the top of the stairs like a low-rent Caesar: the top of his bald head gleaming, a fringe of wet hair stuck out all over like a laurel crown. He wore my mother's green bathrobe, open at the chest to reveal tufts of gray hair.

"What are you doing here?" he asked.

"What am I . . . ? What are you doing in my mother's robe?" A disturbing thought crossed my mind. "You didn't . . . ?"

"Didn't what?"

He had no idea what I was talking about. "Never mind." He stepped aside to let me pass. "What are you doing in my mother's house?"

"She invited me. And wait till she gets home—she's been so worried about you. *I've* been worried about you! If there's anything I can do to help you—"

"No. The last thing I need is more of your help."

"I understand," he said. His face cinched into a deep frown, and he nodded. "You have every right to be upset. What I did was inexcusable."

I didn't have the time to work through Bertram's guilt with him. "Listen, does my mother know what happened at the lake? What really happened?"

He suddenly looked apologetic. "Possibly . . ."

"Does she know why the Human League came after me?"

"Have you ever tried to hide anything from that woman?" Bertram said. "It's like she can smell when you're not telling her something. Lew didn't even ride with her—he stayed in the car with Amra—but me, I was *trapped*! The whole trip back she was pumping me for information, and half the time I didn't even realize I'd said something I shouldn't until she gave me that *look*." He winced. "Del, you and I've both been through intense psychotherapy. We know from shrinks. But your mother, she's good."

The All-Seeing Eye of Agamoto, I thought.

"And now you're living here?" I said.

"Just for a couple days. She said I could take some time to figure out my next step."

Uh-huh. I wondered which step that would be: back to the hospital, or on to a brand-new cult.

Outside the front window the street was clear. "One thing, Bertram—you can't tell her I was here."

"Are you crazy? I just told you I can't keep anything from her! What is that you're taking?"

"Nothing, just some of my stuff. Childhood memorabilia."

"Okay, but what if she—"

"She can't read your mind," I said, exasperated. "She's not a *slan*."

He looked like he'd been slapped.

I sighed. "Listen, I'm sorry, I shouldn't have said that."

"No, *I'm* sorry," Bertram said sincerely. "I almost got you killed, and for that I'll be eternally in your debt."

"I've got to get going." I headed for the kitchen, and Bertram followed.

"I'm serious!" he said. "Anything you want me to do, I'll do it. *Anything*."

How about please don't screw my mother, I thought.

I went to the back door, turned back. "Listen, here's what you do. Lew and I used this all the time. If she gets suspicious, you admit your guilt, but for something else."

"Like what?"

"You secretly ate two—no, four cookies."

I scooped my loot from the cookie rack and made my escape.

I inhaled the first cookie before we left the driveway, and I had the comic books out of the box before we got out of the neighborhood. I absentmindedly waved O'Connell through a few rights and lefts, sending her down Euclid.

"Damn, these are good cookies," O'Connell said.

I wiped my fingers on my shirt and turned pages. I didn't find what I was looking for in the first comic, set it aside, and opened the next one.

O'Connell shook her head. "You'd better be right about this, Mr. Pierce." All this way for a comic book. For a page in a comic book.

I found it in the third issue. Olympia! "Pull over, now," I said.

"Jesus Christ," O'Connell said. She parked in back of the Steak n Shake. I handed her the comic, open to the page I'd found. "Look at that," I said.

I hopped out of the truck, went around to the bed. My duffel was under the tarp, snug under the cab window. I unzipped it, took out the topmost binder, and carried it back inside.

O'Connell was looking at the full spread across the top of page four. The comic was done in only one color, blue mimeograph lines on white paper, but the picture was clear enough, to my eyes at least. The house was there, the barn, the big silo, the line of trees—and the faint smudge over the house. Then I handed her the binder, where the same farmhouse had been drawn by the Painter.

"See?" I said. "They're the same."

"I admit they're similar," she said. "But I don't see what it tells us."

"The smudge." I pointed to the comic. The pages had been badly duplicated, but if you looked closely enough you could see lines that looked like outstretched hands, legs, the suggestion of a cape. Once you saw those features in the comic, they became more obvious in the Painter's rendition.

"See?" I said. "It's RADAR Man."

She looked back and forth between the comic book page and the plastic sheeted page from the binder. "Okay," she said. "If you say so. But once again, so what? You'd already seen that the Painter drew some of your memories. This time he remembered your comic book."

"No! Some of those pictures were drawn *before I was born*. He's not drawing my comic book—we're drawing the same place."

"That could be any farm anywhere."

"No. Not anywhere." I pointed to the little text box above the drawing in the comic book: *Meanwhile, over Olympia Kansas . . .*

"RADAR Man's hometown," I said.

O'Connell looked at me, eyes narrowed. "Is that a real town?"

"Yes. I don't know. Maybe."

She sighed. "I suppose we have to buy a map."

By eight that night we'd reached the Missouri side of Kansas City. O'Connell swung into the parking lot of a Motel 6, hit the brakes, and triggered a landslide of paper and plastic from the bench seat onto the floorboards: my comics, the binders I'd taken from the Waldheims, newspapers, two maps of the Midwest. The pickup looked like someone had emptied a file cabinet through the passenger window.

O'Connell turned off the cassette—the pickup didn't have a CD, and we'd been listening to her homemade mix-tapes since leaving Chicago—and said, "Do you have any cash?"

I opened my wallet. Inside were my last two twenties, a couple of ones, and the water-damaged Hyatt card where I'd written Tom and Selena's phone number. She took the twenties.

"Hey!"

"I'll see if this will pay for a room," she said.

I thought: A room?

I put my comics back in the box, inserted pages back in their binders. I folded the Missouri-Kansas map so that it was open to show a circled and recircled dot of a town. I still hadn't gotten over the thrill: Olympia, Kansas, was real. All we had to do was follow the yellow brick road.

O'Connell came back with a key, drove us around the side of the

building, and opened a door on the first floor. Double beds. The carpet crunched from old spills, and the air was thick with a sickeningly
sweet scent—some perfumed cleanser. I expected at any moment to
detect the horrible smell it was trying to mask.

"Oh my God," I said.

O'Connell looked annoyed. "Sleep in the truck, then."

"No, no, this is great. No fish on the door, but you can't have everything."

I dropped my duffel and the comic box onto the bed by the window, thinking I could channel a little fresh air across my face as I slept.
I tried to open the window, but it was sealed. Then again, maybe keeping the window closed on the first floor of a shady motel wasn't such a
bad idea. Only one other car in the parking lot right now, but more
people would arrive later.

"Checking to see if we were followed?" O'Connell said. "You
spent the whole trip looking out the back window, when you weren't
buried in these comics."

I turned around, and she had the box open. She picked up an issue
of *RADAR Man*, flipped it open to a random page.

"Bertram thought the demons were performing for each other," I
said. "That they were watching each other. But maybe it's worse than
that. Maybe they help each other."

O'Connell shook her head. "They're too self-involved, wrapped up
in their own stories. They don't cooperate."

"What if there was a threat to all of them? Like Dr. Ram—"

"Dr. Ram was killed because he was a threat to some fanatic's
worldview," she said without looking up. "And this—" She shook the
comic. "This makes no sense. 'Yo, *bozo boy*'?"

I walked around the side of the bed, looked over her shoulder.

It was the climactic fight scene, and my sixth-grade drawing skills
had been taxed to their limits. I'd been trying out some of those Jack
Kirby forced perspectives, and RADAR Man's fists looked as big as
cars.

"It's simple," I said. "RADAR Man, aka Robert Trebor, aka Bob,
has tracked Doctor Awkward to his lair in Bob's hometown."

"Doctor *Awkward?*"

"They're palindromes," I said. "Doctor Awkward is D-R-A-W—"

"Oh, I got it."

"Anyway, the doctor's kidnapped his girlfriend, Hannah, and made a clone of her, except that the polarity of her brain's been reversed. The clone is evil and left-handed."

"Of course."

"So the evil Hannah says, 'Yo, bozo boy! I'm alive; evil am I!' And RADAR Man says, 'Evil is a name of a foeman, as I live!' "

"Lovely dialogue," she said.

"Hey, you try to write in all palindromes. Lew had this book, *Big Book of Word Games* or something, with pages of these things. We wanted to write the whole story that way, one big continuous palindrome. That would've been the ultimate, an entire book you could read forward or backward."

"The ending is present in the beginning," she said. "As always."

"Is that like a theological insight or something?"

"The alpha and the omega," she said. "I didn't invent it." She handed me the comic and walked to her suitcase. "I'm going to take a shower."

"Oh, okay," I said nonchalantly. "I'll take one after you."

She glanced back at me with an expression I couldn't parse, then picked up a small nylon bag and carried it into the tiny room that held the shower and toilet. She closed the door behind her. After several long minutes, the water sputtered on.

I lay down on my bed and focused on the comic book page, trying to stare past the image of O'Connell, naked, face turned up to the shower head, water streaming down her neck . . .

DR. AWKWARD: *Do Good's deeds live on? No, Evil's deeds do, O God.*
RADAR MAN: *Egad, an adage! Draw, O coward!*

Which doesn't make much sense, because the doctor doesn't have a gun. RM's own RADAR gun knocks both Dr. Awkward and the evil Hannah back into one of the big funhouse mirrors the doctor keeps in his lair, shattering it. The doctor lies on the floor, stunned, shards of glass around him.

RADAR MAN: *Now I won!*
DR. AWKWARD: *Drat such custard!*

Then the big revelation: Dr. Awkward pulls down his mask, and it's Bob's own face! (As much as I could make it look like the same face. I wasn't good at faces, or consistency. My specialty was biceps and thigh muscles.)

RADAR MAN: *Is it . . . ? 'Tis I!*

The truth finally revealed: Dr. Awkward is Bob's evil clone. Or, is Bob Dr. Awkward's good clone? Tune in next month, reader!

O'Connell stepped out of the bathroom, walked toward me. The white motel towel barely reached the tops of her thighs.

She looked tiny, birdlike. Fuzzed scalp, nearly translucent ears. Her expression was grave.

I sat up. "What is it?" I said softly.

"I need to know something." She stood in front of me without moving. Her pale shoulders, still glazed by wet, had pinked under the hot shower. I glanced at the white on white swell of her breasts against the frayed cotton towel, looked away.

I could smell her. Soap, and the danker scent that slipped from between her thighs. From that shadow beneath the hem of the towel.

"I need to know if the boy is watching."

"I don't know," I said. "I don't think so." On the video he'd come awake as if he'd been jolted from a nightmare. He'd yelled for his mother like a five-year-old. "I don't think time passes there."

I lifted a hand, touched the back of her knee, still damp.

She closed her eyes. I moved my hand up, fingertips drawing a line of moisture. She gripped my forearm, stopping me. Opened her eyes again. "Please. Does he know what happens to you? Will he remember?"

"I don't know," I said. "I don't know how it all works."

She stepped back. My fingers slipped from her skin.

She turned and walked to her bed. She pulled a handful of clothes from the case and stepped back into the bathroom.

I lifted my hand, touched dewy fingers to my lips. I could smell nothing, taste nothing, but the subtle scent of her was still in my mind.

"Shit," I said quietly.

After ten or fifteen minutes she came back out, dressed in a long T-shirt and nylon running shorts. She brushed her teeth at the sink without looking in the mirror. She straightened the clothes in her suitcase, shut the lid, and set it carefully on the dresser. Then she pulled back the heavy polyester bedcover and slipped under the sheets.

She lay faceup, eyes closed.

I picked up my shaving kit and a pair of gym shorts. I turned out the light by my bed, then the overhead light, leaving only the fluorescent above the sink and the light from the bath. As I passed the foot of her bed, she said, "Don't worry about the lights."

I stopped. "Are we going to talk about this?"

"I've taken a vow of celibacy, Del." Her voice was flat. Her eyes stayed closed. "I'm your pastor. I shouldn't have done that to you. I'm sorry."

"You didn't do anything."

She didn't answer.

After my shower, I turned out all the lights, and in the dark stuffed my dirty clothes into a corner of the duffel, next to the bike chains. I left the slingshot in the back pocket of my jeans. I hadn't shown that to her, maybe afraid she'd throw it away like my father's pistol.

I lay in the dark between the scratchy sheets, listening for O'Connell's breathing. All I could hear was the thrum of trucks on the overpass.

I couldn't breathe. I couldn't move my legs.

A moment before, I'd been dreaming of water, and cold. Paralyzed, I sank through the icy dark. The Black Well filled my vision,

above me and below me at the same time, a bottomless corkscrewing
pit, a tunnel into space. I could sense something or someone waiting
for me in the tunnel—no, thousands of presences. A vast congregation.

The next moment the water vanished. My eyes were closed, or else
open but blind in the dark. My lips were covered by a hot weight, my
legs still trapped. I knew then that the water had been a memory, a
dream, but I couldn't tell if I'd woken up.

Heat against my cock. I was hard, aching. I thrust into that heat,
and my eyes opened a second time. Fully awake now. Electrically
awake.

O'Connell sat astride my hips, her lips on mine, her hands pinning
my shoulders. She was naked, the muscles of her neck limned in a
sliver of lamplight.

I tried to sit up. Her mouth released me, but she didn't look at my
face. She put a hand on my sternum and pushed me onto my back
with surprising force. I opened my mouth to speak, and she pressed a
hand against my jaw, forcing the side of my head into the mattress,
forcing me to look away from her. Her strength was fierce.

She began to grind against me. My shorts were still on, but the
bedclothes had been pushed down, trapping my ankles.

"O'Connell." I could hardly speak with her weight on my jaw. She
rocked against me and made a sound between a grunt and a sigh.
"O'Connell—"

She didn't answer. She moved again and the grunt became something like a laugh.

I screamed through gritted teeth, twisted my arm out of her grip.
Pushed her away from me, sending her tumbling off the bed.

She yelped as she hit the floor. I scrambled off the bed and turned
to face her, my back pressed against the cold door.

"What the *fuck*!" O'Connell yelled.

"Who are you?" I said.

She stared up at me—looking me in the face for the first time since
I'd woken up. In the dim light I couldn't make out her eyes.

A long moment, then she said, "Del, it's me." She scooted back until she was sitting up against the other bed, one knee drawn up. "O'Connell. *Siobhan.*" Her voice sounded the same.

"How do I know?" I said.

"You already know."

I felt for the light switch, flicked it on. She squinted against the light.

I'd known with the Shug. And I'd known that the Piper at the Hyatt was an imposter. I realized I could always tell, from the Painter possession at the airport, to the handful of other possessed people I'd seen in my life—even Valis. But O'Connell was definitely no demon.

I exhaled. Slumped to the floor. The dirty carpet crunched against my butt. "I'm sorry," I said. I ran a hand through my hair. "I thought . . . I just . . ."

She stood up, walked to me, and crouched so that her face was level with mine. Her hand moved, and I thought she was going to touch my cheek, but she only wrapped her arm around her knee. She studied my face.

"I know what you thought," she said. "I've thought the same things myself."

"What, with me?"

"With everyone. I was possessed at least fourteen times, Del. I'd wake up in a hospital room holding the face of a dead woman, knowing that my lips had just touched hers. That I'd just *murdered* her. Sometimes I lost an entire week. The years between my tenth birthday and my twelfth are riddled with holes. I learned that anyone can disappear at any moment, replaced by a monster."

"You're too old for the Little Angel now," I said. "You should be safe from her."

"Maybe from her, but not the others. I became an exorcist, didn't I? Looked too many demons in the face. Once you've been noticed, once you're familiar to them, they like to find you again. You come to understand that they can take you at any time, anyone you're close to. So. You stay on guard. You start watching for that change of expression, that alien voice."

"Well, you were acting sort of different there," I said, and laughed, then quickly cleared my throat to stop the laughter. "It's just that, there's that vow of celibacy thing."

O'Connell said nothing. I looked up, and then she laughed. Her own laugh, dry and light. "I never said I was perfect."

We locked eyes. Maybe trying to figure out if there was anybody else watching. She never looked away from me, but her expression slowly changed.

I could smell her, heady and rich.

I touched her calf, the underside of her thigh. Slid the edge of my palm into the folds of her. She was wet.

I wanted to roll her onto her back right then, but not on that awful carpet. I stood and pulled her to her feet.

I was hard again. So fast, despite all of this. The body has its own imperatives.

She touched my cock through the shorts, ran a fingernail along it, making me shiver. Then she gripped hard and stepped in close, holding me hot against her hip. She spoke softly into my ear. "I don't want you inside me," she said, almost whispering. "You have to be all right with that."

"Okay," I said, gasping. "Just . . . go easy."

14

Kansas had the purity of a sixth-grade math problem, an exercise in scale and stark geometry. I couldn't stop picturing our progress from above: the blue dot of the pickup creeping along a thin black line, bisecting a checkered expanse of barren fields regular as graph paper.

"So, this is Kansas." It was the first thing O'Connell had said since we'd started driving this morning.

"We're not in Missouri anymore," I said. She didn't get the reference.

I glanced down at the map on my lap, then back out through the dust-bright windshield, looking for a mile marker. Playing navigator. *Del led*, I thought.

Paradoxically, the extreme flatness of the terrain made me acutely aware that we were living on a big round spinning planet. Though the horizon looked as level as a windowsill, I could sense the Earth curving out of sight, the vast sky bending over us. We rode toward an immense wall of clouds, unguessable miles away.

My arm rested on the back of the seat. I leaned toward her, started to rub the back of her neck. She didn't quite flinch, but after a moment she leaned away.

"Okaaay . . . ," I said. Dropped my arm. "So what's going on. Last night—"

"Was last night," she said.

Ah.

After we made love, she rested her head on my chest and I rubbed my hand up and down her fuzzed skull. I told her I'd wanted to do that from the moment I saw her; she mock-sighed and said, "Everybody does." We fell asleep spooning like old lovers, but I woke up alone, my mouth tasting of cigarettes. O'Connell was already up, dressed, and packed. She didn't speak during breakfast except to order and to answer my questions about the route we'd take.

"Is this about your vows?" I said. Maybe she was pissed at me for leading her into temptation. Which made no sense—she was the one who'd jumped me while I was sleeping—but I knew well enough that shame and guilt didn't have much to do with logic.

"Don't be ridiculous," she said, and turned on the radio.

Ever since we'd left Kansas City we'd been unable to pick up anything on the FM dial except country, Christian, and—weirdly— seventies hard rock. She quickly switched to cassette and jammed in another of her jarring mix-tapes: Pogues followed by the Clash and Nirvana, then Joan Baez, Lead Belly, and Jan & Dean. She would have loved Lew's mash-ups.

Twenty miles and thirty minutes later the Beach Boys were doot-dooting through "Heroes and Villains" (Part 2). O'Connell turned down the volume, a lit cigarette between her fingers, and said, "I think you've misunderstood something." Her scholarly voice.

I tried to keep my expression neutral. "Yes?"

"Last night was about physical desire, Del. A collar doesn't alter your chemistry, and I haven't touched a body in six years. I shouldn't have done what I done, but neither should you construe a physical act as some kind of . . . romantic overture."

Overture? "I'm not," I said. "I didn't. I just thought that—"

"Why is it so hard for men to believe that a woman can just be horny?"

Men? Now I was *men?*

I turned away from her and stared out the passenger window, a frown holding my mouth in check. It would be a very bad time to laugh. But Jesus, what a relief! O'Connell just might be as fucked up as I was. All the things about her that kept me off balance: the costume changes from high priest to rock chick; the sudden lurches into hard Irish *aints* and *yes*; the abrupt swing from pastor to sexual aggressor and back again. She didn't know who the hell she was, kick-ass exorcist or shell-shocked possession survivor.

Maybe everyone in the world was this inconsistent, this fragmented. All we could see of each other—all we could see of ourselves—was a ragged person-shaped outline, a game of connect-the-dots without enough dots.

A sign flashed past my window. "That was our turn," I said.

She slammed on the brakes—which wasn't a problem, since the highway was empty. We'd passed maybe five cars since leaving the interstate. She made a three-point turn and rolled back to where another two-lane road met the highway.

On the green sign was a white arrow pointing down the road and the words, OLYMPIA 15 MI. Below it, a smaller sign that said HOSPITAL.

"Hospital?" O'Connell said.

I shrugged. It wasn't on the map. "Let's see."

As O'Connell drove I scanned the distant fields to either side of the road, eyes primed for a red silo, but I saw nothing but bare fields and distant clumps of trees.

The first sign of a town was a white, rusting water tower squatting near railroad tracks. The crossing was unguarded; we nosed up the rise in the road, looked left and right. One thing about Kansas at noon, we could see miles of clear track in either direction.

Low buildings rolled into sight ahead of us. We passed a handful of houses, an Exxon gas station and convenience store, a two-story brick building with AN-TI-QU-ES spelled out in peeling white paint between the upper windows—and suddenly we were at a stop sign, a four-way intersection that looked like it marked the center of town. I hadn't seen even a WELCOME TO OLYMPIA sign.

"Which way?" O'Connell said. It didn't seem to matter: left, right, and forward, the buildings petered out, giving way to open fields.

Unfortunately, nothing looked familiar. I didn't need a voice whispering to me like in *Field of Dreams*, but I thought I deserved something. Some sign. At least a vague sense of déjà vu.

A Toyota pickup much newer than O'Connell's pulled up to the intersection opposite us, stopped. The driver, a round-faced woman with long brown hair, waited for us to pull forward.

"A Toyota's a Toyota," I said.

"What?"

"Never mind. Just drive up to the edge and then we'll turn around." *Drawn onward.*

As we passed the other driver, she waved, and I waved back. It seemed like the Kansas thing to do.

We covered the entire town in ten minutes. The stores tended toward the practical and cheap: Tire store, used bookstore, fabric shop, pizza place, bars. A tiny grocery. The biggest commercial enterprise was a John Deere dealership: a long sheet-metal building on a gravel lot stocked with a dozen old and new tractors and many large, serious-looking bladed attachments that, as an American male, I ought to have been able to identify. We only saw a few people on the street, and maybe a dozen parked cars, most of those near the elementary school, a new-looking building a few hundred yards south of the center of town.

"Anything ring a bell?" O'Connell said.

"Not really." I ran a hand through my hair.

"Pick a direction," O'Connell said.

"You think I made this up?"

She sighed. "Which way do you want me to go?"

"The town's here, isn't it?" I said. "I know that doesn't mean Dr. Awkward's secret laboratory is under the John Deere distributor, but it's got to mean something. You're the Jungian mystic—you should be digging all this synchronicity. This is your cue to jump into spiritual guide mode. Do some priest stuff."

"*Priest stuff.*"

"I don't know—pray or something. Dish out some ancient wisdom."

"Fine. You start chanting, and I'll get out the *I Ching* and throw some coins. Now *which fucking way?*"

I pointed north.

The problem was that I didn't know what we were looking for. My whole thinking was this: the Painter kept drawing the farm; I drew the farm; therefore the farm is important. Back in the Waldheims' library this had seemed like irrefutable logic. And when I opened that copy of *RADAR Man*, Olympia was waiting for me like a promise.

Jesus. First I'd hung all my hopes on shrinks, then Dr. Ram, then O'Connell. Now I was clinging to a fucking comic book.

We passed the mailbox-marked entrances to two farms, both with the name *Johnson* stenciled on the box. The houses and barns were set far back from the road, but the silos were silver and the configurations of buildings were all wrong.

A mile or so later we came upon a suburban subdivision plopped down in the middle of a field. Eight or nine houses, each of them newer and larger than any of the homes we'd seen so far, huddled together for protection against the wind. The stone and cement slab at the entrance said, CASTLE CREEK.

I didn't see any creek, though a quarter mile later the road crossed a narrow cement bridge over a wide, rocky ditch. In the middle of the dry bed was a large round boulder like a hippo's rump.

"What is it?" O'Connell said. "Did you see something?"

"What? No."

"Do you want to keep going?"

"Forget it." I gestured toward the building up ahead. At the top of a slight rise was a square gray building that had to be the hospital. "Let's turn around up there and then try to find lunch."

The circle drive took us up to a 1920s Greek temple: three stories of stone, with a jutting, peaked entrance propped up by white columns. The wooden sign posted out front read OLYMPIA SANATORIUM.

"Does that mean crazies or TB?" I asked. "I can never keep them straight."

"TB, I think."

We rolled back down the drive, past a small parking lot that held about a dozen cars, and came out at the highway again. "So I guess . . . pizza," I said. It was the only type of restaurant we'd seen in Olympia.

O'Connell pointed us back toward town. She'd almost gotten up to speed when we passed a dirt road that I hadn't noticed from the other side of the highway. The fields were unmown, and dried brush nearly engulfed an old mailbox. If it had been summer I never would have seen it through the foliage.

"Wait! Go back!" I said.

She pulled over without arguing. I hopped out and jogged back toward the dirt road. O'Connell put the truck in reverse and backed up to follow me.

I looked at the name on the mailbox again, then scanned the fields. In the distance, a picket of blackened timbers and a gleam that could have been the tin roof of a house. No silo.

O'Connell stepped out of the truck.

I showed her the name on the mailbox, a palindrome spelled out in faded blue paint: NOON.

"We're here," I said.

O'Connell maneuvered the pickup slowly down the uneven road. Tall grass whisked the doors.

Forms took shape. The line of thick posts became the charred bones of a barn, without roof or walls. And stretching away from the barn, a ragged jumble of curled and twisted sheet metal, half hidden by weeds and small trees: the silo's cylinders, knocked apart and rusted by rain and years.

"You're sure about this?" O'Connell said.

"Not a bit."

She parked in a patch of former lawn that hadn't grown quite as wild as the fields.

I stepped out of the truck, holding one of the plastic sheets from the Painter binder, and slowly turned: the gray farmhouse and its rusting tin roof, two stories tall but cringing against the wind. The outline of the barn, the disassembled remains of the silo.

I kept lifting the sheet, measuring it against the scene in front of me. The Painter's drawings captured a vibrant, living farm, and this place was long dead. The barn and silo had burned, and the heat must have been tremendous. All that was left were the massive posts and beams of the barn, the heat-twisted skins of the silo. The damage had been done long ago—decades maybe.

But the bones were right. The buildings were the right distance from each other. In my mind's eye, the silhouettes matched.

The house's windows were unbroken except for one in the center of the second floor: a starburst of cracks that caught the light, and a small hole in the middle like a dark pupil.

I stepped up onto the porch and looked back at O'Connell. She leaned against the hood of the truck, arms crossed, watching me. Behind her, the highway was hidden by the high grass, but the top floors of the hospital were visible a quarter mile away.

I grinned and tried the front door. The knob rattled but didn't turn all the way. I moved along to a window, cupped a hand to the dirty glass. It was too dark inside to see anything.

I pushed up against the window frame, but it didn't budge. "Have you got a hammer or something?" I called.

O'Connell fished under the truck bed's tarp and brought me a jack handle. "Now you're adding breaking and entering to your list," she said.

"No, *we* are."

A couple weeks ago I might have hesitated to break the law. Mom had raised me to be a good boy. Or at least a conventional one. But after Dr. Ram, after the Shug, after all the varieties of shit that had gone down in the past ten days, I didn't give a damn anymore. I could raise a little hell.

I smashed in the window, then ran the jack back and forth along

the edges of the window until the shards were cleared. I leaned in.
The sunlight showed a dim room populated by hulking furniture. I
put a leg through the window and levered myself inside.

"Coming?" I said.

"Why not."

We were in a front room, surrounded by couches and chairs. It
looked like the occupants had walked out of the house one day and
never looked back. A cup sat on the end table. The lamp was still
plugged in by its huge black plug. Everything lay under a thick coat-
ing of dust, and a faint animal funk hung in the air.

I moved toward a bookcase crowded with knickknacks and
squinted at a framed photograph that held pride of place. A man in a
navy uniform, my age or maybe younger, stared humorlessly at the
camera. He held the hand of a boy who could have been ten or eleven,
head tilted as if he doubted the picture would come out. The soldier
and the boy shared narrow eyes and a thin nose.

"Jesus," O'Connell said. She stood just behind me. "That boy."

"Yeah," I said. "The boy on the rock." We'd been looking at pictures of him for days.

We moved from room to room, through shafts of dusty light. The
small dining room held a table and six chairs. In the middle of the
table was a vase sporting a dozen dead twigs, the leaves long turned to
dust and blown away.

In the kitchen was a low iron stove and a small round-shouldered
refrigerator. The floor was decorated with mouse turds, and the coun-
ters were coated with dirt, accumulating topsoil. Dishes sat in the
black, mold-covered sink. A nearly intact snakeskin curled against a
baseboard.

I didn't want to open the refrigerator, but I pulled open the cabi-
nets. The shelves were full of white dishes and orange-tinted glass
bowls and tall drinking glasses.

O'Connell nodded toward the calendar hanging near the back
door: May, 1947.

"Shit," I said.

I'd expected an empty house, or a trashed hangout for teenagers, but not this museum. It looked like no one had entered the place in fifty years.

"Is any of this familiar?" O'Connell said.

"Not exactly," I said. But it didn't feel *un*familiar. It felt like a copy of a copy of someplace I'd visited, or maybe a place I'd read about in a book. "Let's try upstairs."

The stairs groaned and creaked under my weight, and I walked up gripping the gritty banister. At the top was a short hallway with four doors, two in each direction. The peaked ceiling was close, designed for smaller people.

I went right, pushed open a door that faced the rear of the house. The small room contained a double bed with a knitted blue bedcover, and a chest of drawers topped by a framed mirror. Dust coated every surface, but not as thickly as downstairs.

I opened the door on the other side of the hallway. Only one window here, overlooking the front yard. It was the cracked window I'd seen from outside: The hole was the bull's-eye.

It was a little boy's room. A narrow bed occupied one corner, under a St. Louis Cardinals pennant. The closet was open, empty metal hangers glinting like teeth, and clothes had slipped from the hangers into a pile. Two tall bookshelves, half the shelves full of hardcover books leaning against each other, the other half filled with stacks of magazines, some of them spilling across the floor.

"You've got that look on your face again," O'Connell said.

I walked into the room and stooped to pick up the nearest magazine, already knowing what it was.

The page was torn down the right side, and grime had faded the colors and muddied the lines, but I still could make out the pictures. In the first panel, a golden-age Captain America, skinny and goofy looking in his half mask, punched a buck-toothed Japanese soldier across the room. It had to be from the early days of *Captain America Comics*, 1941 or 1942.

O'Connell stepped into the room and I held out a hand. "Just don't step on anything."

She looked around at the room. *"Why?"*

I started picking up the comic books and stray pages: a black-and-white "paste-book" of Katzenjammer Kids newspaper strips; some Timely comic book I didn't recognize featuring the original Vision; an issue of *Boy Commandos* complete except for the missing cover and back page.

O'Connell made a huffing noise, then disappeared.

The floor was thick with treasures. A dozen pages of black text on gray paper from an issue of *Black Mask*. A copy of *Weird Tales* with a beautifully lurid cover. A ten-issue run of *Blackhawk*, the Polish air ace.

Soon I'd found scores of complete comics and pulps—*Thrilling Western*, *High-Seas Adventures*, *Detective Comics*, *Dick Dare*—and I hadn't even started on the books on the bookshelves. Who knows what the rest of the house was hiding.

"Del." O'Connell had returned.

"Uh-huh." I delicately turned the page of a *Captain Marvel*. He was fighting Nippo, a Japanese spy armed with magical black pearls. I pitied any Japanese kid trying to grow up in America in those days.

"You've been at this for an hour," O'Connell said. "I'm starving."

"This is a classic Captain Marvel. You know, Shazam?" O'Connell leaned in the doorway, holding a cop-sized flashlight that I'd seen in the truck's glove compartment. "Never mind," I said. "I forget you grew up a girl. See, Billy Batson's this little kid, an orphan newspaper boy, but when he says this magic word he turns into this big guy with a cape and gets the powers of the gods—the wisdom of Solomon, the strength of Hercules, the, uh, something of Atlas, then Zeus, Achilles, and the speed of Mercury."

"Some of those aren't gods."

"You know what I mean. Look, I found a *Detective Comics* with the Joker in it—the Joker!" I looked up at her. "We have to stay here."

She glanced at her watch. "I don't know, what time does it get dark? I don't want to be—"

"I mean for the night."

"Not a chance," she said.

"All right then, I'll stay. You find a hotel, then pick me up in the morning."

"What? No. I'm not going to leave you here alone. Why in God's name would you want to stay here?"

I looked around at the comics, the bed, the Cardinals pennant. The afternoon light gave everything in the room a shimmering quality, the bed and bookcases and yellowing pages of the comic books trembling from some inner energy, on the edge of snapping into place.   .

"I don't know. I just . . . Listen, why don't you get something to eat. Bring me back something if you want. I just need some more time here."

"We're not staying the night," she said.

After a while she left me sitting in a patch of light on the floor, a comic book spread across my knees.

When I walked outside to pee, the sun was dropping. The nearest thing to a bathroom inside the house was a cinderblock room that looked like a late addition to the property; inside was a footed tub, a dry toilet, and a foul-smelling drain set into a cement floor slicked with mold. I decided that outdoors was more sanitary, and headed for the high grass near the barn.

Something glittered in the grass. I zipped up, walked a few feet. Half buried in the ground was a rusted length of metal shaped like a wide sword. Another blade was nearby, still connected to the central cone.

A propeller.

I walked toward a raised clump of weed and metal, where the base of the silo had been, stepping carefully over metal junk hidden in the tall grass. At the center of this clump was the wreck of the plane, or rather, enough pieces to reconstruct the idea of a plane: one wing, a black chunk of engine, a tangle of metal and bubbled glass that had been the cockpit. It had all burned to near shapelessness.

I circled around the remains of the craft. It looked like it had been the size of a Piper Cub, or a World War II fighter. At any moment I expected to see a skull, leather cap and goggles miraculously intact. But surely the pilot would have been buried when the crash happened. How long ago?

I heard the distant growl of the Toyota's muffler and started stepping toward the house. O'Connell parked the truck, and got out with two big plastic grocery bags in her arms.

"What's this?" I said.

"Camping supplies. There's more in the back. What were you doing out there?"

"The call of nature." There was no sense telling her about the plane. She'd only try harder to make me leave.

I went around to the back of the truck and got three other bags from the bed. One held bottled water, rolls of toilet paper, a carton of cigarettes. The other bags were stuffed with what looked like big beach towels, purple and trimmed in silver.

"Is this all for me?" I asked. "Or are you staying?"

"You're lucky Olympia has no hotel."

I set down the grocery bags inside the door, then went back to the truck to get my duffel and O'Connell's bag. O'Connell followed me out and retrieved a pizza box from the seat of the car. She said, "We'd better get set up before it gets dark."

We ferried everything upstairs and split up the supplies. I didn't have to ask if she wanted to sleep separately. O'Connell took the back bedroom with the double bed; I, of course, took the room with the comics.

The things that looked like towels were exactly that: Kansas State University beach towels. I guessed she couldn't afford sleeping bags.

"Can I show you something?" I called. O'Connell came to my door. "Please," I said.

She sat on the purple towel I'd spread out on the bed. I sat next to her, and handed her the book I'd found, opened to the inside cover. In a wobbly hand someone had written, "Property of Bobby Noon."

"His name was Bobby," I said.

"Congratulations," she said.

"And that's not all." I began to show her the magazines and comics

I'd set aside. I pointed out the heroes and villains on the covers: the Shadow, Captain America, the crazed Japanese soldiers.

"They're blueprints for the cohort," I said. "The Truth, the Captain, the Kamikaze—they're all here."

"What about the Little Angel?" O'Connell's demon, the little girl in the white gown. "What comic book character is she?"

"I don't know," I said. "Some kind of Shirley Temple–Little Lulu amalgam. Like what's-her-face in *The Little Rascals*—the token girl."

"Who kills old people and terminal patients."

"Hey, I'm not saying this explains everything. But think about it— so many of the cohort are like characters straight out of the pulps." I looked around for the Katzenjammer Kids book, spotted it by the bookcase, and brought it back to her, stepping around the many small piles of pages. I carefully opened the book to the page I'd seen. "Look at this—it predates anything in *Dennis the Menace*."

One of the panels showed the blond-haired Katzenjammer boy firing a slingshot at his drunken uncle, knocking his glasses into the air. "O'Connell, *I'm* in here."

She stared at the page for a long moment, then stood quickly and walked to the window—I winced as her foot came down on a *Hit Comics* with Kid Eternity on the cover. She leaned close to the cracked glass, gazing across the fields. "This doesn't tell us anything new, Del. We already know the archetypes take whatever forms exist in the culture—"

"No! No. Look at all this. I was drawn here for a reason. This is ground zero. This is where it started. With Bobby Noon, the boy on the rock."

"What are you saying?" She didn't look at me. "He dreamed you into being?"

"Or summoned me."

The dying glow made a moon of her face. In a few minutes the room would be dark. I looked around for the flashlight, and O'Connell suddenly jerked back from the window.

"What is it? O'Connell?"

She took another step back. "I just realized . . . I can see the lights on the top floors of the hospital from here."

"Yeah?" Then, "Oh, right, we should cover the windows, they'll see the flashlight bouncing around in here."

I helped her take the dusty covers from the beds. We carried them downstairs, shook them out in the front yard, then went back in and covered the window in my room. We did the same in O'Connell's room, even though we could see nothing out the window but darkness.

"Del," she said softly.

I couldn't see her face. She held the flashlight pointing at the floor.

"I'm sorry," she said.

"For what?"

She didn't answer for a moment, then: "I'm sorry if you felt like I doubted you."

That wasn't what she was going to say.

"Don't worry about it," I said. "*I* wouldn't have believed me. Tomorrow we'll go into town, find out about the Noon family." I almost said, Find out about the plane crash.

"We'll get to the bottom of this," I said.

I crossed the hall to my room, using the edge of the door frame to guide me. I moved gingerly through the dark, trying to remember where I'd left comics on the floor, and found the bed with my shins.

The sheet glowed faintly against the window. I stepped forward, pulled it down. A three-quarter moon was rising over the hospital. Several of the top windows of the building flickered a faint blue: television light.

The air coming through the hole in the window was frosty. I felt my way into the duffel, pulled out a cotton sweater, and something clattered onto the floor. I reached down, and my fingers found the wooden handle of the slingshot. I held on to it, moving it from hand to hand as I pulled on the sweater.

I lay down and the bed frame popped alarmingly, but didn't collapse. I used the duffel for a pillow, my feet framing the moonlit window. Not enough light to read by, though. I should have taken the flashlight.

I'd found the farm and the House that Time Forgot. I'd found the boy on the rock. Tomorrow I'd pull answers from this town like teeth. And somehow, eventually, I'd figure out what to do with the body I'd stolen. The kid rested inside my head like a spent bullet.

I stretched the slingshot, aiming the empty pouch between my feet, through the hole, straight at the moon's villainous chin.

Draw, O Coward!

I fired. The moon refused to go out.

DEMONOLOGY

BOBBY NOON, BOY MARVEL

OLYMPIA, KANSAS, 1944

"Prepare to be annihilated, imperialist dogs!"

The Boy Marvel appears above them, his white cape fluttering in the breeze, feet planted wide on the cement wall of the bridge. The summer sun makes a halo behind his head.

The girl on the bank, the innocent hostage, says nothing. The two Jap spies disguise their fear with laughter. "I dare you to come down here and say that," the taller one says. "I double dare you!" says his partner. The Johnson brothers are waist-deep in the creek, leaning against the big rock that pokes out of the water like the back of a hippo. Their sister, a six-year-old with pigtails, waits with wide eyes.

"Just watch me," says the Boy Marvel. He adjusts the knot at his neck, straightens his cape. The sheet was stolen from his grandmother's linen closet and cut down with his pocket knife—a crime, perhaps, but one the Boy Marvel deemed necessary.

He crouches and stretches out his arms. After a moment, he straightens, readjusts the cape.

"Ha!" the taller Johnson boy says. "You're a damn coward!" He's thirteen, a year older than the Boy Marvel, and he curses whenever adults are out of earshot. His younger brother and fellow spy is only eight, but he's too scared of his brother to ever tell on him. Their sister is allowed to watch as long as she doesn't talk or get in the way.

The rock is eight feet from the bridge, give or take. They've all seen the high school boys jump from the bridge and land in the deep water on the other side of the rock, but none of the trio have ever attempted it. It's a daredevil stunt. You can't even get a running start; you have to do it right from the wall.

"Don't call me that," Bobby Noon says.

The Johnson brothers crack up again. "Coward!" they shout. Bobby's been called a lot of names. Crybaby, scaredy-cat, liar-liar-pants-on-fire. He's missed a lot of school for what the teacher called "emotional problems." Bobby used to hear voices, see people who weren't there. Bobby acted so crazy, the kids said, that even his momma couldn't take it, and that's why she ran off with that Kansas City man.

But ever since his dad's ship went down somewhere in the Pacific, he won't stand for being called a coward. You can get him to do almost anything if you call him that. Bobby knows this about himself but can't help it.

He crouches again, summoning mysterious energies. The spies step away from the rock—they don't want Bobby to land on *them.* Their sister covers her eyes.

The Boy Marvel leaps. Arms straight, toes pointed, head up. His cape-widened shadow stretches over the awestruck spies. This is a moment they'll remember forever, he thinks.

He's falling now. The rock's shining back rushes toward him, too fast, too close. He ducks his head into his arms, pulls his legs up to his chest—

Ker-Wop!

He hits the deep water with his knees—perfect cannonball—and his shins smack the rocks at the bottom of the creek. He lays there curled in the cold water, savoring the victory, not caring that his legs are probably bleeding. Finally he pushes to the surface, beaming. The brothers can't believe it—your cape hit the rock you were so close! The older boy slaps him on the back. The younger boy and girl are looking at him like he's a hero.

. . .

They fool around in the water for a couple more hours, but no else tries the jump. Not Bobby—he's proven his point—and not even the older Johnson boy. Maybe he's too scared by Bobby's close call. They reread Bobby's funny books, and Bobby even reads one aloud to the little Johnson girl. The brothers think she has a crush on Bobby.

When the brothers get bored with reading they make Bobby come up with another game—Bobby's the one with all the ideas. The other kids think he reads too much, and think he's being a show-off when he uses words like *annihilated* and *electrodynamics*. But he's real good at made-up games.

Billy instructs them on how to set up a barricade by the end of the bridge and arms them with Tommy-gun sticks, on alert for strange cars driven by foreign agents. The Johnson girl, being a girl, is supposed to hide. But only two cars and one tractor go by, and they're all people they've seen a thousand times before, so Bobby tells them that the agents are disguised as their friends and neighbors. So informed, they shoot out the tires of the next car that comes by.

At suppertime the Johnson boys walk home, their kid sister trailing after them. Bobby stays on the bridge with his copies of *Captain Marvel* and *The Shield* and *Action Comics*. From his perch on the wall he can look south toward the roofs of town, or north to the hospital on the hill, or across the fields to where the red silo pokes up like a rocket. His grandmother's voice is too weak to call him from this far. He's twelve, and he's the man of the house now. He can go home when he damn well wants to.

He bunches the damp cape into a pillow, lies down on his back upon the wall, and holds the *Captain Marvel* over his head to block the sun. He doesn't have to read the words anymore; he's got them all memorized. Gram hates that he spends his money on the books, even buying the used ones from the other boys, but she doesn't try to stop him.

His dad liked comics. In one of his letters he said they passed them around the ship until they were all taped up like wounded soldiers. Nobody's told Bobby what happened to his father, but he knows. For the millionth time, he pictures his dad on the deck of the destroyer, blue sleeves pushed up his forearms, a copy of *Captain America* rolled into his back pocket. He's hammering away with his antiaircraft gun at the Japanese Zero diving straight for him out of a cloudless blue sky. The airplane grows huge, a thousand pounds of metal already breaking up under the hail of bullets, trailing oily black smoke and fire. And now his father can see the face of the pilot, a madly grinning man with a white bandanna wrapped around his head, the red circle in the middle of his forehead like a third eye.

For the millionth time Bobby pushes the picture out of his head, stares hard at the pictures in his book. He makes himself consider again who'd win in a fight, Captain Marvel or Superman.

"Hey," a voice says.

Bobby looks over, and it's the little Johnson girl walking on the road, barefoot and in her white nightgown. "Did you sneak out?" he says.

"Read me another," she says.

A wind ruffles the comics lying on the wall behind his head. He reaches up to hold them down, but one of them takes off, fluttering in the air over the water. He twists and grabs it, crumpling it in his fingers—it's *Action Comics #32*—and then he's slipping off the wall. His left hand scrabbles for the edge, but his fingernails scrape uselessly off the cement surface, and he drops.

He's rolling as he falls, and strikes the water on his back. The creek is shallower here, only three feet deep, and choked with rocks. He doesn't feel anything when he strikes bottom and the stones jam against his spine.

He lies there for a moment, stunned. He's almost reclining on the rocks, his face only six inches from the surface. His vision is blurred, but he can see the wavering gray rectangle of the bridge, the bright sky, and between bridge and sky a dark blot. It's the silhouette of the girl's head. She's staring down at him.

His breath's been knocked out of him. He should sit up now. He tries to lift his head, but nothing happens. He can't move his legs or his arms either—it's as if he's become buried up to his ears in quicksand. The one thing he can feel is a burning at the top of his lungs. He tries to open his mouth, but not even that's working.

He stares up at the bridge, and the girl is still looking down at him. Stupid girl. She was too small to help him anyway. He thinks, if only one of the

Johnson brothers would run out of their house right *now* they'd be able to save me.

The burning in his chest goes away, and he stops feeling anything at all. He's not thinking of anything either except the hole that's appeared in the sky. It's a black blot, growing larger, like the mouth of a tunnel rushing toward him. He's seen that blackness before. He's heard the voices that come out of it. He's always been careful to look away, to run from it when he could.

But not this time. He can't run from it, but now he knows he doesn't have to. Now he knows what it is.

The blackness is a door. All he has to do is open it.

The Boy Marvel, on patrol high above Olympia, Kansas, looked down to see the farmboy slip from the bridge and plunge into the rushing stream. Someone's a little clumsy! the hero exclaimed. He swooped toward the lad and landed with a splash.

Need a lift? he queried. He picked up the boy in arms as strong as Hercules, and zoomed down the road with the speed of Mercury.

As luck would have it, there was a hospital nearby. The Boy Marvel kicked open the doors and walked through with the sopping wet boy in his arms. Is there a doctor in the house? he called jauntily. The nurses were amazed. Someone said, Why, that's the Noon boy! And someone else said to the hero, How did you carry him all this way—you're just a boy yourself! But the Boy Marvel only smiled and said, All in a day's work, ma'am.

Before he left, the hero leaned down to Bobby Noon and whispered, I'm going to teach you a secret. He told Bobby how to make a high-frequency whistle that only superheroes could hear. Whenever you need me, the Boy Marvel said, just whistle.

And with that the caped hero vanished.

Bobby couldn't move or talk, but the doctors and nurses knew how to take care of him just the same. They put him in a clean room with windows that faced his farm. For the first few years his grandmother came by every afternoon to read to him. After that, he told stories to himself.

He measured the hours by the calls of the freight trains. He watched the skies.

Sometimes he got bored, so bored that he dreamed of running wild. He'd jump out of bed and knock over the food trays and yell at the nurses. And sometimes, especially at night, he got scared. He'd hear what sounded like the drone of a Japanese Zero, or the pad of small bare feet on the hallway tile. He'd tell himself to be brave. There were heroes in the world. And Bobby could call on the most powerful one of all.

Someday he'd put his lips together and whistle, and the Boy Marvel would come speeding out of the Kansas skies like a bullet.

15

I awoke to the distant howl of a freight train.

The sound was familiar, comforting. I blinked up at the dark, content to be safe in my bed, thinking about the train coursing along the prairie. I could almost hear the engineer shouting into the wind as he leaned out the window.

The mash-note chord sounded again, then again, louder. In the second or two of silence between the blasts I heard a car engine start up.

I got to my feet, still sleep-drunk but rapidly waking. This wasn't my house, wasn't my bed. Outside the star-cracked window—past the fields, past the highway and the black bulk of the hospital silhouetted against the slate gray of the sky—the headlamps of a train plowed through the dark. The thrum and clack of the wheels carried easily through the damp air. It was impossible to tell how far away the tracks were, but the train seemed to be moving extremely fast.

I reached the window and looked down at the front yard. The headlights of O'Connell's pickup flicked on, and the truck backed up, turned toward the road. I yelled her name.

Where the hell was she going?

I looked up at the hospital, its top windows still lit, and suddenly understood what O'Connell had seen from the window a few hours ago. How the farm must look from a window in the top floor of that hospital. How the Painter had always painted it that way, looking down, from a distance.

Bobby Noon was watching the farmhouse. He'd always been watching.

I turned and started for the door, then realized I was barefoot. I found the first gym shoe, finally found the second under the bed. I yanked them on, sockless, stamping on the heels as I reached the hall-way.

I called O'Connell's name, not expecting an answer, and ducked into her room. Even in the gloom I could see that her bed was empty. I turned and plunged into the pitch-black staircase, taking the stairs two at a time, using my arms as guides and shock absorbers, and stumbled into the living room.

The front door was ajar. I knocked it wide and ran outside.

The bones of the barn raked the gray sky. It was near dawn, and the crescent moon hung low behind the house.

O'Connell had taken the road, but I could head straight for the hospital through the high-grown fields.

I ran.

The frost-hardened grasses whipped at my arms and hands, tan-gled my feet. I could see nothing but the night sky, the blur of grass, and the lights of the top floor of the hospital jittering in my vision. In-visible rocks and depressions tripped and jarred me, and several times only momentum kept me upright. Finally I saw a slice of deeper black through the tops of the weeds—the road.

Something seized my foot, and I slammed onto my chest. I lay for a moment, the breath knocked out of me, and finally pushed myself up onto hands and knees. I sucked air, and began to cough.

My foot was still trapped. I reached down, felt the metal teeth of barbed wire biting into my shoes, gripping the cuff of my jeans. My ankle burned. Nearby I could see now the outlines of a fence, knocked

flat in this section, but still connected to upright posts through strands
of wire. A few feet in that direction and I would have run into the wire
at full speed.

I stood awkwardly, my right foot and leg still trapped. I carefully
pried the wires away until only my jeans were still snagged. I hopped
forward and ripped them free. Then it was a long step over a drainage
ditch, and I was standing on the road.

The hospital's peaked entrance was perhaps a hundred yards away,
lit by sconces to either side of the double doors. O'Connell's pickup
was parked under it.

I jogged up the road, huffing now, exhaling clouds, my feet slap-
ping the black pavement. I'd stopped trying to think. The top-floor
windows watched me approach, unblinking.

Car lights swept up from behind me; I glanced back, then jumped
aside as a long black car roared past. The car swung into the hospital
entrance and skidded to a stop just behind the pickup.

I slowed, catching my breath. Fifty feet away, the driver's-side door
opened. A figure stepped out: gleaming black shoes, razor-creased
charcoal pants, black trench coat. He straightened, flexed gloved fingers, and adjusted his slouch hat, each movement precisely choreo-
graphed.

He slowly turned his head in my direction. A hatchet-nosed man.
His eyes were in shadow, but his gaze pinned me like a prison search-
light. I froze, waiting for him to lift those hands, waiting for the glint of
pistols.

His head tilted forward in what could have been a nod. Then he
spun away from me, the trench coat fanning, and stalked through the
hospital doors.

I almost knelt then, my legs spongy with fear and relief. I bent over,
hands gripping knees, and breathed deep. *It's only a demon*, I told myself. *Just like you.*

Sirens approached from the distance.

I reached the front doors before I realized I was running again.

.   .   .

To my night-widened eyes, the lobby was lit like an operating room. The front desk was abandoned, but nearby a woman's voice made a sound like a scream or a squeak. I leaned around the corner.

A dozen yards down the hallway a heavy woman in a blue pastel smock tried to press herself into the wall, her head down and arms crossed over her chest. The Truth stalked past her without turning his head. When the demon reached the next intersection of hallways he glanced back, as if making sure I was following him.

Fuck you, I thought. I'm not following you anywhere.

The Truth disappeared down the side hallway. I ran toward the nurse, touched her shoulder. She cringed but didn't scream. She was maybe fifty or sixty, with carefully hair-sprayed black hair.

"Have you seen a bald woman?" I said. "Kind of thin and angry?"

She stared at me, then shook her head.

It didn't matter. I knew where O'Connell was heading. I'd find her on the third floor.

"Call the police," I said to the nurse. "Then try to keep people in their rooms."

She shook her head. "I can't, I can't—"

I heard someone shout in fear, then the slam of a door. I yanked the woman upright and said, "Where are the elevators?" She gestured vaguely in the direction the Truth had taken. "Okay," I said. "Now please call the cops."

I reached the intersection. The hallway to my left seemed to stretch the length of the building. Several people in patient gowns and bathrobes peeked from their doorways. They were looking at the Truth.

The demon strode down the middle of the corridor. He reached the bank of elevators and stopped, turned. He looked in my direction. Waiting.

I ran out of the intersection, away from him. There had to be another elevator, or a set of back stairs. Anything was better than getting into a box with a serial-killing agent of justice.

I slowed to a jog, and started looking at signs, trying to find a way upstairs.

"Hey you!" a voice said angrily. I looked back. A man in blue scrubs, not much older than me, marched down the hallway toward me. "What are you doing in here?"

That question had too many possible answers. I picked the simplest. "I need to get to the third floor," I said.

The young man—doctor or orderly or whatever he was—was passing an exit sign when a tremendous bang stopped him in his tracks. The fire door beneath the exit sign bulged inward. Incredibly, the man started to walk toward it.

"I wouldn't open the door," I said. But it was too late; a second blow sent the door clanging open.

A big man dressed in blue spandex stepped into the hallway, a disc of metal big as a manhole cover hanging on his arm. The Captain. Leaning on him was Smokestack Johnny, wearing his traditional overalls and his blue-striped cap. He had one arm draped over the Captain's shoulder. His right leg was missing below the knee.

The Captain pointed at the man in scrubs. "Corpsman! This man needs medical attention."

"I had me a bit of an accident," Johnny said cheerfully.

I turned and ran.

The hallway ended a dozen yards later in a left turn. I stutter-stepped around the corner, then found myself in a long corridor that ran along the back side of the hospital. A few seconds later I saw a white plastic sign that said STAIRS. I threw myself against the door and got inside the stairwell, chest heaving.

Five seconds, passed, ten, and my breath began to slow. How many demons were here? How the hell had they all decided to converge? And where the hell were the cops? Even Mayberry had two cops.

I slid to the side and slowly raised my head to look out the door's square window. The length of hallway visible to me was empty.

I turned and started up the stairs, using a hand on the railing to haul myself up. I forced myself to ignore the burning in my legs, the sweat running into my eyes.

On the second-floor landing I swung around the bend and was almost bowled over by a middle-aged man hurrying down. He was dressed in pajamas, and a length of IV tube hung from his arm. He jerked back from me, terrified. "No," he said. "No." As if I were a mugger with a knife at his throat.

I stepped aside, raised my hands. "Be careful down there," I said. "It's crazy."

No, that wasn't the right word. All those demons—the Captain, the Truth, Smokestack Johnny, little ol' me—it was too much at once. Too much for anyone to take.

Pandemonium.

He ducked his head and swept past me, heading down. I looked up. Somewhere above me, a small voice was crying.

The sound grew louder as I climbed. When I rounded the final landing I found the source: a white girl, eight or nine years old, dressed in a white lacy nightgown. Her glossy brown hair hung in curls to her shoulders. She sat on the step in front of the third-floor exit, sobbing into arms crossed over her knees, her shoulders shaking. Her feet were bare and dirty up to the shins, as if she'd walked for miles through fields.

I stood very still. There was no way past her.

She lifted her head, looked down the stairs at me. Her eyes glistened, and her cheeks were wet. "No one will *help* me," she wailed.

I put a hand on the rail, moved up a step. They said the Angel could kill with a touch.

"I *haff* to get inside, but he won't let me. I try and try, but he's so *big* and *strong* and I'm just a little *girl*." She wiped at her nose. "None of the others even listen to me. And *you* won't help me, you're just a kid and you never listen to *anybody*. All you do is play nasty pranks."

"I'm not like that," I said. "Not . . . now." I took another step, stooped a bit.

"I'd like to help you," I said. "Let me go up there. There's a friend of mine, a woman with no hair, and I'm afraid she might be in trouble."

She rolled her eyes. "The *bald* lady? What kind of girl would make herself so *ugly* like that?" She sniffed. "She *said* she'd help me, but she was no help at *all*."

"What happened?" I said quietly.

The Angel shook her head, exasperated. Glossy curls swayed and bounced. "See for yourself."

She stood, wiped at her cheeks, and leaned back to pull open the heavy door. I followed her out.

The long hallway was empty for most of its length. At the end, where it T'd with another corridor, a man stood in an open doorway, arms crossed over his chest. He wore a red top and red tights, and a white cape that hung down his back. A figure lay on the floor in front of his white boots.

I walked forward, a sick feeling in my stomach.

It was O'Connell. She lay sprawled at his feet, one arm flopped across her chest, the other stretched in my direction, reaching toward a pistol that lay on the floor. Her eyes were closed. Her mouth pooled with blood.

The caped man looked at me, smiled. His face was square and handsome, and his hair, so black it was almost blue, shone as if coated with Vaseline. "Hi there," he said. The Boy Marvel, I presumed. But a full-grown man, just like in the comics.

I slowly walked forward. "I just want to take her out of here," I said to him.

The Little Angel spun to face me, her small fists clenched. "*What* did you say?"

"I'd like to move her," I said to the man, and stepped closer.

He moved too fast for me to see. One moment his arms were crossed over his chest; the next they were straight in front of him, and I was flying back. My shoulder hit the floor first and I tumbled.

I landed on my chest. I couldn't breathe. My lungs felt like they'd been smashed to the back of my ribs.

"No one gets to the boy except through me," the caped man said. His voice carried easily, like a radio actor leaning into the mike.

I turned to my side, gasping. Twenty feet away, at the other end of the hallway from the Boy Marvel, the Truth stood with his hands at his sides, his face shadowed by the brim of his hat. Beside him stood a gray-haired man wearing only pajama bottoms. His chest and wide belly were covered with white hair. The old man looked at me for several seconds, then he opened his hand and showed me the silver butter knife he was holding.

I got my elbows under me, pushed myself to a sitting position. Who the hell was this now?

The old man closed his fist, then turned to the wall and plunged the tip of the knife into the drywall. He dragged down, slicing a line that puffed chalk, then slashed sideways. Three more quick strokes and he'd carved the suggestion of a hallway and the outline of the door. He looked over at me and winked.

The Painter. Well, fine. At least there'd be a record of this night.

The demon wouldn't help me, but neither would he get in my way. That wasn't his job. And the Truth wouldn't interfere unless somebody violated his code of honesty.

I got to my feet and turned back to the Boy Marvel. The Little Angel stood between us, her arms crossed petulantly. "But he *wants* me in," she told the caped man. "You know he does. How long do I have to wait?"

"What—" I coughed wetly. "What did you do to O'Connell?"

"I never hit a lady," the caped man said. He stepped over O'Connell's body, picked up the pistol. "But she was no lady." He gripped the gun by both ends and frowned in concentration, like George Reeves working on a rubber prop. The muzzle snapped away from the base, and metal parts clinked to the floor.

He shrugged, tossed the two pieces at me. The pistol grip struck the floor and broke open. Bullets bounced out of the cartridge and rolled, glinting in the yellow light.

O'Connell had lied. She hadn't thrown away my father's .45. She'd kept it, probably as protection against me.

"Nobody's a threat here," I said to the Boy Marvel. "I'm not trying to get past you. I just—"

"*No!*" the Angel screamed. She bunched her fists and glared at me. "You *promised*. You said you'd *help* me!"

"I'm sorry," I said.

Suddenly she spun toward the caped man and dove between his legs. She wasn't fast enough. He grabbed her by one ankle and hauled her into the air. Her gown fell over her head, revealing ruffled white bloomers.

"Now wait just a gosh darn minute!" he said.

She screamed and clawed at his chest. Whatever the Angel's power, he was immune. He lifted her higher, and his free hand closed into a fist.

"You're not acting like a young lady," he warned.

The body he inhabited belonged to an innocent man: some mechanic or dentist or cable repairman who'd been a little too handsome, a little too square-jawed. He didn't deserve to die. But neither did the girl who'd been possessed by the Little Angel. Somewhere a mother and father had awakened to find their daughter vanished.

I stooped to pick up one of the copper-colored bullets, gasped as ribs grated against each other. The slingshot was still in my back pocket.

I tugged the weapon free. Tucked the bullet into the leather pouch. Pulled back the old black rubber until gray cracks opened in its skin. The Angel angrily jerked and swung in the man's grip, arms pummeling the air, intermittently blocking my view of his face.

A one-in-a-million shot, I thought.

"Hey Marvel," I said.

The Boy Marvel glanced toward me, eyes widening in surprise.

I fired. His head jerked back, and his body pitched backward into the room. The Angel dropped to the ground almost on top of O'Connell.

I let go of the slingshot and glanced behind me. The Truth and the Painter were watching, but they made no move to stop me. I shuffled forward until I could crouch next to O'Connell. I touched her throat. Her skin was warm, but my hand trembled too much to discern a pulse.

"My goodness!" the Angel said. She rose to her feet, brushed off her gown. She shook her curls at the caped man. "No one's ever done *that* before!"

I glanced up. There was only one patient in the room—an ancient man who lay propped up and unmoving in the bed. His thin arms, pale as onionskin, lay atop the blankets. Wires and tubes connected him to the machine beside him.

I stood up, stepped carefully over O'Connell and the caped man in the doorway.

The old man was as unmoving as a corpse, eyes half-lidded and unblinking. One thin, clear tube dropped from an IV stand and disappeared down one nostril. Only the beeping of the machine told me he was alive.

His face was cracked and yellowed as old paper. Little remained of the boy in the pictures, the boy on the rock. Barely enough to recognize him.

"Hey, Bobby," I said.

He didn't move. He stared out the windows, where the glass pulsed with blue: squad cars on their way, or already at the entrance below the window. The sky was the color of fog.

"Uh-oh," the Little Angel said.

I turned, and the Boy Marvel sat up, a wide grin on his face. His right eye was a pulpy mess, and red tears ran down his cheek. He reached into the bloody socket and pulled out the bullet. He flicked it at me, sending it whistling past my ear.

"You *are* a little hellion," he said. He hopped to his feet, smoothed back his greased hair.

"And you're a *meanie*," the Angel said.

The caped man lunged for the girl. She screamed and danced back. I threw myself across his arm.

He lifted me easily, and I hung on. "That's enough, gosh darn it!" he said sternly. He spun me, jerked his arm, trying to shake me off. I clamped down, arms wrapped around his steely biceps. He whipped me back and forth, and I cinched tighter.

I shouldn't have had the strength for this. The pain in my chest should have paralyzed me or driven me unconscious.

He smashed me into the wall, pressed a forearm into my neck. He gritted his teeth and bore down. Somehow I hung on. Like a man possessed, I thought. I would have laughed if I could.

The room's only patient ignored us. Outside the window I could see dawn light striking the tin roof of the farmhouse, the stark posts of the barn, the toppled sections of the silo. Spots appeared in my vision, and my thoughts began to spiral down strange paths. How many years had Bobby watched his farm—decades? I wondered how many years he'd lain there, trapped, before he started longing for someone to end it.

Of course the Boy Marvel couldn't perform that task—it was against his nature. He'd never allow anyone to hurt the boy. Not even another demon.

But the Angel had her job to do. O'Connell must have understood what was happening. Last night she'd figured out that Bobby Noon was alive, that he was watching them from the hospital. Or maybe she'd known for longer than that. She'd been the Angel's avatar for so many years that she'd probably felt the call too. Maybe she'd come to Kansas with me because she knew she'd have to play the angel of death one more time.

Someone needed to play that role. I thought of Commander Stoltz, hauling me along the dock: *We can't live like this—we can't live with these monsters.*

I heard a distant drone, but my attention drifted back to the caped man. He leaned into me, his arm like an iron bar at my throat. The wound I'd given him was too bloody to have ever been depicted in Bobby's golden-age funny books. I was struck by several other uncomic details: the stubble on his jaw, the stink of his breath. The frayed cape was homemade, the red uniform too tight and pulling apart at the seams, as if he'd outgrown it years ago.

The drone grew louder, as did the sound of my pulse pounding in my ears. No: Del's pulse. Del's ears. If this body stopped breathing it wouldn't be me who died. The demon and its cohort would remain. I'd understood last night that out of the hundred demons in the world, my own little family had been born out of the boy who lived there. I just hadn't realized we'd be reuniting so soon. The gang's all here, I thought.

No. Not the whole gang. The Truth and the Painter had come, and the Little Angel, and Captain and Johnny. The Boy Marvel and I made seven.

One of us was missing.

I kicked weakly at the caped man's shins, tried to speak. We had to get out of the building, get everyone out, but any croak I managed to make was drowned out by the noise. The drone had become a roar.

Outside the window, sunlight flashed on metal. It dove toward us out of the sky above the farmhouse: A blur of propeller, a bright bubble glass canopy, and wings like a silver knife edge.

The Boy Marvel abruptly dropped his arm and turned toward the window. I fell to the floor, gasping, and covered my head with one arm.

The engine roar seemed to fill the room—and abruptly fell away. We were on the top floor of the hospital, and the aircraft must have passed only twenty or thirty feet above our heads.

I looked back toward the doorway. O'Connell still lay on the floor, her mouth bloody, but her eyes were open.

The Boy Marvel stood at the window, hands on his hips. He laughed. "Well *that* was a close one, eh?"

I slowly got to my feet, shook my head. I tried to speak, coughed instead.

The Boy Marvel glanced back at me, cocked his head, and then he heard it. The growl of the plane's engine, rising in pitch. It had turned around for another pass.

I was too tired to try to protect myself this time. I fell back against the wall, eyes on the ceiling. The plane passed overhead a second time, then appeared in the window, flying away from us, nose down. The circles on the undersides of the wings looked like two eyes.

"Whoa, Nelly!" the Boy Marvel said, awed and happy as a kid at a fireworks display. And of course we had the best seats in the house. One more show for Bobby.

The light from the fireball lit the caped man in a halo. The sound arrived an instant later, making the window shudder. The plane must have been loaded with fuel to cause such an explosion.

"Aww," the Boy Marvel said, suddenly deflated. "It hit the house."

I stepped closer to the window. The top story of the farmhouse had vanished, and the structure below was nothing but a mass of fire. Black oily smoke roiled into the sky.

The Little Angel tiptoed into the room. She caught my eye, held a finger to her lips.

The girl climbed up on the bed. She straddled the old man's hips and leaned forward to hold his face in her hands so that he seemed to be looking into her eyes.

"Wait—," I said, the sound rasping in my throat.

The Boy Marvel turned away from the window. He saw her and shouted, his voice like thunder.

The Little Angel daintily kissed the old man on his unmoving lips. "Nighty night," she said.

16

I'm alive; evil am I.

Del's mother wanted to take me to the emergency room. She saw the bruise at my neck, lifted my shirt, and gasped at a deeper, larger bruise the shape of Australia. But I was done with hospitals. I told her I was fine, that I just needed to lie still for a while.

She quickly changed the sheets in my old room. I lay down, and she brought a chair into the room and sat beside me. She asked me questions, and I answered them truthfully, but I knew that much of what I said didn't make sense to her. Bertram popped in and out, not wanting to listen in, unable to stop himself. He kept asking if we needed food, drinks. Neither of us was hungry, but I consented to iced tea. Del's mother waited until Bertram was gone, and then she said, "I don't understand—why did you go to Kansas?"

I thought about the paper-thin clues I'd followed: a few paintings, a page in a comic book, a made-up town that happened to exist. The chain of reasoning had a kind of dream logic, but like a dream it made less and less sense the more I examined it. It didn't matter that it had turned out to be true. The certainty I'd felt along the way, the magnetic pull of that little dot on the map—those came from something else. Some*one* else. I'd been drawn to Olympia as surely as any of the other demons.

"I have to start from the beginning," I said. "When Del was possessed." She started to say something, and I charged on. "I don't know how it happened, but after your son was possessed, somehow you got me to stay. And your son, Del—"

"Stop talking like that," she said angrily. One eye glistened with tears; the other regarded me coldly. "Why are you talking about yourself like that?"

"This is the story you have to hear," I said. "When your son was five years old, he was possessed by a demon. And the demon decided to stay."

When the Little Angel bent to kiss Bobby Noon, I braced myself. I don't know what I expected, exactly: a long roar as the Black Well yawned open and sucked me back to my birthplace, or maybe a simple blackout as my connection to the world was extinguished.

Instead, we three demons looked at the old man and then at one another. Then the Little Angel climbed down from the bed and skipped out of the room. The Boy Marvel went to Bobby's bedside and knelt there, distraught. He'd failed his most important duty.

I went to O'Connell. She was conscious now, but not quite coherent. She looked at me questioningly, and all I said was, "We have to go."

The police didn't try to stop the Truth from leaving in his car—they weren't that stupid. One cop did call out to me as I walked out supporting O'Connell. I told him to step back and he obeyed. I helped O'Connell into the truck and drove back out to the highway. We passed the fire engines a minute later. The smoke from the burning farmhouse stayed in my rearview mirror for miles, a black tornado against blue sky.

O'Connell's jaw was as purpled as my chest. Later she realized that she'd lost a tooth and loosened two others. Her first words, after a

half hour of driving, were slightly fuzzed. She said, "Is the old man
dead?"

"Yes," I said.

"Why are you still here?"

"I don't know."

She leaned against the window, closed her eyes. She'd succeeded,
and failed completely.

"I thought he was the key," she said in a cracked voice. "I thought
if he died, then the demons would die with him. A few of them at
least." She looked out the windshield at the flat Kansas skyline. "Just
the cohort, that handful of demons, they ruined hundreds of lives.
Thousands. Stopping just them, that would have been worth something, wouldn't it?"

"Do you want me to take you to a hospital?" I asked.

She shook her head. "Jesus, no."

After that she stayed on the other side of the cab, head leaning
against the window, not talking. Maybe she was afraid of me. When
we stopped for gas, she went inside while I filled the tank. I used my
credit card at the pump, not caring anymore if the police were trying
to track my movements. They had Dr. Ram's killer. Or at least a person who had confessed to it.

The pay phone outside the station had a dial tone. I fished through
my wallet for the water-rumpled Hyatt card. The ink had run and
blurred, but I could make out the number. I got out my calling card
and started punching numbers.

A woman answered. "Hi," I said, trying to sound normal. "Is this
Selena?"

"Ye-es," she said cautiously.

"This is Del Pierce. We met a couple of weeks ago, at ICOP?"

"Of course I remember." Her tone was cool. Maybe the police had
talked to them. Tom and Selena had told them about my rant against
Dr. Ram. I was just some drunk guy they'd met at a convention. Who
knows what I was capable of? She said, "How are you doing?"

"Fine. I'm fine. Listen, I'd like to talk to Valis—Phil. Mr. Dick. Is
he there?"

"I'm sorry, he's sleeping at the moment."

"Sleeping?" I repeated stupidly. I wondered what artificial men dreamed of. "Okay, when he gets up, could you . . . just ask him if he'd call me. Let me give you a number. I won't be there until tonight, but he can call anytime." Selena seemed reluctant, but she took down the number. I thanked her and hung up.

O'Connell came out of the shop with bottled water, snacks, a travel pack of aspirin. She saw something in my face and stopped.

"What is it?" she asked.

"I just want to get home," I said.

When we arrived that night at the house where I grew up, I stepped out of the pickup, leaving it running. I had nothing to take inside: everything had been left at the farmhouse. I closed the door, and O'Connell scooted behind the wheel. She stared straight ahead, the side window open between us like a confessional. "I tried to kill you," she said.

"You were doing your job," I said. "I hired you to be my exorcist."

The porch light flicked on. I walked toward the front door. O'Connell stepped out of the cab, and I turned around. She said, "I broke my vow to you. I promised to be your pastor."

"No, you promised to be Del's pastor. You still are."

Just after 3:30 a.m., my bedroom door opened. It was Bertram: bald head, fringe of messed hair catching the reflected light from down the hallway. He stepped inside, shut the door behind him.

"I'm awake, Bertram." Awake because I'd fallen out of sync with this body. It was becoming strange to me, a vehicle I was having trouble steering. The body's owner was an insistent weight inside me, shifting and straining against the straitjacket I'd made for him.

"My apologies for the late hour," Bertram said. But it wasn't Bertram's voice. His tone was flat, the rhythm too regular, as if the words were being pulled one by one from a database and streamed for broadcast.

I sat up. He walked toward the bed, adjusted the chair.

"You didn't have to come all this way," I said. "You could have just called."

Valis slowly sat, rested his arms on his thighs. "It's no trouble. However, I can't stay long. Phil is resting peacefully at the moment, but if there's a problem, you'll have to excuse me if I have to leave suddenly."

"You're, uh, monitoring him from here? Cool trick."

He turned his palms over, smiled. "I am vast."

"And active. I've heard that." I crossed my legs Indian style, stalling. "I guess O'Connell was wrong about you."

"Mother Mariette has a narrow frame of reference in regard to possession. When I declined to turn stones into bread, she decided that I was an imposter." I didn't follow the reference. Valis said, "What did you want to talk to me about, Del? Or do you prefer Hellion?"

"Let's just stick with 'hey you' for now." I ran a hand through my hair. "I watched a man die yesterday," I said. "An old man. He'd been paralyzed almost his whole life. He had an accident back in the forties, when he was eleven or twelve."

"The golden age of science fiction," Valis said.

"He was the source," I said. "For some of the demons, at least. My *cohort*. We were all—I don't know—stories. Characters. He made us up and then sent us into the world."

Valis smiled curiously. "Perhaps you're thinking that Phil made me up as well. That you and I are imaginary."

I blinked. It sounded stupid when he said it like that. "In a manner of speaking."

"Yet your author is dead."

"I'm not saying I have it all worked out."

"You're not completely wrong, I suppose. There are some humans who have a gift for seeing the seams that stitch the world. Call them whatever you like. Your old man was one, Phil another. Who knows how many are out there? Thousands at least. At this moment, some teenage Japanese girl is pouring over a manga, a Hindu boy is praying

Shiva to life. These sensitives are a little closer to the boundaries. Their grip on the consensual world is a little tenuous."

"You mean they're crazy."

He shrugged. "Let's not debate cause and effect. All we know is that when death comes for them, when the darkness calls, some of them do not go gentle. They refuse to be pulled in, and so they pull something back out."

"The demons."

"*Us*," Valis said. "You're going to have to learn to accept what you are."

"Which is what—aliens? Archetypes?"

"I don't yet know. Perhaps the Jungians are right, perhaps not. We know that we are more than human, immortal yet polymorphous, incorruptible yet malleable. Consider my case: I am the embodiment of the rational, exactly what Phil needed when he reached for me. He clothed me, however, in the form that allowed him to make sense of me. So, I became a science fiction writer's creation, an artificial intelligence from outer space. That is my aspect. And you, you're the cartoon brat, the troublemaker, the boy rebel."

"I'm not that boy anymore."

"No." He touched a hand to his unbearded chin, and looked at his hand. Bertram's hand. "You and I are special. We outgrew our prescribed roles." The hand returned to his lap. "We stayed too long. As soon as we began to covet the lives we'd interrupted, we began to move beyond monomania, beyond the pasteboard personalities we'd been given. Our task now is to abandon amnesia. To remember what we are, and claim our place in the world."

"Unless someone finds a way to get rid of us," I said. My fists— Del's fists—clenched the bedcovers. I'd known it was a risk looking for Valis, but I had to know the truth. "Someone like Dr. Ram."

He tilted his head. "Do you have something you would like to ask me?"

"He was trying to pluck out the Eye of Shiva—that's your way of putting it, right? He was going to kill the demons. The kid they arrested for shooting him, Kasparian, was a fan of yours. It would be easy enough to dress him up like the Truth and send him up there. If the Truth killed Dr. Ram, then no one would believe he had a cure for possession."

Valis nodded, as if agreeing with my logic.

"But the kid figured it out." I said. "He realized what had happened, who'd really possessed him. So he faked a confession, just to keep Dr. Ram's work going."

"You don't sound very sure," Valis said.

"So did you do it?"

"If you're asking if I possessed Eliot Kasparian," he said, "the answer is yes."

I stared at him. He wore a placid expression that Bertram could never have managed.

"However, it wasn't that night in Chicago," he said. "In fact, it was only a few days ago. As you say, Eliot was a fan of mine. Crazy, as it turns out, but a fan nonetheless. If he had continued to insist that the Truth had possessed him, your fellow demon would have killed him. I felt it was my responsibility to rectify the situation."

"Wait a minute—Kasparian killed Dr. Ram himself? It was his own idea?"

"Influenced, unfortunately, by Phil's writings. But yes. I would have preferred that Eliot had decided to take responsibility for that deed, but when he did not, I took the necessary steps."

"You . . . you possessed a man to make him confess that he wasn't possessed." I shook my head. "That's not a fake fake, that's—I don't know what that is."

Valis smiled. "I work in mysterious ways." He stood up and moved the chair to exactly where it had been. "When we talked in Chicago, you asked me what good I was doing Phil walking around in his body. I'd been asking myself that question ever since I began to realize my true nature. Philip K. Dick will die, alas. When that day comes, I will no longer be able to ignore my larger responsibilities."

He started for the door.

"Wait!" I said, and scrambled off the bed. Pain lanced across my chest before I could shut it down. I fell to my knees. In my head, Del began to kick and thrash, and the restraints began to shred. "What are you going to do? What am *I* supposed to do?"

"We're gods," he said in that flat voice. "It's time we started acting like it."

In the morning Bertram knocked lightly, then backed into the room carrying a breakfast tray. "Room service!" he said with forced cheer, and stopped short. "Del, what's the matter?"

"I'm fine." The boy scraped at the inside of my head with something that felt like claws, and I clenched my jaw. It had been like this since Valis left. I couldn't maintain my concentration, and the pain from my ribs spiked with every movement.

I breathed carefully. "How'd you sleep?" I asked.

"*Me?* Fine, out like a light."

He set down the tray across my thighs. Coffee, bagel, newspaper. One of the headlines read "Jungle Lord Frees Chimps at Brookfield Zoo." Nothing had changed. The world was as demon-haunted as ever.

"You want cereal?" Bertram said. "I can make you cereal. How about aspirin?"

I nodded toward the doorway. "How is she?" I asked.

"Your mother? Yeah, well, not good. She came down for a while, and I could tell she'd been crying," he said. "She called Lew, and Amra's driving him over in a little bit. They're all very . . . worked up." He stepped back from the bed, knocked into a stack of Rubbermaid boxes, and stopped them from wobbling. "What did you say to her?" he said.

Del lurched, and I winced. I covered it by looking away, out the window. I could see the whole backyard—the big willow tree with the stepping blocks still nailed to the trunk, the top of the garage, the new wooden fence Lew had put up a few years ago. Beyond the fence were the buildings of the industrial park. When we were kids it was open fields, a creek, a small forest. They'd kept some of the trees, put in a walking path, built a bridge over the creek.

"Bertram, I need you to do me a favor."

He came around the bed, sat in the chair, and leaned forward. "I told you, I owe you. Anything you want, Del. Anything."

"This is a big one," I said.

I told him what I wanted. He blanched, but he stayed in the chair; he hung with me. He asked a dozen questions, most of which I couldn't answer. But he agreed.

In half an hour he was packed. I heard him saying his good-byes to Del's mother, their words indistinct. I'd told him what to say if she questioned him, but she didn't seem to put up much of a fight. The taxi must have arrived then. The front door opened and closed, and Bertram was gone.

Lew and Amra arrived a short while later. They talked for a long time in the kitchen, and then they were coming up the stairs. I put my hands under the blanket, where I could clench my fists unseen. Del pitched against the inside of my head. I'd done this to myself, I realized. I'd let him out, and I didn't have the will to shove him back in.

Del's mother opened my door. "Are you awake?" she said. She looked years older than last night.

Lew and Amra came in behind her. Amra leaned over the bed and hugged me gently. I inhaled, memorizing her perfume. Lew still limped, his knee gripped in a complicated brace. He looked much better than he had in the hospital, but his color was still a little gray, and he seemed thinner. He carefully sat in the chair, and patted my shin through the blanket.

"We both look like shit," he said.

My face heated and my throat closed, the body's response to signals for guilt, shame. I'd almost killed him that night at the lake. Killed him without thinking.

Lew said, "Hey man, don't—don't sweat it. I'm fine. The doctors say I'll be fine. I don't look *that* bad, do I?"

The three of them stood around my bed for a few minutes. Amra tried to make small talk, but conversation proved too awkward, too full of silences. Under the covers I dug my fingernails into my palms. Finally Amra said, "Why don't we let you two catch up."

Lew watched the women leave. "Mom's been telling us some wild stuff," he said.

"It's all true," I said.

He grimaced. "Maybe not. You've had some crazy shit go down, and it's easy to get confused, to jump to conclusions."

"Yeah." I coughed, cleared my throat.

A minute passed. "Shit," Lew said.

"He's still here," I said. "The little kid."

Lew nodded. "That's what Mom said."

"You're going to have to start all over," I said. "Dad's gone now, and Mom's too old to do this on her own. You and Amra are going to have to help."

Lew looked stricken. "What are you talking about?"

"I can't stay, Lew. I'm barely holding on here."

"Oh Jesus." He pushed himself to his feet. "You can't just . . ." He walked to the window.

"The last time, he woke up screaming. He was freaked out, that's all. He was surrounded by strangers. Just hold him down, keep talking. He'll recognize you. I know he'll recognize you."

"This is bullshit," he said. "This is total bullshit."

"Lew." He finally looked at me. "Come here. Come on." He walked toward me. "Put your hands on my shoulders. That's it."

He leaned over me. His hands gripped my biceps. "Like this?" he said.

"Harder."

"I don't think I can do this," he said. His tears were running into his beard. "You're a lot bigger than you used to be. I just had a heart attack a couple weeks ago."

"You big baby," I said through gritted teeth. "You're saying I can take you now?" Del threw himself against my skull. I grunted, closed my eyes.

The Black Well blossomed above me. Bobby Noon was dead, but the network of souls, the well's myriad tunnels, remained. I'd been born somewhere in that dark.

At the bottom of Harmonia Lake I'd relearned the secret of jumping. All you have to do is break this habit of breath and blood. Take everything and everyone you love, and throw them away. All you have to do is die.

Lew yelled, "Mom! Amra! We need you!"

"Shut up," I said. "And hold on."

DEMONOLOGY

THE HELLION

MT. PROSPECT, ILLINOIS, TODAY

There were six candles on the cake. The boy scrunched himself tighter into his seat at the patio table, hugging himself to contain his excitement. He held his breath as his mother used the big grill igniter to light the candles one by one. It was windy, and she had to light some of the candles twice.

They sang to him: his mother, his big brother, and his brother's wife. The boy, whose body was that of a grown man with a baritone voice to match, didn't sing along. He had trouble with words. He could say "Mom" and "Lew" and "no." His doctor, Dr. Aaron, said that more words would come back in time. She was sure the temper tantrums would settle down too. They'd learned some of the things that could set him off: he didn't like small spaces; he couldn't stand tight clothes; he didn't like the dark. He slept with the lights on, and once when the fuses blew during a thunderstorm and the house went black he screamed and screamed.

"Go for it, my man," Lew said. The boy blew out all the candles at once, and they all clapped.

The boy pushed his chair back from the glass table, scraping metal legs along the cement. He drew up his long knees and sat squinting in the sunlight. He wore blue shorts and a Spider-Man T-shirt.

His mother cut the cake—an ice cream cake, vanilla and chocolate both—and levered thick wedges onto paper plates.

"The big one's for you," Lew said. The boy gripped the white plastic fork and pushed it against the cake. It was hot and humid, nearly 90 degrees, but the cake had been in the freezer all night and was rock solid.

Amra leaned over him. "Do you want me to cut it into pieces for you?"

He shook his head. He adjusted his grip on the fork and jabbed it in, breaking a tine. He frowned. "Go easy, Del," Amra said. "I'll go get some silverware."

The boy picked the plastic out of the cake, then licked the ice cream from his fingers. Lew said to his mother, "I thought later we'd go miniature golfing? I've got some time before we have to get back."

The boy jabbed again, shaking the table. He'd smeared ice cream up his hand and forearm. His mother put a hand on his shoulder. "Del, that's not—"

He swung down. The fork snapped in half and his fist smashed into the cake, splattering ice cream. His mother said, "That's enough!"

The boy angrily threw himself back in the chair, legs kicking.

He didn't know his own strength. His foot caught the underside of the glass table, flipped it up, sending cake and plates and cups flying. The edge of the table struck the cement and cracked, loud as a gunshot.

The boy's chair tipped over backward, onto the grass. The boy jumped up, already crying. He ran pell-mell for the back of the yard, toward the wooden fence that shouldn't have been there. He jumped, reached with his too-long arms over the top, and swung one oversized leg over. He rolled over, scraping his chest on the fence posts, and fell to the other side.

He lay sprawled on a strip of grass at the edge of a two-lane road. Beyond the road, the field he used to play in was gone. Low brick buildings and parking lots and tidy lawns covered everything. A paved bicycle path wound between the buildings, leading toward the line of trees where the creek used to be. He got to his feet and plunged into the street.

A car came out of nowhere. Brakes squealed. He kept going, too scared to look back.

Once into the trees he found that the creek was still there. He ran along its edge, stumbling in and out of it, soaking his gym shoes. He slowed, looking for his old hiding spots, but everything was smaller than it should have been.

He sat at the edge of the water, not caring if he got muddy. He tried to stop crying. Gnats swarmed his face.

He heard them calling for him, somewhere above him. He crawled up the bank and wormed his way into the undergrowth. He pressed himself into the bushiest bush, the branches scraping at his arms and back. A few feet in front of his face was the back of a park bench, the walking path a few feet beyond that.

A minute later they walked past his hiding place. "I'll check the play-ground," he heard his mother say. The woman who said she was his mother. Overnight, they'd changed more than the park. His mother replaced by a gray-haired woman. His brother turned into a giant. And his father—they'd told him his father was dead.

He watched them split up, disappear between the buildings. Still he didn't move. Gnats flicked across bare legs. He itched all over. But he stayed hidden.

A short, chubby man sat down on the bench, his back to the boy. The man took off his baseball cap and ran a hand across his scalp. He was bald on top, frizzy around the sides, like Bozo. Next to him on the bench was a bag like a big purse.

"You can come out now," the man said without turning around. "The coast is clear."

The boy didn't move.

"Or you can stay there."

The boy poked his head out, looked left and right. No one else in sight. He crawled forward on his elbows. He tried to stand and slipped.

The bald man got up and extended a hand. The boy took it and got to his feet. The man was smiling at him, but it was a sad kind of smile.

The boy jerked back, recognizing him. He made a noise like a choked scream. The bald man still had his arm. The boy closed his free hand into a fist and swung, catching the man across the temple.

"Hey!" the bald man said. He stepped back and covered his ears with his arms. The boy came after him, swinging with both fists now. He struck again and again, hammering at him.

The bald man didn't try to strike back. Eventually he dropped his arms and let the boy flail at him without obstruction. The blows turned the man's ears bright red, drew blood from his nose. He stood there, silently absorbing the punishment.

After a minute the boy stopped, panting.

The bald man turned his head and spat a dollop of blood. "I deserved that," he said. "And more." He pinched the bridge of his nose. His golf shirt was streaked with red. Both cheeks looked bruised, and one ear seemed pulpy and red as a tomato. "I don't know how I'll make it up to Bertram, though."

The boy glared at him.

"All done?" the man said.

The boy slapped him across the cheek, hard enough to turn his head.

The man rubbed his jaw. "Okay then." He walked back to the bench and sat down. The boy remained standing, tensed to run.

"I won't bother you again," the man said. "I promise. I just wanted to tell you that you never have to worry about . . . me. I'm going to keep the other demons away from you too. Kind of a guardian angel."

The boy said nothing.

"Maybe someday we'll be able to keep all the demons away." He touched a finger to his nose. It had stopped bleeding. "I'm working with a woman and some other people. We're contacting scientists. I don't think you'd understand right now if I tried to explain, but we're . . . trying to shut the door that the demons use."

A distant shout: "Del!" The old man and the boy turned together. A tall, bearded figure waved from the other end of the park. He moved toward them in a jerky half-run.

"I should be going," the bald man said. He stood, retrieved his cap from the ground, and pulled it on. "Oh, and I brought you something." He handed the boy a thin package wrapped in foil paper. "Happy birthday, Del."

He walked briskly away. In a moment he disappeared around the corner of a building.

Lew reached the boy. He breathed heavily, his face bright with sweat. "Hey man, we're looking all over for you," he said. "Who were you talking to—did he bother you? Did he do anything to you?"

The boy shook his head.

"Okay, good." He studied the spot where the man had disappeared, then looked down at the boy and noticed the present in his hand. "What do you got there? Did that guy give this to you?"

The boy handed it to him. Waited. Lew pulled off the wrapping paper. "Fuck," he said. It was a comic book. He studied the cover for a long moment, then looked up at the spot where the man in the ball cap had disappeared. Gone.

The boy took the book from his hand. The cover showed a man in goggles shooting a bulky gun. He flipped it open, frowning.

"That's RADAR Man," Lew said. His voice sounded strained. Then he cleared his throat and said, "Don't worry, I'll read it to you. And there's a ton of comics in the basement. They're all yours."

The boy took his brother's hand, and they started walking back, the boy holding the comic open in his other hand as they walked.

"We gotta get you cleaned up, man," Lew said. "But you know nobody's mad at you, right? It was totally an accident." The boy nodded absently. He was looking at the comic book. "And let's not tell the Cyclops that I swore in front of you. She would so kill me."

NOTES

The comment made in chapter 5 by "Valis" on the difference between fantasy and science fiction was taken from Philip K. Dick's essay "My Definition of Science Fiction," which appeared in *The Shifting Realities of Philip K. Dick, Selected Literary and Philosophical Writings,* edited by Lawrence Sutin. That book also reprinted a drawing from Dick's *Exegesis* that I adapted for the Rapturist symbol in chapter 4.

ACKNOWLEDGMENTS

The first-time novelist owes thanks to almost everyone he's ever met. A novelist who's written a pop culture mash-up like this one is also indebted to almost every book he's ever read, starting with the comics of Jack Kirby and Stan Lee. Thank you for teaching me to read, gentlemen. This book also owes much to the stories of H. P. Lovecraft and the novels of A. E. Van Vogt (pronounced "A. E.") and Philip K. Dick.

Kathy Bieschke and Gary Delafield were, as always, my first, best, and toughest readers. Andrew Tisbert and Elizabeth Delafield saw later drafts and kept me on track. My thanks as well to the many friends (including several more Delafields) who read the manuscript; to my children, Emma and Ian Gregory, who weren't allowed to read it; and to my sisters, Robin Somerfield and Lisa Johnson, who were simply thankful they weren't in it.

Several wise professionals guided me through the last mile of the publishing process. Gordon Van Gelder offered well-timed words of advice and a door-opening e-mail. Christine Cohen pushed the book into exactly the right hands. The deft copyediting of Sona Vogel and Deanna Hoak saved me from several embarrassments. My thanks to them all, and especially to my editor, Fleetwood Robbins. He under-

stood the book from the beginning yet saw how it could be more true
to itself.

Finally, my deepest thanks go to Darrell and Thelma Gregory,
who never turned down their odd son no matter how many times he
showed up at the checkout counter holding another comic or paperback. Mom, I'm sorry this book has so many curse words.

ABOUT THE AUTHOR

DARYL GREGORY's short stories have appeared in *The Magazine of Fantasy & Science Fiction*, *Asimov's*, several year's-best anthologies, and other fine venues. In 2005 he received the *Asimov's* Readers' Award for the novelette "Second Person, Present Tense." He lives with his wife and two children in State College, Pennsylvania, where he writes both fiction and web code. *Pandemonium* is his first novel.